Praise for

A BookPage Best

A Goo K OF 2011

"[Bohjalian] earns a place alongside Stephen King as the master of the Halloween beach book. This ghost story is expertly and, at times, beautifully written, deliciously creepy, and, like a bag of trick-or-treat loot, silently calls out to you when it's languishing on the night table."
—*Boston Globe*

"A good read for those who like a dash of creepiness." —*New York Times*

"Boasts all the trappings of a classic Gothic horror story, reminiscent in places of the spousal secrets in Nathaniel Hawthorne's *Young Goodman Brown*, the thrills of *Rosemary's Baby,* and the psychological frights of Daphne du Maurier. That *thump thump* you hear as you read is only your heart leaping from your chest." —*Washington Post*

"Shades of *The Shining* make for a haunting tale . . . A modern-day ghost story worth losing sleep over." —*Family Circle*

"A delicious and haunting tale." —*Minneapolis Star Tribune*

"This unsettling latest from master storyteller Bohjalian will keep you up at night." —*People* magazine

"Good 'n' spooky." —*Good Housekeeping*

"*The Night Strangers* has all the hallmarks of a good ghost story, but . . . Bohjalian has put his own 21st-century spin on the supernatural genre in his frightening new novel." —*CNN*

"A gripping paranormal thriller . . . Meticulous research and keen attention to detail give depth and character to [the] eerie world. . . . Bohjalian is a master, and the slow-mounting dread makes this a frightful ride."
—*Publishers Weekly*

"A page-turner of uncommon depth. Guilt, egotism, and fear all play parts in this genre-bending novel." —*Booklist* (starred review)

"Compelling . . . a practical magick horror story." —*Kirkus Reviews*

Chris Bohjalian

The
NIGHT
STRANGERS

A NOVEL

Broadway Paperbacks   New York

BROADWAY

This is a work of fiction. Names, characters, places, and incidents either are the product
of the author's imagination or are used fictitiously. Any resemblance to actual persons,
living or dead, events, or locales is entirely coincidental.

Originally published in hardcover in slightly different form in the United States by
Crown Publishers, an imprint of the Crown Publishing Group, a division of
Random House, Inc., New York, in 2011.

Library of Congress Cataloging-in-Publication Data
Bohjalian, Christopher A.
The night strangers : a novel / Chris Bohjalian.—1st ed.
p. cm.
1. Air pilots—Fiction. 2. Herbalists—Fiction. 3. Twins—Fiction. 4. Domestic
fiction. 5. New Hampshire—Fiction. I. Title.
PS3552.O495N54 2011
813'.54—dc22   2010045401

ISBN 978-0-307-39500-9
eISBN 978-0-307-88886-0

Printed in the United States of America

Title and part title photos: Mark Simms/Shutterstock.com

Book design by Lynne Amft
Cover design by Jessie Sayward Bright
Cover photograph by Kamil Vojnar

10 9 8 7 6 5 4 3 2

First Paperback Edition

For Shaye Areheart and Jane Gelfman

Our bodies are our gardens, to the which our wills are gardeners.

WILLIAM SHAKESPEARE, *Othello*

Dead . . . might not be quiet at all.

MARSHA NORMAN, *'night, Mother*

THE NIGHT STRANGERS

The door was presumed to have been the entry to a coal chute, a perfectly reasonable assumption since a small hillock of damp coal sat moldering before it. It was a little under five feet in height and just about four feet wide, and it was composed of barnboard and thick pieces of rough-hewn timber. Its most distinguishing feature was not its peculiarly squat visage—and if a person were predisposed to see such things in the dim light of the basement, the knobs on the wood and the character of the planking did suggest the vague shadow of a face—but the fact that at some point someone had sealed the door shut with six-inch-long wrought-iron carriage bolts. Thirty-nine of them ringed the wood and it was all but impenetrable, unless one were feeling energetic and had handy an ax. The door glowered in an especially dank corner of the basement, and the floor before it was dirt. The fact was, however, that most of the basement floor was dirt; only the concrete island on which sat the washing machine, the dryer, the furnace, and the hot-water tank was not dirt. When most prospective buyers inspected the house, this was their principal concern: a floor that seemed equal parts clay and loam. That was what caused them to nod, their minds immediately envisioning runnels of water during spring thaws and the mud that could be brought upstairs every time they did laundry or descended there to retrieve (perhaps) a new lightbulb or a hammer. It was a lot of largely wasted square footage, because the footprint of the house above it was substantial. As a result, the door was rarely noticed and never commented upon.

Still, the basement walls were stone and the foundation was sturdy. It capably shouldered three stories of Victorian heft: the elegant gingerbread trim along three different porches, which in the greater scheme of things weighed next to nothing, as well as the stout beams that weighed a very great deal but stood invisible behind horsehair and plaster and lath. Though the first-floor ceilings were uniformly twelve feet and the bedrooms' and sitting rooms' that marked the second and third floors no less than ten, the height of the basement ceiling wavered between six and eight feet, and—underneath an addition from 1927—a mere four feet. The floor rose and fell like beach sand. Further capable of inducing claustrophobia there were the immense lengths of copper tubing for gas and hot water, the strings of knob-and-tube electrical wiring (some live, some dead), and the horizontal beams that helped buttress the kitchen, the living room, and the dining room. The den. The library. The bright, wide entry hallway and the thinner, dark corridor that snaked behind the kitchen to the back stairs and the pantry. The copper tubing looped together in Gordian knots near the furnace and the hot-water tank. This piping alone scared away some buyers; it certainly scared away many more than did that door. There were strategically placed jack posts in the tallest section of the basement and a railroad tie turned vertical in the shortest.

In the years the house was for sale—one real estate agent attributed her inability to sell it to the unwillingness of the cantankerous, absentee owner to accept anything but the asking price, while another simply presumed it would take time for the right sort of family to express serious interest—all of the prospective buyers were from out of state. A great many were from Boston, enticed north into the White Mountains to see a house advertised in the *Globe* real estate section as the perfect weekend or retirement home for families that would appreciate its sweeping views of Mount Lafayette or the phantasmagoric foliage offered each autumn by the sugar bush to the south and the east. It was only twenty minutes from a ski resort. Still, almost no one with any familiarity with the property—and that was the right term, with its connotations of acreage (nineteen acres split between forest and meadow cut by a neighbor for hay) and outbuildings (two, including a garage that had once been a carriage barn and a small but workable greenhouse)—showed any desire to buy it. No one from the nearby village of Bethel even looked at it, viewing it as a house with (and this was the euphemism they were likely to use) a history.

At the same time, few of the agents who brought flatlanders from Massachusetts, New York, and Pennsylvania to see the house ascribed its years on the market to the door in the basement or the thirty-nine carriage bolts that sealed it shut.

When your airplane hits the flock of birds, the passengers in the cabin behind you feel the jolting bangs and the aircraft rolls fifteen degrees to its starboard side. The birds are geese, and it is not uncommon for you to see them from the flight deck as your plane begins its climb out of Burlington, Vermont. In this particular departure corridor, you see geese, crows, seagulls (lots of seagulls), and ducks all the time. The geese are flying perhaps forty miles an hour, traveling in formation from one feeding area to another, angling south from Malletts Bay, the animals always careful to keep near their cohorts. Today your aircraft is a Bombardier CRJ700, a regional jet that seats seventy passengers, two pilots, and a pair of flight attendants. This flight has forty-three passengers and three attendants, two on duty who have been with the airline for over a decade and a half, and another who is merely commuting home to Philadelphia and has almost as much experience. Both working flight attendants are, by any standard, immensely competent. You do not know them well, but you have gotten to know them both a bit over the last four days together. Likewise, the pilots (if you may be so bold) are skilled, too, though your first officer has only been flying for three years. (The reality is that you and Amy have not been doing your jobs as long as the flight attendants have been doing theirs.) But Amy Lynch is smart and funny, and you have enjoyed working with her the last few days, as you have flown between Washington, Pittsburgh, Charlotte, Columbus, Philadelphia, and finally Burlington. She has nearly thirty-five hundred

hours of flying time, twenty-one with you over the last four days. You
are a veteran who has been flying for fourteen years, and you have finally
lasted long enough for there to be talk that soon you may get to start
training on an Airbus simulator and begin your climb to a considerably
bigger plane and a considerably bigger salary. You have twin daughters,
and in eight years they will start college: That bigger paycheck matters,
as does the esteem that comes with a 154-seat jet.

This afternoon you see the birds, each with a wingspan almost the
length of a man, just a second after your first officer does. She happens
to be handling the takeoff. But the moment you fly through the drapes
of geese—there it is, the sound you have always likened to a machine
gun, the violent thud as each animal careens like a bullet into the metal
and glass of your aircraft—the plane wobbles briefly to its side as first the
left engine and then the right flame out. Most of those geese must weigh
ten or eleven pounds each, and when they careen into the engines, the
animals' bones and feathers and flesh are turned almost instantly to jam
and then almost as quickly incinerated. The passengers don't know what
they are smelling, but they know there is a stench in the cabin that they
have never inhaled during a takeoff before, and combined with the way
the aircraft has pitched to starboard, they are experiencing what even the
most frequent flyers would describe as an uh-oh sensation as they peer
out the fuselage windows.

Meanwhile, you say "my airplane" and you take the controls. You
flip on the APU, the backup generator in the tail of the plane, because a
few years ago Chesley Sullenberger did this when his jet plowed through
geese over the Bronx, and now turning on the APU is a part of the emergency checklist. You tell Amy, "Ignition on," although you are quite
sure that the wrecked blades have completely ripped the engines apart
and neither will ever reignite: You can see on the instrument panel that
the engine speeds are at zero. Nothing inside the turbines is spinning
because whatever metal is there is now scrap and shard. But it can't hurt
to have your first officer try to restart the engines while you find the best
spot to bring the plane down. "Airspeed, two hundred and forty knots,"

you say, the best glide speed for this jet—the speed that will give you the longest possible glide.

And while radio communication is your lowest priority this second, you do tell the tower that there has been a bird strike. You begin with words that sound at once foreign and cinematic in your mind because you never anticipated saying them: "Burlington, we just had a bird strike and are declaring an emergency."

"Roger. What do you need?" a cool female voice in the tower responds.

"Stand by," you tell her simply, trying to focus. After a moment, she offers you a heading in the event you want to return to Burlington.

And, indeed, your first instinct is to make a wide, sweeping circle and land back at the airport. You left to the northwest on runway 33; perhaps you could loop back around and land on runway 15. But making a turn that large will cause the plane to lose a lot of altitude, and right now you're only about twenty-five hundred feet in the air. You weren't quite half a mile above the Champlain valley when that flock of geese darkened your windshield like a theater curtain. Your instincts tell you that you are never going to make it if you try for runway 15.

"Not happening," you tell the tower. "We have no thrust in either engine." An emergency landing at the airport is impossible.

And when you hear that voice from the tower next, you detect a twinge of panic in that usually professional façade: "Roger. State your intentions."

You project alternate flight paths, scanning the Champlain valley. Maybe instead of Burlington you could glide across the lake to Plattsburgh—to the airport there. The old Air Force base in upstate New York. You can see the area in the far distance to the right, and the angle of the runways looks promising. But it's not likely you have anywhere near the altitude or the speed to make it. And even if you do coax the crippled airliner across the lake, you will still have to adjust your approach: The angle of the runways is promising, not perfect, which means you might be crash-landing in a populated area. Moreover, the CRJ has very low wings. Not a lot of clearance as you scoot along ground that isn't a long, flat patch of pavement. It would be easy to catch a wingtip and lose control. You have seen your share of videos of planes cartwheeling along the ground into fireballs.

But you have to bring the plane down somewhere, and you have to bring it down soon. Neither engine has restarted.

You know well how that other captain managed to crash-land a powerless jet—and that was an Airbus 320, an oil tanker compared to this relatively petite CRJ—in the Hudson River one cold but crystal clear January afternoon. It was considered a miracle, but mostly it was just excellent flying. Chesley Sullenberger had flown commercially for twenty-nine years and prior to that had been a fighter jock. Twenty-nine years versus your fourteen. Arguably, a considerable difference. But you still have a boatload of hours in the air.

Likewise, you know the story of the Lockheed Electra turboprop that sailed into thousands of starlings—some people estimated as many as ten thousand—on October 4, 1960. The plane and the birds collided seconds after takeoff from Logan Airport, only four hundred feet above the water in Boston Harbor. The engines stalled and the plane plummeted into the water, no more than two hundred yards from shore. This was no gentle, seemingly slow-motion glide. There were seventy-two people onboard. Miraculously, ten survived, largely because of the flotilla of small boats that descended on the wreckage.

And now it is August, and though the sky is that same cerulean blue as it had been that January day over New York, it is downright muggy outside. Before you looms Lake Champlain, wider than the Hudson but still long like a river. You notice two ferryboats, one venturing west to Plattsburgh and the other motoring east to Burlington. There must be a dozen sailboats. And there is the crystalline surface of all that warm August water. Warm. August. Water. You will bring your plane down there—nose up so the aircraft doesn't flip—because it is your best option. It is, perhaps, your only option. You have two dead engines and the speed of the aircraft's descent is accelerating. You will do precisely what Sullenberger did on the Hudson. You've read all about it. All pilots have.

The tower is asking you again where you want to land. That voice once more brings up Burlington. She tells you that they have stopped all incoming and outgoing traffic there. Then she suggests Plattsburgh.

"I'm going to use the lake the way he used the river," you tell her evenly, not specifying who *he* is because you don't have time and, really, you were just thinking aloud when you added that to your tower communication. And already you are turning your plane from the northwest to the south and watching the water start to rise up.

You wish it were possible to dump the fuel on this CRJ, and not simply because you fear an explosion and fire; you know that the plane would float longer if there were more air in the tanks. Still, the plane should float long enough if you do this correctly. And so you descend as if you were approaching an ordinary runway, nose up, flaps full. The ground proximity warning system kicks in, and a computerized voice starts repeating, "Terrain. Terrain. Terrain." Soon it will become more urgent, insisting, "Pull up. Pull up." As if you didn't know. Behind you, your passengers in the first rows hear it, too.

In a moment you will give the command every captain dreads: "Brace for impact." Then you will skim across Lake Champlain, landing from the north a few minutes past five on a summer afternoon, and your passengers will be rescued by those ferryboats and sailboats. They will not face the frigid waters of the Hudson River but will instead wait on the wings in the gentle summer bath of a New England lake or bob on the waves in those garish orange life rafts.

"Thrust levels all idle," Amy tells you, shaking her head, just a trace of anxiety in her usually giddy, usually playful voice.

Without thrust, landing the plane will be all about pitch. Lowering the nose will give you more speed and a longer glide; raising it will slow the aircraft and shorten your time in the air. You want to belly into the lake as gently as possible, though *gentle* is a relative term. The water can feel like granite to the underbelly of a jet if you hit it at the wrong angle.

"No relight," Amy tells you, essentially reiterating what she shared with you just a moment ago, speaking louder now because, in addition to having to be heard over the synthetic Cassandra telling you to *pull up, pull up, pull up,* your flight deck is alive with emergency chimes and bells and a controller who wants you in Burlington or Plattsburgh or (Did you hear this correctly?) the interstate highway in New York that runs parallel to the lake. But the asphalt linking Albany and Plattsburgh is no more an option than the asphalt on the runways at the airports on either side of the water. No, you will use the lake the way Chesley Sullenberger used the river, and soon your passengers will be wrapped in blankets on the decks of the ferries.

The plane is eighteen rows long along one side but only seventeen on the other so there is room for a second lavatory at the front of the aircraft. There are two doors at the front of the plane and two over the wings at row fourteen (though that is actually the unnamed thirteenth row). Everyone in the passenger cabin is agonizingly aware of their proximity to those four exits, but perhaps no one is more focused upon them right now than Ethan Stearns as he sits in an aisle seat in the very last row, barely a foot and a half from the rear lavatory. It is not his own safety that has him calculating in his mind the speed with which he will be able to fight his way through the chaotic, merciless swarm to those exit windows, assuming the plane actually remains intact after it hits the surface of the lake; it is the safety of his young daughter, Ashley, who is sitting in the window seat beside him. His wife, Ashley's mother, is ten rows ahead of them. The plane is not full, but it seemed like a lot of work to have the gate agent reassign their seats so they could be closer together on the short trip to Philly. So, instead of his wife in the row ahead of him, there is a man he knows nothing about and a woman who, based on something she said into her cell before the doors were locked and armed, had just interviewed at the IBM facility in Essex Junction, Vermont.

His wife, he realizes, is five rows from the exits over the windows and just seven from the front doors of the plane. He and Ashley are five rows from their only real shot from the aircraft, the window exits. His mind has already done the triage and the odds: His wife is more likely to survive than either he or their eight-year-old daughter. His eyes meet his wife's when she turns back to glance at Ashley and him. He smiles; somehow, he smiles. He reminds himself as he gazes around his lovely little girl's head—which is pressed so close against the glass that he can barely see out of it—that the guy who landed an Airbus in the Hudson got everyone out alive. It's not like they're about to slam into a mountain or a skyscraper. He makes sure that her life jacket is tight around her waist and he understands how to inflate it once they are outside the plane. He had barely had time to find it under her seat and figure out how to pull it from its bag and unfold it. He never did find his. He guesses no more than three or four other passengers have donned life jackets.

"Brace for impact!" the flight attendant is telling them. "Brace for water landing! Heads down, heads down, heads down!"

"When we come to a stop in the water, we are going to race for that window exit," he tells his girl gently, whispering into her ear, trying to sound as serene as the flight attendant sounds urgent. "Okay? I am going to lift you up and carry you like we're racing through the crowds on Main Street in Disney World. You remember, when the park's closing for the night after the fireworks and we're racing for spots on the monorail?"

"But I can't swim that far," she stammers, her voice a little numb.

"That's why you have a life jacket," he tells her. "The key is to scoot out of the plane with me, that's all. Your mom will already be waiting for us because she's a little closer to the exit." Then his eyes go back to his wife's, and her terror is like an electric shock. The cabin is eerily quiet because the engines aren't working, and the passengers are mouthing their prayers or texting or staring in mute wonder as the plane seems to be descending beneath the Burlington skyline to the east and the Adirondack foothills to the west.

"Do not wait for us!" he finally says to his wife, uncaring that it is like shouting in a cathedral during silent prayer. "I'll have Ashley! Just get out of the plane!"

Once he has spoken, broken the spell, others start offering advice.

Someone, a man, yells for the women and men in the exit rows to be prepared. Someone else starts yelling out how many feet above the lake water he believes they are.

Ethan finally pulls his daughter's head from the window, kisses her on the cheek, and then pushes her down into the brace position. Then he joins her, but he wraps his left arm around her shoulders, as if he actually believes he is strong enough to protect her from the impact of a passenger jet augering into a lake at 150 miles an hour.

The captain never thought the door in the basement in any way resembled the over-wing exit doors on an airplane. Or even a main cabin door. Which, of course, it did not. But much later his new therapist, when the captain and his family had moved from Pennsylvania to New Hampshire, would probe this connection. A squat door? A pilot with PTSD? How could a psychiatrist not mine this possible connection? But of all the things the captain saw in the door in that dusky corner of the basement in the house they had bought, a locked and armed passenger jet door was never among them.

And, indeed, a Hudson River–like landing is precisely what might have occurred, and you might have wound up a media darling just like that Sully Sullenberger. But soon after you have told the cabin to brace for impact and your plane has skimmed onto the lake—tail then underbelly then nose, a hard landing but picture perfect—there is a high wave. It curls up from the wake of one of those ferryboats—the one that had been churning its way west—as it starts to turn around to aid the plane that is bearing down fast upon the water. The crest is just tall enough and just sudden enough that it smacks the left wingtip of the aircraft. For a tiny fraction of a second you are eye to eye with the foam. And then, before you know it, the one thing you had wanted to avoid is occurring. Suddenly the CRJ is not coasting along the glass of the lake as you had planned—had envisioned—but is vertical to the water. And then it is somersaulting, slamming down hard, that great metal underbelly facing the sun, and the passengers, who had been merely terrified into a prayerful silence, are now disoriented and screaming. You hear them through the metal door of the flight deck. Others already are dead, though you will only learn this later, because when the plane bangs back into the water that second time, it breaks into halves and the passengers in rows ten through fourteen are slammed headfirst into the fuselage as it collapses or are decapitated by the jagged metal edges. Others are starting to drown that very instant as the lake water—yes, warmer than the Hudson that day in January but still a shock to the system if you are upside down in an airplane and strapped tight by a strong nylon belt into a seat—begins filling the two halves of the blackened cabin.

But the fuel does not explode and the surface of the lake will not become a firestorm. And so not everyone will die. Of your forty-three passengers, four crew members (including yourself), and one dead-heading flight attendant, nine will survive. Nine somehow will manage to unhook their seat belts, though in some cases their heads already are underwater, and claw or swim their way the six or eight yards to those gaping holes in the fuselage. (All that talk in the plane about exit doors, all that calculation about proximity and survival? None of it mattered for most of the passengers, because the plane split in half like a baguette torn in two.) They will push past those who are already dead, past dangling wires, laptop computers, briefcases, backpacks, magazines, seat cushions, slim plastic bags with uninflated life vests, and the daggerlike shards of metal, everything—the harmless and the murderous—bobbing together amidst the bubbles like jellyfish. Despite broken bones and deep cuts and sprained legs and arms, they will kick their way away from the plane before the largest pieces start to disappear completely underwater.

As, somehow, will you. Reflexively you will release your five-point shoulder harness (it will only be later that you will see and feel the eggplant-colored bruise the buckle left just below your sternum), and you will unbuckle your first officer, squinting in the tiny flight deck that already is filling fast with lake water, not completely disoriented because there are streaks of light to your left that must be afternoon sky. You hope

Amy is merely unconscious and not dead (only that evening will you look back on the moment and realize by the way her skull was dangling that her neck was broken and your efforts were meaningless). Then you pull open the door to the cabin, initially twisting the chrome knob the wrong way because you are upside down, and the water rushes in and knocks you and your first officer against the back of your seat, but you wrap one arm around her and take a deep breath and swim into it, your eyes above the surface of the water and then, suddenly, not. So you swim with physical references, a combination of muscle memory and what you saw before the water was over your head, feeling along the flight attendant's jump seat (he's not there, a good sign, perhaps) and then to the exit door. You pop your head above the roiling water inside the aircraft, desperate for air, discovering that what had been perhaps three feet of air is now down to inches because of the speed with which the plane is sinking. You take another deep breath and paw your way down the metal until you have found the door's emergency lever. Again, momentarily you forget that the aircraft is floating upside down, and you can't understand why you can't open it. But then you recall where you are and manage to flip the lever and shoulder the door free, and with Amy still a great, dead rag doll in your arms, you shimmy through the opening against the water, briefly catching the cuff of your uniform pants on an edge, and out onto the surface of the lake. Miraculously, you are free. You are alive. Perhaps everyone is alive. (Later, you will wonder how you could possibly have thought that for even a moment.) You hold Amy under her arms, treading water madly, strangely aware of your shoes, gulping in great gasps of air, your throat and your sinuses on fire from the water that has gone up your nose, until there is someone beside you—no, above you and beside you—in a sailboat. Someone is in the sailboat, the sail a beautiful, billowing red canvas that is blocking out the sun, and he is reaching down for you. And someone else from that sailboat is jumping into the lake, a fellow perhaps half your age, and together they are lifting your first officer from your arms and into the small craft. There are sirens you hear clearly, and so automatically you turn your eyes to the east, surprised by how well you can see the Burlington waterfront and the crowds that are forming along the ferry dock and along the bike path and along the walkway beside the aquarium. Boys in T-shirts and shorts, and girls in wispy summer dresses. It's as if they are lining the streets and expect a parade.

Again, however, this is an image that only registers in your mind later, when you are on a boat. One of those ferryboats. Perhaps the one that had inadvertently finished up what the geese had started, destroying your aircraft once and for all. Mostly what you are seeing as you kick through the agitated ripples and waves, the water in your mouth at once earthy and bitter with jet fuel, are the two halves of your plane starting to disappear, and how the starboard wing is gone. Just gone. Is it already wafting its way in slow motion to the bottom of the lake, alongside all of those seventeenth- and eighteenth-century cannons and warships and Abenaki canoes? Apparently. You are aware of your few surviving passengers, one in an uninflated life jacket, swimming or dog-paddling toward the boats, which now seem to be everywhere. But not all of the survivors are trying to work their way through the water made choppy by all those boats and a plane that doesn't belong. There is a woman, perhaps thirty-five, looking around madly and crying out someone's name as she treads water. It is a girl's name. Ashley. And you have a sick sense that she is crying out the name of the child you happened to notice board the aircraft with a Dora the Explorer backpack. She had blond spit curls and was seven or eight years old. Perhaps two years younger than your own little girls. Your and your wife's twins. She had peered into the flight deck and smiled at you, and so you had smiled back. There is a man whom you pegged as your age, somewhere around forty, who keeps coming up for air and then diving back under the water, and finally starts swimming back toward the slowly disappearing rear half of the jet. And so you swim that way, too, once your first officer has been lifted from your arms, to see if there are other survivors you can pull from the fuselage, swimming past and between the floating bodies of people in short-sleeved sport shirts and summer-weight business jackets. But you don't get far because out of nowhere two strong-armed college boys appear in the water beside you and are—as if they are lifeguards—pulling you away from the wreckage of the plane. Your plane.

You try to resist them, to explain to them who you are, but you haven't the strength and your words are lost in the sobs and wails and the idling engines of the ferries and a Coast Guard motorboat that now has arrived on the scene. Besides, they know. They know precisely who you are. You're wearing your uniform, all but the jacket and the cap. So, you allow yourself to be brought to that ferryboat and hoisted aboard. And there you stand in silence, suddenly aware of the great gash along your forehead (all that blood you had presumed was simply water) and how there is something wrong with one of your ankles and how your ribs hurt like hell. You stand there, most of your weight on your good ankle, wrapped in a blanket you're not sure you need, and watch the rear half of the plane, still belly up, recede once and for all beneath the surface of the lake.

It would be the captain's wife, a lawyer two years younger than the captain who specialized in estate planning and did the heavy lifting when it came to raising their twin girls, who would see the advantages of finding a house that offered both relative seclusion and vistas that might feed her husband's battered soul. Emily Linton was two years shy of forty when Flight 1611 flipped onto its back like a killer whale at a SeaWorld performance. Her husband was not deemed responsible for the tragedy (that onus would be hung round the remains of the cooked birds), but neither was he Sully Sullenberger. The media's interest in him would wane once it was clear that he hadn't made an egregious mistake but neither had he successfully ditched a commercial jet on the water. And their lack of attention was precisely what he desired as he mourned the dead in the lake and pondered the long, painful litany of might-have-beens. Chip Linton would second-guess this critical three minutes of his life for as long as he lived, aware always that he was not Sully Sullenberger. He would, Emily knew, compare himself to that older pilot he had never met and always come up lacking. The psychiatrist from the pilots' union and a preternaturally serene young woman from the Critical Incident Response Team warned them both of this; they seemed to want to counsel both her husband and her, and she was grateful.

Their children were fifth-graders named Hallie and Garnet: Garnet because her newborn hair had been the deep red it was even now and Hallie because it was the name of the infant's grandmother—Emily's mother. Hallie and Garnet were not identical twins, though they certainly were close and took pride in their sisterly camaraderie. They were each other's best friend. The family had lived outside of Philadelphia, in the mannered suburb of West Chester, but at different points in their lives both Emily and Chip had spent sizable chunks of time in New England. Emily's grandparents had had a summerhouse in Meredith, New Hampshire, and she had fond childhood memories of Julys and Augusts in the brisk waters of Lake Winnipesaukee. Chip had spent four years in Amherst at the University of Massachusetts, though by his senior year he was spending far more time at the Northampton Airport than he was in classes: He would devote whatever money he made working overnight at the university switchboard to flying lessons there in Pipers and Cessnas and, eventually, in a twin-engine Beechcraft Duchess. The first mountains he flew over—foothills in all but name—were the thousand-foot peak of Hitchcock and the eleven-hundred-foot summit of Norwottuck, which were no more than five miles from the edge of the runway.

Consequently, the idea of retreating to New England after the disastrous water landing grew slowly but inexorably—rather like a seed germinating in water in a bathroom glass—in the minds of both the captain and his wife. Any state but Vermont, the site of the crash, would do. Neither of them particularly liked the idea of uprooting their children, but they also didn't believe that remaining in Pennsylvania was an option after the captain's sudden retirement from flying. They needed to start fresh someplace new. Emily thought she could take the bar wherever they resettled, and Chip presumed it didn't matter at forty whether he started a new career in New England or the Mid-Atlantic. The girls would make friends wherever they found themselves. Children were resilient. Didn't families move all the time?

Still, they had barely begun to search the Web for possible homes in New England when they heard from a real estate agent. A fellow named Sheldon Carter called, describing some town they had never heard of in northern New Hampshire. Bethel. Sheldon, of course, along with every other sentient adult in the country, was aware of Flight 1611 and the captain who wasn't Sully Sullenberger. He knew precisely who Emily was. He said that he had seen her name among the possible buyers who requested more information on the agency's Web site in Littleton, New Hampshire, and that he had the perfect house for them. His voice was serene and warm, and it sounded as if he really did have an intuitive sense of what the Linton family needed: a world where they would be far from both the stares—some judgmental, some pitying—and the averted eyes. A world where people were not defined by their successes and failures. A world that was, in some ways, oblivious to the inexorable media—the twenty-four-hour news cycles, the relentless blogs, the wonder walls of gossip and innuendo and supposition on the Web—that constantly had stories likely to trigger self-hatred and despair in the captain, even though it wasn't his fault.

The house he had in mind, the Realtor said, had character, space, and absolutely spectacular views. It sat alone on a hill up the road from the village. And the town had a first-rate public school system. Sheldon actually described the property as regal before sending Emily a link to it on the agency's Web site.

Consequently, the Lintons agreed to visit Bethel, New Hampshire. They drove, though the captain insisted he had no fear of flying. They drove because this way they could look at four other possible houses along the Connecticut River, two in western Massachusetts and two in New Hampshire.

All of those houses were intriguing in some fashion, and all of them felt more authentically Yankee than the development Colonial in which they lived in Pennsylvania—a house that wasn't that much older than the stadium where the Phillies played baseball. But none of them cast a spell over Emily or Chip or their girls. They were too small or too damp or simply not as interesting as they had seemed on the Web sites. Two of them were in a condition that was almost too good. It felt to Emily as if they were strolling inside the pages of *Martha Stewart Living* and there was no need to fix the place up and make it their own. It seemed like someone was about to walk in the door and ask them to take their shoes off. Consequently, the Lintons' expectations were not especially high when they finally reached a sparsely populated corner of northwestern New Hampshire and met the real estate agent in the driveway of the house just outside of Bethel. The Canadian border, Chip realized, couldn't have been more than forty-five or fifty miles distant.

Sheldon was delightful and he was obese. His stomach pillowed over his belt like a beanbag chair and he walked with a cane. He said he was sixty-eight, but he was diabetic and Emily doubted he'd reach seventy. But he was charming, and immediately he commented upon young Hallie's remarkable cheekbones and Garnet's thick mane of red hair. Emily presumed this was his way of trying to build commonality with prospective buyers. And if she was being manipulated, Emily decided that she didn't mind; anyone who complimented her daughters made her happy. But the girls were far more interested in the greenhouse and the barn on the property than they were in the kind words of a grandfatherly real estate agent. They were intrigued by the idea that the house came with a carriage barn. Then the whole family wandered through the Victorian's three floors, the rooms and the corridors handsome, though even Sheldon admitted that they were a little dark once they went beyond the entry foyer. The air was particularly musty in the bedrooms, but it was thick everywhere with emptiness and disuse. They listened attentively as the real estate agent explained how it would be deceptively easy to lay down a concrete pad across the entire basement floor, and how the three stories above were not nearly the fiscal nightmare to heat in the winter that a person might fear they would be. There was, for instance, that beautiful soapstone woodstove in the den. Supposedly, it alone heated the den, the kitchen, and the dining room.

But neither the captain nor his wife was troubled by the basement with its dirt floor and low ceiling or how costly it might be to heat the massive structure above it. They saw only a magnificent three-story Victorian with that gingerbread trim and its fish-scale clapboards along the three porches. They saw only its carriage barn and that greenhouse. They saw only its views of Mount Lafayette and the cannonball-shaped foothills that rippled beneath the mountain's tectonic heft, and the house's proximity to a village green with a gazebo and a Civil War cannon, an immaculate white clapboard firehouse for the volunteer firefighters, and an iconic, squat brick library built with Carnegie money in 1911.

If they noticed a door with thirty-nine carriage bolts partially hidden by a moldering pile of coal, the image never registered in either of their minds. It certainly didn't register in the minds of their daughters. And so the Lintons offered more or less what the absentee owner was asking for the property—they chalked up his unwillingness to budge much on the price to the fact that he had grown up in the house, and with both parents and his lone sibling dead attributed profound sentimental value to the brown and red clapboard walls and elegant slate roof—and he accepted. The very next day, Sheldon Carter died of a heart attack. But the closing was still seamless, and the Lintons moved in on Groundhog Day.

It was only on their third afternoon there, when Chip Linton descended the basement steps with their first ever load of laundry in their new home, that he would sense something from the corner of his eye and turn toward it, realizing as the hairs on the back of his neck began to prickle that behind all that coal in the corner was a door.

Part I

Chapter One

You see the long, wide, perfectly straight strip of asphalt before you, the hangar to your right with the words GREEN MOUNTAIN BOYS painted in billboard-size letters along the side. You recognize it as Burlington's runway 33, facing to the northwest. When your first officer lifts your plane off the ground, you know there will be a slight bump in about eight or nine seconds as you rise up and cross over the ravine churned out by the Winooski River. There is always a slight updraft there, even on a muggy afternoon such as today's. The sun has begun its descent in the west but is still high above the Adirondacks.

Already, however, you feel yourself sweating, and so you know on some level this must be a dream. But, unfortunately, you don't know how to wake yourself up. No idea. Emily, your wife, can do that, but not you. Still, you wouldn't be sweating unless this were a dream because in reality you never broke a sweat when you were flying. Why would you? And if it is a dream—*that dream*—you know what's next. Your heart starts pummeling your ribs even before they appear. And then there they are. The geese. You are upon them or they are upon you. Doesn't matter. You're somewhere between two and two and a half thousand feet above the ground, and there are the Bonnie and Clyde–like machine-gun blasts as you plow through them. (Why Bonnie and Clyde? You're unclear on this, too, but your therapist has told you with a smile what an odd place the unconscious world is. And so it is Bonnie and Clyde's Browning automatic rifles that you think of when you think of that sound.) Your engines will go—one in flames, one with grinding, steel-cutting-steel immolation, in both cases the nine-, ten-, even eleven-pound birds displacing the compressor blades and sending them spinning like shrapnel through the engines—although your forward thrust will bring you to about twenty-five hundred feet before you will begin your glide and start to lose altitude.

By then, of course, it is your plane. At least it was in reality. You had taken the controls.

So why is it now that it isn't—why is it that you aren't flying the jet? In this strange, dreamy version, no one is flying the aircraft, not even Amy Lynch, your first officer. Instead, the jet is immobile in the air, as if teetering on a high wire or balanced on its belly on the top of a great triangular obelisk. And then it becomes—and here is that expression a friend of yours who is in the Air National Guard and flies F-16s uses to convey his own fighter's absolute lack of glide prowess—a lawn dart. The nose turns down, straight down, still well east of the lake, and you are looking down at trees and grass and death in the sort of cataclysmic fireball after which only small fragments of body are ever recovered and identified. A finger with a wedding band. A foot as far as an ankle, still strangely wearing a black Converse sneaker. A quarter of a jaw with a few bottom teeth.

Only then do you wake up. Apparently, you really can't die in a plane crash in your dreams. A myth proves accurate. You find yourself cradled in Emily's arms in the small hours of the night, your whole body wet with sweat and your heart that relentless jackhammer.

When your Philadelphia therapist refers to this as a flashback, you wonder if you should correct her. It's a nightmare, not a flashback. In reality, you didn't actually auger into the ground.

They decided they would take a break from the boxes they had been unpacking and the wallpaper they had been scraping to go skiing and snowboarding. It was the Lintons' first Sunday in New Hampshire, and they woke, took their equipment from the massive pile of athletic gear they had deposited unceremoniously in the mudroom off the front entryway, and Chip hooked everything into the rack on the top of the station wagon or wedged it into the back. They would drive to Cannon Mountain, where they would buy day passes for the family. Emily would snowboard with the girls while Chip skied alone. After five days of steady work, the stacks of boxes had begun to shrink and the corridors composed of cardboard had begun to diminish in both height and length. The cartons marked HALLIE and GARNET and KITCHEN were largely (but not entirely) gone, flattened and taken yesterday to the transfer station. On the other hand, they hadn't even started on the boxes in the living room because they had made the decision that the wallpaper there—a repeating image of horses and hounds and a fox that looked disturbingly like an eel with fur—had to go and they might as well deal with it sooner rather than later. Nor had they started on the boxes in the dining room or the guest bedrooms. In the other rooms (and this house, they realized, really did have a lot of rooms) they had made varying degrees of progress, though all still had at least two or three unopened moving cartons.

Emily found herself fascinated by the traces that remained of the family who had lived in the house before them: Sometimes she was bemused, other times slightly disturbed. Parnell Dunmore had been buried nearly seven years now in the cemetery a mile away with the elegant wrought-iron fencing and the gates with the ornate trelliswork, and his wife, Tansy, had been in that graveyard almost four. Tansy had lived in the house not quite fifty years and, with Parnell, raised two sons there. Twins, which Emily viewed as either an irony or a coincidence. One of the sons had taken his own life as a twelve-year-old decades earlier, but his brother, now an ornery fifty-four-year-old named Hewitt, lived about forty minutes away in St. Johnsbury. Though almost all of the Dunmores' furniture had long been cleared by the time the Lintons moved in, a certain amount of detritus remained that either the son had forgotten or hadn't bothered to pack—or, in some way, was inextricably linked to the house. Sometimes Emily would find the sort of thing you might discover in the back of an antiques store, such as the broken but handsome sewing machine from the late nineteenth century. It was made of cast iron and mahogany and had a treadle in the bottom of the cabinet that demanded both feet to operate. It looked like a desk and might have weighed as much as a small car. Emily found it in the attic and couldn't imagine how anyone could possibly have carted it up the rickety steps that descended from a trapdoor in the second-floor ceiling and was the only link between the attic and the rest of the house. Not far from the sewing machine were rows of old wine bottles—over two dozen—with either plastic flowers or melted candles emerging from the tops. Some were forty years old. Among the items they found in the basement (all far from the corner with that peculiar door) were old wooden sap buckets, great coils of deteriorating rubber garden hose, a plastic model of an Apollo rocket, a brass door knocker, and three separate birdhouses. The girls found a couple of old teacups hanging from hooks in the very back of a cabinet in a dining room wall and porcelain figurines of elves and trolls and skiers in a box in a corner of the walk-in closet on the third floor.

Meanwhile, the carriage barn had everything from long lengths of rusted barbed wire to a Betty Crocker wall calendar made of canvas from 1973. There were empty paint cans and barrels of bobbins because once, decades and decades ago, there had been a bobbin mill along the river at the base of the hill on which the house sat. Apparently, every house in Bethel had barrels of bobbins. There were a boy's bow and a quiver of arrows, the tips blunt, and tall piles of what might have been the house's original shutters (there must have been fifty of them). There was a collar for a draft horse. Emily phoned Hewitt Dunmore in St. Johnsbury and asked about this miscellaneous silt from the house and the barn, even offering to drive the articles (including, somehow, that sewing machine) to his home, but Hewitt raged that he couldn't have been expected to empty the house completely, not with a back as bad as his and with knees that were cranky at best. He suggested they keep whatever they liked and bring to the dump whatever they didn't.

Even the small greenhouse hadn't been fully emptied. It still had its four wooden tables for plants, and the girls seemed to view it as their playhouse, even though it really wasn't all that warm right now; in fact, Emily was quite sure that the temperature was no more than four or five degrees warmer than outside. But the twins already had swept off the tables and deposited their American Girl dolls there, as well as most of the dolls' furniture. They had carted their bins with dress-up clothes there, too, as well as their plastic trolls (which they insisted they had outgrown years earlier but nonetheless had brought with them to New Hampshire). The cat, meanwhile, seemed to spend her time in the barn. She hadn't caught anything, as far as they knew, but she seemed to be stalking mice there.

The items that left Emily troubled were the crowbar, the knife, and the ax. She found their presence alarming and was relieved that it was she who had come across them, rather than Hallie or Garnet. She found the crowbar in the back of the closet of the second-floor bedroom that once had belonged to one of the Dunmore boys, a room that was going to be a guest bedroom now. It was upright in a corner and might merely have been there for years, forgotten. The knife was a carving knife with a pearl handle, and while the handle was discolored with age, the blade, though rusted, was sharp as new. Emily found it underneath a wrought-iron heating grate in the master bedroom—what was now her and Chip's bedroom—and she only noticed it because she was considering replacing the dingy black grille with something more attractive from a home restoration catalog. And so she happened to spin the grate and there it was. Some of the metal latticework had been sawed off, allowing the knife to be slipped into place—and quickly removed. And, finally, there was that ax—a hatchet, really. She found it behind some ancient (and scarily toxic) cleaning supplies that Hewitt Dunmore had left underneath the kitchen sink. It was the length of her arm from her elbow to the tip of her finger.

She showed each of the items—the crowbar, the knife, and the ax—to Chip as soon as she found them. He suggested that perhaps Tansy Dunmore had been especially unnerved by the murders, some years earlier, of a pair of Dartmouth College professors by some local teen boys. Dartmouth was a ninety-minute drive to the south, and the double homicide had left everyone in Vermont and New Hampshire on edge. Or, perhaps, Tansy had always been easily frightened.

"But we know that Parnell Dunmore had a hunting rifle," she replied, and he, in turn, surmised that she probably didn't know how to shoot.

"Trust me, most women aren't Lizzie Borden," Emily argued. "If a woman has a choice between killing someone at close range with a carving knife or an ax or shooting that person with a rifle, she is always going to pick the gun." But she saw that Chip was unconvinced. He remained more baffled than alarmed.

And, soon enough, her alarm passed, too, or perhaps she was so fixated on the day-to-day logistics of anchoring her family. Registering the twins for dance classes and school. Finding Hallie a new teacher for the flute and one for Garnet for the violin. Doing what she could to get them acclimated to their new classroom and teacher and (she hoped) friends. And then there was the ongoing vigilance when it came to Garnet's seizures. In most ways, they were minor: She would go into a trance and leave them for perhaps half an hour. Sometimes it would be less, sometimes more. It was a variant of epilepsy: Electrostatic discharges in her brain—solar flares on the EEGs—would interrupt her thinking, and her mind would become, in essence, a frozen computer. The issue, according to the neurologists (and they had seen three over the years), was whether the seizures might be symptomatic of a condition that would worsen as she grew, the seizures both lengthening and occurring with greater frequency. But, they reassured Chip and Emily, they were just as likely to disappear forever as Garnet approached adolescence. For a while she had been treated with Valium, but in doses that Emily knew would have left most adults wobbly-kneed and walking into walls. Somehow, Garnet handled the dosage just fine, despite the reality that she weighed barely half as much as her mother. The child had been off Valium for a year now and she hadn't had a seizure since October, but Emily never stopped watching.

Then last night they had lost power in a windstorm and the four of them wound up huddling for three hours in front of the woodstove. The novelty of the outage had worn off quickly, and the event had proven to be the last straw. They needed to get away for the day, and a Sunday at the nearby ski resort seemed like the ideal prescription.

As they were stowing their gear in the wagon midmorning, the air brisk but not uncomfortable (the thermometer outside the kitchen window, a dollop of mercury in a tube that was held by a brass relief of either a portly chimney sweep or Saint Nicholas, they couldn't decide, read thirty-one degrees), Emily saw a battered pickup truck rumbling its way up the long driveway. Most of the year the driveway was gravel and dirt, but by this point in the winter it was a solid glaze of packed snow and ice. The drifts along the side were so high that she couldn't see the truck's wheels, and it looked as if the vehicle were skimming across the top of the snow. She didn't recognize it. As far as she could tell it was red, but it was so streaked with white from road salt and brown from spread sand that she wasn't entirely sure. But it seemed to be losing a back panel to rust. And it definitely needed muffler work. It announced its presence with a roar, even though it was navigating the curling driveway with some care.

"You know who that is?" Chip asked. He had just finished pulling shut the clamps that locked the girls' snowboards to the roof.

"Not a clue," she said, and now she could see it was a woman driving, her hair a lustrous gray mane that was parted in the middle and fell well past her shoulders. Her parka was blue. The woman coasted to a stop in a section of driveway in front of the carriage barn, actually driving past their station wagon. Emily looked at her husband and saw he was already walking over to the pickup, and so she followed. The girls were bundled up and ready to go, but—as usual, when there was daylight and they weren't in school or unpacking boxes in their bedrooms—they were in the greenhouse.

"Good morning," the woman said, pushing open her door and jumping down onto the driveway with an obliviousness to the coating of snow there that was somewhere between foolhardy and confident. Emily still found herself moving gingerly along it. They had snow in

Pennsylvania, but not like this. Not all winter long. There the snow came and it went. Here? You'd never know that Greenland was melting faster than a Popsicle in July. Here were the winters she recalled from her childhood: snow and cold and winds that numbed her cheeks. Leafless, sinuous maples.

She noticed that the woman was holding a long, flat Tupperware tin in both hands and, on top of it, a similarly shaped baking dish covered with aluminum foil. Emily understood instantly that this was a neighbor bringing food. More food. A lasagna and brownies, she suspected. She guessed that the woman was almost a generation older than she and Chip: probably fifty-five or sixty. Her face was lovely but lined, and her eyes looked a bit like her parka: They were the color of moonstones. She wasn't wearing gloves. "I'm Anise," she said. "I'm a friend of Reseda Hill," she added, referring to the woman who had taken over as their real estate agent after Sheldon Carter died so abruptly.

"Emily Linton," she said. "This is Chip, my husband." Emily found it interesting that, ever since the plane crash, she had been more likely to introduce her husband than he was to take the social lead and introduce her. He wasn't a failure—not by a long stretch when she contemplated the traumas that had marked his childhood—but he had confessed to her that he felt like one. These days he defined himself entirely by a single moment, and that moment was not about the nine people who had lived but was instead about the thirty-nine who had perished. He defined himself almost wholly in the negative: It was not who he was, it was who he was not. Now she watched the tentative way that he gave this friend of their real estate agent his hand and mumbled a soft greeting.

"Oh, I'd know your face anywhere," Anise said with a broad smile that revealed a layer of upper teeth that were just beginning to cross over one another and a row of lower ones that were starting to yellow with age. The woman hadn't meant anything by the remark, but it had become one of those statements that Emily knew made Chip anxious. Yes, for a time his face had been everywhere. For a time it had been all over the Web, the cable news networks, and the newsweeklies. After all, he was the pilot who had failed to do what Sully Sullenberger had accomplished. People never meant anything when they said that they recognized him. And sometimes it was even better when they came right out and acknowledged that they knew who he was, as Anise just had, rather than simply staring at him and saying nothing. Chip had told her once that silence without verbal recognition seemed like even more of an indictment.

"Can I help you with those?" Emily asked, and she pointed at the tin and the baking dish in Anise's arms.

"If you promise to eat them," said Anise. "There's a lentil-nut loaf in this one and carob-chip brownies in the other."

"Vegan?" Emily asked.

"Yes. They taste better than they sound—I promise," Anise insisted, and she handed the items to Emily with particular care because Emily was already wearing her ski gloves. "The brownies have names on them. One for each of you. Hallie is spelled with an *i-e*, right?"

"Yes, that's right. Really, this all sounds scrumptious. Thank you. It will be such a gift not to have to cook tonight."

"Reheat the lentil loaf in a three-hundred-and-seventy-five-degree oven for twenty minutes."

"Or microwave it for, what, three minutes? Four?"

Anise tilted her head as if this were a math equation that was puzzling her. "Huh. I don't have one of those. Too scary. I put those in the same category with cell phones and aspartame. You're just asking for brain cancer."

Emily noticed that her husband hadn't said a word, but now he was eyeing the woman's vehicle. She had been married to him long enough to know that he was probably wondering how this woman with her fear of carcinogens in diet soda and radiation from a cell phone could drive around in that rusted-out, carbon-monoxide-spewing tank.

"It looks like you're about to head to the mountain," Anise observed, just as the pause was about to grow awkward.

"We are," Emily told her.

"With the girls?"

"Yes," she said, momentarily nonplussed by the idea that she and

Chip might be leaving the girls behind. Of course they would be bringing them. She wasn't going to leave a pair of ten-year-olds alone for the day—especially in an unfamiliar house in which once had resided an apparently sociopathically skittish old woman who left knives and hatchets in corners. But then she reminded herself that Anise was a friend of Reseda's, and there was every reason to presume that Anise was simply trying to make conversation. Show some interest. "It's a family outing," Emily went on. "An escape from Box Hell."

"You lose power last night?"

"We did. Did you?"

"I did. I was surprised because I live in the valley. Living up here on the hill, you'll lose it more often than I will," Anise said. Then: "Well, I don't want to keep you. I live on the road to the Notchway Inn. It's the brick Georgian with the greenhouse and the overgrown paddock with the white fence. I don't have horses, but a previous owner did. Don't be strangers."

"You know much about this house?" It was Chip speaking, and because it was the first time he had opened his mouth other than his softly murmured how-do-you-do, both she and Anise found themselves turning toward him with a combination of intensity and expectation.

"A little bit. I knew Sawyer and Hewitt Dunmore. It's an interesting place, isn't it?"

"Can I ask you a question?" Chip said.

"Absolutely," answered this friend of their real estate agent.

"In the basement is a door. I noticed it the day before yesterday when I was bringing a load of laundry down there."

"Okay," she said, shrugging. "Where does it go?"

"I don't know. I was hoping you might."

"Nope."

"It's sealed shut."

"Sealed?"

"With bolts. Lots and lots of carriage bolts."

"That's interesting. Based on the design of the house, where do you think it goes? Back up to the kitchen, I'd wager. I know the house has a back stairway linking the first and second floors. Why not one linking the basement with the kitchen?"

"Not likely. The kitchen would be above the other side of the basement. It seems to be a door to nothing. It's at the edge of the house. All that's above it is the screened porch. And that porch is just built above dirt."

"I'll bet it was a ramp, in that case. A wheelbarrow ramp."

"There's one of those on the other side of the basement—on the north side of the house."

"Maybe it's a coal chute then."

"There is some old coal lying around it," he admitted.

"There you go, mystery solved. The Dunmores—or the Pierces before them—probably built that screened porch after they stopped heating with coal."

He nodded, but Emily knew that her husband wasn't entirely convinced. The two of them had discussed the likelihood that it was merely a coal chute the afternoon he first noticed it. Certainly it was possible that's all it was. But why would you use thirty-nine carriage bolts to seal it shut? (Emily feared the coincidence that there were the same number of bolts as there were fatalities on Flight 1611 was only going to exacerbate her husband's fixation on the door.) Chip had removed one of the bolts, but it had taken an awl with a beveled point, a screwdriver, and a hammer—and nearly twenty-five minutes of struggling. It was six inches long. When he realized that the remaining thirty-eight were probably identical and might demand the same labor—kneeling in dirt and moldy, crumbling coal—he twisted the carriage bolt back into place and returned upstairs to unpack some more boxes. Over cups of decaffeinated coffee late that night, sitting on the floor in the den because here was one room where the wallpaper was a soothing pattern of blue and yellow iris, he and Emily discussed calling Hewitt Dunmore to ask about the strange door. But when Emily had phoned Hewitt yesterday about the possessions they'd come across in the house, everything from that extraordinary sewing machine to those eccentric figurines, she had found herself incapable of asking him about it—or, for that matter, about the crowbar, the knife, and the ax. He seemed too damn ornery. Besides, it was just a door to a coal chute, wasn't it? She decided another time, perhaps.

"Yeah, that's what we figured," Chip said finally. "A coal chute."

"What else could it be?" Anise agreed, and she raised her eyebrows and smiled once more. "It's not like the Dunmores hid bodies down there."

No, of course not, Emily thought.

"It must feel wonderful to be here," Anise continued.

"It's nice," Emily agreed, carefully modulating her tone. Nothing in her life felt particularly wonderful right now. Besides, she hadn't been here long enough to have any sense at all of whether moving to Bethel had been the right decision.

"Are you going to garden?"

"I don't know."

"Did you garden in Pennsylvania?"

"Not really."

Anise motioned at the greenhouse. "You'll want to take advantage of that. Tansy did for a while. Then she stopped. She shouldn't have."

Emily thought about this. "I presume you're a gardener," she said finally. "You said you have a greenhouse."

"We're all gardeners," Anise answered, and there was something in the tone that was oddly salacious. A moment later, the woman was climbing into her battered pickup and Emily was carrying the lentil-nut loaf and four carob-chip brownies with their names on them into the kitchen and calling for the girls. Chip remained outside by their car, staring up into the sky and, she presumed, watching for birds or the white trail of a jet high overhead.

You do watch for birds. You do stare at the plumes of the jets high overhead. You will, you know, never fly again. Not as a pilot and not as a passenger. Never.

You have confessed only to your psychiatrist in Philadelphia that, suddenly, you are afraid of flying. As well, you discussed with her at length what physicians have determined are the psychosomatic or phantom pains in your neck and your back and your head: the lingering whiplash. The occasional daggerlike spikes in your left kidney and abdomen, a sensation you have likened to a horizontal barb impaling you through your back and your stomach. The way your skull sometimes feels as if the frontal bone—that great helmet beneath your skin—has been crushed, smashed into the brain in one moment of life-ending trauma.

She told you they would pass. Eventually.

Instead they have gotten worse this week since you arrived in New Hampshire. You tell yourself it is because of the work of moving your family from one house to another. All that lifting. All that stress. It was bound to aggravate whatever is going on in your back and your neck and your head. Your mind.

Moreover, the dreams seem to be changing here. Oh, you still have the dreams where you crash CRJs in catastrophic, steel-melting infernos—though, of course, you always wake a split second before impact. You still have the nightmares with dense tropical forests filled with palm trees and oxygen masks dangling like strange, tubular plants.

But last night there was a dream with a little girl, not either of your daughters. She was sopping wet, drowned—dead, you knew it even in your sleep—but she didn't know she was dead and she was nattering on and on about her backpack, which she wanted you to help her find. This was new. So was the dream on Thursday night with some burly guy your age who was standing behind you and Amy, your now dead first officer, on the flight deck of the CRJ as you were about to start down Burlington's runway 33 for the last time. He was telling you to wait, wait, wait—to goddamn it, wait!—because if you waited just a couple of seconds you wouldn't hit the goddamn birds. But you ignored him and started your roll, turning around to command him to take his seat in the passenger cabin, noticing for the first time when you turned that he, too, was dead and hadn't a clue: A round metal shard had pierced his skull like a long spike of rebar, and another was protruding from just beneath his rib cage. Only in a dream could he stand.

Soon enough, the nightmare ended as they all do: a fireball occurring just as you open your eyes and stare up at the diaphanous shadows of your bedroom at night.

O ne time, if only to change the dynamic with your psychiatrist in Philadelphia, you told her about a broad broad brought abroad. A joke at your mother's expense when you were in the fifth grade. Your mother was terrified of flying. Absolutely petrified. Had to be hammered to get on an airplane. Had to have her good-luck charm bracelet on her wrist and her Saint Christopher's medal around her neck. Had to be wearing a specific pair of sunglasses as a headband to keep that long and lustrous black hair off her face. Tony Swoboda and his wife, Kaye, were driving you and your family from Stamford to Kennedy Airport the time you all flew to Spain and Portugal on a two-week tour. One of those vacation packages that took you to a half dozen cities in barely a dozen days: Madrid in two days and Lisbon in thirty-six hours. An afternoon for Toledo. It was your last vacation as a family—you and your parents and your younger brother—because it would be soon after your return that your father would start up the grand staircase at Grand Central Terminal around 8:35 on a Tuesday morning and die right there on the steps of a ruptured cerebral aneurysm. (His last conscious vision? You like to believe it was Paul Helleu's Mediterranean sky, but at the time the ceiling had not yet been restored. The stars that day had still been obscured by soot.) He was walking from the train station to his office at the ad agency on Forty-eighth Street, as he had almost every workday of his life for twenty years. It was the end for him, but only the beginning of the end for your mother. Somehow, her husband's life insurance had lapsed and their savings and investments were clearly inadequate to keep her and her two sons in a four-bedroom house near the water in Greenwich, Connecticut. They would cut back, then they would move. A smaller house in Stamford, at the edge of the city. It wouldn't have been so bad for the three of them if the combination of widowhood and diminished resources hadn't conspired to turn a social drinker (a very social drinker, in hindsight) into a drunk.

Ah, but your father was still among you when you went to Kennedy Airport for the final time as a family of four. And Tony was teasing your mother that afternoon, trying to make her smile because the idea of fly-ing across the Atlantic Ocean at night had her on the verge of vomiting. Tony and Kaye were great friends of your parents. Had been for years. "Yeah," Tony was saying to your mother, as he and your father carted the great suitcases into the terminal from the parking lot (you realize when you focus upon the details of this memory that Tony and Kaye have not dropped you all off at the curb before the departure doors; they have parked their massive station wagon and are crossing the garage with you), "you're just a broad broad brought abroad." Your mother couldn't quite bring herself to smile, but she finally put out her cigarette and stared at something other than her fingers or the smoke or the length of the ash, and marched into the terminal. This was at the very end of the era when people dressed for flying as if the airplane were a synagogue or a church. Your mother was wearing a gray cashmere blazer and a black skirt, and even as a ten-year-old boy you knew it was far chichier than the uniforms that some of the airlines had their stewardesses wearing. And you, of course, were in your navy blue sports jacket—the only blazer you owned because you were a boy and how many sports jackets does a boy really need?

Unlike your mother (and, to a certain extent, even your father), you had never been scared of flying. Not even the tiniest bit. From your very first flight, a Boeing 727 to Florida, you would always sit hypnotized in your seat, staring out the window as the plane accelerated down the run-way and gently lifted off. The windows invariably were scratched, but still you would watch the world grow small and wait for the jolt as the plane cracked the edge of the clouds. You built plastic models of fighter jets, passenger jets, and the lumbering bombers the United States used in the Second World War. For hours at a time you played a video game—one of the first of its kind—in which you were a pilot with a rudimentary jet console before you.

That night you flew with your family to Europe, your mother sit-ting in the seat beside you, gripping the armrests during takeoff, con-vinced that nothing as heavy as this—a Boeing 747—could possibly get off the ground or (if somehow it did) remain aloft. Meanwhile, you only studied the lights along the runway and the landmarks of the terminals nearby. Your mother believed that bad things happened at thirty-five thousand feet, and her terrors were exacerbated rather than relieved by all that Scotch she would consume when the plane reached its cruising altitude. She was always a little pale when she flew. A broad broad brought abroad.

You, however, loved the experience. The speed. The vistas. The peace. Later you would understand the physics of flying, but that never lessened the magic. Even when the plane would be cruising on autopilot and you were swapping out Jepp charts in your binder—tedious work you seemed to be doing at least twice a month—you would occasionally glance out the window and find yourself a little awed by the beauty of the world so very, very far below you.

Ten-year-old Hallie Linton thought their new greenhouse in Bethel was a bit like the walled garden in that story *The Secret Garden*. It was an enchanted place, but—just like in the novel and the movie— right now you couldn't see its possibilities. It was wintry in there at the moment and empty, except for those four tables and the stacks of flimsy plastic pots, and it smelled musty. There was so much black dirt on some of the big glass panes that a person could write her name in it. But she loved the building. Even now, the sun six weeks shy of the equinox and much of the glass opaque with grime, the greenhouse glowed with a bluish tint at the right time of the day. Hallie studied the way the long metal beams sparkled at noon, especially after she and Garnet had taken some Windex and paper towels yesterday and gingerly stood on the tables and scrubbed a few of the windowpanes. (Cleaning all of the windows was going to be a major project, both because there were so many and because the dirt, in this temperature, seemed to have been quilted over with glue. Nevertheless, she had every intention of making the effort when the days had gotten a little longer and the sun had started thawing the grime.)

She knew Garnet didn't have quite as much interest in the building as she did, but dutifully she had helped cart out their dolls and the doll furniture; she seemed to appreciate the idea that at some point this was going to be their playhouse—or, at least, a playhouse that they might share with their mom and dad's plants. Their parents had not evidenced a particular interest in gardening in West Chester, but recently their mother had said something about starting tomato seedlings in here. She had said she might even take up flowers as a hobby. It didn't matter to Hallie. How much time could a grown-up really spend in a building like this? Besides, their mom had taken a job with a couple of other lawyers in Littleton. And their dad? Hallie couldn't begin to imagine what was going to interest Dad now that he was no longer a pilot. She was pretty sure that planes were all he knew and all that interested him. He liked to fly—or had once. She certainly didn't see him gardening or growing flowers in here.

Of course, she wasn't precisely sure what was going to interest her either in New Hampshire. She knew that she was outgrowing her dolls, but she had no idea what might replace them here in the mountains. Probably not ballet and probably not the flute. Though she was only ten, Hallie grasped the reality that these would be just hobbies for her, even if she pursued them vigorously; she was no prodigy and there was no point in approaching either ballet or music with passion. This revelation neither saddened nor slowed her. She presumed someday she would find something else, and in the meantime she would go to dance class and practice her flute with the same dogged acceptance that compelled her to attend to her homework.

She had noticed already that she didn't seem to have quite as much homework in Bethel. That might change. But at least over their first few days here, her new teacher hadn't assigned nearly as much math or spelling or reading as Mrs. Leeds had in West Chester.

Moreover, there weren't the massive shopping malls here that there were in the suburbs of Philadelphia. Or the community theater groups for their mom. Or even the Phillies—which, she had to admit, interested her mostly because they had interested her dad and some of her friends at her old school. Had they remained in Pennsylvania, she and Garnet were going to get cell phones for their eleventh birthday this coming summer, but cell phones seemed less important here: There wasn't any coverage at their new house, so how could they text their friends—assuming, of course, they eventually made some new ones? Hallie imagined bringing a laptop out to the greenhouse and getting a page on something like Facebook, just like the older kids, and surfing and posting and chatting for hours, but the router would have to be mighty powerful. She guessed they would spend a lot more time snowboarding here than they had in Pennsylvania. After all, the mountain was only twenty minutes away; they could see it from one of the house's porches. And yesterday they had seen—and heard—snowmobiles racing across the farthest edge of the meadow, and so she thought it was possible that maybe she'd take up snowmobiling.

Now, here was something that might interest Dad: snowmobiling. The connections in her mind were the roar of the engines and the sense of speed. Like a jet, a snowmobile was fast and it was loud.

Based on the few days that she and Garnet had been at their new school and their first visit to their new dance studio, it was clear that she was going to have to take the lead if she and her sister were going to make any new friends. That probably was to be expected. She had always been more popular than Garnet back in Pennsylvania, so why wouldn't that be the case here? Hallie understood that her sister was going to be a part of any group largely because she herself was. Moms seemed to love Garnet's red hair, but kids thought it was almost too red. This wasn't strawberry blond stuff. It was more like just strawberry. (Hallie was thankful every day that they were fraternal twins only; she liked her dark brown hair much more than Garnet's, and she knew she had a much prettier nose.) And then there were the trances. And those overnight stays at the hospital over the years for EEGs and testing. It was only a matter of time before Garnet would have a seizure here and the kids would view her simultaneously with the contempt wolves feel for the wounded and lame, and with the terror they feel for someone who is chronically ill.

And yet the sense that Garnet was an outsider, a little different, also gave her twin a certain control over her: Hallie knew that often she would defer to Garnet's wishes when they were alone, the motivation existing somewhere in that realm between sympathy and loyalty.

So far they hadn't brought any of their new schoolmates—her new schoolmates, really—over to play. Not Molly or Lily or Adele. There hadn't been time. But she guessed she would soon. Molly, perhaps, who sat at her classroom table, even though she and Molly really didn't have all that much in common. Or maybe it would be Lily. She hoped she and Lily would become friends. Good friends. Lily was nice. So was Lily's mother, though the woman seemed to hover a lot. When they were introduced at the school and Lily's mother figured out that she and Garnet were twins—*the new twins,* she had cooed—she had been weirdly excited. Hallie could tell that it had made the school principal, who happened to be in the classroom at the time, a little uncomfortable. But Lily's mom was friends with Reseda, the lady who'd wound up being their real estate agent after Mr. Carter died, and Reseda seemed to be nice enough. She was sweet—and she was very, very pretty, in an exotic sort of way.

Hallie heard Garnet calling for her now, yelling that Mom and Dad said the car was packed and it was time to leave for the mountain. As she closed the greenhouse door, she made a mental note to ask Mom if she was making new friends. She hoped that her mom and Reseda would become pals.

When the girls had been in the second grade, a plane had crashed outside of Harrisburg, Pennsylvania, killing all forty-four people onboard. Apparently, a combination of ice and wind and inexperience had been the culprits. It was a turboprop—a Dash 8—not one of the planes Chip flew. But it crashed on approach to the airport, and so it was near enough to civilization that news crews were on the scene in moments and footage of the fiery wreck was on television for days. Chip had been gone at the time, in the midst of three days of flying around the Northeast and the Mid-Atlantic. Emily recalled the ways she had tried to shield her girls from the images—as she did always when there was an accident—but this time the twins had gotten wind of the crash and become frightened. She had had to sit Hallie and Garnet down in the living room, the three of them in what had become their accustomed spots on the massive, L-shaped couch with the upholstery of lovebirds, and reassure them that they needn't worry. Their father was safe. Their father's plane (and even though Chip flew many planes, they seemed to discuss Chip's work as if he always flew the same exact jet) was not going to crash. Because she harbored her own small superstitions, Emily did not want to jinx Chip by stating that his plane was *never* going to crash. It was a small, semantic distinction, but it reassured her; it gave her the sense that she wasn't really tempting fate. (Still, in even her worst, wildest dreams, she didn't honestly believe that someday his plane might pinwheel into a lake minutes after takeoff.)

And she had managed to comfort the girls that day. Other planes might crash—but not Daddy's.

She wondered now if when the twins were alone they discussed that afternoon on the couch three years ago. She assumed they remembered it. She considered whether they felt betrayed by their mother, whether they had come to the conclusion that her reassurances were meaningless. That she would say anything to calm them down. But what mother wouldn't? The fact that neither girl had reminded her of the conversation meant nothing to Emily.

She was glad they lived three hours east of Lake Champlain. She could never have tolerated a move to New England if Bethel had been anywhere near that lake.

"Garnet?"

The girl opened her eyes when she heard her name and swam slowly to the surface of wakefulness. At first she presumed she was home. West Chester. The room overlooking the front walkway and the apple tree, the two windows on one wall opposite the foot of the bed. The homes of their neighbors—the Morrisons and the Browns—visible if she craned her neck to the left or the right. But here, she noticed, there was only one window at the foot of her bed, while there was a second one to the right side of it—both horizontal. She saw the wallpaper in the night-light, the green and red plaid that looked like Christmastime wrapping paper. She saw the moon, a day or two short of full, through the glass and the gauzy curtains that her father had hung the day before yesterday. And finally she remembered precisely where she was. New Hampshire. Not home. No, that wasn't right. She *was* home. It was just that home now was New Hampshire. She and Hallie had the two bedrooms on the third floor of this house. The floor with the attic (though you couldn't get to the attic from either her or Hallie's room; you had to pull down that trapdoor in the ceiling in the hallway on the floor below them). Their old home, she recalled, had only the two floors. For a moment her eyes focused on the last remaining moving box that she hadn't yet begun to unpack, and she tried to remember what was inside it. It was a big one. Barbie dolls and the Dream House? Summer T-shirts and shorts and bathing suits? That seemed right. It had clothes and dolls and the Dream House.

The day and the evening slowly came back to her. Snowboarding. The tram with her mom and Hallie, and the way the snow on the pine trees at the top of the mountain reminded her of vanilla cake frosting. Hot chocolate at the base lodge. Then there was the dinner at home that was completely inedible: a bean loaf followed by bad-tasting brownies that some woman had baked for them, though Hallie had liked the brownies more than everyone else and had been so hungry after the main course that she had ended up devouring the brownie with Dad's name on it as well as her own. Then they had watched a DVD of some teen boy who learns he's a prince, a movie they'd long outgrown that made both girls wish they had the satellite dish hooked up so they could watch regular TV instead.

"Garnet?"

There in the doorway stood Hallie.

In an instant, the second that Garnet had pushed herself ever so slightly off the mattress and glanced at her, Hallie had realized that her sister was awake and raced across the room like a sprinter and dove into bed beside her. She burrowed under the quilt, and Garnet could feel how cold her sister's feet were.

"Your toes are icicles," she said to Hallie. Then: "What are you doing?"

Her voice a whisper, Hallie said, "You don't hear them?"

Them? Mom and Dad? "Who?" she asked anyway, presuming that of course her sister was referring to their parents.

"I don't know. Listen," Hallie murmured urgently. "Just listen."

And so Garnet did. She heard the slight whistle of her sister's breathing through her nose and she heard the occasional soft bang from the ancient radiator that sat like a gargoyle on the wall nearest the bed. But there was no wind outside and the cat, wherever she was at the moment, wasn't making a sound. There was no noise at all coming from Mom and Dad's bedroom on the floor below them.

"I don't hear anything," she said finally.

"You must!" There was an urgency to Hallie's voice that was rare.

"What time is it?"

"It's like three. Listen!"

"What should I be hearing?"

In the moonlight Garnet could see her sister's eyes, wide and alert, and she thought once again of their cat. Dessy, short for Desdemona. They had gotten the cat from the animal shelter when they were three and Mom had done a Shakespeare play with a character with that name. The cat's orange fur had reminded their mom of the color of the gown she had worn for much of the production.

"You really don't hear it?" Hallie asked in a small but intense voice. "You really don't hear them?"

There was that word again: *them.*

"No."

Hallie was lying on her side, but her head was elevated, her ears well above the pillow. "Wait, it's stopped."

"What?"

"Shhhhhhhh."

"No, don't shush me. Tell me! You're scaring me!" Rarely was Garnet ever this insistent with her older sister. Though Hallie was only minutes her senior, Garnet always deferred to her as if the chasm that separated them was two or three years.

"I'm scared myself."

"Of what?"

"I heard people."

"Really?"

Hallie nodded. "Two or three. I don't know. But definitely one was a girl—like our age. Or maybe a little younger."

"In the house?"

"I guess."

"You guess?"

"It doesn't make sense."

"Of course it doesn't. The nearest house must be, like, a mile away."

"No, that's not why it doesn't make sense," Hallie said.

"Then why?"

"I don't know, but the people were mad. Or scared. That's it, that's why they were so loud: They were scared. I think they were more scared than mad. And I heard water. Lots of water. Waves and stuff."

"You were dreaming."

"I heard it when I was talking to you just this second."

"What did you hear?"

"The water and the people and someone was, like, choking—"

"We don't have a pond," Garnet said, cutting her off. "We don't have a pool. We don't even have a brook like we had in West Chester. It had to be just a nightmare."

"I don't have nightmares. You do. I don't." She made it sound like a failing, Garnet thought, like Hallie viewed it as an accomplishment that she didn't have bad dreams. But Garnet also had to admit that she was indeed far more likely to have nightmares than her sister. It had always been that way. Supposedly the nightmares had nothing to do with what the adults referred to as her epilepsy or her seizures, but she wasn't so sure. When she was having one, it was like she was asleep and the waking world—the real world—was a dream.

"Besides, it wasn't the water that made it so scary," Hallie went on.

"No?"

"No. It's that the people were drowning."

"What?"

"They were, like, screaming for help and choking. Especially the girl. And just now when I came in here? It was like she was gagging. I could almost feel it."

Garnet considered this for a brief second. Then she took Hallie's hand and pulled her sister from the bed, dragging her along the short corridor on the third floor and then down the steep, thin stairway to the second floor, with their parents' bedroom. On the way, she switched on every light in the halls between the two rooms.

Chapter Two

Emily's separation from her firm was perfectly amicable, and she was able to bring some of her practice with her from Pennsylvania to New Hampshire. She passed the White Mountain bar in the winter months between when she and Chip made an offer on the house and when they and their daughters moved in. But she also joined a small firm in Littleton so she would have an office and an assistant and at least a shadow of the legal amenities she was accustomed to. Their new real estate agent, Reseda Hill, had essentially brokered that deal, too, introducing her to John Hardin, the firm's paterfamilias. Now Emily would have a place to go during the day, which was something she needed; she didn't see herself as the sort of attorney who was capable of working from her house.

But at nights and on weekends, when she was in their new home that February, she found herself studying her husband carefully. She was not precisely sure what she was looking for and worried about, yet she was incapable of suppressing a demonstrable anxiety that filled her on occasion when she saw him. He was sleeping badly, even worse here in northern New England than he had in their rambling Colonial in the development outside of Philadelphia in the weeks after the crash. The psychiatrist from the union had warned her that this would happen. She had said it was likely that Chip's appetite might all but disappear. It had. And his bad dreams continued, despite the prescribed pharmacological intervention, and all it took was the ethereal plume of a plane high in the atmosphere to cause his heart to race. He broke out in a sweat at Cannon Mountain when the ski lift they were riding stalled halfway up the mountain and they dangled in their seats perhaps forty yards above the well-groomed snow. He became nauseous sometimes when he heard the birds that remained through the winter months outside the kitchen window in the morning. And he would grow a little dizzy whenever he came across a news story about the airline industry or an airplane—and there were always news stories about the airline industry and airplanes. Always. And, finally, there were those phantom pains throughout his body that continued to plague him. He'd had all the testing imaginable back in Pennsylvania: CAT scans and MRIs and dyes injected everywhere. He had seen all manner of chiropractors and physical therapists. And none of the tests had shown anything wrong.

The real strangeness? His ankle and two of his ribs—the former sprained badly, the latter broken and cracked—had healed completely and he felt absolutely no pain there. Same with the spot on his head where he had actually been cut. The top of his head, he reported, often hurt like hell—but not his forehead, which had been cut when his head slammed into the right prong of the control stick. Moreover, these aches and pains had only gotten worse since they had moved to northern New Hampshire.

They both understood that a degree of PTSD was inevitable. How could it not be? He had captained a plane that had crashed and four-fifths of the people onboard had died. It wasn't his fault: He wasn't fatigued, he hadn't been distracted or inattentive, he hadn't pulled back on the control yoke when he should have pressed it forward to recover from a stall. (Once, years earlier, he had had a plane stall on him when the wings iced over, and calmly he had pushed the yoke forward, accelerating the descent but restarting the engines, and landed smoothly. None of the passengers onboard had ever known there had been a problem, but he had been roundly applauded by his airline. And how many times had he successfully aborted landings at the last minute because there was a truck or a plane on the runway that wasn't supposed to be there and performed a go-around? At least once for every seven or eight months he had been flying.) That didn't make the visions and memories that came

back to him—illuminated suddenly like trees in the dark made clear by
great bolts of lightning—any easier to shoulder. But, still, she watched
him when she wasn't at her new office in Littleton, aware that this was a
reversal in their roles: In the past, he had been the one to watch over her
during those intervals when he wasn't flying.

Meanwhile, Hallie was sleeping badly, too, and no one from the
union or the airline or the Critical Incident Response Team had advised
her to expect this. There was that strange night when her daughter was
convinced she heard people—a child—drowning. It had been three in
the morning and had been the worst sort of nightmare: so real that she
was convinced she was hearing the child for long minutes after she was
awake. And Hallie had never really had nightmares before. Bad dreams
had always been far more likely to dog Garnet than her sister in the small
hours of the morning.

Consequently, when Emily wasn't watching her husband, she was
watching her daughter. And when she wasn't watching Hallie, she had
to remain vigilant around Garnet: She always had to be prepared for the
next seizure. It was a wonder she was able to get out of bed in the morning, much less find the energy to get her girls out the door for school and
then drive into Littleton for work. But she had to. She had to. Someone,
somehow, had to keep it together.

You are curious about the hallways in this house in the White Mountains because the one on the third floor of the structure seems slender compared to the ones on the second. Or, for that matter, the ones
on the first. You really didn't notice this when you were looking at the
house with Emily and Sheldon. And so you track down the tape measure in the carton with the tools you have been using as you settle into
the house but have yet to organize in some fashion in that basement
made largely of dirt. You find it in the living room, where you were wall-
papering yesterday, and begin by measuring the corridor that links the
front hall with the seventeen steps to the second floor. (A thought: That
strange, thin back stairwell that links the kitchen with the second floor.

Is that seventeen steps, too?) Then you climb those steps to measure the hallway outside of your and Emily's bedroom. Finally you start up the fifteen steps to the third floor. There you kneel and stretch the tape measure across the corridor outside of Hallie's bedroom. It wasn't your imagination or an optical illusion: The hallways are thirty-nine inches wide on the first floor (there, again, is that number), thirty-seven on the second, and thirty-four on the third. Five inches is not a great distance, but it is enough to make that corridor feel claustrophobic—or, to use the word Emily and the girls have used as your twins have started nesting like barn swallows on this small, third floor, *cozy*. The third floor has but three rooms: two bedrooms that share a walk-in closet in the hallway (neither bedroom has a closet of its own) and a bathroom with a lion's-foot tub but no shower. The attic exists on the same level, but a veritable Berlin Wall separates it from this small nook of rooms. The house narrows between the second and third floors, with that elegant fish-scale trim that marks the screened porch reestablishing itself on the third-floor exterior. Hallie's and Garnet's bedrooms are characterized by the house's sloping roof, snug knee walls, and horizontal windows.

You put the tape measure down on the wooden floor and sit.

She deserves friends.

A man's voice. You have heard it periodically since you came here. You try to recall if you heard it in Pennsylvania as well, and you decide . . . maybe. Maybe not. You turn to see if anyone is with you in the corridor, and, as always, you are alone. But you know, in reality, you're not. There is the voice you have just heard of this man roughly your age and the voice of a girl no older (and, perhaps, a bit younger) than your lovely daughters and the voice of a woman perhaps ten years your junior. And there are the cacophonous shrieks and wails of all the women and men who died on Flight 1611. Should you have told Hallie that you knew precisely who she heard your first Sunday night in this house? Maybe. But how could you without further terrifying the poor child? You wish you knew what it meant that she heard their voices, too, and try to take comfort in the reality that she hasn't reported hearing them since.

You sigh. You note the sunshine through the hallway window and the opalescent light it casts upon the wood paneling. This third-floor hallway is paneled with maple, like some of the first-floor corridors; the second floor is merely painted Sheetrock. You find yourself slowly pulling your knees into your chest and contemplating how, other than that voice—now gone—the house is quiet. The girls are at school and Emily is at work. It must seem to the world that you are all alone.

You wonder if you will ever work again. You wonder what you could do. All you have ever done professionally is fly airplanes.

Somehow, despite the way your grades tumbled after your father died and your mother was aged quickly by bottles of very bad Scotch, you made it into the University of Massachusetts. It might have been the University of Connecticut, but when you were fifteen your mother lost her driver's license for the last time and your aunt and uncle in Framingham, Massachusetts, decided that you and your eleven-year-old brother would be better off with them. Your mother agreed. It had gotten to the point where it didn't matter that you watered down the Scotch, every other day pouring out perhaps half an inch—a portion of the schooner sail or cliff-side estate that gave character to the label—of the whiskey and adding just that much tap water. Your mother would drink just that much more.

And your little brother? He's doing fine. He used to be considered fragile. Wounded. Scarred. Done in by the abrupt and early death of your father and the virtual mummification of your mother. He's doing better than you, these days. He teaches history at a high school in Berkeley. Got as far away from Connecticut and Massachusetts as he could.

Now it is you who everyone presumes is so fragile. Wounded. Scarred. Maybe they're right. Perhaps you are.

A nursery rhyme comes into your head, and, like an egg, you allow yourself to topple onto your side, your legs still pulled hard against your torso. You lie like that a long while, watching the chrome shell of the tape measure sparkle until the sun moves.

She deserves friends.

You nod. She does.

Chapter Three

G arnet came down the stairs with her math workbook and a couple of pencils. They were supposed to convert miles into yards
or feet and vice versa, and Hallie was incapable of explaining to
her how to do it when the answer wasn't obvious. Their dad was excellent at math, although neither girl had availed herself of his abilities since
the accident because they did not want to burden him with one more
thing. From conversations they had overheard their mother having with
friends on the telephone and the things they had seen their father doing
(or, in some cases, not doing), they feared that asking him to help them
with math just might put him over the edge. But they had been in New
Hampshire for a couple of weeks now, and maybe things would be different here. More normal. Their mother and father talked about how
they were starting here with a clean slate. And based on the changes that
would occur in the house when they were at school—some old wallpaper gone or some new wallpaper hung, a banister stained or another
room painted—their dad had emerged from the funk that had left him
cocooned and immobile in his bathrobe in West Chester. And so Garnet
figured now was as good a time as any to come down the two flights of
stairs and get some help with her math. It might even be good for Dad.

When she found him, he was in the kitchen, but he wasn't making
dinner even though it was nearly five in the afternoon. They seemed
to eat earlier here than they did in Pennsylvania, in part because Mom
didn't have such a long commute and got home earlier, but also because
everyone here just seemed to do everything earlier. In Pennsylvania, Dad

had usually done the cooking in those three- or four-day periods when he had been home and Mom had fed them when Dad had been flying. Of course, Mom's dinners had been pretty likely to be frozen food or take-out pizza—which was absolutely fine. She was, essentially, a single parent half the time. And then there were those seasons when Mom was in a community theater drama or musical. Often those nights when Dad was flying, Garnet and Hallie would color or play games or do a little homework while eating deli sandwiches in the back of whatever gym or community center where Mom's theater troupe was rehearsing.

When Garnet got downstairs, she found her father on his knees, rummaging through the cabinet beneath the kitchen sink. His head and shoulders were invisible inside the cabinetry, and around his legs were the bottles and jars and brushes that usually were stored under there.

"Dad?"

Carefully he withdrew his upper body and sat on his heels. His hair was disheveled, and she noticed a thin trickle of sweat on his brow. He had a mug with cold coffee beside him.

"Hey, princess," he said. He called both her and her sister *princess*. It was a term of endearment, but no more specific than *honey* or *darling*. "What do you need?"

"Can you help me with my math?" She held out the workbook like an offering, both of her hands beneath it as if she were presenting a sacred text to a rabbi or priest.

He was silent for a moment, and she wondered after she had spoken if this might be one of those instances that would be important years from now: the first time her dad had helped her with her math after the accident. A great step forward in the march back to normalcy. But when the moment grew long and still he had said nothing, she decided she was wrong: This would instead be merely one more of those times when her dad's behavior would suggest it was going to be a long, long time before he was better.

"I mean, if you're busy, I can probably figure it out myself," she continued. She knew that sometimes she made people uncomfortable when she grew quiet. They feared she was about to have a seizure and go into a trance. Especially lately. But often it was just easier to say nothing and let everyone else do the talking, the deciding, and the . . . worrying. And it was nice to daydream. She liked the visions that sometimes marked the seizures. She wondered if her dad now had them, too.

"Oh, I'm not doing anything important," he said finally.

"Cleaning?" she asked. "Organizing?"

"Something like that. I keep expecting to find a secret compartment back there."

She nodded, intrigued by the idea that there might be one. She understood why her father might have such a suspicion. Sometimes she found strange things in this house and the barn and the greenhouse.

Abruptly he stood to full height and rubbed his hands together, a habit of his when he was excited about something. "Well," he said, his voice robust and happy. "What have you got there?" Then he placed his palm on her back and escorted her to the dining room table, where together they tackled the two pages in the workbook.

Reseda Hill stood in her greenhouse a few steps in front of Anise, inspecting the scapes on the coral root she had transplanted earlier that winter. She kept the plants and spices for cooking cordoned off from the herbs for healing. Basil and parsley had no business mixing with hypnobium, belladonna, or amalaki. Her tomato seedlings in late April, prior to being transplanted into her vegetable garden, would not do well near the pungent aroma from the angel's death. The greenhouse was pentagonal and divided in half: On the right side, as one entered, were those herbs and spices that were common to any chef with even a modicum of culinary education; on the left side were those rare tropical plants from South America and India that only experienced healers, herbalists, and shamans were likely to use. In the center of the pentagon was a fountain with a stone creature holding a vase that dribbled water into the catch basin. The creature stood about three and a half feet tall, half man and half goat, with great, batlike wings on his back and a trim and pointed Vandyke running from his chin to his ears. Reseda did not bring it home from a compound in Barre, Vermont, that sold mostly (but not exclusively) tombstones and have it transformed into a fountain for her greenhouse because it bore a distinct resemblance to Baphomet. The truth was, she wasn't a Satanist or attracted to most satanic rituals; but she was a bit of a bomb thrower, and she liked the idea that designing her greenhouse in the shape of a pentagon and placing what looked like a stone demon smack in the center would fuel rumors among the sorts of people who were never going to be her friends anyway. Besides, she liked goats and she liked handsome men with their shirts off. She thought both were cute in a diminutive sort of way.

"I find the twins very interesting," Anise was saying, her parka draped over her folded arms.

"You've spent too much time with horror movies and pulp paperbacks. You always find twins interesting. I'm a twin. The world is filled with twins. Trust me: We're not interesting."

"These ones are prepubescent, and they have been traumatized. They're like the Dunmore boys. You know the tincture. You know the recipe."

Reseda bent over the patchouli and rubbed one of the egg-shaped leaves between her thumb and forefinger, breathing in deeply the perfume. Patchouli made her feel young. "The Dunmores were well before my time," she said after a moment. "Besides, it was the girls' father who was traumatized. We don't know if Hallie and Garnet were."

"You're not a mother; I am. Their scars are different from their father's, but nearly as deep."

"The pair struck me as rather resilient."

"I'm sure they are. But their father is an airline pilot who survived a plane crash. Most of his passengers died."

"You really don't like to fly, do you?" Reseda observed.

"You know I don't."

"When was the last time you were on an airplane?"

"I was twenty-three. Laurence and I flew to Aruba on our honeymoon. It took three planes to get there back then."

"Was it pleasant?"

"The honeymoon? Absolutely. But I was scared to death every moment I was in the air. Of course, I didn't know then what I know now."

"I don't like that expression: *scared to death.*"

"It's apt."

"It demonstrates both fear and naïveté."

"Perhaps in my case it's a control phobia—or the lack of control. That's why many people dislike flying. But I think my point is still valid. Captain Linton crashed a plane into a lake."

Reseda went to the table with the motherwort and the hypnobium. She felt Anise's eyes on her back. Anise loved working with hypnobium. She was one of the few women who was capable of using it in food as well as in potions. She was almost able to mask its bitterness with dark chocolate and sugar; no one could hide the taste completely, but Anise was able to make it edible. "The captain had help," Reseda reminded her. "It wasn't his fault."

"True. But here is what I keep thinking about: The family came to us. The *girls* came to us. Sheldon Carter was an old fool selling a house. He had no idea what we needed. Lord, he had no idea even what we are."

"What you are. I wasn't there."

"Sometimes I think you don't approve of us, Reseda."

"Just because you can do something doesn't mean you should."

"My point is simply that it wasn't you who found the family and enticed them north. They found the house on the Web and Sheldon responded."

"That's true."

"And so it must mean something. You of all people should see that."

"Perhaps," Reseda murmured, but she didn't turn around. She honestly couldn't decide if it meant anything at all. The world was awash in coincidence and connection; usually, it took time to deduce which was which.

*   *   *

Chip told Emily that the worst of the flashbacks were of the moment when he was upside down, disoriented, the water starting to enter the flight deck through the edges of the door to the cabin, and he suspected the plane behind him had broken apart. But he had other flashbacks, too, such as when he was pulling his first officer through the upside-down door of the flight deck and saw how deep the water already was in the fuselage. He said he didn't recall seeing any passengers strapped in the bulkhead seats, their feet above the waterline, their heads below it, either drowning or drowned. But he knew one woman had been there. She would manage to unbuckle her seat belt, but apparently she did so before registering where the exit was and, upside down, she went to the side of the plane with the lavatory. She had been sitting right beside the exit, and yet she would drown pressed against the floor of the fuselage, which, as this piece of aircraft fell to the bottom of the lake, had become its ceiling. Chip presumed he would have seen her when he was opening the door had she remained in her seat or not swum in the wrong direction.

What would remain a mystery to Chip and Emily and everyone who investigated the ditching was why the flight attendant had unlatched himself from his harness and not tried to open the exit. He had survived the initial impact, that was clear, and yet his body would be found lodged in the third row of seats. One possibility? He, too, had been disoriented when he was upside down and underwater, and he'd simply gotten lost when he tried to find the exit. Or, perhaps, he had tried to help someone. That seemed likely to Chip. He hadn't known Eliot Hardy well, but in the few days they had flown together before the crash, he had found him patient, firm, and good-humored—precisely the characteristics that defined a professional flight attendant. His cause of death was drowning, but based on his broken nose, there was some thought that he may have hit his head on debris or been kicked in the face by a passenger. Even if the impact hadn't knocked him out, it may have caused him to swallow great gulps of water, and that was the beginning of the end.

But the other flashbacks that Chip described to her were equally as disturbing in Emily's opinion, beginning with the flameout of the left engine and ending with the half dozen corpses that somehow had been flung like scarecrows and wax figurines from the wrecked aircraft and were floating around him like buoys in Lake Champlain.

In some ways, the flashbacks were all worse than the nightmares. "I seem to know when it's a dream and I seem to know that I'm not going to die—though there are times when I think you all would have been better off if I had died," he said.

"You don't mean that," Emily told him. "I wouldn't want to live without you. Hallie and Garnet would have been devastated to lose you. We all still have a lot of years before us."

But she had been coached well by his therapist in Philadelphia and by friends that she should expect this. It was survivor guilt. No, it was worse than that: It was survivor guilt exacerbated by the reality that he was a captain who had survived the wreck of his plane. The captain had not gone down with his ship. She could remind him that he had saved eight other lives, but it never did any good. He was focused on the thirty-nine people who had died. The fact that it wasn't his fault may have been some consolation, though the comfort it offered wasn't as healing as she wished it would be. He was constantly second-guessing everything he had done on that flight, constantly reliving every decision he had made and contemplating whether there was something he should have done instead or something he could have done better. Maybe he should have tried for the highway. Maybe he should have tried gliding to Plattsburgh. Maybe his pitch was a degree off. Maybe. Maybe. Maybe . . .

One time that winter he confessed to her that he had wondered prior to Flight 1611 if in some fashion his whole career as a pilot had been snakebitten and it was only a matter of time before he had an accident. He presumed that, by the time he was forty, he would have been flying an Airbus 320 or a Boeing 737. He'd be on track to be captaining triple-seven heavies internationally, flying between Philadelphia and Rome or San Francisco and Tokyo. He had been born in 1972 and graduated from college in 1994. But it had taken him until 1998 to finish flight school, because twice he ran out of money and had to find other jobs to fund his flying: Once it was banging nails into shoddily built town houses in a development in Orlando, Florida. Next it was as a bellman at a hotel in Disney World. Anything to make some money and be near the flight school. He and Emily met his first year as a first officer, when he was flying Dash 8 turboprops between Virginia, Ohio, Pennsylvania, and New Jersey, and by 2001 he was married and convinced his career was back on track. But advancement as a pilot is based entirely on seniority, and his airline suffered as much as any carrier after 9/11; he was among the junior pilots laid off in 2002, losing his job while Emily was beginning her third trimester with twins. He would finally latch on with another airline in early 2003, and took comfort in the idea that unemployment had meant he and Emily together had diapered and fed the twins their first few months in this world. Emily had been on maternity leave from the law firm for three months and he had been out of work nine. He had loved that period, though both he and Emily had fretted over money. But it also meant that, when he was forty years old and Flight 1611 was flipped by a wave in Lake Champlain, he was still flying regional jets.

E mily thought Chip was functioning rather well most of the time— at least on the surface, he was. Some days, it even seemed as if he were getting better. Not all of the time, of course. Far from it. But most of the time. She noted carefully, as if she were a physician or nurse, that it seemed to be the smallest of things that might set him off. After he had sent some signed documents back to the airline and the pilots' union via Federal Express, he confessed to having had an almost disabling occurrence of heart palpitations: Federal Express meant airplanes, and there had been that Tom Hanks movie with that all too grim scene of a plane augering into a body of water—which brought back to him his own failed ditching. He said he had sat in the car for forty-five minutes after sending the papers, trying to catch his breath. He admitted that he had almost driven himself to the emergency room at the hospital in Littleton, and she had felt bad that she hadn't been there for him.

Actually, she felt a little guilty that she wasn't with him most days as he worked all alone in their new house, tackling the small and large projects. She encouraged him to take time off and drive into town to join her for lunch, but always he passed. One morning she suggested, her voice as offhand and casual as she could make it, that he visit a career counselor to see what else he might want to do with his life—but only, of course, when he was ready. She tried to respect his fragility and his need to withdraw from the world. She only nodded when he said he was fine—absolutely fine—at home.

Home. She understood this Victorian on a hill in a distant corner of the White Mountains was now their home, but in her office in Littleton she felt a distance from it that transcended the buyer's remorse she had anticipated. There was a randomness to the house that originally had seemed quaint, as if an eccentric old aunt rather than a trained architect had designed it, but now seemed at once useless and disturbing. Why was the third-floor attic inaccessible from the two third-floor bedrooms? What really was the purpose of those rickety stairs that ran from a kitchen nook to a shadowy corner of the second floor? And then there was the Dunmores' absolutely horrific taste in wallpaper: Had they chosen it consciously to terrify their two sons? Good Lord, Emily feared she might have killed herself, too, if she'd had to grow up near the carnivorous sunflowers in one room or the viperlike mammals in another. Like Tansy, she might have wound up so squirrelly that she would have hid crowbars and carving knives in the house's myriad crannies. Moreover, every floor seemed to have odd drafts and squeaking doors. It had that basement made of dirt.

She wondered if she had made a monumental mistake uprooting her family: Sometimes it felt to her as if she had sacrificed her daughters for her husband. Could their new elementary school really be as good as the one in West Chester? Not likely, she feared. And, yes, the girls would make new friends and develop new interests, but would there be the same sorts of opportunities for them here that there had been in an admittedly tony suburb of Philadelphia? Already she questioned the capabilities of the music teachers she had found for the girls. Moreover, she missed her friends—her co-workers at the firm on Chestnut Street and the self-proclaimed theater geeks with whom she would dress up in period costume and sing and dance—more than she had expected, and for the first time in her life began to experience real depression. She thought often of the last show she had been in before Flight 1611 had crashed into Lake Champlain. It had been *Hello, Dolly!* She had been called back for Dolly but hadn't gotten the part and been cast instead as one of the four middle-aged women expected to add multigenerational authenticity to the chorus. She didn't care. This was, it seemed, her new function, and she milked the role for all it was worth. The last time she had had a lead had been as Anna in the *The King and I,* and that had been three years ago. Now she was thirty-eight. Lord, she had become "a community theater actress of a certain age," which was far worse than being a real actress of a certain age.

But it was she who had, in fact, initiated this move to northern New England. Chip was only forty. With any luck, they had decades together ahead of them. A half century, even. The key was starting over someplace new. Someplace where mere acquaintances (and some total strangers) wouldn't want to talk about the accident with her when they came upon her squeezing avocados at the supermarket, while her closest friends, after those first days, didn't know what to say. Someplace where people were not bewildered by Chip's ongoing near catatonia (for God's sake, his plane had crashed) but nonetheless surprised by it. After all, this was Chip Linton. Captain Linton.

And Chip's own family? There wasn't much. There was his mother, who, somehow, was still alive despite a liver that had to be nothing more than a cirrhosis-ridden briquette of scar tissue. Up until the accident, Chip had still visited her every six or eight weeks (every third of those seemingly at the hospital), trying to find a semblance of the mother he could recall from before his father had died, but the girls hadn't seen their grandmother since they'd been in kindergarten. The woman terrified the twins with her alcoholic rants or her disastrous attempts at grandmotherly affection: scalding Garnet when she tried (and failed) to make the child herbal tea or accidentally setting a dish towel (and nearly the kitchen) on fire when she thought it would be fun to bake brownies. Emily's brother-in-law, meanwhile, was living in California. Chip thought it was wonderful that his brother was a schoolteacher, but she knew the truth: He was among the most juvenile and selfish men she had ever met. He had completely cut himself off from his mother and was, clearly, a teacher because it was the way he satisfied his insatiable need for attention. His social life was a mystery, but she feared it involved a string of eighteen- and nineteen-year-old girls, some in college but some still in high school. He was too smart to sleep with one younger than eighteen, but he had said just enough to give her a sense that his tastes ran to women not yet old enough to drink. And, like her mother-in-law, he had been useless and invisible since Flight 1611 had crashed.

Her parents, Emily believed, would have been better. They might have been awkward, but they would have been . . . present. They would have tried. One of the great sadnesses for her was always going to be that they had never gotten to meet Hallie and Garnet. She had been a first-year associate, fresh from law school, and Chip was a young first officer when they fell in love, and she anticipated that together they would build a life that was stylish and romantic and productive. Then her parents got sick, her mother from ALS and her father from colon cancer. She spent three years watching them die up close and at a distance, while she and Chip dated, got engaged, and eventually wed. She was an only child, and in those first months after Flight 1611 fell from the sky, she missed her parents as much as she had at any point in all the years they'd been gone.

The sad truth was, however, that some days it seemed to her that she was no better than everyone else when it came to knowing what to say to her husband. She hadn't a clue. In the autumn, in the season after the accident, when the days were growing short and rainy and damp, they would walk past each other in the corridors of their Pennsylvania house like sleepwalkers and avoid eye contact over dinner as if they were travelers at an airport restaurant who spoke different languages. Even the girls would often sit silently at the table, worried and ill at ease.

One time she found Chip sobbing in Hallie's empty bedroom while the twins were sleeping over at a friend's house, a sight that was almost tragic in her mind since he was a man who never cried. Had been a brick as her parents deteriorated and died, supported her in every way that she needed. Had handled Garnet's condition (somehow, she preferred that term to *illness*)—the strange early seizures, the batteries of tests, the diagnosis—in a fashion that was at once unflappable and sensitive. He, it seemed, had always known what to say to her. At least until the accident. Everything had been different after the accident. And it was different in ways that she didn't like. Not one single bit.

And when something wasn't working, you changed it. Breakdowns lead to breakthroughs. Wasn't that what the legal consultant with the Armani suits and the ponytail had said to her when he was working with her Chestnut Street law firm?

Indeed. Breakdowns lead to breakthroughs.

And so here they were. In New Hampshire. Far from everything that had been her life as recently as 5:04 P.M. on the afternoon of August 11, the minute that Flight 1611 began its descent into Lake Champlain.

Chapter Four

In the days when you were a first officer, after your aircraft landed, you would meticulously go through the shutdown checklist with the captain and then walk around the plane. It was your responsibility to eyeball the aircraft and make sure that nothing was leaking or out of place. Sure enough, once you did spot a crack in the skin near the nose, and that aircraft subsequently was taken out of service. But you never spied anything leaking.

What you noticed often, however, and always on the leading edges of the plane—the wings and the nose and the vertical climb of the tail— were bits of dead birds. One time there was a dent in a wing the length of a couch cushion, likely the result of a collision with a goose. In hindsight, you can't say whether you noticed the spots monthly or perhaps even more frequently than that. But you know the birds that brought down 1611 were certainly not the first birds to collide with an aircraft you were flying.

Some days you find yourself Googling the details of the Lockheed turboprop that was brought down by starlings at Logan Airport in 1960 when sixty-two people would perish. It fascinates you that when a pair of Airbus engines were destroyed by geese nearly five decades later, so little mention would be made of that earlier nightmare. But that was the accident that led aircraft designers to start firing birds into engines to test their capabilities and the FAA to set requirements for how many birds an engine had to be able to swallow before choking to death.

*   *   *

On the school bus, Garnet was aware of a sixth-grade boy staring back at Hallie and her. They were sitting beside each other in what had become their accustomed side (the left), and she was in her accustomed spot: cocooned beside the grimy window, her sister buffering her from the world. The boy was the older brother of a girl in their class named Sally. Finally he spoke: "You do and you don't look like twins," he said, his bare hands on the back of his seat as he looked at them. He was two rows ahead of them, but the seat between them was empty. The long bus was never more than half full.

"I have no idea what that means," Hallie told the boy. "You do and you don't look like Sally's big brother," she then added belligerently.

But Garnet knew what the boy had meant. She understood precisely what the sixth-grader was trying to say. Perhaps because she was always following Hallie or deferring to Hallie, she was always looking at Hallie. Watching her. And while they were not physically identical twins, there was an air of identicalness about them. They were like puppies from the same litter. Hallie, Garnet knew, glided through the world with far more confidence than she herself ever would have, but still their mannerisms were eerily similar. They gnawed at the nails on their pinkies with the same affectation, extending their thumbs as if they were hitchhiking. They stretched the same way in class or while watching television, extending their legs and toes and raising their arms like long, slinky cats. And though their hair was two very different colors, it was equally fine, fell to the same spot on their shoulders, and today was kept out of their eyes with the same robin's egg blue headbands. And, Garnet knew, they had the same delicate chins and the same almond-shaped eyes. She had been told (warned, actually) that because she was a redhead eventually she would have great constellations of freckles, but so far she had been spared and she and her sister had the same invariably tan complexions.

"It means," the boy said, his voice betraying his unease with Hallie's challenging tone, "that you look like you're more than just sisters. That's all." Then he turned around and stared out his own window. He was, of course, absolutely right. Garnet knew that Hallie had in fact also known just what he was driving at. But sometimes Hallie needed to assert herself. Procure for herself a little distance. And that was fine. Besides, just as Garnet had anticipated she would, at that moment her sister discreetly took her hand and gave it a reassuring squeeze.

Reseda sat alone in the butterfly position—her back straight, the soles of her feet touching, her fingers gently grasping her toes—on a silk pillow on the gravel path in her greenhouse. She was vaguely aware of the sound of the water from her fountain and the occasional clicking from the baseboard radiators, and she felt the sun through the glass against her eyelids. She inhaled the fragrance of the nearby rosemary. Still, she was uneasy: Her mind kept circling back to the Linton twins, and she wondered what this meant. As she had reminded Anise, she herself was a twin. What was it about this pair that seemed to have such . . . potential? What might make them more suitable—more useful—than other twins? The tincture demanded the blood of a traumatized twin, but that may have been nineteenth-century drama or alliteration. Moreover, no one had ever been able to tell her what "trauma" Sawyer Dunmore had endured. The girls were still prepubescent, that was true. But the reality was that the tincture was from the second volume, a book that Reseda found deeply disturbing. It was filled with concoctions and cures that demanded animal hearts and human blood. Anise was a vegan, but she was willing to make exceptions for recipes found in the second book—especially when a tincture was as effective as the one leavened years earlier with Sawyer Dunmore's blood.

Anise—all the other women, actually—had been interested in another set of twins three years earlier. Again, fraternal, childlike, and possibly traumatized. Boys, that time, like the Dunmores. They had moved to Littleton because their father was going to be the superintendent of a nearby correctional facility. They were eleven when they arrived, moving with their parents and two younger sisters from Nashua to the White Mountains. When they had been toddlers, their town house and the adjoining town house had burned down in the small hours of the morning, and the fire had begun in the very bedroom they shared. The wiring behind their night-light had been defective and set the night-light and then their bedding on fire as they slept. But their father had smelled the smoke before they succumbed to it and gotten the twins and his wife safely out of the house. The next-door neighbors had not been so fortunate: They were an elderly couple, and both succumbed to smoke inhalation in their sleep.

Sadly, no sooner had Anise gotten to know the twins' mother—a deferential and mousy little thing, and thus rather perfect—than the father was involved in a very public, gloves-off sort of fight with the state legislature over funding for the correctional facility and ended up quitting in a huff. The family moved back to Nashua, and whatever opportunities those twins might have offered were gone. They couldn't possibly try outside of Bethel; they couldn't possibly try at such a distance. People would notice. They would watch. They would intervene.

She sighed. It wasn't simply that the earth here in Bethel felt sacred to Reseda—though it did. It was liminal. Connected. A bridge, in her opinion—or, better still, a passageway. She thought of the Egyptian doors to the afterlife, six- and seven-foot slabs of granite found in some of the ancient tombs. Often carved into granite was a series of concentric doorways, suggesting an infinite corridor.

But Bethel was also isolated, and that mattered, too. It was, in the end, why she stayed here. The soil was at once blessed and undiscovered—at least by most of the living.

Sometimes people from other parts of the country found her. They wanted her to host everything from goddess workshops to rites of passage retreats. These strangers had heard rumors about her and wanted to learn from her, though they never wanted to learn anything she wanted to teach. Politely she would direct them to shamans she knew who were legitimate healers and—unlike her—comfortable as teachers. Unfortunately, the world also was filled with hundreds (thousands?) of people who claimed to be shamans and had Web sites, and would be content to take their money and teach them to handcraft a shamanic rattle or drum. Maybe help them to try to make sense of their dreams. The truth was, she wasn't especially interested in the living. These days, she knew, she was far more fascinated by the dead.

Once again she saw in her mind the faces of the Linton girls and then the face of their father. She saw him flinching reflexively when his plane flew into a cloud of geese. And, finally, she thought of the geese themselves, rising up from a marsh or inlet or patch of swampy soil and flying thousands of feet into the air only to collide with a jet plane. One of the other women in a group she had joined before retreating to New Hampshire had had an eagle for a power animal. But no one, as far as Reseda knew, had ever had a goose. She wondered if those geese had been part of a plan. Had they been sent? Had there been a reason for the sacrifice of the thirty-nine passengers aboard the aircraft?

She resolved she would watch the twins more attentively and she would wait. Unlike the family of the correctional superintendent, she doubted the Lintons were going anywhere soon.

Occasionally, you recall the unsolicited comments that passengers would offer as they boarded the plane and you were in the midst of your preflight checklist. There was that exchange with a Southern belle as you prepared to lift off from Charlotte. She was a blond debutante, attractive and slim at middle age, and she stood beside the flight attendant, her elegant Burberry carry-on bouncing against her tanned knee and the edge of the galley.

"You do know what you're doing, don't you?" she asked, peering into the flight deck, her Southern accent emphasizing each and every *d*.

"I do," you said.

"I hope so. I have four children at home," she told you, and you were struck by the way she had managed to lose all that weight four times. "And I want to make sure we get there safely. So you all be sure and tell me if you need any help, okay?"

You had to ask: "Are you a pilot?"

"No," she answered, shaking her head and smiling. "But I am a *very* fast learner."

When you arrived in Philadelphia, she again peered into the flight deck as she was exiting the aircraft. "Thank you," she said, "well done." Then she gave you a thumbs-up.

E mily was leaning aimlessly against the counter at the diner on the main street in Littleton. It was lunchtime, and she had ordered a grilled cheese and tomato soup—comfort food in her opinion, even when one was nearing forty—that she was planning to bring back to her office. She would eat at her desk and work.

"Are you Emily Linton?"

She turned and saw before her an attractive woman somewhere around fifty. The stranger had ash blond hair that was cut short and a lovely, aquiline nose. She was wearing a down overcoat that fell to mid-shin and leather boots stained white from salt on the sidewalk.

"I am," she said.

"I'm Becky Davis," the woman said, pulling off a leather glove and extending her hand to Emily. She smiled, but Emily could sense that she was a little wary. "Do you have a second?"

Emily glanced at the rectangular cutout in the wall behind the counter and peered into the chaos in the kitchen and the plates lined up on the brushed metal sill. It didn't look like her grilled cheese was up. "Sure," she said.

Becky studied the patrons in the diner—mostly senior citizens and mostly men in green John Deere ball caps—and seemed to be considering where they should talk. Then she spied an empty booth not far from where they were standing and motioned toward it.

"I really can't stay," Emily said. "I was planning to bring my sandwich back to my office and work through lunch."

"Oh, I have work to do, too," Becky told her, and she slid onto the red leather cushion. Reluctantly Emily sat across from her. She couldn't decide whether she was about to get an earful now about her husband the pilot or whether this woman was about to try to invite her to visit a church or join a women's group of some sort. Becky seemed normal enough, but the way her eyes had darted around before deciding they should sit suggested that looks in this case might be deceiving; perhaps she was one of the town crazies. She seemed a little flushed—the cold, perhaps—but she was fidgeting nervously with the zipper on her coat and her unease was palpable.

"You're Hallie and Garnet's mother, right?" Becky asked. "You just moved here from Pennsylvania."

"That's right," Emily admitted, understanding this would not be about Flight 1611. It was, she decided, instead going to be about joining the elementary school's parent-teacher organization. Maybe they needed her to bake cupcakes for something. In West Chester, it seemed she was always baking cupcakes for something. Still, she smiled and raised her eyebrows. "You'll have to tell me why you've done so much homework."

"Oh, everyone knows. Bethel is a small town. I live in the brick house with the white shutters about two miles from you. I imagine you pass it every day on the way in to Littleton. Still, our paths weren't going to cross unless I introduced myself to you, because my boys are well beyond the elementary school. One is in high school and one is in college."

"Where do you work?" Emily asked.

"I work at Lyndon State. It's a long commute, I know."

"Not by Philly standards."

"I guess. And obviously I'm not there today. My parents are coming north from Asheville for the week and I took the day off to get the house ready. That's my work this afternoon." Now the woman was glancing behind her and peering out the large glass windows of the diner.

"You expect to see them on the sidewalk?" Emily asked. She couldn't resist.

"What?"

"Your parents. You were looking around just now like you expected to see them wandering up Main Street."

"No. Look, I'm taking a chance talking to you. Reseda Hill sold you your house and you work in John Hardin's law firm. So, obviously, it's crossed my mind that you might be . . ." She paused, the half sentence lingering awkwardly amidst the clattering dishes and burble of conversation in the diner.

"I might be what?"

"There's no graceful way to say it: You might be one of them."

"One of them? One of who?"

"But there's obviously a lot about you on the Web—because of your husband," she went on, ignoring Emily's question. "I've read a lot. And I know the principal at the elementary school, of course. Doris LeBaron. She's been the principal since before my older boy started there. And she's told me a little about you, too."

"Why was Doris talking to you about me? I mean, I hate to sound paranoid, but . . . why?"

"I could lie and say it's just because of who your husband is. I'm sure you know, people talk about that. It's human nature. But that wouldn't be the truth—at least not the whole truth. Doris and I are friends. We walk together in the summer. We're in the same spin class in the winter. And she's seen you with your girls. And we both have the sense that you're not one of them. Now, if I'm wrong, well then I guess I have just seriously—"

"One of who?" Emily asked again. "You didn't say."

"The herbalists," she said, leaning in as she spoke and then pulling away. It was as if *herbalists* was a dirty word.

"Oh, I get it," Emily said, and she had to restrain herself from rolling her eyes. "Those women who have the greenhouses. I mean, I've heard something. And Anise and Reseda are indeed trying to look out for us. They've both been very helpful."

"Anise, too," Becky murmured thoughtfully, as if this were additional bad news.

"She seems eccentric—but nice. Really."

Becky craned her neck to glance over Emily's shoulder and abruptly stood up. "God, I've completely lost track of time. I'm so sorry, but I have to go."

"You didn't order anything. Aren't you eating?" Emily asked.

The woman shook her head. "If you ever want to talk, call me," she said. "My number is in the book." She pulled on her gloves and strode purposefully down the diner corridor between the booths and the row of swivel seats at the counter, and then out the door. On her way out, she almost bowled over a regal looking fellow with massive shoulders and a bald head the shape of an egg as the two of them nearly collided at the front door. Emily saw the waitress was beckoning her from the register and holding up a white paper bag with her lunch. She rose. She couldn't imagine how a woman like Becky Davis could seem so normal on the surface and so clearly unstable underneath. She didn't expect she would ever have a reason to phone her.

A nd what of God? You pause in your work in the kitchen, replacing the paint roller in the tray and sitting back on your heels as you wonder: *Where was He when Flight 1611 crashed?*

The thing is, you went to Sunday school as a little boy, but by college you were no longer capable of reconciling childhood cancer, genocidal warfare, and mudslides that obliterated whole villages and buried babies alive with any kind of divine presence. Sometimes you and Emily worry that you have made a mistake not introducing your girls to any religious tradition at all—wouldn't it at least have helped them to hone their moral compasses?—but between your travel and Emily's work, Sundays really were nothing more than days of rest. Besides, half the time you weren't even home on Sundays. When the girls were toddlers and Emily was alone with them, the last thing she was going to be capable of on a Sunday morning was getting them up and dressed and off to church. And certainly the geese that appeared before your windshield just above two thousand feet on August 11 have done nothing to reinvigorate your faith. Nothing at all. The thirty-nine people who died that day in the water died through no fault of their own. They were as innocent as the many millions who die every year of disease and starvation. The many millions more who have died throughout human history in war or been killed in genocidal slaughters. The casualties of fire, water, air. The victims of car accidents, train collisions, and . . . plane crashes.

And yet still . . .

Still . . .

Since the failed ditching in Lake Champlain, you have found yourself pausing as you gaze up at thunderheads and rainbows and at the snow that transforms these leafless trees in Bethel into skeletal sculptures of black and silver and white.

No one has brought up church here in New Hampshire. At least not yet. Everyone did back in West Chester after Flight 1611 broke apart in Lake Champlain. Maybe folks here are more circumspect. Still, it has left you surprised. Apparently, the Congregational church in the village has sparse attendance at best. You noticed few cars in the lot when you drove past it that first Sunday morning on your way to the ski resort. Maybe everyone here goes to the Catholic and Methodist churches in Littleton, or the Baptist one in Twin Mountain.

You shrug and dip the paint roller into the tray once again and resume work on the corner of the kitchen behind the pumpkin·pine table and deacon's bench. The irony that you own a piece of furniture called a deacon's bench is not lost on you. In your old house, Desdemona would doze on it in the afternoons, when the sun would warm the long cushion. In this new house, the bench sits in a corner unlikely to see much sun, even in June and July. You wonder where the cat will doze now.

Emily drove up the long driveway that led to a house where an elderly couple named Jackson lived, the girls in the backseat behind her. She didn't know the Jacksons, but the twins' teacher, Mrs. Collier, wanted the girls to catch up with the rest of the class on a science project: The students were growing bean sprouts and carrot tops in glass jars, but they had started a little more than a week before the Lintons arrived in Bethel. Ginger Jackson, a retired food chemist from New Jersey, was also an avid vegetable gardener, and she had provided the class with the materials for their project. She had informed Mrs. Collier that she had extras she had started herself to follow along, and she could give them to Hallie and Garnet so they could have plants at the same stage as their peers'.

Emily felt an unexpected pang of melancholy when she reached the house, and she wondered what it was in the structure that was affecting her so. The oldest, original parts of the house dated back to 1860, Reseda had said. It was a Gothic Revival cottage, though the term *cottage* suggested a modesty the building had probably lacked even before two additions increased the size by roughly a thousand square feet. Now it was shaped like a rectangular U with four fireplaces, one in each of the shorter wings and two in the long center. The chimneys reminded Emily of the pictures of the funnels she had seen on massive cruise ships in port, and the house's roofs were slate and descended gently like sand dunes. A snug and inviting bay window anchored each tip of the U, and Emily could imagine one of her daughters curled up with a book in each of the window seats.

And that, she understood suddenly, was why she was feeling a great pang of sadness. This was the sort of house she wanted—not the melancholy crypt she and Chip had bought.

"Does she know we're coming for the plants?" Hallie asked her mother from the backseat of the car.

"I called and left a message," Emily answered. She coasted to a stop beside the garage. "But it doesn't look like anyone's home," she said, talking to herself as much as she was informing her daughters. She climbed from the Volvo and looked around. No sign of any other vehicles. She walked gingerly over the ice on the driveway and peered through one of the glass windows in the garage door. There was no car in either bay.

"I'm sorry, girls," she said when she returned, settling back in behind the wheel. "We'll have to try again another day."

"Are you disappointed?" Garnet asked her.

"Oh, only for you girls," she said, worried that her own disenchantment must have crept into her voice.

Garnet shrugged. Hallie had her chin in her hand. "We'll probably just come back tomorrow," she said. "Or the next day. Why not? There's not a whole lot else to do around here."

"Sometimes when I went to New Hampshire to visit my grandmother, I felt exactly the same way," Emily confessed. "The stores were boring, there was no TV reception. I didn't know the kids there so I didn't have any friends. But the place kind of grew on me."

"You were just visiting, Mom."

"I know. But . . ." She stopped speaking when she heard Hallie's small sniffle, and she turned her full attention on the child. The girl missed her friends in West Chester. Both twins did. "Oh, sweetie, I know it's hard. But you'll meet kids, I know you will. You'll make new friends. I promise."

Hallie nodded and wiped her eyes with the palm of her hand. Garnet patted her sister on the knee. And neither girl said a word. If they couldn't put into concrete sentences the reasons why their family had moved, they understood how brittle their father had become and the need to retreat from Pennsylvania. From civilization. And they accepted that, because they were his children, this move was a part of their lot.

The notion made Emily want to cry, too.

You find yourself studying the transcript of the final seconds of your final flight and hearing over and over in your head the actual recording that was played in the NTSB hearing. You sat through all three days of the investigation, you listened to the tapes, you watched the computer simulations. You were transfixed by the cell phone video made by a tourist who happened to have been eating an ice cream cone at the Burlington boathouse when you ditched your plane in the water. (She would drop the ice cream on the wooden dock when she saw the regional jet bearing down amidst the boats on the lake.) Then, those nights on the news, you watched yourself in the hearing room staring at that video or listening to testimony or—one day—testifying yourself, and you were struck both by how much your hair had thinned and by how impassive you seemed in your rolling chair beside that long mahogany table. You wore your uniform (again, a last time) when you testified.

You always sounded calm and controlled in the recording. You never raised your voice. You never panicked. Same with your first officer. Amy, like you, was a study in professionalism. Yes, she screamed reflexively when the wave careened into the wingtip of the jet and you went perpendicular to the water. But you didn't. You didn't curse, you didn't cry out (though the woman recording the cell phone video certainly did, exclaiming, "Oh, my God, oh, my God, it's flipping! It's flipping!"). You kept your composure even then, even when death appeared imminent. There was an involuntary grunt because the sensation was not unlike being punched hard in the stomach and the chest, and the yoke slammed up into your thumbs with such force that it's a small miracle they didn't break. But otherwise you stayed with your controls until all control was completely out of your hands. You flew your aircraft until, pure and simple, you couldn't.

And then, the day after the crash, you endured the interrogation by the NTSB. It was all about alcohol, sleep, and food. Thank God, you recall thinking at the time, you hadn't had even a glass of wine the night before the plane hit the birds. And you clicked shut your hotel door that evening and fell asleep watching a Red Sox game on a hotel cable station. When you flew your three legs that day, you had been sober and well rested; you had eaten well.

People have told you that you would have had a better chance of succeeding that August afternoon in an Airbus than in a CRJ, because the Airbus uses more fly-by-wire technology: A computer prevents a pilot from flying either too fast or too slowly and assures that the aircraft's pitch and turn angles never exceed the plane's capabilities. But the issue wasn't bringing the plane safely to the lake: You did that. You and Amy did that together. In the end, the issue was, son of a bitch, that wave.

Still, it seems indecent to be alive today when four-fifths of your passengers and your crew are dead. You have no plans to rectify that and join them, of course: Haven't you done enough to scar your two children already? The last thing they need now is for their father to kill himself. But when you see in your mind the black box—and you see it often, though not as frequently as the dead as they bobbed in the water and the fuselage slipped under the waves—you see also that the only place for you to live is a place like this: a sparsely populated hill in a sparsely populated corner of a sparsely populated state. You are living in exile. As an exile. Emily doesn't view Bethel quite this way. It was her brainchild to come here in the first place. But you do. You view it precisely as an exile. Your own personal Elba.

One day when Emily is at her office in Littleton and the girls are at school and you have just been to the hardware store to get lightbulbs and Spackle and have yet another window shade cut, on your way home you decide to detour toward the office of the real estate agency where the agents—first Sheldon, then Reseda—who sold you the house work. You coast into the parking lot of the dignified mock Tudor that houses the agency and sits beside the brick library and across the street from the post office. You stare for a moment at the town common, with its pristine white gazebo and creosote black Civil War cannon, the heavy gun's small mounted plaque honoring the White Mountain veterans of that war and the ones that followed in Europe and the Middle East. You gaze at the maple trees—willowy, sable, spiderlike—with a dusting of snow on the wider branches from last night. You wonder precisely why you have veered here and what you are going to ask.

But in you go, and there is Reseda Hill seated behind her desk with her landline phone against her ear and the screen on her computer showing a modest house for sale just off the main street in Littleton. The agent smiles when she sees you, and you stand there awkwardly, not wanting to appear to be eavesdropping on the conversation but not wanting to seem to ignore her, either. There doesn't seem to be a receptionist, but out of nowhere another agent appears from a backroom, a woman in her mid-thirties—Reseda's age, too, you believe—who is wearing black pants that are provocative and tight and a cashmere sweater with pearls.

She has hennaed her hair and placed it back in a bun and is wearing a perfume that reminds you of lilacs. She introduces herself to you as Holly, but, before the conversation has proceeded any further, Reseda has motioned to her that she will be off the phone in a moment.

"Would you like some tea?" asks Holly, but you decline. You hear yourself telling her your name, and she says, "I know." And you're not taken aback. Not at all. Of course she knows your name.

"Coffee?"

"No, I'm fine. Really." You tell her you can come back, it's not important, because deference now leaches from you like perspiration.

"I'm sure Reseda would want to talk to you," she insists. Then: "I've always thought being an airline pilot must be very glamorous. Is it?"

You find yourself smiling. It is a popular misconception. "It once was—but that was years before I started flying. The generation of pilots before me had it a little easier: They certainly weren't eating cheese sandwiches on the flight deck."

"The airline doesn't feed you?"

"My first years, it did. We had vouchers. But no more. The vouchers disappeared with my pension. So, on my first leg—I'm sorry, my first flight—I would usually be eating a brown bag lunch I packed myself before leaving home. I remember some mornings, I would make three identical sandwiches: one for me and one for each of my daughters. I have two. Twins. My daughters would bring theirs to school, of course. But you know what? I liked those cheese sandwiches. I really did. You get to your cruising altitude and you eat and enjoy the view. It's actually rather pleasant. I loved to fly."

"Were you gone a lot?"

"Probably too much. I was usually flying four days and home three. The rules for rest are complicated, but I might fly a dozen legs those four days. Sometimes, it would be less: seven or eight. Either way, I would say I ate half my meals between thirty and thirty-five thousand feet with a paper napkin in my lap."

"And that was safe?"

You nod. "That was safe. I was always a stickler for safety."

Just about then your real estate agent laughs at something and hangs up the phone. She rises from the seat behind her desk, and you are struck by the suede and fur, burgundy-colored boots she is wearing, and how they haven't any heels at all: This really is a woman who knows how to navigate her way through a White Mountain winter.

"Chip, how are you?" she says, smiling, her eyes that beautiful, disturbing cobalt blue you noticed the first time you met and you think of whenever you think of her. Reseda is tall and trim, a slight ski jump to her nose, and her cheekbones are almost as prominent as her eyes. Her hair is darker than the chest-high wrought-iron fence that surrounds the cemetery at the edge of the village. She takes one of your hands in both of hers, and you always have the sense around her that, if you were in a big city, she would be the type who would want you to greet her with polite air kisses on both of her cheeks. Her palms are dry and cold, and yet the sensation, the touch, makes you a little warm.

"We're settling in well, I think," you begin. You describe your breakfasts with the view of Mount Lafayette from the kitchen and skiing periodically the past couple of weeks at the nearby resort. You make a small joke—and the joke does seem to you to be woefully inadequate—about the numbers of boxes you have unpacked and yet the numbers that remain. You wonder as you listen to the sound of your voice—a voice that once inspired confidence at thirty-five thousand feet—whether you are capable of asking the questions that have brought you here. They seem ridiculous now. Absolutely ridiculous. But, finally, you start: "You ever notice that door?"

She angles her head slightly, justifiably confused. The world has a lot of doors. Your house alone has twenty-seven (yes, you have counted), and that doesn't include the closets and the cupboards and the pantry. "What door?"

"There is a door in the basement. It—"

And then there it is, that slight smile and sympathetic nod you have seen so often from people since August 11, and she is cutting you off. You are now in everyone's eyes an emotional invalid. They need to be . . . gentle . . . around you. "Oh, Anise told me you were asking about that," she is saying. "The coal chute."

And you realize that once more they have been talking about you. Anise has told Reseda that you were nonplussed by a . . . coal chute.

"I must confess," she continues, "I never did notice it. But then I rarely showed that house. Still, it must be a guy thing. I never heard other agents mention it. I guess women notice how much light a kitchen gets in the afternoon and men notice the coal chute in the basement. But sit down and tell me. What about it?"

You sit in the chair opposite her desk, and it feels good, if only because you have been working very, very hard scraping wallpaper and Reseda is indeed lovely to look at. The chair is leather and the smell is vaguely reminiscent of the aroma of the seat on the flight deck: human and animal all at once.

"I just can't imagine why someone would have sealed the door shut in such an enthusiastic fashion," you begin, careful to smile back both because Emily has told you that you have a handsome smile and because you don't want to sound like any more of a lunatic than you already must.

She shrugs. "Hewitt Dunmore is a bit of an odd duck," she says simply, referring to the previous owner.

"So you think he was the one who closed it up?"

"Oh, I don't know. I don't know him well. Anise does. She knew his parents and his brother, too. Maybe his father was the one who sealed it up. You know, that's actually more likely. I imagine it was years and years ago that they stopped heating with coal. It's LP gas now, correct?"

"It is. And there's also that woodstove."

"I love that woodstove. Soapstone. Palladian windows on the doors, right?"

"Right. We've been so busy unpacking we've only started a fire in it a couple of times."

"That must have been cozy," she says, and there is something vaguely seductive in the sibilant way that she finishes her sentence. Those magnificent eyes widen just the tiniest bit.

"It's not really a cozy house."

She sits upright behind her desk, that lovely oval of a face abruptly looking alarmed. But you're not at all sure that the alarm is genuine. She *looks* alarmed, and it is that same disingenuousness that marked the bad acting of so many of Emily's friends in Pennsylvania when they pretended to be actors in their community theater dramas and musicals. "Oh, I hope you're not regretting the move already. We're all so happy to have you here. You and Emily and your beautiful twins."

"No, not at all. It's a wonderful house. I didn't mean to suggest I had any regrets. I think Emily and I will be very comfortable there. I think the girls already are adjusting quite well. Especially Hallie. She loves that greenhouse."

"That's important. Is she sleeping well? Are you all sleeping well?"

You recall Hallie's bad dream that first Sunday night. You recall a second she had more recently. You wonder simultaneously whether a couple of bad dreams would suggest your child is not sleeping well and why the real estate agent would ask such a thing in the first place. Has she heard something from someone? Did Emily mention something to another attorney in her firm who mentioned it to Reseda? Did Hallie tell her teacher in school, who, in turn, told this real estate agent? Is the town really that small? Is it possible that people really talk *that* much?

"We're all sleeping fine," you respond, which is, more or less, the case with your daughters and your wife. A couple of nightmares, you decide firmly, does not constitute sleeping badly. And while you yourself haven't slept well in six months, your nightmares and flashbacks are really none of her business. Besides, you don't want to appear any more damaged to Reseda than you already must.

"But right now you and Emily are only . . . comfortable," she murmurs, repeating one of the words that you used, and you detect a slight sniff of disappointment. No, not disappointment: disapproval.

"Sometimes, happy is asking a lot." You say this with no particular stoicism in your tone; it's a glib throwaway.

"Oh, I hope that's not true. Personally, I don't think it is. I understand what you've been through. But I would like to believe that happiness is a perfectly reasonable expectation here."

"Perhaps."

"Have you taken the door off?" she asks, her eyes growing a little more probing, a little more intense.

"It would demand a lot of effort."

"Have you talked to Hewitt?"

"About the door?"

She nods.

"Nope."

"You should," she says.

"Probably."

"Or . . ."

"Yes?" You realize for the first time that there is a scent in the office that is reminiscent of lavender. Burned lavender. As if it were incense. You have inhaled a small, lovely dollop of Reseda's perfume.

"You could ask Gerard up to the house and have him just rip that door down. That would be easier than removing all those bolts."

You pause for just a moment before responding, because you don't believe you have mentioned the bolts. But then you get it: "Anise must have told you about the bolts."

And for just about the same amount of time that you paused, so does Reseda. Her face remains waxen, unmoving. Then: "Yes. She did."

"Who's Gerard?"

"Anise's son—and a very nice young man. A little quiet, a little intimidating even. He's a weight lifter. Belongs to the health club in Littleton. He will probably be the one haying your fields this summer. He's big and tall and very, very strong, and I'm sure he could rip that door right off its hinges."

You contemplate this notion. The advantage is that you would learn what's behind the door pretty quickly. The disadvantage is that you would be in violation of an unspoken rural code: You are an able-bodied man and you are having another able-bodied man handle a household chore that you should be capable of managing on your own. You could take an ax to that door as well as this Gerard. You are not that old and infirm. And so you tell Reseda, "Thank you. I think I can handle this one. Maybe I should just rip the door off myself."

"Well, if you change your mind, his shoulders are pretty broad. He's pretty resourceful."

"Good to know. Thank you."

"Tell me: How is Emily enjoying Littleton? The second floor of a little brick building beside a bicycle shop and a bank must feel like a very big change from a top floor of a skyscraper in Philadelphia."

Has Emily told Reseda this, too? Has she told her that her old firm dominated the twenty-fifth and twenty-sixth floors of a building on Chestnut Street? Or is this conjecture on the part of the real estate agent? "It is a change," you say, "but she finds the pace very pleasant."

"And I'm sure the drive in to work—the commute—is a lot more civilized."

You nod agreeably. "It is. And a lot shorter. About fifteen minutes, door to door. Can I ask you something else?"

"Absolutely," she says.

You turn around in your chair because you remember Holly is there and what you are about to ask feels . . . private. Holly is at her desk and moving her mouse as she stares at her computer screen. But she senses you are gazing at her, and so she looks up and grins. Instantly you turn your attention back to Reseda.

"Hewitt Dunmore's twin brother," you begin awkwardly, unsure precisely how to broach the subject. "Sawyer, I think his name was. He took his own life, right?"

"That is what people say."

"How? Why? What do you know about his death?"

"Well, I didn't know Sawyer. I wasn't even born when he died. But Anise knew him. She knew the whole family."

"Is there anything you can tell me?"

She shrugs and shakes her head, her face growing a little sad. "Teen-

age or pre-teenage depression, I assume. He was what, twelve or thirteen? Back then, it wasn't really understood or treated."

"And the . . . means?"

"He bled to death."

"He slashed his wrists?"

"Something like that. But, honestly, my sense is that it was more
complicated. Anise might know the details."

Honestly. The word sounds insincere to you. Deceitful, maybe.
How could she not recall the way a local boy had killed himself, even if
it was before she was born? Wouldn't it be a part of the lore of this small
village, the sagas and stories and secrets that everyone shared? But, perhaps, you are being unfair; perhaps it really isn't discussed around here.
New England reticence. Propriety. And it was a long, long time ago.

"You must be looking forward to spring," she says suddenly, her
voice lightening. "It might be my favorite season. I love it—although I
understand that for many people around here spring is a very mixed bag:
mud and more mud. Lots of gray days. I tell you, crocuses this far north
must have a death wish. No sooner do they poke their pretty little heads
through the grass than they get hammered with eight inches of very wet
snow. But there will also be some absolutely glorious days. Just wonderful! And there is sugaring to look forward to. I don't sugar myself. But I
have friends who do. You must bring your twins to a sugarhouse. I think
they would love it: Sugar on snow, the aroma of maple. The samples.
No child can resist a sugarhouse!"

"We will. Anyone's sugarhouse in particular?"

"I think you should stop by the Milliers'. Claude and Lavender Millier. It will be weeks before there's a sugar run. Or it might be a month.
You never know. But I'll introduce you between now and then."

"Thank you. Do they have children?"

"Grown. But I know their son will scoot up from Salem for a few
days to help with the boiling. He's a doctor. A pediatrician. He's part of
a beautiful practice in a big old barn of a house with fantastic views of
the ocean."

"Anyone with a sugarhouse and children roughly Hallie and Garnet's age?"

"Of course. I'll just have to think a moment. I hear they're doing very well in school."

"You hear a lot," you say, a reflex, and wish instantly that you could take the remark back. It isn't like you. It's just that everyone always seemed to be talking about you back in Pennsylvania this past autumn and winter, and now everyone seems to be talking about your whole family here in New Hampshire.

"Oh, you know how people chat in a small town. We haven't anything better to do—especially this time of the year, when the days are short as a pepper plant." She looks out the large picture window and continues, her voice a little dreamy. "Soon the geese will be coming back. We'll see them flying north in just a few weeks. I love geese. Big, powerful birds. They're another sign of spring." Then she turns back to you and makes eye contact. "Tell me: Would you and Emily and your beautiful twins like to come to my house for dinner this weekend? Perhaps a casual dinner on Sunday night? Something easy and light?"

This is an enormous amount of information to try to make sense of: There is, as Emily would say, text and subtext. No one can use the words *goose* and *geese* around you without knowing that they connote profoundly disturbing images. They do not provoke a PTSD sort of flashback—you do not find yourself sweating when you hear them, they do not induce heart palpitations—but they do conjure for you the destruction of your airplane and the deaths of thirty-nine people. Thirty-six adults, three children. Including one with a doll dressed as a cheerleader. That, too, wound up floating in Lake Champlain, the eyes open, the hair the color of corn silk fanning out like seaweed in the waves. And then there was the girl with the Dora the Explorer backpack. All of the children were, you would learn later, younger than Hallie and Garnet.

At the same time, there is that dinner invitation, proffered out of the blue. An unexpected kindness.

You are not at all sure what to make of the juxtaposition. Was the invitation a spontaneous gesture provoked by guilt? Had she brought up the birds without thinking and then, after realizing what she had done, hoped to make amends with dinner?

"Well, that's very sweet of you," you hear yourself murmuring. "Thank you. Let me check with Emily and get back to you."

"It will be very casual. Maybe some others will come."

"I'm free!" says Holly from behind her desk, though she doesn't look up when you glance back at her. "I want to come!"

"Of course," says Reseda.

You find yourself struck by the names of all of these women around you. Reseda. Holly. Anise. You decide that either you have stumbled upon a secret society of florists or gardeners or all of their parents were hippies. Or, perhaps, they're part of a coven. You are bemused by that notion in particular and conclude the synaptic link was triggered by the mention, a few minutes ago, of Salem. You always think of witches when you hear the name of that small city. Everyone does. The burning times. The hangings. The women (and men) pressed to death by stones.

"You're grinning," says Reseda.

"I just had a funny thought."

"Can you share it?"

"I like your name. I like all of your names here."

"The reseda is among the most enticing and fragrant flowers in the world," she says, and you realize that you're not in the slightest bit surprised.

When you leave a few minutes later, you have in one hand Gerard's phone number and in the other a thick espresso-chip cookie from a batch that Anise had baked that very morning and dropped off at the real estate agency. You doubt you will ever call Gerard, at least about that door. But you are glad that you have the cookie. It's delicious. You hadn't realized how hungry you were.

Chapter Five

A bird became trapped in the woodstove. It flew in through the top of the chimney just as the late winter sun was starting to thaw the thin skins of ice on the shallow puddles in the driveway. No one was awake in the house. The animal worked its way lower and lower in the Metalbestos prefabricated chimney—a sparkling, cylindrical metal tube that was nine inches wide—from the opening nearly four feet above the twelve-by-twelve pitch made of slate and through the tube that cut through the attic and the second floor, darting finally through the rectangular vent to the catalytic converter and then into the soapstone stove with its regal glass windows. The windows were caked over with soot from fires long ago as well as from the few logs the Lintons had burned, and so the bird flew around and around in the near total dark, its wings frequently clipping the iron walls or the black stains on the glass. Desdemona, the Lintons' cat, was aware of the animal before anyone else, and she stared alertly at the stove, her haunches raised ever so slightly and her tail occasionally brushing the floor.

Emily was the first one downstairs that morning, and when she saw the cat watching the stove as if it were a mole hole in the yard back in Pennsylvania, she didn't know what to think. But she switched on the lamp beside the couch and two heavy boxes of unpacked books, and instantly the poor bird made another effort to escape, thwapping into the door because the flue was open just enough to create thin slats of light. Emily knew instantly then what was so interesting to Desdemona. She screamed upstairs to Chip because she was afraid of birds and knew that, once she opened the woodstove door and the bird flew out into the room, she would be utterly useless. And yet it was only when she heard him on the stairs, asking her what was wrong, that she knew how strange and inconsiderate it would be to tell him her panic had been caused by a bird. One small bird. But with the competence that formerly she had taken for granted, he opened the window nearest the stove and closed the door between the living room and the dining room—the room with, perhaps, the strangest, darkest wallpaper, a series of sunflowers that grew from the hardwood floor to the height of a grown man and, over time, had become brown with age and made her think of the elongated, damned souls in an El Greco painting—and used a bath towel to whisk the bird in the direction of the open window. It was a chickadee. She noticed a little black soot on its gray wings and the white of its nape. Instead of flying through the open half of the window, however, the bird darted straight into the solid pane above it, breaking its neck and falling dead onto the carpet.

As Chip gently picked it up, using his fingers to sweep it into the palm of his hand before Desdemona could cart it away in her mouth, Emily started to cry. She thought on some level it was just because it was so small, so very small, but she knew in her heart that there was more to it than that. Much more. Chip brought the bird outside, though where she didn't know, and then he came back inside and sat down beside her. He put his arm around her. He didn't say a word, he just rocked her a little bit and sighed, and she let her tears fall against the plaid top of his pajamas until they both heard their girls on the stairs. Abruptly they stood, and she told the children that she had been crying because the bird in the woodstove was just so little, but she was fine now. She was, she really was. They were all just fine.

You stand in blue jeans and a gray sweatshirt with the logo of your old airline emblazoned across the front and shovel coal for nearly thirty minutes, moving the pile a solid five feet from that basement door. It was possible to stand amidst the coal earlier this month when you were merely tinkering with one of the carriage bolts. But if you're going to get medieval on that door with an ax this morning, you need a little more space. A little more room. Before you know it, you're sweating, even though it is the first week in March and you are working in a dank basement in a badly insulated house that's nearly a century and a quarter old. But the furnace emits a little heat, even here, and it's no more than a dozen feet away.

When you have finally redistributed the coal, you sit on the basement steps to rest and sip from the plastic bottle of soda that has grown warm. Your heart is thumping from the exertion as you study the door and the bolts and wonder what precisely you will find behind it. You didn't tell Emily you were going to do this when she left for work this morning, you didn't mention it to the girls before school. You weren't sure this really was a part of your agenda. You had expected you would tape the doorframes and windowsills and paint another wall in the kitchen. Roll that soothing sienna Emily picked out over the freshly spackled Sheetrock.

You find it interesting that the ax you are going to use to bring down this door came with the house. It's the one Emily found hidden behind the ancient cleaning supplies in the cabinet underneath the kitchen sink. You could have used the ax you had brought with you along with a litany of other gardening tools from Pennsylvania: the rake and the hoe and the shears and the wheelbarrow. The clippers. The netting for the blueberry bushes. After all, you wandered out to the barn to retrieve the shovel you're using now and you could have carried the ax back inside the house, too. But instead you pulled down the trapdoor and climbed up into the attic and found the box where Emily had stored those three, strange implements of self-defense: The crowbar. The knife. The ax. For reasons neither of you could precisely articulate, you couldn't bring yourselves to cart those old items to the dump. But neither had you any desire to leave them where they were or to use them yourselves. Until now. Until you realized you needed an ax for this morning's project.

And you like the symmetry. It's as if the Dunmores left you this ax for precisely this purpose—which, of course, means there might be purposes as well for the crowbar and the knife. Now there's a macabre thought.

This coming Sunday night, two days from now, you and Emily and the girls are having dinner with Reseda and Holly and whomever else the real estate agent will invite. You sip that cola and contemplate how satisfying it will be to inform them that you took the door down on your own—no need for this Gerard character that Reseda recommended—and found behind it . . . what?

You just can't imagine. You have absolutely no idea what might be back there.

E mily's mood had been sinking for days, ever since that chickadee died on their living room rug (though she told herself that there was no connection; her mood was going to deteriorate regardless of whether that bird made it out of the house). She knew it was never a good sign when she found herself poring over the obituaries she found in the *Philadelphia Inquirer* or—now that she and her family were ensconced in northern New Hampshire—in the weekly edition of the *Littleton Courier.* The old and the middle-aged and, in some disturbing or terrifying cases, the young. The faces in the photographs that were now being worked on by a mortician or moldering in a grave. Or cremated. It was the first thing Emily did this morning when she arrived at work and sat down at her desk in the room that not all that long ago had probably been someone's bedroom. She sipped her coffee and thought of how she had uprooted her children and how her husband was a shell of the man he had been a mere seven months earlier. She thought of her friends she missed—those at the large firm where she had risen to partner, and those in the ridiculous, narcissistic, but bighearted theater community that offered such a wondrous change from her legal practice—and she contemplated how it had all come to this: a dusky office with three other lawyers she barely knew, a sweet young paralegal named Eve, and a secretary her own age named Violet, whom the lawyers shared and was dauntingly competent and not a little intimidating. She thought of how the days just didn't get long fast enough here in northern New England. Right now back in West Chester, people were having their ride-on mowers tuned up.

On the stairway she heard footsteps, and a moment later she looked up and saw John Hardin peering in. John's name was first on the firm's shingle. He was over seventy, but he had the big hair of a Russian commissar. It was entirely white now, but he was a vigorous man who still skied and jogged and seemed to have no plans to retire. He didn't work all that hard—none of them did—but they also didn't make all that much money. In theory, however, that was precisely the point of living here rather than in, say, a suburb of Philadelphia like West Chester. Your paycheck was considerably smaller but your quality of life was so much better. You could age with the grace of John Hardin—though Emily knew that her and Chip's dotage might not be quite so serene if either she didn't find a way to make a little more money than she was earning now or Chip didn't find a second career. The reality was that she had earned considerably more than her husband when they lived in Pennsylvania: Estate law was vastly more lucrative than commercial aviation in this day and age. Now that her income had taken a severe nosedive and his was—at the moment, anyway—nonexistent, they had not put a penny into their girls' college funds in nine months and their savings would be long depleted by the time they were receiving their first solicitations from AARP. (And even that assumed the annual needs of a cranky old house on a hill in a frigid corner of northern New Hampshire did not grow particularly onerous in the coming decade and change.)

This morning, perhaps because it was a Friday and the fashion bar at the firm fell even lower, John was wearing blue jeans that were a little baggy, a gray tweed blazer, and a novelty T-shirt from the town in Mississippi that claimed the world's largest aluminum and concrete catfish. Apparently, based on the photo on the shirt, you could walk inside the attraction and "Live Just Like Jonah!" The T-shirt was neon yellow and blue and clashed mightily with the jacket: It was like he had wrapped the Swedish flag around his torso. His parka was slung over his shoulder, and he was holding a paper cup of coffee in his free hand.

"It's going to snow tonight," he said, and the prospect clearly delighted him.

"And tomorrow?"

"Skiing."

"Okay, then."

"How are you doing, Emily? Honestly?" He had paused on the far side of her desk, and his voice took on the cast that she imagined he used when, before settling into a practice that revolved around real estate closings and trust modifications, he wanted to convey an avuncular sincerity to a jury. Convey to them how he could only represent a client who was innocent. She could tell he had noticed that her newspaper was open to the obituaries.

"No complaints," she lied, shrugging.

He peered over her desk and pointed at the face of the teenage boy who had died in a snowmobile accident. "There's little in this world worse than the death of a child," he murmured.

"I agree."

"I think everyone would. And yet it's the damnedest thing: History is filled with human sacrifice—child sacrifice. Can you image? Anise and Reseda have come across some of the strangest cults and traditions in their botanical and shamanic research," he said.

"Anise and Reseda? I know they grow a lot of bizarre plants. I know Reseda has introduced some very exotic flowers to this area. But human sacrifice? Where in the world does that fit in?" She wondered at the connection in John's mind that would lead him to link the death of a boy in a snowmobile accident with human sacrifice.

"Well, it isn't their specialty," he said, and he raised his eyebrows mischievously.

"That's a relief: No one likes to learn that one's new friends are into human sacrifice."

"I just meant that Reseda's other work—her shamanic work—has led her to hear of ideas from other parts of the world that most people around here would find rather disturbing. Anise has, too."

"Are Anise and Reseda both . . . shamans?"

"Oh, no."

"Just Reseda?"

"That's right," he said. "Of course, even in this corner of the globe we've had our share of strange doings. Trust me: Some people think the woods around here are just filled with witches." He shook his head a little ruefully and then smiled. "Tell me, do you and Chip have anything special planned this weekend?"

"I think we'll do something different and scrape some wallpaper. Maybe unpack a few boxes. And, as a matter of fact, we're having dinner with Reseda on Sunday."

"How's it coming? All that scraping and unpacking?"

"Just fine."

He nodded. Then: "Do you have dinner plans on Saturday, too?"

They didn't, but she wasn't sure whether she felt up to two dinner parties in two days. She also understood, however, that it would probably do both her and Chip some good to get out tomorrow night and spend some time with this partner in the firm and his wife and whomever else he decided to invite at the very last minute.

"No."

"Then come to Clary's and my house for supper. Nothing fancy. We should have had you over weeks and weeks ago. We're derelict. I'm derelict."

Supper. A quaint word. Provincial, but sweet. She heard herself murmuring that yes, they would like that, thank you, but only if they could bring the girls because they didn't really have a babysitter yet.

"Of course," he said. "We can set them up in the playroom upstairs and they'll be happy as can be. We already have an awful lot of high-tech toys and video games up there for our own grandchildren. Or, if the girls would be more comfortable, they can be downstairs with us."

"Okay, then. Thank you. What can we bring?"

"Smiles. That's absolutely it."

"A bottle of wine?"

"Sure. I will never say no to a bottle of wine. That would be perfect."

It all sounded so civilized, she thought. So . . . normal.

Unfortunately, it also sounded now as if she were hearing both of their voices underwater. And that, she knew, was not a good sign. She feared that it would take more than two dinner parties in two days to pull her back from the lip of depression. Two in two days might be precisely the sort of push that would send her spiraling over the edge.

You may be kidding yourself, but you have always presumed that your passengers that August afternoon weren't quite as terrified in their last moments of life as other people who died in other plane crashes. This assumption is based on the reality that they knew an awful lot about the miracle on the Hudson, too. They had seen the color photographs of the passengers as they stood in the icy water on the Airbus wings. They had seen the way the great plane had floated long enough for 155 people to exit the aircraft. And so as your CRJ was gliding—though inexorably descending—toward Lake Champlain, they must have clung to the hope that they, too, would survive; that they, too, would exit the cabin in an orderly fashion and slide into the life rafts or wait for their rescue on the wings. Or, perhaps, tread water for a few brief moments until a boat picked them up, because this was August and the lake would be warm.

And, indeed, this view has been partially corroborated by the statements of at least two of the passengers who survived. Behind you, as you struggled to bring the crippled jet safely back to earth, the cabin was calm. Yes, there were people praying. There were people who were texting what they thought might be their final messages to spouses and parents and children. But some of the passengers were coolly reaching for the life jackets under their seats and pulling them over their summer shirts. Some, inevitably, inflated them inside the cabin, which they weren't supposed to do, and which might have hastened their death when the water rushed in and they were unable to dive under the surface and swim to the holes in the jet. But they weren't panicked.

Yes, they were scared. But unlike you, they were largely oblivious to the stories of the water ditchings that were disasters. None, for example, had watched the absolutely horrific video of Ethiopian Airlines Flight

961, a Boeing 767 that attempted to land in the Indian Ocean off the coast of Comoros in 1996. The plane had been hijacked and had, finally, run out of fuel. Its left wing slammed into the water first, no more than a few hundred yards from the beach, and the aircraft broke into thousands of pieces. As you watched the video, you found it amazing that only 125 of the 175 people onboard died. You would have expected everyone to have been killed.

The truth is that airlines don't have pilots practice water landings on their simulators. The reason? There is so little data about how a plane performs when it hits the water that it's difficult to program the simulation. Besides, what's the point? Why waste precious training and practice time on an eventuality that's so very rare?

And yet, thanks to Sully Sullenberger, many of your passengers that August afternoon probably believed they were going to survive what is, the vast majority of the time, an absolutely unsurvivable event.

Heads down, heads down, heads down!

Then, that new voice: *She deserves friends.*

You sip your soda and stare at the door, unsure which of the voices are real and which are only in your head. You rub your aching neck and the top of your skull: phantom pains. Nothing more. Nothing to do with the shoveling. Really, it's nothing. Nothing at all.

Hallie watched Mrs. Collier lean against the wall beside the chalkboard, her checkered smock dress a little white with dust. The woman's eyes scanned the students, and Hallie knew they were going to pause when they reached her. This was part intuition and part experiential knowledge. Hallie could tell Mrs. Collier had decided pretty quickly that she liked her and had figured out that she would give a pretty good answer to whatever question had been posed. And, sure enough, the teacher spotted her at her table—the classroom had five tables, each with four or five children, because Mrs. Collier preferred communal tables to neat rows of individual desks—and pushed a stray lock of her sandy brown hair away from her eyes and behind her ear. Then she said in that breathy voice she used whenever she spoke her name, "Hallie, what do you think?" They were discussing what effect having so many rivers and lakes had had on the early settlement patterns in Vermont and New Hampshire. One wall was filled with postcards the class had collected of Squam, Sunapee, Winnipesaukee, and Umbagog. There were two of Lake Champlain (the name of which alone made Hallie uncomfortable) and Lake Memphremagog. New Hampshire's nearby Echo and Profile lakes were tiny compared to most of the other ones they had looked at in northern New England, but they were still of great interest to the class and there were postcards of each of them, too. Echo was located right beside the ski resort, and sometimes people were allowed to ski off the trail and onto the ice. And Profile was underneath a ledge where a rock formation called the Old Man of the Mountain used to be. Apparently, the Old Man was a cliffside made of granite that once had resembled the face of a cranky-looking old man. In 2003 it had fallen apart, and the pieces had plummeted thirteen hundred feet to the ground. Hallie was fascinated by the way New Hampshire used it on their quarter and on stamps and in all kinds of literature. She wished it were still up there above Profile Lake. She would have liked to have seen it for real.

Now she looked up at Mrs. Collier and answered that she thought the rivers had been more important than the lakes, because the rivers could power mills and help people get around. The teacher nodded and proceeded to compare the Connecticut River, which flowed north-south along the Vermont–New Hampshire border, to the interstate highway that these days ran parallel to it. After that, the class might have moved on with the lesson in how geography affected development, but Hallie noticed that the boy beside her, a rail of a child with a mop of dark hair that curled in great, swooping tendrils, was drawing a picture of an airplane dropping like an arrow toward a lake. His name was Dwight. He was using a yellow Ticonderoga pencil and a sheet of three-hole loose-leaf paper, and coloring in the water as she watched. The pine trees along the shore and the plane already were in place. There was smoke coming from at least one of the aircraft's two engines.

It surprised her that, despite all of their discussions of lakes throughout the week, someone hadn't thought of her father sooner. She was relieved that Garnet sat at a different table, because she feared her sister would find the drawing far more upsetting. That was just how Garnet was wired. Whenever they talked of the plane crash, Garnet would wind up sad or scared or strangely distant. These were not the neurological seizures that looked to most of the world like trances—there she was, just staring at the same page in a book or at the same Web site on the computer or at something outside the window only she seemed to see— though at first Hallie and her mother had feared that they were. (Hallie recalled now how one time the previous autumn Garnet had spent so long on the window seat in her old bedroom in West Chester, her knees at her chest and her arms around her knees, her eyes open but not seeing, that Hallie had had to rush downstairs and bring their dad upstairs to her sister. See if he could snap her out of the seizure. He had. Sort of. The girl made eye contact with him and nodded that she was okay, they didn't need to go to a doctor. But it was another ten minutes before she was off the window seat and back at the computer they shared.) Still, Garnet would retreat to someplace in her mind and sometimes not say a word for a minute or two. She would ignore everyone, her eyes morose. These were not the ten- or fifteen- or even twenty-minute trances that marked the seizures. But they were nonetheless worrisome. Consequently, Hallie tried not to bring up the plane crash—which, she guessed now, might explain why today's classroom discussion of lakes hadn't made her think of Flight 1611 until she noticed the drawing.

Abruptly Mrs. Collier was at her table, standing right between her and Dwight and exuding anger and pain. Fiercely she grabbed the piece of paper with the sketch of the plane from the tabletop and stared at it. Then she glowered at the boy and said, her voice only barely controlled, "Did you hear one single word I was saying? Or one single word your classmates were saying?"

The boy looked terrified. His hands were buried in his lap, and his head and shoulders had gone limp like wilting flowers. Hallie didn't think he had meant anything by the drawing. He knew about her father—everyone knew about her father—but she didn't believe that he had been trying to frighten her or tease her in some fashion. He was just a boy, and boys seemed to like drawing airplanes—and, sometimes, those planes seemed to crash.

"Uh-huh," he murmured finally.

"Uh-huh, what?" Mrs. Collier pressed.

"I was listening."

"What was the last thing I said?"

Hallie knew it was the comparison of the river to a highway, but it was painfully clear that Dwight had indeed been in his own world and hadn't a clue. The duration of the silence grew excruciating as Mrs. Collier waited for an answer she was never going to get.

And that's when it happened. Abruptly Garnet was on her feet, too, and she was crossing the classroom to their table and standing beside their teacher and Dwight. Reflexively Mrs. Collier started to pull the paper toward her chest, crinkling it into a ball, but Garnet was too fast for her. She had an edge of the drawing in her fingers and then the whole picture in her hands. Out of nowhere she revealed a red plastic cigarette lighter, and then she was igniting the wrinkled sheet, holding it so that in seconds the flames had climbed up the image and incinerated every bit of the pulp. The children were either gasping or eerily silent, and Mrs. Collier was demanding that Garnet put it out, put it out now.

But already it was out. The last black wisps floated to the tile floor as gently as snowflakes, and Garnet stepped on them with her clog. Then she handed Mrs. Collier the lighter and said, her voice sweeter than warm syrup, "If you want, I can go to the principal's office. I know where it is."

Hallie had never seen her sister do anything like this. Not ever. She presumed that, if either of them was going to pull a stunt like this, it would have been far more likely to have been her.

Later, when they were walking up their driveway where the school bus left them off each afternoon, Garnet finally told her sister where she had gotten the lighter. She said it was in the far back corner of the walk-in closet they shared in the hallway between their bedrooms and she'd found it the night before when she was trying to find places for all of her boots and shoes. She added, "I didn't know it was a picture of Dad's plane at first. I really didn't. I just knew it was making Mrs. Collier unhappy. And I guess I just wanted to try out the lighter." Given what the picture was, however, and how the adults all presumed Garnet knew that the image was Flight 1611 plummeting into Lake Champlain, neither the principal nor Mrs. Collier felt a serious inclination to discipline her. They simply told her that the school didn't allow students such things as lighters, and then the principal tried to call Dad at home and Mom at her office. Hallie pointed out to Garnet how she'd received absolutely no punishment at all, and her sister nodded. "You and I can probably do just about anything we want and get away with it," Hallie added, and it was only after she had spoken that she realized she was stating the obvious. Garnet, it seemed, had known this for months.

You stand tall as you swing the ax hard into the door made of barnboard, your pants and sneakers positively black with coal, your hands and forearms streaked with sweat and muck. You convince yourself that the knobs and lines on the wood really look nothing like a face. Nothing at all. When you pause for breath you recall a historian you once heard speaking on the radio about the testosterone it must have taken to clear great swaths of New England of trees in the seventeenth and eighteenth centuries. The forests that greeted the first Europeans were substantial, and the tools the men used to clear them were primitive. They swung axes for hours and hours a day.

And now you are slamming the steel blade into the wood, conscious of how different this tool is from the electrical and mechanical ones that kept your airplanes aloft for nearly a decade and a half. The timbers around you quiver with each blow and the barnboard begins to splinter. When you hit the wood just right, there is a high-pitched groan after the crash of the blade that sounds a bit like a tree branch swaying in a fierce wind. But the groan may be your imagination or your mind playing tricks on you for any number of reasons. You are tired, you are lonely, you are—and the notion surprises you momentarily because until this second you hadn't realized it was the case—worried about Emily. Tending to you—taking care of you—has begun to wear on her. You can tell.

Or maybe what sounds precisely like a moan from the door is a new manifestation of your PTSD: anthropomorphizing the timbers that were used to board up a coal chute.

And then, of course, the whimpers may be real: This may be precisely what shattering wood sounds like.

Regardless, soon enough, you have hewn a hole in the door. With your hands you pull the pieces apart, a chest-high hole that is large enough to reach in far if you want (you don't). You take the heavy metal flashlight you bought at the hardware store for precisely this purpose (not, as you murmured to the woman behind the counter, because you seem to lose power so often here on the hill) and shine it through the uneven fissure.

And all that you spy are what look like wooden walls. Aged horizontal timbers that resemble a part of the foundation of the house. Otherwise, it is an empty . . . and what is the word you want? Compartment? Fruit cellar? Bin? The floor, you notice, is dirt, just like the rest of the basement.

But you have determined it is not a coal chute. At least you think you have. You're not completely sure. Perhaps it had been a coal chute for a time and then it was walled off in this manner and used to store vegetables or fruit. Hard to say unless you tear down the door completely. And so you will. You allow yourself to rest for a moment, aware of the way your heart is thumping in your chest—from effort this time, rather than from anxiety—and then you resume your efforts, raising the ax and smashing it so hard into the timbers that you wonder if this is what the retort from a rifle feels like against your shoulder. But you continue to slam the ax into the barnboard over and over and over, until you have reduced a sizable section of it to kindling. You pull apart the remnants of the lumber with your bare hands as if you are parting the leaves in the trees at the edge of a great forest. It's that simple. And then you drop the ax and pick the flashlight up off the dirt floor. You bow down just enough to twist your body through the passage you have created, careful as you step not to tear your jeans or catch your sweatshirt on the sharp points of the shredded wood.

And before you know it, you are in. The thirty-nine carriage bolts are still surrounding the frame like the bulbs on a movie marquee, but you are in. It took no more than an hour and a half, including the time you spent shoveling the coal like a stoker on a steamer.

You run the flashlight over the walls and the ceiling, aware that somewhere very far away the phone is ringing. (Later you will learn it is the principal at your daughters' elementary school; you will be told that Garnet had brought a cigarette lighter into the classroom and reduced to ashes a drawing another student had made. Only after nearly ten minutes of obfuscation on the part of the principal will you discover that the drawing had been of a plane crashing into a lake.) No matter. The answering machine upstairs will get it. And with the flashlight you study the walls made of horizontal beams ten inches thick and easily two inches—two legitimate inches, not the two inches of the modern two-by-four—wide. If, long ago, this really had been a coal chute, the sluice has been boarded up solidly. You tap on the wood behind which the chute most likely would have existed, and it sounds pretty solid on the other side. Earth solid. No hollowness at all. And so you sit down in the dirt, your back to a wooden wall, and contemplate—now, where does this memory come from?—the pit of despair. That's what it was called, when the researchers weren't using its technical name: vertical chamber apparatus. You learned about it in college. In a psychology course. Harry Harlow designed it for baby monkeys to see what he could learn about depression. It was a stainless-steel trough in which he isolated the animals alone for months at a time. Even a year, in some cases. And, you recall, he learned only what one would expect from isolating a sentient creature for months in a box. The monkeys were wrecked when they emerged. Depressed. Psychotic. Really couldn't be salvaged once they were set free. Rarely recovered. Well, this cubicle could be a pit of despair, too. You recall the sensation of lying in bed under the sheets this past autumn. After the accident. There were days, your children at school, thirty-nine dead in the water, your career over and done, when you didn't get up until three in the afternoon, when the girls got home. Some days you didn't get dressed at all. After all, what was the point? Really? What . . . was . . . the . . . point?

You pull your knees into your chest, if only because you believe this is the posture that behooves one in the midst of a stint in the pit of despair. You think of Poe and amontillado. A cask. Building stone and mortar. A trowel. Or, in this case, barnboard and thirty-nine six-inch-long carriage bolts. You bow your head against your drawn knees and breathe in the aroma of cold, cold dirt and mold. The air is a little stale.

In the unlikely event the cabin loses pressure, an oxygen mask will descend . . .

How many times had you heard that—or some version of that—in the cabin behind you while you were waiting to leave the gate? You always will miss that. The calm before . . . not the storm. The calm before the serenity of flying. How you loved flying.

You feel a sharp spike in your lower back, as if you have leaned against a protruding nail, and reflexively you wince. Just in case, you sit forward and run your hand over the wood behind you. It's rough against your fingertips, but there is nothing spiking out from the beams. This pain is—as you presumed when you felt it—merely one of those strange, mystery aches that have dogged you since August 11.

"It was noisy under the water."

Your head swivels instinctively toward the voice at the same time that your body jerks away from it, and your shoulder smacks hard into the gritty timbers beside you. But the voice is more startling than frightening. There, sitting next to you in the pit, is the child from the plane with the blond spit curls, her hair now wet with lake water and flattened against her scalp, who had boarded Flight 1611 with the Dora the Explorer backpack. The backpack is, in fact, in her arms even now, and she is sitting almost the way you are. Her arms are around her matchstick-like legs. You notice a bruise on one knee and a scratch on the other. Kiddie knees, Emily would call them. Too much tree climbing. Her uninflated life jacket looks like a bib.

"When I would have my head underwater at the swimming pool, it was always quiet," she continues, her voice offhand, as if the two of you have known each other for years, "but that day in the lake? It was really, really noisy."

When you think back to that moment, you realize she's right. It was noisy. There were those ferryboat engines, which were much louder when you were in the water than when you were up on the deck, and the screams and shrieks from the passengers and the rescuers. There was a Coast Guard boat's ululating siren. There was the chaotic, unorchestrated thwapping of the churned-up water and waves. And so you nod like a dad and tell the girl she is correct. You agree. Then you hear yourself asking the child her name, as if she is a slightly younger friend of Hallie and Garnet and you are sitting in a school classroom or, perhaps, at a Brownie picnic. (You wonder: Will your girls find a Girl Scout troop here or will this passage to the north lead them to leave the scouts altogether?)

"Ashley. I have two cats and a dog," she tells you. "Your cat is huge. Much bigger than mine. Do you have any other pets?"

"Nope. Just Dessy. It's short for Desdemona. And you're right: She is a very big girl."

"My cats are Mike and Ike. I didn't name them. The animal shelter did. They were from the same litter, and the shelter named them after some candy because they loved each other so much as kittens and they were, like, always together. My dog is named Whisper. I got to name her. She's a mutt, but she looks a little like a beagle."

You wish you had gotten another dog after your chocolate Lab, Maxie, passed away the year before last. You would have liked to have had a dog here in the country. You would have liked to have had one to walk this past autumn when you were sleepwalking through life in Pennsylvania in the months after the crash. Desdemona might not have minded. She'd always seemed to like Maxie. But if you'd gotten a new dog, it would have been a puppy, and it's possible that Desdemona would have had far less patience with the hysterical antics of a three-month-old Lab.

"Ashley's a pretty name."

"I don't have a Mary-Kate."

"I didn't think so," you tell her. You find yourself smiling, even though the child's wet clothes are making the dirt between you turn to mud. Only recently have your daughters outgrown the Olsen sisters. "But you know what? My children are twins. I have twin girls."

"I know."

Of course she does. She knows about Dessy. Why wouldn't she know about Hallie and Garnet?

"Most people think twins always look the same," she tells you with great earnestness. "But I know that only happens sometimes. I have cousins who are twins, and one's a boy and one's a girl. It would be pretty weird if they looked identical! My family sometimes jokes about how Andrew—he's the boy—is older than Becca. But it's only by, like, a couple of minutes. Who's older in this house: Hallie or Garnet?"

"Hallie but, like Andrew, only by minutes. Hallie is named after her grandmother. And her sister is named Garnet, because her hair was so very, very red when she was born."

The child nods, taking this in. "Those are very pretty names."

"I think so."

Ashley stretches out her legs so she can open her backpack. She unzips the top and peers in for a moment. Then she turns to you, her face growing sad, and you reach out your arm to rub her shoulder, to console her. Suddenly she bends forward, bowing almost, grimacing, and your eyes go to her lower back, that precise spot on your own back where only moments ago you had felt a sharp sliver of pain. And then you gasp and, as if she were your own child, turn the girl away from you so you can examine more carefully the wound and see what you can do to help her. There you see a twisting corkscrew of metal nearly the size of a skateboard, a part of it adorned with the sky blue paint your airline uses to brighten the exterior fuselages of its jets, impaling the child from her back to her front. Perhaps seven or eight inches of the metal is extending from just beneath the front of her ribs—you must have missed it earlier because of her life jacket and knapsack—and at least a foot reaches out from her back like a shelf. Her clothing is awash in blood and flesh, and there are tendrils of muscle twitching like small black snakes from the holes that have been gashed through both sides of her shirt.

You can't imagine what you can possibly do to help her—you can't imagine what anyone could do—you can't think of anything you could say to ease her agony and her fear. But, still, you reach for her because, after all, you are a father. Because you are an adult and you have to do something. Gently, so as not to jostle her and cause that great shard of metal to move inside her and cause her yet more agony, you wrap your arms around her. But when you press your fingers on the back of her shirt, you feel only air and she is gone.

You sigh. Your heart slows. You drop your hands to your sides and then, a moment later, touch the pinpricks of pain at the small of your own back.

She was never really there, you tell yourself. Yes, you recall there was a child on the plane named Ashley. You know this from the passenger manifest. You know this from the list of the dead. Ashley Stearns. She was seated beside her father, Ethan Stearns. But of course you just fabricated in your mind this whole brief conversation. You will be careful not to tell Emily. Or Michael Richmond, your new therapist here in New Hampshire. Already you worry them both. So, you will share this . . . this vision . . . with no one.

You run your fingers through the dirt, reassuring yourself that it was always this moist. This damp. You press them in a little deeper, digging abstractedly, when—And how did you not know this would happen, how could you possibly have not seen this coming? Isn't this why you broke down the door in the first place?—you feel a long, coralline tube of bone. You pull it slowly from the ground and study it, grateful on some level that, unlike Ashley Stearns, it is no apparition. No delusion. This bone is as real as the ones in your forearm and probably as long as the radius and ulna that link your elbow and your wrist.

Chapter Six

"There's another one," Hallie was saying from the backseat of the Volvo.

"I saw it, too," Garnet said, "and I saw it at the same time as you."

"I called it, I get it," Hallie insisted.

Emily stole a glance at her daughters in the rearview mirror. "Saw what? Get what?" she asked.

"Greenhouses," Garnet answered. "There are greenhouses everywhere here. I bet there are even more greenhouses than silos."

They were driving home from dance class Saturday morning, and it was starting to snow, great white flecks that hit the windshield and instantly were transformed into droplets of water. It wasn't quite noon, and Emily was a little relieved to be talking about something other than that damned cigarette lighter. Counting greenhouses? The number in Bethel was odd, there was no doubt about it, but hearing the girls bicker as they counted them felt like a return to normalcy after yesterday afternoon's and last night's conversations about the lighter and what, as a family, they should do about it. The conversations had seemed endless. She and Chip had both had to speak to Mrs. Collier on the telephone, and then the two of them alone had debated what to do. She had come home from work early, and they had talked to Garnet soon after she got off the school bus. Then they had spoken with Garnet and Hallie together. Both girls had always been so well behaved that she and Chip really didn't have a lot of history with discipline: Even when the girls had been toddlers, neither she nor Chip had sent either child to the "time-out chair"—one of the ladder-back chairs that was actually a part of their regular dining room furniture—more than two or three times. Good Lord, Garnet had been more likely to send herself to the time-out chair, which she had done at least twice when Emily was alone with the girls while Chip was flying. It was as if Garnet had somehow deduced that her mother was not merely outnumbered, she was outmatched by three-year-old twins and had reached the breaking point: She needed one of the girls to sit still for a few minutes while she tried to straighten up the board books and stuffed animals and baby dolls (and baby doll clothing) that coated the floor of the house like fallen leaves in October, or make a dent in the shaky skyscraper of disgusting dishes that rose high from the kitchen sink. In the end, Emily and Chip had chosen not to discipline Garnet for hiding her discovery of the lighter from them—and from Hallie—and then for bringing it with her to school: Between the plane crash and being uprooted and brought to New Hampshire, it was a wonder that there hadn't been far more and far worse instances of acting out. She wished that Garnet had evidenced more contrition, but clearly her daughter accepted that she had made a mistake. And even the girl's schoolteacher seemed to believe that the boy who had drawn the picture of the plane was just asking for some sort of off-the-grid reaction.

"And the greenhouses are all in Bethel. Not in Littleton or Franconia," Hallie was saying. "You see one almost the second you get off the highway."

"And then another and another," Garnet added.

"Well, winters are long here," Emily said, speaking as much to try to make sense of it to herself as to try to explain it to her daughters. "And that means the growing seasons are short. You want to start plants as early as you can in a greenhouse and then give them as long a growing season as possible."

"But why just here?" Garnet asked her.

This was a perfectly reasonable question, and she wished she had a good answer. She recalled that woman from the diner, Becky Davis, and how Becky had referred to the local women as the herbalists—as if they were a cult. Emily presumed that each of those women had a greenhouse. And that group, apparently, included Anise and Reseda and Ginger Jackson and John Hardin's wife, Clary, since she knew that all four of them owned greenhouses. And that also meant, perhaps, that even Tansy Dunmore at some point had been one of them—whoever *they* were—because she and Chip now owned a house with a greenhouse.

Of course, as loopy as all those women might be about vegetables and herbs, Becky herself hadn't seemed a paragon of stability that afternoon in the diner.

"Well," Emily said, trying to focus on Garnet's question, "it could be as simple as the fact that someone around here builds greenhouses. You know, maybe someone in the community owns a company that makes them. That's all. Or it could be a . . . a club."

"Even Mrs. Collier owns one," Hallie added, referring to the girls' schoolteacher. Emily felt Hallie tapping the back of her seat with her foot absentmindedly. It drove her a little crazy some days, but now she was taking comfort in the idea that her daughter had kicked off her snow boots when she climbed into the car and so at least she wasn't leaving brown marks from road sand and mud on the tan leather. "What did she tell you about hers?" she asked. In her mind she had already added another person—another woman—to the group. She wasn't sure how she felt about the idea that the girls' teacher was one of the women (and the club really did seem to include only women). "Anything special?"

"No. She just said she might take us there later this spring to show Garnet and me some of her special plants."

"You mean the whole class?"

"No, not the whole class," Hallie answered. "I think she just meant Garnet and me."

Emily wondered what the teacher had meant by *special plants*. Some people used greenhouses to grow tomatoes or phlox. What were these women using them for? Comfrey and crampbark? Hawthorn? Elder? She knew there were all sorts of people floating around remote corners of New England, some New Agers and some old-timers, who would still put a little comfrey on a cut or a bruise. She recalled a woman from her visits to her grandmother in Meredith, an elderly friend of the family: Before she would join her grandmother and her friend for walks around the lake at twilight, the woman would rub some leaf on her arms and no mosquito would ever come near her. Not a single one. And it smelled heavenly. Like perfume. Emily tried to recall now what it was and couldn't.

She slowed as she took a corner and the road's shoulder all but disappeared, and she noted the way the snow was starting to stick to the pavement. She had hoped it would have stopped for the season by now. But they'd gotten another three inches in the night, and John Hardin and his wife were probably on their fourth or fifth runs of the day at the mountain. Soon, she presumed, the couple would be calling it quits and heading home to prepare for their small dinner party that evening. Behind her, Hallie stopped kicking her seat.

"Maybe we should put some interesting plants in our greenhouse," Emily said to the girls, trying out an idea. Maybe one of the benefits to living here in northern New Hampshire would be the chance for the girls to reconnect with the natural world. She imagined taking them on nature walks and teaching them the names of the wildflowers that grew along the side of the road. Of course, that would mean she would have to learn the names of those wildflowers first.

"No, let's not," Hallie said, mimicking the derisive voices of the teenagers she saw on sitcoms on TV.

"Yeah," Garnet agreed. "We want that to be our playhouse."

"Can't it be both?" Emily asked, though now she was really only teasing them. If they felt that strongly about wanting it to be their private world, she had no objections at all.

"No way," Hallie said. "It's a playhouse—not a greenhouse."

"Okay, then," Emily agreed. "Playhouse: not a greenhouse." She glanced out the window at a handsome white Cape with evergreen shutters. In the backyard she thought she spied a greenhouse.

*   *   *

You could tell your wife about the bone. Bones, actually. When you dug around in the dirt a little more, you found three bullet-size phalanges that you are quite sure came from a human hand. A human finger.

Perhaps you even *should* tell your wife about the bones. But you don't. You did not tell her yesterday when she came home from work and you will not tell her when she and the girls return from dance class this morning. And while you could devise any number of reasonable excuses for withholding the discovery—Emily is a little depressed, Emily already has a basket case of a husband, Emily is questioning her decision to bring the family north to New Hampshire—the main reason is essentially this: You have a macabre fascination with the bones. This house is brimming with strangeness and purposeful surprises. You want to investigate this on your own. See what it means. Talk to Hewitt Dunmore yourself.

Besides, why scare Emily? She was disturbed enough by the crowbar, the knife, and the ax. Why risk agitating her—and, thus, the girls? Because when Emily is anxious, the girls are anxious. That's just how it is.

And so you wrap the long bone in sheets of newspaper (the *Philadelphia Inquirer,* the same pages that days ago pillowed the china plates that had come into your life in the weeks and months after your wedding) and place it upright in the very back of your mahogany armoire. It reminds you of the way that crowbar had been leaned up—hidden—in a corner of a closet in another bedroom. You place the pieces of fingers in a Ziploc bag beside it.

You find yourself smiling a little ruefully when you shut the armoire door. Perhaps you are more like Parnell or Tansy or Hewitt Dunmore than you realized. You hide things.

At some point soon, however, perhaps even this afternoon, Emily is going to go downstairs to the basement, and there she will see that you have torn down that door. She will see that the coal has been moved and the door is in ruins. And so you decide you will tell her about that part of your little project. You will tell her when she gets back from the dance studio with your girls. You will say you initiated this small home improvement this morning. Not yesterday. Today. After all, if she thinks you took care of the door yesterday and chose not to tell her until now, she might ask questions. And, before you know it, you might reveal that you have found some bones. Or, worse, that you may have reconnected with a dead girl with a Dora the Explorer backpack.

O n Saturday afternoon, the sun trying and failing to burn off the high overhead quilt of oyster white cirrus, Reseda misted the hypnobium, epazote, and derangia in her greenhouse. Then she gazed for a long moment at the arnica, appraising the plants. They looked like daisies, but the flowers were an orange just a tad more vibrant than terra-cotta. They smelled slightly like sage. On Monday she would harvest the arnica for a tincture. Most people only used arnica externally as an anti-inflammatory. They rubbed it on sprains and strains. They feared its toxicity when taken internally: A large enough dose was lethal. And while Reseda knew that you could kill a person with arnica, the truth was you could kill a person with plenty of medicines if you overdid it. Hence the word: *overdose.* She used a thousand times more arnica than the bare trace element you might find in a homemade homeopathic tincture or pill, but not enough, apparently, to ever have killed a person.

She wondered what she would prepare for the Lintons tomorrow night when they came to her house for dinner, and she put down her mister and wandered across the greenhouse to the section with the herbs she used in cooking. She noted how healthy the rosemary looked and inhaled its fragrance. Lamb, she decided that moment. Yes: She would serve lamb.

She recalled the way Captain Linton's mind had roamed among shadows when he dropped by her office, how he seemed to be living now only in gloaming. She understood; she had her own trauma. She had had her own extended moments with the dead. His depression and disorientation were products of the accident, and with a little luck and the right counsel he would recover and resume a safer path. She found it significant that she was most attracted to the stories of the captain and his wife, while Anise and the other women were obsessed only with their girls.

She paused when she felt a prickling at the outer edge of her aura and stood perfectly still. She hadn't imagined it. Consequently, she stepped over the shin-high stone statue of the amphisbaena, careful not to trip over either of the serpent's heads (in myth, amphisbaena meat was an aphrodisiac; its skin could cure colds), passed by her Baphomet, and knelt. She peeled off her gardening gloves and spread wide her fingers, stretching her arms and straightening her spine. She stared up through the glass at the nimbus of light in the hazy western sky, closed her eyes, and randomly said aloud names of the living as if they were parts of a mantra or prayer. In a moment, whatever—whoever—was trying to cloud her aura was gone.

It was a source of unending interest to her: How could she—given all that she knew and all that she had endured—be so attuned to the thoughts of the living and so mystified by the thoughts of the dead?

They were only on the interstate for two exits on Saturday night, but they passed a pair of signs warning drivers of moose. One advised urgently, *Brake for Moose: It may save your life.* The first time Chip had seen that one, the day after they'd moved to Bethel, he'd remarked, "I suppose they're afraid most people will accelerate when they see a moose. Look, honey, there's a moose on the road: Let's speed up and see if we can hit it!" He didn't joke much these days, and so it always comforted Emily when she saw a glimpse of his humor. It was difficult to recall now, but before the accident he had actually been a rather funny man.

The Hardins' house in Littleton was a white Federal that resided with princely elegance in the town's hill section above the main street. The driveway had a circular portico and the front yard a stone fountain, the basin of which, because it was winter, had been removed and placed against the pedestal like a giant mushroom cap so the water pooling inside didn't freeze and crack it. There was another car in the driveway, and Emily suspected by the way the front windshield had been defrosted that this vehicle was a recent arrival, too, and not one of the Hardins' automobiles.

"There will be other people," she said to neither Chip nor the girls in particular as they stood for a moment in the driveway. She found herself worrying for her husband. Worrying about her husband. It seemed that morning he had taken an ax and destroyed that squat, ugly door in the basement. The exertion had left him exhausted, though Emily was troubled more by the fury he had brought to the task: Why in the world had he used an ax instead of simply removing the carriage bolts from one side and then prying the door open with a crowbar? He had told her there were too many bolts and they were too long: Removing even a third of them would have taken hours. She took him at his word, but she couldn't help but fear it was the fact that there were precisely thirty-nine of them that had prevented him. He had seemed unduly disturbed by the coincidence, the notion that there was one bolt for every fatality—as if each length of metal corresponded exactly with one human soul. One night over dinner he had expressed his wonderment at the connection, and she had smiled and told him this was magical thinking, a symptom of an obsessive-compulsive disorder. He, in turn, had told her that magical thinking was also a symptom of depression and there was something enigmatic in his response: Was he signaling to her that he knew she had demons, too, and to allow him this indulgence? Or was he alerting her to the idea that she was right and he had done a little Web diagnosis on himself and understood that his consideration of the bolts was at once irrational and explicable?

And what had he discovered from all that sweat, what had he found on the other side of that barnboard? Nothing. He said there wasn't a single thing behind that creepy door—which, when she was honest with herself, left her a little relieved. If she could find knives and axes hidden beneath heating grates and under the sink, what in the world might Tansy Dunmore have hidden behind the door in the basement? A cannon?

"Will there be other kids?" Garnet was asking. It was spitting snow once again, and the slate path had enough of a dusting that their boots were leaving tracks in the fine white powder. Emily looked up and focused instantly on her daughter when she heard the unease in the child's voice. Garnet could be shy, and other children had not been a part of the plan. Quickly Emily inventoried the rest of the law firm in her mind and tried to catalog the possible children. In the end she couldn't decide and answered that she honestly didn't know, but she expected that the girls would be able to cocoon upstairs with a movie or two just as John Hardin had promised.

And, it turned out, there were no other children. But there was another couple present whom Clary Hardin, John's wife, thought Emily and Chip would enjoy. When the pair saw the Lintons awkwardly removing their snow boots in the front entryway, they rose from their perch on a sofa with plush pillows and serpentine arms that looked like it belonged in a French villa and went with the Hardins to greet them. They seemed to be roughly the age of their hosts: Emily pegged the couple as somewhere in their late sixties, though both—like John and Clary—seemed almost impeccably well preserved. They introduced themselves as Peyton and Sage Messner.

"And you two, quite obviously, are Hallie and Garnet," said Sage, kneeling down before the twins. It looked like she was drinking Scotch, and the ice cubes tinkled against her glass as she moved. With her free hand she surprised Garnet by stroking her hair, and Emily hoped that only a mother would sense her child's discomfort with a gesture this intimate from a stranger. "Your hair is every bit as extraordinary and as beautiful as I'd heard," Sage went on.

"I told Sage at bridge club," Clary said quickly.

"And I had told Clary," John added, chuckling. "I told her it was remarkable, a shade of magical titian that only a practiced Renaissance dye maker could concoct."

"And you knew your share of them, old man," Peyton Messner chided him.

"I am old, but not that old—thank heavens," John corrected him.

Emily handed John her overcoat and glanced quickly at Chip. He was staring at the chandelier that was dangling from the dining room ceiling, and so she glanced at it, too. The bulbs were faces, she realized, though because they were lit one couldn't really study them. But there seemed to be at least three or four different characters, one as sad as the classic drama mask signifying tragedy and one as hysterical as the mask denoting comedy. And then there was one that seemed . . . terrified. She thought of the Edvard Munch painting of the scream. She guessed there were twenty bulbs, each the white of a cotton ball cloud, and they seemed to exist like flowers at the ends of slender but tangled wrought-iron vines.

"Don't you just love it," Clary said, when she noticed Emily gazing at the chandelier. "John and I found it in a lighting store in Paris. We saw it for sale in a shop window in the Marais and just had to have it."

"It's pretty eccentric," she said.

"I've always found it downright hypnotic," said Peyton, his voice deep and plummy and rather hypnotic itself.

"Where in the world do you get replacement bulbs?" Emily asked.

"I hope we brought a lifetime supply back with us," said John, and he punctuated the sentence with another small laugh. "But I do fear someday we may run out."

"When my father's construction company was building the first greenhouses, he was investigating the best grow lights. I wonder what he would have thought of bulbs like these," Peyton said, pointing at the chandelier ever so slightly with one of his long, elegant fingers.

"Tell me something," Emily asked. "Why are there so many greenhouses in Bethel?"

"Do you girls want some juice—or cocktails?" Clary asked the twins, and Emily had the distinct sense that she was consciously avoiding the question by turning her attention—everyone's attention—to Hallie and Garnet. "John makes a mean Shirley Temple."

"I make a mean everything," her husband said, raising his eyebrows rakishly.

Emily saw both children looking at her, trying to gauge whether she approved of their having cocktails. The word was such a throwback to another era that she wasn't sure either girl even knew what it meant. "Why not have Shirley Temples?" she said to them. "You always like them at the airport." Funny, Emily thought now: The girls did like Shirley Temples, but she and Chip only thought to order them for the children when they were traveling. She recalled almost at once all of the restaurants and bars and lounges along the concourses at the Philadelphia airport.

"Okay, I'll have one," Hallie agreed.

"And you, Garnet?" asked John.

"Yes, please."

"I have cherries, but the red won't be as magic as your hair," he said to her and then retreated to the kitchen.

"Where would you like the girls to settle in?" Emily asked her hostess.

"Well, wherever they'd like!" said Clary, waving her arm at the living room as if she were a fairy godmother with a wand. "The couch, the divan, the carpets. Wherever they'd like!"

Emily recalled John's invitation at the office—the way he had stressed that there was a playroom upstairs where the twins could escape the grown-ups. The last thing Hallie and Garnet wanted this evening was to sit like dolls on the divan. And so, even though it was awkward, she said to her hostess, "That's really very sweet of you, but I know the girls are tired. They had dance in the morning and were doing yet more unpacking this afternoon. John said something about a playroom. Would it be okay if they just curled up there and dozed in front of a movie? They brought some of their DVDs."

"Oh, of course. Just let us have them for a few minutes," Clary said, and she smiled at the children. Her eyes hadn't wavered, but in those two short sentences her voice had lost its saccharine lilt and grown demanding. *Just let us have them.* The words echoed in Emily's head, and they sounded vaguely threatening. This was, she understood, a ridiculous and completely unhealthy overreaction. Still, she wanted her children to have a quiet evening upstairs. It was what she had promised them—and what she had been offered.

Reflexively Emily turned toward Chip for help, because the old Chip would have found a diplomatic way to have the girls excused as soon as John returned with their drinks. But the moment she saw him with that odd new posture of his—his left arm dangling down at his side, his right arm bent across his stomach, and his right hand cradling his left elbow—she knew there would be no cavalry approaching from that direction. He was still gazing at that bizarre chandelier. And so she grinned at her children and did nothing as Sage pressed her palm behind Garnet's back and Clary did the same with Hallie, and the two older women guided the girls into the living room. Emily followed them, feeling a little obsequious and a little put upon. For a second she was afraid she was going to have to escort Chip into the room, but abruptly he pulled himself together and followed her.

"No one asked you two what you would like!" Peyton said to her. "That's John for you—always the grandfather. Oblivious to adults when there are children present whom he can spoil. Would either of you like some wine? I brought a couple of very nice Malbecs from Sonoma."

"That would be lovely, thank you," she murmured.

"Chip?"

He waved his hand as if brushing a fly from his face. "Oh, that's fine."

Peyton nodded approvingly, clearly pleased to have a task, and went to the kitchen, where John was concocting the Shirley Temples.

"Now," Clary was saying, sitting both Hallie and Garnet down on a round velvet pouf the color of a raspberry in August. "Tell me how you're enjoying New Hampshire." She and Sage sat on the floor before the children, as if the girls were storytellers or—and when the word came to Emily, she thought it, too, was an unhealthy connection—royalty. Clary was sitting with her legs straight before her while Sage had curled hers underneath her. Emily was impressed with the woman's elasticity. She contemplated recommending to her daughters that they offer their hostess and her friend the pouf, but there were plenty of other places where these ladies could sit. They had chosen to sit on the floor before her daughters.

Hallie and Garnet glanced briefly at each other, deciding who should answer, and then Hallie rocked forward a bit and replied simply, "I like the greenhouse."

"Me, too," said Garnet.

"I am not at all surprised," Sage said.

"Why?" Emily asked. She realized the moment the word had escaped her lips that it sounded like she was cross-examining the woman. But Sage didn't seem to be disturbed by the tone.

"What's not to love in a greenhouse?" she answered. "Think of the beauty and the magic inside and the fact the world is always new in a greenhouse. It can always be spring. You can have flowers every day."

Emily noticed Hallie looking at her and nodding. She was reminding her of their conversation in the car ride home from dance that morning: Bethel had more greenhouses than the neighboring communities.

"Well, I'm not sure that's why the girls love the greenhouse. We've discussed what we will and won't do with the building, and Hallie and Garnet are pretty clear about this: It will be their playhouse, not my greenhouse," Emily said. "Besides, I think this village must have enough greenhouses already devoted to tomatoes and phlox and whatever."

"Tomatoes and phlox," Sage said slowly, pondering Emily's response. She didn't seem especially happy. "We do grow both. At least some of us. But we also grow a fair amount of . . . whatever."

"Really, why are there so many greenhouses in Bethel?" Emily asked. "There must be a reason."

"There might be more than in some towns, but there's no mystery to it," Clary answered, jumping in. "There used to be a very active garden club in the village—women from Bethel won embarrassing numbers of blue ribbons at the county fairs for flowers and herbs and vegetables— and Sage's father-in-law happened to own a construction company that specialized in them."

"In greenhouses."

"And solariums. And sunrooms. And he gave us all the 'friends and family discount.'"

"But *whatever* it is that we grow," Sage added, still smarting from

Emily's offhand dismissal of what they cultivated in their greenhouses, "more times than not it tends to be more interesting than mere tomatoes and phlox. Some of us bring in cuttings and seedlings from all over the world. I have all sorts of things thriving in my greenhouse right now that most Americans have never even heard of—would never even have dreamed of! And Anise? Her work is even more extraordinary. Anise is brilliant: You simply can't imagine. The things either of us could tell you about the power of herbs and tinctures and blood and—"

"Yes, Sage," Clary said, squeezing her arm and cutting her off. "We all know that you grow some remarkable things. But we don't want to bore the girls!"

"What do you mean by blood?" Emily asked. "I presume you don't put blood in tinctures or potions."

"Oh," Sage said, her voice more measured than a moment ago but still edgy, "I only meant the effect a natural remedy can have on the blood—on a person's health."

"Herbs and tinctures and blood," Chip said, and because he had barely spoken since they arrived, everyone turned to him expectantly. Even the girls. He sat down in an easy chair upholstered with images of honeysuckle vines. "Sometimes I think I could use a good herbalist these days."

Emily could tell there was a subterranean layer of sarcasm in his remark, but only because they had known each other so long. She was confident that only she had even an inkling that he might be mocking the need for an herbalist. Moreover, she also believed that it wasn't precisely that he lacked faith in herbal medicine; rather, it was that he had problems of his own that in his opinion far transcended the powers of cohosh and ginseng.

"Tell us, Hallie: What specifically do you like about the greenhouse?" Clary asked, not exactly ignoring Chip but not responding to his remark, either.

"Well, it's, like, Garnet's and my own special place," the girl answered.

"It *is* your own special place, isn't it? Places have auras, and I am so glad you appreciate the aura of that greenhouse."

"We haven't spent a lot of time there yet," Garnet added. "It's kind of cold right now."

"Of course it is. But Sage and Anise and I will be happy to help you decide what to grow there. We can bring by seedlings and starters and roots. We can—"

"I was serious," Emily said, careful to smile as she interrupted Clary. "I think the girls want it to be a playhouse. Dolls and games and secrets—that sort of thing."

Sage stared at her, the woman's eyes narrowing just the tiniest bit. "You know that Peyton's father built that greenhouse. You know it was on land that was carefully dowsed."

"I didn't know that. But, still, it seems to be metal framing and big pieces of glass with a good southern exposure. It's beautifully built, and your father-in-law's company did very good work: I don't know much about greenhouses, but I can tell that for sure. You can be very proud. But, well, it's a greenhouse—not a nuclear power plant."

"No, it's certainly not. But tell me, Emily: Could you design a greenhouse?"

"No, but I could call a company that makes them and order one."

"There was more to it than that," Sage told her, her tongue clicking hard on the last word, and Emily was just about to say she agreed, she understood, she was just being glib. It wasn't that she actually believed she had said something that might merit an apology; rather, she simply wanted to deescalate the conversation. But before she had opened her mouth, John and Peyton returned with the girls' Shirley Temples and her and Chip's glasses of red wine.

"You're going to like this, Chip," Peyton told her husband.

"And you girls are going to love these," said John, leaning over and handing each of the twins a wide tumbler blushing with grenadine syrup. "It's my secret ingredient."

"And that is?" asked Chip.

"A magician never reveals the secret behind an illusion. And notice I did not use the word *trick*."

"Any special reason?" Emily asked.

"A trick suggests I have taken advantage of people or fooled them. Played a joke of some sort on them. I prefer to leave that sort of bad behavior to my work as an attorney."

"Just so long as it's not an herbal narcotic or magic hallucinogen of some kind," Chip remarked. "Drink up, girls."

Everyone turned to him, a little nonplussed by the inappropriateness of the comment. But he simply raised his wineglass in a silent toast and took a sip. "You were right, Peyton. This is a delightful wine. A great selection."

And Peyton nodded and the girls sipped their Shirley Temples, a little tentatively at first but then voraciously, as Peyton told the grown-ups how he and Sage had discovered the vineyard on a tasting tour in Northern California last year, and how the Malbec was a new varietal for these wine growers. Chip's strange admonition was ignored, and the small party quickly regained its footing. Emily was relieved. She had the sense that everyone was. Before the children had finished their Shirley Temples, John was escorting them up the stairs to the playroom, and Emily told herself that Sage and Clary were only following her daughters with their eyes because the girls were twins and they were indeed adorable. There was nothing more to it than that.

"So, tell me," Chip was saying. "What's Clary short for? Clarice?"

"Oh, it's not short for anything at all," the woman said, pushing herself to her feet and then sitting on the spot on the pouf that Hallie had vacated. "It's just Clary. I was named after the herb."

"Clary? I don't believe I know that herb," Emily confessed.

"Treats women's problems," Peyton said, and he laughed, even rolling his eyes.

"Oh, stop it, Peyton, you know it does much more than that," Clary chastised him, though it was evident that this was a long-running joke between the two friends.

"I do. I do, indeed," he agreed.

There was a short lull in the conversation, and in the pause Emily listened to the low murmur of John's voice upstairs as he showed the girls how to work the DVD player and then she heard the sound of the television. She couldn't make out the program, but the girls laughed either at something the lawyer had said or at something on the screen. It really didn't matter which. They sounded content enough, and so she turned her attention to her hostess and her new friends and settled in for the evening.

You wake up when you hear the murmuring voices. You pull your way like a swimmer from the torrents of another sleep burdened by dreams of airplanes crashing hard into the earth, and you sit up in bed. There beside you, your wife slumbers soundlessly. She is curled on her side and has heard nothing. It doesn't strike you as the slightest bit odd that you are confident the voices are neither burglars nor intruders. Almost abstractedly, you scan this room in the foothills along the western spine of the White Mountains, your bedroom—but still not a room that offers even a shadow of the familiarity and intimacy you associate with that word: *bedroom*. This still is but a room with a bed. The digital clock on Emily's dresser reads 2:55. Not quite three in the morning. You left the Hardins' about eleven and were in bed by midnight. Asleep then by 12:15. You still have the faint taste in your mouth of Peyton's wines from Sonoma and the special canapés that Clary kept passing to you. (*I know you will like these, Chip. I just know it.*)

The voices are coming from someplace in the house below you, not from the floor above. And so it seems that the speakers are not Hallie and Garnet. Besides, they're grown-ups. You knew that the moment you awoke. Still, isn't it conceivable that the girls are watching something on television at three in the morning and the grown-ups are characters in a movie or Disney Channel sitcom or whatever is being beamed into your house that moment via a satellite and a dish? But then you remember:

You don't have a dish yet. You had one in West Chester. Not here. You have one on order, but it is not going to be installed until this coming Tuesday morning. And so if these sounds are indeed grown-ups, then the girls must be watching a DVD.

And yet that wouldn't be like your daughters. Not at all. They're ten—still four months shy of eleven. You really can't imagine them tiptoeing down these strange stairs in this strange house in the middle of the night to watch a DVD. Besides, the distant murmuring doesn't sound like typical sitcom fare: It sounds like a woman and a man who are embroiled in a dispute. Arguing about something, and not in a playful, comedic, all-problems-will-be-solved-in-twenty-two-minutes-of-television sort of way.

Your plane always had a low altitude warning system on the altimeter: Whenever you were a mere thousand feet above the earth, even on a normal approach to a normal landing, it would tweet three times. You wish now your brain had a similar warning system, a way of alerting you that you were about to experience another of these . . . visions. Or, perhaps, visitations. After the accident, you had been warned of the flashbacks and the sleeplessness and the loss of appetite. The nightmares and the guilt. The inability to focus. But no one had told you of the visitations.

Now you climb from beneath the quilt, a little nonplussed by how cold the room is. For a brief moment you wonder if the furnace is out and you will need to relight the pilot. (You see in your mind an image of yourself in your captain's uniform and wonder: Why is it called a *pilot* light?) Your feet are bare, and the floor feels a little rough and chilly on them. When you were a child, you had pancake-flat feet. Not an arch to be found. And so from an early age you wore special orthopedic shoes; as a toddler and a small boy, you slept with a steel bar linking your ankles. You had to hop instead of walk when you awoke in the night, and you hopped in your bare feet. There was a wooden floor in the house just like this one. It was the room in your parents' house that they (and you, eventually) called the playroom. When you were a boy, once a month you would visit your orthopedist in Stamford and strip down to nothing but a pair of white underpants, and the doctor would roll marbles down a long corridor that ended in his practice's waiting room. While he watched your feet and your ankles and your hips, you would run after those marbles. That corridor had a carpet that was thick but firm. At first you weren't shy about running in nothing but underpants into that waiting room, chasing after marbles that were white as cue balls and shiny like ice. Eventually, however, the indignity of the practice began to dawn on you and you grew hesitant. Then diffident. Still, the doctor always convinced your mother to persuade you to run, and so there you were, even in the first and second grade, being run like a monkey down a hall until you emerged into a roomful of strangers in nothing but underpants. Your feet never developed perfect arches, but whatever that doctor did was not ineffective. By the time you stopped scampering after marbles, your arches were at least good enough. Oh, you were never going to be a fighter jock, but when you chose to become a commercial pilot, your feet were never an issue.

The discussion below you has grown a little more agitated, and you pause in your pajamas in the frame of your bedroom door. The hallway is lit by the moon through the corridor windows. You ponder the narrow stairs up to Hallie's and Garnet's bedrooms and wonder if you should check on the twins before going downstairs: see if they are indeed in their beds, because if they are, then it's clear that the voices below you are not coming from a DVD.

And so you move slowly and quietly up that thin stairway to the cozy and snug third floor of your house. You press your fingers against the wall for balance because this stairwell is so cramped that there is neither a handrail nor a banister. The girls' doors are both open, and you peer into each room for a long moment, watching each child sleep in the red glow of her night-light. You have always loved watching your children sleep. Some nights in Pennsylvania—before the crash, when life was filled with only routine and promise—you and your wife would stand in the doorway and watch first Garnet and then Hallie sleep, your

souls warmed by the uncomplicated domesticity conveyed by the perfume in a baby shampoo. You would watch the way Garnet's small hands
would be embracing a stuffed teddy bear she had named Scraggles, or
the way Hallie would be lying flat on her stomach, her arms burrowed
deep beneath her pillow. In the winter, the girls often slept in red and
white Lanz nightgowns that matched one of their mother's. Tonight
they are sleeping in pajamas: Garnet's are patterned with evergreen trees
and Hallie's with Japanese lotus flowers. Now, at three in the morning,
you wander as silently as you can into each child's room, first pulling
the comforter back up and over Garnet's shoulders and then placing the
stuffed gray rabbit Hallie named Smokey beside her on her bed. The
bunny had fallen to the floor.

Up here, the voices are the same indecipherable buzz they were on
the second floor. This strikes you as interesting. You would have expected
the sound to be more muffled—perhaps even inaudible—when you are
another floor higher. Here you may even have heard what sounded a bit
like a laugh: a mean-spirited little chuckle at someone's expense.

And so you start back down that narrow stairwell and then along
the second-floor corridor, passing your and your wife's bedroom. At
the top of the stairs to the first floor, you reach for the flashlight you
keep upright beside the trim, but you do not switch it on until you have
reached the bottom step because you do not want to risk waking Emily.
But when you are on the ground floor, you turn it on and spray the
rooms. There in the living room is that wallpaper with the fox that looks
like an eel, the image repeated over and over. There in the dining room
are the walls of statuesque but sickly sunflowers, as well as the two sawhorses and the piece of plywood on which you drape sheets of wallpaper
and then slather them with paste; in this light, with a curtainless vertical
window just beyond the sawhorses, the image resembles a guillotine.
(You built a plastic one from a modeling kit when you were a boy. It
actually came with the pieces for a plastic nobleman with a detachable
head. You were meticulous and glued the device and the victim together
with the same care you brought to your models of jet airplanes and bat-
tleships.) There, in a corner of the hallway, is a stepladder with a gallon

of paint on the top step, and for just a fraction of a second you are sure it's a man.

And, finally, there is the door to the basement, and you find you are nodding to yourself that it is open. The door to the basement is never open. You keep it closed because why would you want the smell of the dirt floor wafting up into the house? Why would you want the heat from the radiators or the woodstove to drift there?

Ah, but it is ajar now. Of course. It has been opened for you. It is open now because that's where the voices are coming from and whoever is down there wanted to be sure that you heard them.

You see in your mind a book jacket: *How to Live in a Haunted House.* No, that's not right: It should be *How Not to Live in a Haunted House.* But then you decide that this construction is wrong, too. All wrong. Both books sound like real estate guides: The first is a manual for finding a house with a history; the second is a handbook for avoiding one. What you are after is an instruction booklet alive with advice for cohabiting with the dead. What to expect. How to cope with the voices that fill the night and the doors that mysteriously open. How to make sense of a house with bones in its basement. Unfortunately, that title eludes you. It hovers like a wisp just beyond your mind's reach.

Perhaps that's because you don't really believe in ghosts. You tell yourself you are not in a ghost story. These voices have woken no one but you. In all likelihood, a draft opened the basement door. Or you left it open yourself: Either you forgot to close it or you left it like this subconsciously. Your therapist would love that. And this conversation below you is only in your head, another invisible wound from the disaster that marked your last flight.

"Hello?" The sound of your own voice surprises you. You hear a slight tremor in it, an uncharacteristic hitch in those two syllables. This is not the tone that told passengers cruising altitudes or directed them to gaze out their windows at the majesty of the Manhattan skyline and New York Harbor or the unexpected expanse of Lake Michigan. This is not the voice that one time (and one time only) told them to brace for impact. Instantly the discussion in the basement grows quiet. "Hello?"

you call again, a little louder, a little more confident. Still, there is nothing but silence. You beam the light down the stairs at the stones in the wall at the bottom, at the coils of hose the moving men happened to dump just to the side of the banister. At the wooden pallets you rounded up the other day and on which you have stacked great jugs of cat sand and cases of soda and juice you bought at the warehouse store in Littleton. You feel for the switch at the top of the stairs that flips on the two naked, sixty-watt bulbs in the basement ceiling—really just pillows of insulation amidst thick wooden beams—and, after the basement is awash in the dim half-light, you start down, your feet still bare. You wish you had thought to put on your slippers. Then again, perhaps not. You can clean your feet under the spigot in the bathtub before climbing back into bed. The slippers would have to go into the wash. You never go into the basement without the sorts of shoes you are likely to wear only outdoors.

At the bottom of the stairs you pause, the flashlight at your side, and then turn slowly toward the pile of coal and the doorway behind which you found the bones. Instantly you recognize the pair of adults standing between the doorway and the coal, and you go to them, switching the flashlight from your right to your left hand so you can shake their wet hands if they choose to extend their wet arms to you. And the man does, even though it is painfully clear that you have interrupted a fight he has been having with the woman. A squabble. You wonder: Perhaps you were mistaken; perhaps you were not supposed to hear them.

"Captain," the man says, but the woman only gazes at you with a worried look in her eyes. A chasmlike gash disfigures the right side of her face, and blood is pooling on the shoulder of her blouse. She is fortunate that she wasn't one of the three passengers on the plane who were decapitated. Her name is Sandra Durant, though her hair—which was honey in the snapshot photos you saw in the newspaper—has been darkened by lake water and muddied by blood: thirty-two years old, a single woman who you learned in the weeks after the disaster had been on your plane because she had just interviewed for a job in Vermont. She worked at a computer company in Cherry Hill, New Jersey, and was considering a job at IBM's Essex Junction facility. She was a public relations manager. Had a boyfriend, parents, two brothers. A cat named Ozzie.

The man is a strong, well-built fellow about forty, and he, too, suffered a horrific head wound: His forehead looks as if someone drilled a hole in it the size of a flute. His biceps stretch the fabric of his green short-sleeved polo shirt. His handshake is solid.

"You're Ashley's dad," you say, referring to the child with the Dora the Explorer backpack. Again, you saw a photo in the newspaper. After he releases your hand, you glance down at the drops of lake water that Ethan Stearns has left on your fingers and palm.

"That's right."

Ashley's mother is alive in a suburb of Burlington, Vermont. You believe it's called Monkton. Ashley and her parents were traveling to Florida to visit an aunt and uncle there before school resumed in September. They would have changed planes in Philadelphia. You recall the voice of Ashley's mother as she screamed her daughter's name in the waves and dove under the surface of Lake Champlain over and over in the seconds after the aircraft broke apart and jet fuel coated the surface like olive oil.

"I'm sorry about Ashley," you tell him. "I'm sorry about everything," you tell them both.

"It wasn't your fault," says Sandra Durant.

"We were so close to being all right," you tell her. "You know that, don't you?" You consider adding, *It was the birds that brought us down, but it was the wake from a boat that did us in.* But you will never know that for certain. What if you had kept the aircraft nose a single degree higher above the horizon? Or, perhaps, a single degree lower? Would a wave still have pitchpoled your plane and killed thirty-nine of your passengers?

The woman looks at Ethan, a little frightened. Behind you the furnace kicks on. This sudden rumbling, a reminder of the bricks and mortar and horsehair tangibility of the house, takes you back to the reality that you are standing in cold dirt and coal dust. You gaze for a moment at the splintered pieces of wood from the door that once had been sealed shut with thirty-nine carriage bolts. Thirty-nine. A day or two after you had counted them for the first time, you returned to the basement and envisioned the door was the diagram for a CRJ700, your old plane. You touched each of the bolts with the tips of your fingers. You worked your way back to the rear of the cabin, attaching names to the bolts wherever you could. When you finally smashed in the door, you wanted to be sure that you did not dislodge the bolts from their spots in the wood. If you managed to break through the barnboard without inadvertently dislodging one, you pretended, you would ditch the plane without a single casualty. Everyone would get out alive. You knew you couldn't rewrite history this way or bring back the dead, but it wasn't precisely a game, either.

"Ashley was smart and beautiful and she had a huge heart," says Ethan Stearns. "She was a kid with unbelievable promise. She was a ballerina."

"All little girls are ballerinas," you tell him. What you meant was, *I know what you mean. I have twins and they're dancers, too.* But the words hang out there wrong in the air, all wrong; they sound antagonistic, challenging—as if you are disputing this angry, grieving dead man in your basement. Impugning his lovely little girl's talents.

"You have no idea what she would have done with her life," he says, his tone the confrontational murmur that first drew you from sleep. His hatred for you permeates every syllable. He blames you for his child's death. The fact that he is dead, too, is irrelevant. This is a good man, you conclude. You would be just as irate if, God forbid, something happened to either of your girls and you found yourself face-to-face with the person you held responsible for the child's death.

"No, I don't," you tell him simply, and though it sounds like a confession, you do not bow your head. You meet him eye to eye. Father to father.

"But it's not just all that potential that's gone," he says. He takes a deep breath and exhales through his nose. The steam rises like mist in the chill of the basement. "It's that she has no one her age. She has—"

"Ethan, stop it," says Sandra Durant, her tone at once determined and pleading. How is it, you wonder, that she hasn't yet finished bleeding out? Her blouse and her skirt have become indistinguishable, one long, saturated tunic the color of those wines Peyton kept opening earlier that evening.

"I won't," Ethan insists. "I want my daughter to have friends again. I want her to have little girls to play with."

"That's cruel!"

"That's fair! She deserves friends!" he snaps back. And that's when you first understand what this pair has been fighting about. They have been arguing over your girls. Hallie and Garnet, the two of them asleep right now in their rooms on the third floor. Ethan holds you responsible for the death of his daughter. For killing Ashley and leaving her with no one to play with. You know you would feel precisely the same way.

"Would you like me to introduce my girls to Ashley?" you ask this father, this man just like you. "They seem to be a little older, but they're good girls, Ethan. Very good girls. Very kind, both of them. They'd be good playmates—and role models."

"Yes, I would like that," he tells you. "Do what it takes." His scowl lessens appreciably, but then Sandra slaps him hard, whatever fear she has of him subsumed by her apparent worry for your daughters, and you feel the spray from the lake on your own face. You bring your fingertips to your cheek and then gaze at the drops of water there that a moment ago were on Ethan Stearns's cheek.

"Chip?" You turn toward the stairs when you hear Emily's voice. She is calling down into the basement from the top of the steps, her concern for you permeating your name. When you turn back to Ethan and Sandra, the two of them are gone.

"I'm here, sweetheart," you call up to Emily.

"What are you doing?"

"I was checking the pilot light on the furnace." Yes, that's it. What else would you have been doing? Then you walk in your bare feet across the moist dirt of the basement and up the steps to your wife, telling her that the pilot is fine and the furnace is fine and the basement is fine. Everything is fine.

Yes, it is. Everything is just fine. Even the pilot.

She deserves friends. Do what it takes.

You kiss her on the cheek and meet her worried eyes. You smile. Then you flip off the light to the basement and grab a wad of paper towels for your feet. No sense in tracking mud between here and the bathtub.

Part II

The girl was another fifth-grader named Molly Francoeur, and Hallie had figured out right away—in her very first hours in the new classroom—that the child was not one of the school's popular kids. She was big for her age, already five and a half feet tall, and she towered over the boys and the girls. As a result, she was gangly, awkward, and could be very shy in the classroom and at recess. She wore a tractor green John Deere sweatshirt most days and reminded Hallie of a Sesame Street character. Her father had run off years earlier, and her mother worked a shift behind the register at the gas station and convenience store by the entrance to the interstate. She had a sister in second grade and a brother in ninth grade, at the high school, a boy who had already gotten into trouble for drugs and "borrowing" a car that belonged to a teacher's aide. But Molly was also much smarter than Hallie had expected when Mrs. Collier was introducing the twins to the class and she sat Hallie down at the table with Molly and two boys. Hallie had slowly gotten to know the girl, and she realized that the kid had been besieged by bad luck since the day she'd been born.

At first, Hallie had feared that she herself wouldn't have a lot of clout in whatever pecking order existed here in northern New Hampshire: She was new, her father was the pilot who crashed the plane into the lake (even if it wasn't his fault), and she was twins with a girl with the freakiest red hair on the planet. It was why she had invited Molly over to their house the first time: She'd figured that beggars really couldn't be choosers. It was only when Hallie had been in the school a few days and realized that Mrs. Collier was strangely excited by the idea that she was a twin and that the grown-ups in this town actually liked the color of Garnet's hair that she began to understand it wouldn't be long before she had reestablished herself as one of the cooler kids in the class. And this mattered to Hallie.

By then, however, she had already become friends with Molly Francoeur and, happily, learned that she might have underestimated this other-child. Now it was early Sunday afternoon, and Molly had just been dropped off at their house for another playdate. Hallie and Garnet had taken the girl out to the greenhouse this time. The snow that had fallen the other night had melted off the roof, and the early March sun was warming the structure, but they still kept on their snow jackets. The three fifth-graders were creating a tableau with Hallie and Garnet's large American Girl dolls and furniture, not especially troubled by the reality that some of the dolls' clothing and tables and beds were supposed to look like they were from eighteenth-century Tidewater Virginia while the other accessories were supposed to replicate the Northern Plains a hundred years later. Molly spoke with the laconic cadences that Hallie and Garnet had come to recognize from many (though not all) of the people they ran into at school, at the dance studio, or with their mom and dad at the supermarket or the hardware store.

They had just decided that the three dolls would be sisters—three beds and three dressers in a row, the dolls in their beds for the night— when Molly folded her fingers under her arms to warm them and said, "Maybe they should be triplets."

"And maybe they're orphans," Garnet said, and Hallie had to restrain herself from rolling her eyes. Garnet loved building games around orphans. Over the years, she had made Beanie Babies, Barbies, and trolls into orphans. It didn't surprise Hallie that now she wanted to make their American Girl dolls orphans, too. Usually Garnet's orphan scenario was straight out of *Annie* or *A Little Princess*. There was an evil lady running an orphanage, and out of the blue a loving and spectacularly wealthy guardian angel would exact revenge on the orphanage director and whisk the Beanie Babies, Barbies, or trolls off to a life of luxury and unimaginable happiness. Sometimes the angel would be a prince, and sometimes there would be two angels—the orphans' parents come to rescue them.

"Okay," agreed Molly, and Hallie decided there was no reason for the dolls not to be orphans. The game would be a little predictable, but it was Sunday afternoon, she was tired from going to Mom's boss's house last night, and she didn't have a better idea. "And maybe they're cursed," Molly added.

Hallie thought about this: It was definitely a new wrinkle. She and Garnet had never put a curse on their American Girl dolls. The closest they had come to using a curse as a device in any of their games had been a brief phase so long ago that Hallie had only the dimmest recollection. It had something to do with a couple of their "ball gown" Barbies and the two Disney princesses who wind up out like a light: Snow White and Sleeping Beauty. "What's the curse?" she asked Molly.

The child's lips were chapped from months of cold weather, and she curled them together while she formulated a response. Garnet looked back and forth between Molly and her, waiting. Hallie had the sense that her sister didn't want to deviate too far from the orphan game. Finally Molly unpuckered her lips and said, "They've been poisoned."

"With an apple?" Garnet asked.

"No, that's too boring," Molly said, and Hallie agreed. The girl pulled her hands out from under her arms and with one of her hands pointed at the greenhouse walls around them. "Maybe something poisonous was grown in here. What's a good poisonous plant?"

"Poison ivy," Garnet suggested, but she crinkled her nose immediately after she spoke, and Hallie could tell it was because Garnet understood that this wasn't at all what they were looking for. She was just brainstorming. They didn't need a poison that made your skin itch; they needed a poison that might kill you.

"It needs to be much worse than that," said Hallie.

"It does," Molly agreed. "What would those freaky women around here have used? Maybe the lady who lived here before you brought weird poison plants back from Australia or South America. A lot of the women do that."

The twins turned to each other simultaneously, and Hallie could see the surprise she was feeling mirrored in her sister's eyes. What in the world would the lady who once lived here have known about poison? From the way their parents talked about the woman, it sounded like she practically never left Bethel. Why would Molly think she knew anything at all? Instead of answering Molly, Hallie asked, "What are you talking about?"

"You know, the woman who lived here. She was a witch. They all are. If there's a greenhouse, there's a witch. That's how you can tell. And this one? Very scary. My mom says her son killed himself."

"She was a witch?" Hallie said.

"I mean she wasn't a real witch. They're not like that. They don't think they can fly through the air on broomsticks or something. They don't run around in those pointy Halloween hats. But they are, like, into witchcraft. Witch stuff. My mom said they make potions out of plants that usually only grow in jungles and deserts. They're all known around here for growing stuff."

"Yeah, like herbs," Garnet said.

"Much more," said Molly.

"Look, I'm sure they grow vegetables and herbs and I guess some flowers," Hallie told her. "You know, tomatoes. Parsley. Daffodils. Not . . ." And she stopped speaking because she had no idea what sorts of things a witch grew.

"It's not like the woman was a real witch," Molly said again. "It's not like any of them are."

"They're herbalists," Garnet told the girl, speaking the word very slowly because she had heard her parents using it one night after dinner, and she had never before said it aloud. It was, she decided, a mouthful.

"What's that?" Molly asked.

Garnet shrugged because she wasn't completely certain. "I guess it's a person who uses herbs for stuff. But for more than cooking, because everyone uses herbs in cooking. Right?"

"What else did your mom say about the woman who used to live here?" Hallie asked.

Molly went to one of the dolls and adjusted the quilt. *She's stalling,* Hallie thought, *because she doesn't know what to say. She wishes she hadn't brought any of this up.*

Finally Molly answered, "She said she was kind of weird. She and some of her friends. They scared people. There were all kinds of rumors about them, and it was like they were hippies, but older. At least most of them were. Not all. But all of them were women."

Hallie thought of the pictures she had seen of hippies: the kaleidoscopic-colored T-shirts, the long hair. The ripped bell-bottom pants. The beads and the peace signs. The marijuana. "Do you mean she grew marijuana?" she asked Molly. "Marijuana's an herb, right?"

The child shrugged her shoulders, which looked even broader and more substantial in her snow jacket. "I don't know. But I don't think that's what my mom meant."

"Then what did she mean?" Hallie demanded, and she knew there was a bullying quality to her voice that teachers would never approve of, but she couldn't stop herself and she really didn't care.

"Well, my mom said that the lady who used to live here and her friends all had these little garden plots or greenhouses where they grew the stuff for their potions. It was all very hush-hush. A lot of people didn't like them, but I guess a lot of others did."

"What kinds of potions did they make?" Garnet asked.

"I don't know."

"Did they make poisons?"

"I said, I don't know! But here's the scariest part. She had twins."

Hallie knew this on some vague level, but because her parents had only mentioned one and he lived in St. Johnsbury, she'd never really thought about it. There was so much other information to try to understand. But now the idea that there had been twins long ago in this house grew more real.

"They were boys," Molly continued. "And one killed himself. At least that's what everyone says. But my mom thinks he was murdered by the women. The police never arrested the lady, and she ended up shutting down her greenhouse—*this* greenhouse. But my mom says the women killed him."

"How old was he? Our age?" Hallie asked.

"A little older. He was, like, twelve or thirteen," she said, and suddenly this big girl bowed her head and her body seemed to collapse into itself, the child almost shrinking before the twins' very eyes. She was, Hallie realized, on the verge of tears. "I wasn't supposed to tell you any of this stuff. My mom made me promise."

"But you did," Garnet said.

"It all just came out," she murmured. "Maybe it's not true. I don't know. But you can't tell anyone I told you." Then: "I want to go home. I should go home. Can I call my mom?" The last of her sentence was smothered by a few pathetic sniffles, and she ran her bare hand across her mouth and under her nose. Garnet reached out to pat the girl's arm, but Molly jerked away and wouldn't look at them. Garnet had the sense that the child was scared—really and truly terrified, despite the reality that it was the middle of a Sunday afternoon and the sun was high overhead.

"Molly, please stay," Hallie said, though she was still profoundly disturbed by the idea that twins had lived in this house before Garnet and her and one of them had either killed himself or been killed. But she also realized that one of her and Garnet's very first playdates here was about to end in disaster. That wouldn't bode well as she and her sister tried to make new friends. And, the fact was, they were stuck here in Bethel; they had to make the best of it. So she took a deep breath and then did what she could to salvage the afternoon. She pulled the American Girl doll from eighteenth-century Virginia from its bed and held it under its arms like an offering. She presented the doll to Molly and said, raising her eyebrows theatrically and trying to add an aura of evil to her sentence—as if she were the scariest witch on the scariest Halloween—"Now, how shall we poison the child?"

*   *   *

Anise handled a pestle with the grace of a gourmet chef wielding a chopping knife. This afternoon she was grinding hypnobium, using her black marble mortar because her wooden ones were far too absorbent for a plant this toxic, pounding and swirling the seeds against the sides of the bowl. It sounded almost as if she were dicing an onion on a cutting board or chopping basil for bruschetta. Clary Hardin was sipping green tea and leaning against the counter in Anise's kitchen, telling her about her dinner last night with John, the Messners, and the Lintons. She was pausing now in her story only because her friend was so intent on her work. Finally Anise looked up at Clary and exhaled deeply. "Tell me more about what you think of the girls," she said.

"I told you, I think they're delightful. John does, too."

"This morning Sage described them as rather philistine. She found their uninterest in plants off-putting."

Clary shook her head at Sage's description. "They're ten. She forgets what it's like to be ten."

"She said they want to use Tansy's greenhouse as a playhouse."

"For now. But I'm sure they'll grow into it."

"And Emily?" Carefully she tapped most of the powder from the mortar into a wide-mouth glass canning jar, holding the jar over the sink in the event some spilled over the side. She reserved a teaspoon, which she dropped into a porcelain mixing bowl already filled with flour and margarine and the very last of her maple syrup. She was baking cookies.

"Emily is far more scarred than she lets on," Clary answered. "Of course, she is nowhere near the wreck that her husband is. Now *he* is seriously damaged goods."

"As he should be. But not the girls?"

Clary thought about this. "Oh, they are. I think they'll do. Really. But Hallie is far more readable than Garnet. I know children are resilient—"

"Children are resilient," Anise said, simultaneously agreeing with her friend and cutting her off. "But often their wounds simply remain invisible until, all at once, whatever is festering there becomes agonizingly apparent."

"Nevertheless, neither seems quite as traumatized as I would have expected. They're going to have dinner with Reseda tonight, and I will be very interested in her take."

Anise pressed the lid atop the glass and then screwed the large ring around the top, sealing the jar shut. "Reseda's talents are overrated."

"You only think so because you are some strange exception to the rule. Trust me: When I'm with her, I spend most of my time pushing all compromising or catty thoughts as far from my mind as possible."

"I can't believe you have thoughts that are catty."

Clary smiled. "But you do believe I have ones that are compromising?"

"Of course," said Anise, and she squeezed past her friend on the way to the walk-in pantry filled with the raw materials for her cooking and tinctures: her powders and seeds and dried leaves. "You're married to a lawyer."

On Sunday night, Emily leaned back against the gleaming steel and marble cooking island in Reseda's kitchen and inhaled deeply the aroma of rosemary and lamb from the oven and the scent of the beeswax candles that seemed to be alight everywhere. It was a wonder the woman had found the counter space to cook. Emily knew she was a little tipsy—maybe even more than a little—but she didn't care. It felt good to relax and let down her guard a bit. She was drinking some sort of hard, mulled cider and it was like candy. The twins were watching movies on the other side of the house in the den while the rest of the adults were in the sunroom that was attached to this two-hundred-year-old Colonial like an architectural afterthought. In addition to Chip and her, Reseda had invited Holly and a young man with a silver loop in his eyebrow who seemed to be Holly's boyfriend, and the Jacksons—an older couple whose attitude toward her daughters was eerily reminiscent of the way Clary Hardin and Sage Messner had hovered over the twins just last night. Emily had joined Reseda when the hostess came to the kitchen to check on the lamb and toss the potatoes that were roasting on a rack below the meat, offering to help but really hoping only to get away from the Jacksons for a moment.

As soon as she and Chip had arrived at Reseda's, she had known who this older couple was. She wasn't sure how because she had never met them. (She hadn't returned to the Jacksons' to get the bean sprouts and carrot tops for the girls' class science project, because Ginger had taken the initiative and brought them to the school.) But, even before Ginger Jackson had opened her mouth, Emily had had a feeling that she was going to recognize the slightly throaty rasp that marked the woman's voice from the answering machine. She pegged the woman to be in her late sixties and her husband, Alexander, to be in his early seventies. She thought she had seen him somewhere before but couldn't pinpoint where or when. Then it clicked: He was the fellow that odd Becky Davis had nearly bowled over the day she raced out of the diner in Littleton. Alexander was tall and powerfully built and, despite his age, could pull off a completely shaved head. His shoulders seemed to be pressing hard against his turtleneck and navy blue blazer. Ginger wore her hair very much like Anise: It was a free-flowing silver mane that cascaded a long way down her back and looked a little wild. She was wearing a peasant skirt that fell to her ankles and rimless eyeglasses with lenses that didn't look much bigger than pennies and seemed to be levitating just over her nose. The two of them, Alexander and Ginger, had been at least as smothering with her twins as the Hardins and the Messners had been on Saturday night. They had been so invasive of Hallie's and Garnet's personal space—what their third-grade teacher back in West Chester had called an individual's bubble—that Garnet had actually backed away from Ginger and sat down on the plush easy chair beside Emily. For a moment, Emily had thought that her daughter was going to crawl into her lap. Then, when the twins had finally been allowed to leave the grown-ups, Ginger had started in on Emily.

And she had started in with an eagerness that was downright relentless. She wanted to know whether Emily had ever gardened and what her plans were for her own greenhouse. She offered to come in with seedlings and starters for the makings of an Italian herb garden, as well as what she called the basics of a tincture patch. She said it didn't have to be exotic at first, but—she assured Emily—it would be soon enough. She admitted that her own greenhouse lacked the powerfully healing aura of Reseda's, though Emily had seen Reseda's that evening, and she honestly wasn't sure what was healing about a greenhouse filled with statues that were either frightening or freakish: A two-headed snake of some kind? A demonic-looking creature that was half man and half goat? A gargoyle clutching tiny humans who seemed to have great, leafy ivy where they should have had hands and feet? Then Ginger had gone on and on about the meadows around her house, comparing it favorably to the home in New Jersey where she and her husband had raised their sons, describing with a naturalist's skill the occasional deer or moose that would wander along the edge of the woods here in Bethel. At one point, Ginger had pulled a compact from the pocket of her jumper and dabbed a watery cream at the edges of Emily's eyes. "I make this myself," she told Emily. "Makes those crow's-feet disappear." Emily had immediately noted Ginger's surprisingly unlined face but still presumed the secret was Botox or a spectacularly gifted cosmetic surgeon—or, perhaps, both. When Reseda had risen, Emily had fled with her to the kitchen. Reseda seemed to understand that Ginger's enthusiasm had crossed the rather substantial line between animated and rabid.

"She means well," Reseda was saying, referring to Ginger Jackson. "I hope it wasn't a mistake inviting her."

"No, it's fine," Emily said. Reseda was wearing a perfectly pressed white button-down blouse, open at the neck just enough to show a hint of the lace on her bra, a black leather skirt that fell to her knees, and charcoal tights. Like Emily, she was not wearing shoes, but otherwise Emily felt underdressed beside her; she was wearing jeans, wool socks, and a blue and green Fair Isle sweater. It was a Sunday night and she had dressed casually. "But it is nice to catch my breath," she continued.

"She does have her share of very strong opinions. And she is very, very passionate about her gardening and tinctures and creams. But you all are, aren't you?"

Reseda smiled but didn't respond to the question. Instead she said with sisterly camaraderie, "I'll see if I can discreetly seat you and Ginger at opposite ends of the table."

"Or in opposite rooms, perhaps."

Reseda nodded. "Chip seems a little better," she observed.

"A little. But PTSD isn't a cold. Depression isn't a cold. It's going to take time." She thought again of the way he had razed that door in the basement and then how she had found him down there in the middle of the night sixteen or seventeen hours ago. She didn't believe for a moment that he was checking the pilot light.

Reseda slid the roasted potatoes back into the oven and shut the door. "I think we're just about there," she murmured and then turned her attention back to Emily. "His name is Baphomet."

"What is?"

"The creature in the fountain in my greenhouse. I rather like him."

Emily gazed down at her drink. Had she mentioned aloud the greenhouse just now? She didn't believe that she had.

"I bought him in a moment of minor anarchism. I knew what people were saying about me, and I thought I would really give them something to talk about."

"I don't understand."

"Some people think he's the devil."

"Baphomet."

"Yes."

"And people think you do . . . what? Worship the devil? They think you're a—what's the word?—a Satanist?"

"Or Wiccan. But, I assure you, I'm neither."

"John said you're a shaman."

"I'm not sure John knows what that means."

"But you are something."

Reseda sipped her mulled cider and seemed to be contemplating her answer, as if she weren't precisely sure herself. Emily was struck by the woman's eyes, which, in the candlelight in the kitchen, looked almost black. Weren't they usually blue? Her lipstick was the color of a ripe fig, and her face was shaped like a heart. Emily realized that she wanted to kiss her, which struck her as odd because she hadn't kissed a girl since she and a friend experimented at a sleepover in ninth grade. But she and Chip rarely made love now. Perhaps that explained her desire. Between his catatonia, her exhaustion, raising the girls, and the logistics of the move, she guessed that they had had sex perhaps a half dozen times since August 11 (and not once since moving to New Hampshire), and each event had been a rather rote affair. It had felt to her—and, she presumed, to him—like they were going through the motions because they were supposed to. They were married, they were in love; they were supposed to have sex. Before the crash, they had always had a rather interesting sex life, fueled by the three- and four-day absences that marked what he did for a living. Alas, romance, it seemed, was another casualty of Flight 1611.

"When I was a teenager, something happened to my sister and me," Reseda said finally, stepping over to Emily so that Emily felt her lower back pressed against the counter. Reseda placed her cider on the marble. "It was violent and horrifying. But I learned something very interesting. Someday I'll tell you."

"But not tonight, I gather," Emily said. She found it difficult to speak with Reseda so close, and her voice was barely above a whisper.

"No. Not tonight."

The woman was standing right in front of her now, and suddenly all Emily could smell was the unrecognizable but absolutely heavenly scent of her perfume—the aroma of the lamb and the rosemary and the candles seemed to have vanished completely—and then the woman was closing her eyes and leaning into her, and pressing those lips the color of figs against hers. Emily was startled, but she closed her eyes, too, and accepted the woman's warm tongue as it explored first her lips and then burrowed gently between them and started teasing the inside of her mouth. She felt Reseda's hand reaching between her legs and massaging her firmly through her jeans; almost involuntarily she started to move her hips, to grind against the woman's fingers.

And then Reseda was pulling away, her eyes open, smiling in a vague, absentminded sort of way. "Sweet," she said softly, and she turned and took a pair of pot holders off the counter and went to remove the lamb from the oven. "This looks perfect," she said.

"I don't know what came over me," Emily said, embarrassed, the words catching in her throat, but already Reseda was placing the great yellow pan with the meat on an ivy-shaped trivet and bringing one long, slender finger to her lips. In the kitchen doorway Emily heard her husband and Alexander Jackson, the two of them laughing about something, and Reseda said to the pair, "Ah, men. Lovely. Could one of you start pouring the wine in the dining room? We're just about ready."

Hours later, Emily woke up in the night when she felt Chip's hands on her rear. She had been asleep on her side, and he had pulled her nightgown up and over her waist, and now his fingers were sliding down the crevice and rubbing her. She felt his erection against her thigh, and her mind moved between images of Reseda's closed eyes and the taste of her tongue and the feel of her husband hard against her leg. When his finger entered her, she was shocked at how wet she was. She pressed her ass against him and heard herself purring ever so slightly. She couldn't recall the last time she and Chip had made love in the middle of the night. No, wait, she could. It had been four and a half years ago, when he had gotten home from a deadhead leg at two or two-thirty in the morning after four days away. She started to recall the details, but now Chip was rolling her onto her back and all she was aware of was the feel of his mouth on her breasts and the way he was raising himself above her—she reached up and grabbed at the sides of his chest, her fingers pressing against his ribs—and entering her. She moaned and rolled her head back against the pillow.

In the morning, while preparing the girls' breakfast with Chip, she tried to make sense of Reseda's kiss and the reality that she and her husband had finally christened their bedroom in New Hampshire—and how, for the first time in well over half a year, the sex had left her satisfied. It wasn't a coincidence, this she knew. There was a connection. But for the life of her she couldn't decide what it meant.

Chapter Eight

The house always seems a little more peculiar to you when the girls are at school and Emily is at work. When you're alone. It's as if it suspects that this is when you're the most receptive. Or, perhaps, the most vulnerable.

It.

One day you stood on your driveway and just stared at it. The windows were eyes, the long screened porch a mouth. It watched you back.

You know the air moves in currents along the hallways like breath, especially in that back stairway to the second floor and the thin corridor along the third floor. One day you came across Desdemona cowering in the living room, her orange body a small ball between the radiator and the corner where the wall angled into the bay window. She was quivering, her fur fluffed and her eyes wide. For the only time ever she hissed at you.

And then there was the time you found her with her collar caught on the pineapple finial on the banister to the front staircase. She was trying and failing to extricate herself and growing panicked. She was hanging herself, choking to death because for some reason the breakaway collar hadn't unclasped. If you hadn't wandered into the hallway at that very moment, in all likelihood the animal would have died.

In the end, you didn't tell Emily about this because you know it would have upset her. There is actually a great deal you are shielding her from.

You realize, of course, that you are giving life to slate and clapboard and horsehair plaster. To bad wallpaper and a door in the basement. There is no *it*. But there is something. There are people. You know what you have found and you know what you have hidden in newspapers in the back of your armoire.

She deserves friends.

It's Monday, the start of a workweek for Emily and a school week for your girls, and once more you are here all alone. You tell yourself it wasn't a bad weekend, despite your encounter with Ethan Stearns and Sandra Durant from Flight 1611 in the small hours of Sunday morning. After all, you spent time with the living, too. You got to know Emily's boss a little better on Saturday night; you had a nice evening at Reseda's on Sunday. Both parties were actually rather pleasant, and you made new friends. Moreover, when you awoke hours before sunrise today, you and Emily made love with an ardor you hadn't felt in months.

So, you tell yourself, in many ways you are managing just fine. For a long moment you sit in a ladder-back chair and stare at the grotesque sunflowers on the dining room walls. These are not the cheerful Tuscan sunflowers of August. They are the dying blossoms of September, brown not merely because the wallpaper is antique. Even brand-new this paper may have been morbid.

The plan today is to continue stripping that god-awful wallpaper. In the past—in this house and in West Chester—you always scraped the old wallpaper off all of the walls before starting to hang the new paper. That is the logical way to proceed. But not this time. The other day you grew so bored with scraping that you started hanging the new paper, a serene (and appropriate) Victorian array of roses, on the wall on which you had removed all the old paper. You expect you will finish scraping today. You have one long wall and a small portion of another to go. Then you will have only one set of sponges and buckets to contend with and one set of tools.

Tools. You gaze for a moment at the sponges and scrapers and box cutters and pause on the word. Each tool has a purpose.

As did that ax that was left for you. It was meant to batter down that door in the basement.

And that would suggest that the crowbar and the pearl-handled knife have specific functions, too. They've been provided to you for a reason. Unfortunately, you see only the barest wisps of that reason; it stretches away from you like the delicate, silken threads of cirrus you gazed upon too many times to count from the flight deck.

You have just steeled yourself to begin scraping for the day when you breathe in through your nose and there it is: the aroma of lake water and jet fuel. (The smell of the jet fuel actually makes you a little nauseous. This is new. You find this reality disconcerting.) You turn, and there on the dining room rug is little Ashley with her Dora the Explorer backpack, sitting with her legs curled up on the carpet underneath her. She looks at you with her big eyes and her damp hair, and you study her wet face. It's not all lake water that is on her cheeks, you realize. You know from the redness of her eyes that she is crying, and her cheeks are moist with her tears.

And so you sit on the floor beside her, your own knees a little creaky. "Hello, Ashley."

She sniffles and folds herself around that backpack. She looks down, and you can no longer see her eyes and her face, just the way her sodden hair is plastered to the top of her head.

"Why are you crying, sweetie?"

The second the words are out there, you regret the question. Why wouldn't she be crying? She simply shakes her head obstinately and ignores your inquiry. Which is when the more practical question comes to you.

"Sweetie," you begin, and the second time you use this particular term of endearment, it dawns on you that this is a name you use often with Hallie and Garnet. "Is there something I can do?"

She deserves friends. Do what it takes.

Again, she offers you only a sad, stubborn twist of her head.

"Are you lonely?"

Slowly she meets your eyes. She nods almost imperceptibly. You recall your conversation with her father: You had offered to introduce this poor child to your own wonderful girls. You need to follow through with that idea of yours. You need to find Ashley playmates. This is something tangible you can do.

"I know you've seen Hallie and Garnet," you tell her, and you reach behind you for the roll of paper towels on the floor. You hand one to the girl so she can blow her nose and wipe her eyes. "How do I introduce you to them? Any idea there?"

She presses the paper towel flat against her face for a moment and chokes back a small sob. Then she pulls it away and looks more composed. "I don't know," she says.

"Tell me: Have my girls seen you?"

"Sort of. But not really."

"Not really?"

"I don't think they can."

"Why?"

"They're breathers."

"Breathers?"

"You know. Like you."

"But I can see you. I can hear you."

She shrugs.

"Well, then," you say in your most gentle, paternal voice. "We have a problem. And problems need solutions. Right?"

She turns from you and gazes out the dining room window. You follow her eyes and see in the clear sky high over the meadow a plume from an airplane. Really, planes are everywhere. Just . . . everywhere. When you turn back to Ashley, she is gone. Reflexively you pat the carpet where she was sitting, and it is still damp with lake water. All that remains is the paper towel, which you pick up. It, too, is wet, and it has the rank odor of jet fuel. So, you wad it into a ball and push yourself to your feet. You know the solution to the problem and you know you have the tools. Or, to be precise, the tool. But you have no intention of tak-

ing the knife that the Dunmores left you and butchering either Hallie or
Garnet so Ashley Stearns can have a playmate.

Wouldn't that be asking too much of you—of anyone? One would
think so. Yes. That is indeed what one would think.

Emily wasn't about to call Reseda because she hadn't the slightest
idea what she would say. She honestly wasn't sure whether she
should be indignant that this woman had kissed her on Sunday night—
certainly she would be if a man had done such a thing—or whether she
needed to say simply that she wasn't interested in her in that sort of way.
She loved her husband and wanted only to be friends. The last thing she
needed to add to her life was some sort of harmless, playful dalliance
with Reseda. Because in the end it wouldn't be harmless. These things
never were.

Besides, she didn't believe that Reseda actually had designs on her.
Emily couldn't decide what the kiss had meant—if, in fact, it had meant
anything.

She realized she had been sitting at her desk, daydreaming, for
twenty minutes. Somehow it had become ten-fifteen in the morning.
She was supposed to be in Franconia for a real estate closing at eleven.
Quickly she rose and gathered the file on the property, a relatively new
gray Colonial with four bedrooms and a pond, and reached for her coat
behind the door. In the hallway on her way out, she ran into John Hardin.

"Emily," he said, "your girls are a dream. Clary and Sage just adored
them. I think they're going to become the granddaughters Sage *still*
doesn't have!"

She nodded. She had thought so much about that Sunday night
kiss that she had completely forgotten how the seniors had swarmed on
her children the night before then. Somehow, that part of the weekend
seemed a long, long time ago.

*   *   *

You pinpoint Hewitt Dunmore's address in St. Johnsbury on Map-Quest and see you can drive there via the interstate in thirty-five minutes—assuming you don't hit a moose. You don't really worry about hitting a moose; you haven't even seen one since you moved here. But those warning signs on the highway make you smile. You consider phoning Hewitt before leaving your house but in the end decide against it; you know he will try to dissuade you from coming. He may even insist that he doesn't want to see you. But the girls—and that friend of theirs, Molly, who is joining them later today—don't climb off the school bus until just about three in the afternoon. And it's only a half hour and change that separates your house from Hewitt's, so you could spend a good forty-five minutes with him before having to turn around. Assuming, of course, that he's home. Since you haven't called ahead, there's no guarantee, and this may very well be a waste of an hour and a quarter.

Still, you don't imagine that he travels all that much, and you have a sense he will be there. And when you coast to a stop on a St. Johnsbury street with the unpromising name of Almshouse Road, the modest house at the address where he lives has a tired-looking minivan—covered with end-of-winter muck, like most cars around here this time of the year—parked in the driveway. The house is a Cape in dire need of scraping and painting, and the roof looks a little ragged, but you like the remnants of red that peel from the clapboards. The color reminds you of a barn.

There isn't a doorbell, and so you remove your glove before you rap on the wood: You expect the sound will be sharper and more likely to carry this way. Sure enough, a moment after you knock, a small man with bloodhound jowls and a gray bristle haircut opens the door, leaning heavily on a cane, and stares out at you through eyeglasses thick as a jelly jar. He is wearing a tattered cardigan the color of coral and a string tie over a blue oxford shirt. He looks like a cantankerous professor from a small, rural college. He is not what you expected, but, since he did not attend the closing on the house, you honestly weren't sure what to expect. Emily had found him ornery on the telephone, but that's really all you know.

"Yes?"

You extend the hand on which you are not wearing a glove. "I'm Chip Linton. My wife and I are the ones who—"

"Yes, yes, I know," he says, taking your hand and cutting you off. "You're the ones who bought my parents' house."

You note in your mind how he altered slightly how you would have finished that sentence. You would have referred to it as his house; he called it his parents'. You wonder if this distinction means anything.

"Come in, come in," he says, his voice resigned. "No sense in standing outside in the doorway."

He takes your coat and tosses it on a coatrack behind the front door as you untie your boots, and then he limps into the kitchen, sitting you down in a heavy wooden armchair before a mahogany table that is perfectly round and rather substantial. The chair is one of four. The appliances are old but spotless, the white on the refrigerator showing a little dark wear only around the handle. The floor has linoleum diamonds, and the cabinets look to be made of cherry.

"To what do I owe the pleasure of this visit?" he says, sitting across from you and folding his hands on the tabletop. In another room there is a radio playing classical music.

"Well, your parents' house is proving to be a bit of a mystery to me," you respond, smiling as you speak. You hadn't planned on getting to the matter at hand quite so quickly, but he hasn't offered you coffee or tea and has come right to the point: Why are you here?

"How so?" he says evenly.

"Well, let's see. There are the items you left behind."

"That old sewing machine? I told your wife to keep it. Same with the sap buckets and all them bobbins. Or you can cart 'em off to the dump. Makes no difference to me."

"There's a very nice brass door knocker. You could use a door knocker."

"I heard you rapping just fine, thank you very much."

You nod. For the first time you have gotten a real taste of his accent. When he said *fine,* you heard more than a hint of an *o* and a second syllable: *fo-ine.* "There were three other items that were real, well, UFOs."

"Pardon?"

"Unidentified flying objects."

"That's right. You're a pilot."

"Used to be."

"You ever see any UFOs?"

"I did not."

"Believe in them?"

"No."

"You should. This universe is a very strange place."

"You know this from personal experience?"

He raises the caterpillars that pass for eyebrows. "So, your new home," he says, ignoring your question. "I would not be surprised by anything at all my mother or my father left behind in that house. As you must know by now, my mother was nothing if not eccentric. And she was mighty ill toward the end."

"No, I didn't know that."

"Huh. I woulda thought she was still a source of gossip up in Bethel."

"Rest assured, she isn't."

Outside Hewitt's door, a town sand truck rumbles by, and the two of you sit and listen. The storm windows rattle.

"She was once," he says. "That's for sure."

"Why?"

He shrugs. "People are just built the way they're built."

You point at a dusty photo on a wall of dusty photos at the edge of the kitchen. It's a teenage boy holding a fishing pole and a brown trout that must be a foot and a half long. "Is that you or your brother?" you ask.

"That would be Sawyer."

"Did your mom become more eccentric after he died?"

"Ayup. I suppose she did."

"How?"

"Losing a son cannot be easy on any mother."

"Do you have children?"

"Nope."

This is starting to feel to you like an interrogation, and you don't like that. But you don't seem to be getting anywhere with your questions. And so you change your tactics. "I like this little city—St. Johnsbury." You are careful not to add a question to the statement, hoping he will offer something back without a prompt. But he just sits back in his chair, pulling his folded hands off the table and into his lap, and stares at you with a face that is absolutely unreadable. You have the sense that, if this becomes a contest to see who can remain silent the longest, you won't have a chance in hell. Suddenly you are aware of how hot he keeps this house, and you look back into the living room and notice for the first time a cast-iron woodstove the size of a dryer. Atop is a black kettle steamer shaped like a sleeping cat. The place seems to be filled with these unexpected, oddly domestic touches. You are pretty sure he is not married now; you wonder if he was once.

"There are a few things in your parents' house that I'm hoping you can explain to me," you tell him finally, when the quiet has become interminable.

"You know, I haven't been inside there in years."

"I didn't know that, either."

"Ayup."

"Can you tell me about the door in the basement?"

"You mean the door *to* the basement? The one in the kitchen? Or the wheelbarrow ramp?"

"Neither. I meant that piece of barnboard with the thirty-nine carriage bolts that goes to nowhere."

He arcs his eyebrows and actually chuckles the tiniest bit. "Thirty-nine, eh?"

"Yes. Thirty-nine."

"Seems a mite excessive. I just guess my father was a tad eccentric, too."

"What was it? Why did he seal it up? Please?"

You hadn't meant for that last word to have such a pleading quality to it; there was an unmistakable tenor of begging to your tone. But, much to your surprise, it seems to have an effect on Hewitt Dunmore. The moment he starts to speak, you realize he is about to say more than he has the whole time you have been with him in this overheated kitchen. He is finally going to tell you a story.

"It was a coal chute. But hasn't been that in years. The way my father explained it, Mother had gotten a little paranoid. Start of her Alzheimer's, maybe. She was afraid of someone sneaking in through the chute. You know, they'd climb through the latticework under the porch, and the next thing you know, they're inside the house. So, as I understand it, my father put a wooden beam across the door and thought, That was that. Didn't do at all, not in my mother's eyes. Mother wanted more. Now, usually my father was very good with her when she got like that. Even before the Alzheimer's, she could be a bit difficult. And she was always like a dog with a bone. Always. Just wouldn't let something go. So, you might say that my father was making a statement with a wall of two-by-fours and all those carriage bolts. Weren't no intruder going to get into the house *that* way, thank you very much." When he is done, he shakes his head and grins. Then: "Thirty-nine, eh?"

"Yes."

"Guess Father didn't have a lot to do that day." He gives you a small smile.

"Tell me, is that how your mother passed away? Alzheimer's?"

"Ayup."

"I'm sorry."

He pulls his hands from his lap and, elbows at his sides, raises his hands, palms up—a universal gesture for resignation. Then he folds his arms across his chest.

"I think, in her paranoia, she left behind some other things," you continue.

"Wouldn't surprise me."

"She seemed to have hidden things."

"That would be Mother. 'Specially toward the end."

"We found a knife under a heating grate. A very sharp carving knife."

He shakes his head. "Oh, I am sorry about that. You have small children, as I recall."

"We do."

"They weren't hurt, were they?"

"No. Emily—my wife—found it."

"I heard after the closing that your girls are twins. My lawyer told me. I didn't know that."

"Yes. Fraternal. Not identical."

"I was a twin."

"I know."

He sighs. He seems about to say something more but manages to restrain himself.

"There's more," you tell him finally. "More things."

"Go on."

"One of my girls came across a disposable cigarette lighter in the house."

"A lighter? Huh. Well, I doubt that was Mother. A workman, maybe."

"And there was a crowbar and an ax."

"Hidden, I suppose."

"Yes."

"Well, I would guess we can pin those items on Mother and on her Alzheimer's. She musta been mighty scared."

"Was she afraid of anyone in particular?"

"Just burglars," he answers simply, though he draws the word out into three syllables: *bur-ga-lers.*

"Burglars."

"Ayup."

"So she hid weapons so she could defend herself."

"So it seems."

"Did your father know?"

"About the weapons? Doubt it. He wouldn't have stood for it. Would have put those sorts of items away where they belonged."

You consider whether to tell him about the bones. But you pause because you haven't even mentioned them to Emily. And you're not sure who Hewitt would tell. But you don't know when you will have an opportunity like this again. "I broke the door down," you begin, but then you catch yourself. "Well, I took the door down."

"The basement door with all them carriage bolts."

"Yes. I took it down, and I found bones in there. In the dirt."

He sits forward, alert for the first time. "From what sort of animal?"

"Human."

"Unlikely."

"Some I am sure are digits from fingers. One is clearly a human arm."

"And you are sure of this because you went to medical school when you weren't flying airplanes?"

This was, you like to believe, merely a harmless dig—he meant nothing especially hurtful. And you're honestly not sure why it seems to cut so deep. "I have some education," you answer simply.

He shakes his head. "I hate to think of the animal that must have dug its way into that corner and then couldn't dig its way back out. Very, very sad."

"You really believe the bones belong to, I don't know, a dog?"

"Or a feral cat. Or a fox."

"The bones are too big."

"Even those little ones you think are finger bones? You're one hundred percent sure of that?"

"Not one hundred percent, no."

"You show them to a doctor or professor? I used to work at the school here in town. St. Johnsbury Academy. I managed the physical plant. You want, you bring me them bones and I can show them to a teacher there. How's that sound?"

It is an interesting idea. "Can I think about it?"

" 'Course you can. I don't expect I'm going anywhere."

"That's a very compelling offer. One thing . . ."

"Go on."

"I haven't told my wife about the bones. I don't want to scare her."

"That's up to you."

"Thank you for understanding."

He shrugs. "Are people making a big deal out of the greenhouse on the property?"

"My girls. They seem to love it."

"I meant the women."

"Not really. There was some talk the other night when Emily and I were at a dinner party. But I think my children have already claimed it as a playhouse."

"Well, that's good. I think you will be much better-off if you keep it a playhouse. My mother . . . Oh, never mind about my mother."

"No, tell me. I'd like to know."

"Nothing to say. You just keep that greenhouse for the girls—the twins. You just keep them twins safe."

"As their father, I try. Is there anything specific I should be worried about?" you ask, recalling the sad fact that his twin brother took his own life.

"No. No, I'm just a morbid old man," he says, and he uses the arm-rests on the chair to push himself to his feet. You remind him that he is only a decade and a half your senior and really not an old man at all, but you can tell by the way he is standing—pressing both hands on the table for support—that your visit is over. A few moments later, as you are outside on his front steps and putting your gloves back on, you hear him speaking in the living room. You are barely out the door and already he has picked up the telephone and called someone. You wonder what this means—whether you have merely embarrassed yourself or whether there will be consequences for revealing what you found behind that door in the basement.

A mong Chip and Emily's acquaintances in West Chester was an FBI agent who had retired early and was now a security consultant. His name was Steve Hopper. At a holiday cocktail party at a mutual friend's house their last December in Pennsylvania, Emily had seen Chip and Steve and a woman she didn't know chatting near the fireplace, and when she joined them the woman was telling Chip, "I just think it's unbelievable you didn't panic. I mean, weren't you scared to death? I would have been shrieking bloody murder."

The woman clearly had had way too much to drink; her words were slurred, and no sober individual would have asked her husband if he had been terrified. Few sober people would even have been willing to bring up the doomed aircraft.

But Chip seemed to view this conversation as merely one more element to the cross he believed he was destined to shoulder. He was nodding, formulating a response, when Steve jumped in.

"I would wager my friend here was too busy focusing to be frightened," he said. "My money is that bravery never entered into the equation. That right, Chip? Good CRM?"

Emily knew that CRM stood for crew resource management, and she wasn't all that surprised that Steve knew, too; he seemed to know all sorts of arcane trivia. But this woman with them couldn't possibly know, and Emily wondered if she would ask. She was swaying slightly, and it was probably a good thing that her glass was only half full; otherwise she would have sloshed some of the alcohol on either Chip or Steve.

"Well," Chip said, looking first at Steve and then at this other woman and then at her, "there was a lot to do and not very much time. Mostly Amy and I were—"

"Who's Amy?" the woman asked.

"She was my copilot."

"She must have been peeing in her pants."

"No, I don't think she was."

"So you really weren't scared?" the woman asked, circling back to her original question.

"No," Chip said. "I think there were two things filling up that part of my brain that might otherwise have been wanting—to use your term—to shriek bloody murder. The first, just like my friend Steve here said, was focus. Amy and I were pretty focused on the tasks at hand."

"And the second?"

Emily watched her husband stare down at the flames in the fireplace for a moment. "I always thought I could do it," he said finally. "I'd seen the Airbus land in the Hudson. I saw in my mind the CRJ landing on Lake Champlain in just the same way."

The woman was about to say something more, but Steve took her by the elbow, said jovially that he wanted to freshen up both of their drinks, and then led the two of them away from her husband.

On the way home from St. Johnsbury, you race into the supermarket because you recall you don't have after-school snacks in the refrigerator for the girls. And since Molly is with them, you want to be sure you have something special. In minutes you have rounded up a six-pack of juice boxes, two pints of ice cream, apples, and peanut butter. In the parking lot on your way out, as you are opening the front door to your car, you run into Anise. She has pulled into the space right beside yours.

"Chip, hi," she says, climbing out of her pickup with a grocery list and a chaotic raft of coupons in her hand.

"No time," you tell her, smiling. "I have to race up the hill and beat the school bus."

"Goodies for the girls?" she asks, motioning at the grocery bag that you have just now plopped onto the passenger seat.

"Absolutely."

"Here, take these, too," she says, reaching back into her pickup and handing you a plastic bag with cookies she has baked. "Vegan," she informs you. "And totally scrumptious. They're maple. There should be a sugar run tomorrow, so I decided it was finally time to use the very last of last year's syrup."

"Thank you, Anise. That's very kind of you."

"Try one," she says, and to be polite you are about to open the bag she has given you. But before you can, she is handing you a cookie that she has, seemingly, pulled out of nowhere. "I baked this one especially for you," she says, and for a split second you are a bit flustered because you presume she is serious. But she winks, and you decide she is kidding. Then you bite into a soft maple cookie that melts in your mouth. It's delicious—far and away the best thing this culinary lunatic has offered you since you arrived here in Bethel.

Emily didn't know Molly Francoeur's family at all, but she wasn't about to say no when Molly's mother, Jocelyn, called, absolutely frantic, to ask if Molly could stay for dinner that night. Emily had just walked into the house herself. It seemed that Molly's grandmother had fallen down a flight of stairs and broken her hip. So Jocelyn Francoeur didn't expect that she would be back from the hospital much before eight-thirty or nine that evening.

"Of course she can stay with us," Emily said, adding that the girl could spend the night with them if need be.

"No, I'll be back before bedtime for sure," Jocelyn said, her tone a little crazed—which made all the sense in the world, given the accident that had befallen her own mother. "If not, then I'll have Molly's aunt come get her. She lives down around Hanover."

"That's almost an hour and a half away!"

"It doesn't matter."

"Well, we have plenty of room and extra pj's if you change your mind," Emily said.

"No. She is not spending the night," Molly's mother said adamantly, and that was that.

Hallie didn't think Molly was all that worried about her grand-mother. In truth, Hallie wouldn't have been especially alarmed if her grandmother in Connecticut had broken her hip, either. She knew a hip was serious, but didn't broken bones heal all the time? Back in West Chester, there had been a boy in Garnet's and her class who had broken an arm falling off the zip line at the playground and, a year later, his leg learning to play ice hockey. Another boy they knew who was three years older than Garnet and she had broken his collarbone playing football.

"I think we need some leaves and grass and stuff," Molly was saying now. "Enough of the snow has melted that we can get some." They had done their homework after having snacks with Dad when they came home from school, and now, after dinner, they had bundled up and come out here to the greenhouse. The place didn't have lights like most of the greenhouses in Bethel, but they had brought two battery-powered lanterns—essentially big flashlights that sat on the floor. It wasn't going to be light enough to read with them, but they were able to build scenes with their dolls. It was a little after eight o'clock, and Molly's mom had called from the hospital and said she would get here around nine-thirty. Emily hadn't wanted the girls to head out to the greenhouse, but Hallie had reminded her that it was come out here or stay inside and play one of the computer games she really didn't approve of or watch another DVD—and they were all bored to tears with their DVDs. And so Mom had relented and here they were. Molly wanted to gather some sticks and leaves because the scene they were constructing for their dolls was supposed to be in the woods. She wanted the dolls to be witches, and while Hallie didn't believe that any of their dolls had the face of a witch, she was happy to go along with the game. They had put the dolls under the spell of witches the other day; making their dolls the witches themselves was refreshing and new.

"I'll go with you," said Garnet, grabbing one of the lanterns, and the two girls zipped up their parkas and wandered from the greenhouse. For a moment, Hallie was surprised at how quickly she had been left alone in the structure. She realized she had never been out here alone after dark and considered joining the girls outside. But even through the steamy, smudged glass she could see the lights of her house, and she could see the glow from Garnet's lantern as it bobbed like a buoy in the dark. And then, abruptly, it was gone. She guessed either Garnet was holding it in front of her and walking away from the greenhouse or they had simply crossed the meadow and wandered into the edge of the woods. Either way, it wasn't a big deal. And so she resumed work on their scene, standing the dolls erect in a circle around a toy copper kettle that was going to be the cauldron. She raised one of the dolls' arms and extended it over the kettle as if it were sprinkling some sort of herb or powder into it. She wondered: Did the women around here who Molly insisted were witches use cauldrons? Or did they mix up their potions in everyday-looking, normal kitchen pots? One day, those pots were boiling spaghetti or potatoes. And the next? Love potions. Or, maybe, some sort of potion that made a person's eyes less blue—or not blue at all. That was it: Maybe there was a witch with blue eyes and she used her magic to make sure that no one in Bethel could have eyes as blue as hers. Whenever a woman was pregnant, that witch would cast some sort of spell to make sure the baby had eyes that were brown or green or whatever colors eyes could be, so long as they weren't blue like hers. Hallie liked this story: It could be the start of whatever scene they created tonight with their dolls.

Hallie had kept her promise to Molly and not told her mother that some people—including Molly's own mom—believed that one of the twins who had lived in this house years and years ago had been killed by the local women. But the story had scared her because she was a twin. It was like when a plane crashed: She felt a connection. And so she had asked her mom whether she thought there might be witches living here in Bethel. Her mom, in turn, had said that the women were merely eccentrics, and then she had explained what this new word meant. She had said there were lots of rumors about what the women did, but there were no such things as witches—just as there were no such things as ghosts or vampires or werewolves. The truth, her mom insisted, was that these women were just very, very interested in plants—flowers and herbs, especially. And, maybe because they took themselves so seriously, they had made some enemies. Or, at least, gotten a reputation for being self-important and strange. But that's all there was to it: Women like Clary and Sage and Anise and Reseda might be eccentric, but they most assuredly were not witches.

Hallie had moved a third doll in front of the kettle and was surveying her work, wondering what to add next, when she saw the house go dark. One moment she had been aware of the glow from the lights that were on in rooms on every single floor of the place, even the third floor, where she and Garnet slept, and the next the house had vanished completely into the moonless night. The greenhouse was still lit by her lantern, but the rest of the world had gone black. She understood that this was a blackout: They had had them once in a great while in the winter back in West Chester, and they had already had a couple of them here in Bethel. Nevertheless, this was scary. Blackouts always were scary. But this was worse because she was all alone out here in the greenhouse and her mind had been wandering among visions of witches. Her first thought was to race for the main house, maybe calling for Garnet and Molly and searching out their lantern as she ran. But she took a breath and reminded herself that either the lights would pop back on any second or—if they didn't—Mom or Dad would be out here to get her and her sister and their friend. And the last thing she wanted was to be caught running like some terrified toddler back to the house just because there was a blackout. So, working very hard to remain calm, she started rummaging through the miniature trunk in which she stored the dolls' clothes, looking for appropriate attire and props for the scene they were constructing.

This is fall-of-man blackness, a despairing, debilitating sort of blindness. You hadn't anticipated the cloak of misery that would descend upon you when you flipped the breaker—a light switch, but a click that is louder, sharper, and considerably more satisfying—and cut the power to the house. But the fuse box is in the basement, on the wall by the concrete pad that holds the appliances, so perhaps you should have known that you would not merely be blind, you would be dealt a body blow of gloom.

She deserves friends.

Usually, everything throbs more here in the basement. The top of your head, your lower back, and abdomen—sometimes the pain there is so pronounced that you see white spots of light and fear you will vomit. Back in Pennsylvania, you told a doctor it felt like you had been gored. But it's not so bad at the moment. You can feel it, but it is more of an ambient twinge.

You are a pilot—you were a pilot—and so you tend always to be thinking ahead. Prior to flipping the breaker, you had counted exactly how many steps it was to the wheelbarrow ramp and unlatched the dead bolt and the chain, and removed the horizontal beam that Parnell Dunmore had used to keep out intruders. Prior to darkening the house— prior to even starting to clean the dinner dishes with Emily—you had brought down from the attic the carving knife that the Dunmores had left behind for you. Yes, for you. Every tool has a purpose. You cut the power with the fingers on your left hand because in your right you are holding the knife. Now you move across the basement, counting the steps in your mind, and in a moment you feel the start of the incline and you are walking up from the coal black basement into the nearly coal black night. There is no moon, but there are stars, and in the greenhouse there is still some dusky light because your beautiful daughters brought lanterns out there so they could play.

She deserves friends. Do what it takes.

And because you are a pilot, you have determined in your mind precisely how you will approach the three girls and who will live and who will die—who will die in addition to yourself. Because you know you can't live another day after you have tried to atone for the deaths of thirty-nine people with a fortieth. Funny: Your mind formed the words *thirty-nine people,* not *thirty-nine souls.* Because you know now that souls don't die. For a person who is not religious, this is a revelation. It has not been a joyful one, however, because along with your discovery that there is an afterlife has come the knowledge that sadness and pain transcend the grave, too. Children live on, their hair always dripping with lake water and jet fuel, their abdomens skewered with the horrific shards of metal airplanes. Dead fathers watch helplessly as their dead daughters pine for playmates. Young women stagger through the blackness of your basement after interviews for jobs they never will have.

The blackness of your basement: no white light there. Perhaps there is no white light anywhere. It's a myth. A vision triggered by dying brain chemicals and desperate endorphins.

Still, no one will ever understand what you are about to do. You could never explain it. You should have died back in August.

In the distance, you watch a silhouette move in the greenhouse, and you wonder why you see only one. Aren't all three girls out there? After dinner, all three went out there to play. Two, you presume, must simply be in corners you cannot see. Or, maybe, the light from the lantern (didn't they bring more than one?) is angled so that you can only see one of the children.

Your mind roams back toward the house. It is possible that one or two of the children has gone back inside for something. You pause and run your fingers over the side of the blade, trying to decide what to do. And then you see the second lantern bobbing at the edge of the meadow a good ninety or one hundred yards from the greenhouse, and then it's gone, disappearing into the brush and the trees. And that's when it all makes sense. Your judgment is suspect, and so the decision has been made for you. There is but a single girl remaining inside the greenhouse, and so, clearly, she is the one. You take a breath and march ahead, resolved.

Hallie ran to the entrance of the greenhouse and stared into the dark when she heard her mother's voice. Her mother was calling out her name and Garnet's, dashing from the house and spraying the greenhouse and the carriage barn and the woods with one of their regular flashlights. Hallie thought for a split second there was someone else out there—someone other than her mom and Garnet and Molly—though she couldn't have said whether it was because she had heard footsteps in the grass or because she had seen a shape change the consistency of the darkness enveloping the chasm that now separated the greenhouse from the rest of the property.

"Garnet? Hallie?" her mother was shouting over and over, and so

Hallie screamed for her mother that she was right here, she was right here in the doorway to the greenhouse, and her mother ran to her and knelt briefly before her, studying her in the light from the lantern without saying a word. Then she spoke: "We've lost power. Again." She rolled her eyes, trying to make light of the way, a moment ago, she had been frantically shrieking their names. Then she looked over Hallie's shoulder into the greenhouse, and Hallie could see the concern instantly return to her face. "Where in heaven's name are your sister and Molly?"

"They went to the woods to get stuff for the game."

"Stuff?"

"Twigs and moss and things."

"At night?"

"Uh-huh."

Her mom shook her head. "I wouldn't want them doing that any night and certainly not now. Not with a blackout. They won't be able to see the house to get their bearings."

"I saw the porch light go out and the house get dark," Hallie told her.

"Which direction did they go in? Do you know?"

"They were just going to go to the edge—to that path at the bottom of the field."

"Okay. You stay here while I go get them. Don't move."

Hallie nodded, but only seconds after her mother started off toward the path, she followed her, suddenly very afraid to be alone in the greenhouse.

"Wait up!" she cried, and her mother paused, shining the light back on her, and Hallie ran through the mud and melted snow. She realized that her mom was navigating this chilly March slop with nothing but socks on her feet. When she caught up, her mom took her hand and pulled her along, crying out Garnet's and Molly's names into a wind that seemed to be increasing, growing more blustery the closer they got to the woods. But it really didn't take them long to find the girls. Within minutes they were upon her sister and their new friend, perhaps a dozen yards past where the grass would merge with the trees. The small copse of pines where they were standing was illuminated by their lantern.

"Is everything okay?" Garnet asked their mother, becoming a little unnerved now herself.

Hallie watched their mom embrace first Garnet and then Molly. She held each child at arm's length and seemed to inspect them, just as she had examined her back at the greenhouse. "I was worried about you," she answered. "I didn't know where you were. What were you two thinking going into the woods at night?"

"We were just getting things to make it look like the dolls were in the forest."

"We lost power," Hallie said.

"We did?"

"Yes, we did," their mother told them, her voice sounding less unhinged than it had a moment ago but also more stern. Abruptly Hallie watched her mother's head spin toward the path that led back to the fields. "Chip?" she said into the dark. "Chip, is that you?" Hallie had heard the sound, too: a rustling, a scuffling among the leaves.

When there was no response, their mother took Garnet by the hand and pointed her flashlight toward the meadow. "Did you girls hear something?"

Molly, who hadn't said a word, suddenly started to whimper. "I'm scared," she sniffled, and she ran the sleeve of her coat across her nose and then wiped at her eyes. "I want to go home."

"Oh, Molly, I didn't mean to frighten you. I'm sorry. I'm sure we just heard a deer or a fox or something," Emily said, but Hallie could tell that her mother didn't believe a word she was saying. "I just got spooked by the blackout. Come on, girls, let's head back to the house."

"Where's Daddy?" Hallie asked.

"I guess he's back at the house, too," her mother answered. "Come on. I'm positive the power will be back on in a couple of minutes and we'll be able to have some hot chocolate." Then they walked purposefully from the woods along the path and up the sloping meadow past the greenhouse—retrieving the single lantern there—and into the dark house.

S ilently you place the knife at your feet and push shut the door to the wheelbarrow ramp, locking it from the inside, your fingers spidering along the wood frame in the absolute dark. You feel around for the horizontal beam and drop it back in place, listening as your wife calls your name in the kitchen above you. She sounds anxious, frenzied. You want to yell up to her, *Down here, honey. Just checking the breakers in the fuse box. Everything's fine!* But Ethan Stearns is standing between you and the stairs, a beacon that is strangely but perfectly visible in the blackness. He is scowling, incapable of masking his disgust.

But, really, what were you supposed to do? Massacre all of them?

You couldn't have done that. You see in your mind an image of the children at daybreak, all dead, Emily, too, their throats cut as they bled to death in the woods—their parkas and sweaters forever stained red. You see it all in your mind with the sun overhead, the sky the same breathtaking summer cobalt it had been on August 11 over Lake Champlain. But this was never supposed to have been a slaughter of that magnitude: three fifth-grade girls and your wife. This had been about a playmate. A single playmate. You kill a child and then you kill yourself. That was the bargain.

But Ethan is shaking his head.

She deserves friends.

Was it always a plural? Friends? He nods. It was, it was.

You kneel and paw at the dirt floor until you have recovered the knife. There you notice little Ashley, sitting with her legs crossed, her eyes sadder than you have ever seen them. Does she understand what she is asking—what it means?

She deserves friends. Do what it takes.

You gaze at Ethan. *No,* you want to say aloud, *no,* but for some reason you are afraid to speak in this dark and crease the blackness with noise. But you do think to yourself: *No. Absolutely not. That is asking too much.*

Upstairs, Emily searches for you. You can feel the way she is moving up the steps to the second floor; the house—*it*—is telling you. Meanwhile, the girls huddle around the kitchen table, Molly alone on the deacon's bench. Desdemona is prowling on that rickety staircase behind the kitchen, the existence of which is, like so much of this house, an absolute mystery. And you? Once again, as you did one morning in the pit of despair on the other side of this basement—Harry Harlow's vertical chamber apparatus, reconfigured for a house on the fringes of madness—you curl your knees into your chest and try to lie there, unmoving as an egg.

Hallie glanced at Garnet, but she couldn't quite make out her sister's eyes in the dim glow of the lantern. She sensed that Garnet had retreated into one of those places where she was gazing at nothing. She wondered if Garnet was about to have one of her seizures—or whether she was in the early stages of one already. She heard their mother call out their dad's name again. Her mother was upstairs now, going from room to room along the hallway. Hallie guessed that she would head up to the third floor and her and Garnet's rooms next. She might even pull down that trapdoor to the attic.

"Where do you think he is?" Molly asked, her voice strangely small on a girl Hallie usually thought of as so very big.

"I don't know."

The girl looked at Garnet. "Garnet?" she said, but her sister didn't respond.

"She's okay," Hallie said, shrugging.

Upstairs they heard a crash, a small piece of furniture toppling over in Hallie's mind, and Hallie watched Molly flinch. She knew that she herself had been startled also. But Garnet remained oblivious.

"I'm okay, girls," their mother called down the stairs. "I knocked into the end table by your father's and my bed, that's all!"

"Okay, Mom," Hallie called back.

"I hope my mom gets here soon," Molly said.

"Yup." Hallie didn't know what else to say. A moment later she heard her mother pulling down the door to the attic, just as she had expected she would, and Molly, unfamiliar with the lengthy groan the hinges made as the door descended, looked a little ashen in the lantern light.

"What was that?" she asked.

Hallie reassured her that it was only the door to the attic, adding, "I know. It sounds really creepy."

Eventually Emily pounded her way back down the stairs, and Hallie asked her, "Did you really go into the attic?"

"No, I just, I don't know, I called and shone my light up there."

"You checked our rooms?"

"Yes, I did check your rooms," she said, opening the basement door. "Chip?" she yelled down the stairs and bent over, peering underneath the wobbly banister and shining the flashlight into the void. "Chip?" When he didn't answer, she slammed the door shut and swore, finally succumbing to the fear and frustration she had been experiencing since they lost power and her husband—and, briefly, one of her daughters and their friend—disappeared into the dark. "Damn it! Where is he?" she asked aloud, clearly not expecting an answer. Hallie feared that her mother was on the verge of tears. Normally she would have told her that Garnet might be having a seizure, but she didn't dare. Besides, what really could her mother do? Most of the time, you just had to wait them out anyway.

"You girls really haven't seen him?" her mother asked, her voice helpless.

Hallie shook her head but then wondered if her mother could see her and said, "No, Mom."

She watched her mother go to the wall where the phone usually hung, running her hand along it. It was as if she had forgotten she had a flashlight. "I can't find the phone!" she was saying. "It's not in the cradle. I want to call the power company, and I can't even find the goddamn phone." A moment later Hallie heard a crash and her mother swearing again, and she knew by the sound it was the casserole dish in which her parents had baked the enchiladas they'd eaten for dinner. But then her mother must have found the phone, because they heard her pressing the buttons. Unfortunately, it wasn't going to work because there was no power. Hallie could have told her that. It was electric. And, as they all knew, there was no cell coverage in this corner of Bethel, which was why her mom had been searching for the regular phone in the first place.

"Fuck!" her mother swore. Hallie had never heard her mother say that word before. "Fuck!"

"Want me to go upstairs and get another flashlight?" Hallie asked. "It would make the kitchen a little lighter."

"God, no! I want all three of you to stay right here with me," her mother said, trying to regain a semblance of maternal composure. "I'm sure the power will come back on any second now and your father will reappear—he's probably outside in the woods this very minute looking for you—and so let's just stay right where we are. Okay? We'll stay right here in the kitchen and wait for him," she continued, and she had barely finished her sentence when, indeed, the lights returned and the refrigerator started to hum and below them the furnace rumbled back into life. Hallie heard the classical music their parents must have been listening to on the public radio station when they were cleaning up the kitchen.

"See what I mean?" her mother said, and she extended her hands, palms up. She looked disheveled, her hair wild, as if she had been awakened in the middle of the night. Meanwhile, Garnet sat perfectly still, absolutely unmoved or unaware or uninterested in the fact that the power had been restored. She was indeed having a seizure, and, given the blackout and their dad's disappearance, Hallie hoped it would be a short one. She looked to see if her mom had noticed yet that Garnet was in her own private world, but her mother was staring down at her feet. She was still wearing only her socks, and they were sopping wet and streaked with mud.

"I guess I'll need to throw these away," she said, looking up, and Hallie thought she might have been about to offer a small smile, but she looked over Hallie's shoulder and gasped, and a second later Molly pushed away from the table and stood, screaming, a ululating, sirenlike wail of terror. And so reflexively Hallie turned around, too.

There in the doorway at the top of the stairs to the basement was their father. His shirt was awash in blood, a great stain spreading from the left of his navel with the speed of toppled house paint on tile. And there in the center of that red tsunami was—and now Hallie started to scream, too—the pearl handle of a carving knife. Her father rolled his eyes up into his head so they looked like golf balls and groaned. Then he fell back against the doorframe, pulled the knife from his abdomen with both hands, and sank slowly to the floor, leaving a long swash of blood against the wood.

Chapter Nine

Garnet felt confused, the way she always did when a seizure had passed: It was as if she had had a nap and missed things that everyone else knew about. But unlike after a nap, she never felt well rested. She felt groggy instead: It was like she had awoken in the middle of the night rather than at a predictable time in the morning.

Now she was aware that her mother was leaving her, speeding down the driveway after their father. The headlights and siren from the ambulance had faded moments ago, and Reseda was here. Holly and Ginger Jackson, too. Her mother had called Reseda and said to come quickly. She had. Before that, however, Molly's mother had come to the house and retrieved her own daughter. The first thing Garnet recalled seeing when she emerged from the seizure was Molly leaning against her own mom, sobbing, as Mrs. Francoeur stood in the front hallway and ranted about what a mistake she had made letting the girl stay here. Only when Mrs. Francoeur saw Garnet's father bleeding on the kitchen floor did her rage dissipate. She went from railing about how Emily clearly was part of something evil to crying that the house was cursed and Emily was merely a fool to bring her family here. Meanwhile, Garnet's mom simply kept pressing dish towels against her dad's abdomen. Then the ambulance arrived, and Mrs. Francoeur finally went home—though not before making it clear that Molly was never going to be allowed over for a playdate again.

Before her mother left, she had told Garnet that she would be back soon. She had said that Daddy would be just fine. He would get some stitches and be as good as new. But whether *soon* meant within hours or the next day, Garnet didn't know, and when she asked, her mother just repeated that one word: *soon.* So, now she sat beside the window in the living room and gazed outside. The yard was dark once more now that all the cars had driven off and—other than murmured voices—the only sound was the occasional rattle of one of the windowpanes in an early spring breeze. Yet the house felt full. Reseda and Holly and Ginger were in the kitchen, discussing how best they could help the family, and it had already been decided that Reseda and Holly were going to spend the night.

Eventually Hallie sat back down beside her. "They're about to have us get in our pajamas and go to sleep," she said, her chin in her hands.

"You were listening."

"Uh-huh."

"You hear anything else?"

"Not really. They knew I was by the door."

"They did?"

"Yup."

"How?"

Hallie shrugged. "I don't know. I mean, Reseda wasn't mad or anything. She just tapped on the door and teased me about it."

"I don't want to sleep upstairs."

"Me, either."

Garnet sighed. "When we were in the woods, do you think he was there?" she wondered aloud.

"Dad?"

"Uh-huh."

"I don't think so. Do you?" Hallie asked.

She nodded. "Yeah, I do."

"There was one second when I thought I saw something. Someone," Hallie admitted.

"If it was Dad, he must have been there to protect us," she said.

"Yup," Hallie agreed, but Garnet had the sense that her sister—like her—wasn't completely certain of that.

*   *   *

Reseda had spent very little time in the Southwest, but one night in Taos she had been part of a fire ceremony. The shamans had burned juniper branches they had soaked in water, and the result was a blaze with hypnotic purple smoke, the air alive with the aroma from the juniper's essential oils. A woman had played the violin while sixty or seventy of them sat or stood around the bonfire and contemplated the colors of the flames against the night sky.

Tonight, with the two girls haunted by the power outage and the image of their father's blood, she was using sage. In her experience, sage cleansed the energy in a space in much the same fashion as juniper: It helped clear away fear and worry and violence. And this was a space that had experienced all three that evening. She added a few more drops of sage oil to the diffuser and lit the tea candle beneath it.

"Candles make me think of blackouts," Hallie said from the couch, her voice slightly petulant.

Reseda knew this was the child's way of asking her to blow out the candle. She sat down on the armrest beside the girl and wondered what it meant that her father had actually cut the breakers: This had been no wind- or storm-triggered blackout. She had gleaned this when she said good-bye to him and to Emily as they left for the hospital. She honestly wasn't sure what to do with this information and, at the moment, had no plans to share it with anyone. "This candle really offers very little light," she said. "It warms the oil in the shallow bowl above it. Do you like the aroma?"

The girl shrugged noncommittally, but Reseda knew that she did. Then Hallie put down the mug with the California poppy and chamomile tea that Reseda had steeped for the twins to help them sleep. She noted that it was almost empty.

"I love sage," said Holly, looking up at the girl from her spot on one of the two air mattresses they had inflated and set on the floor beside the couch. She was planning to sleep tonight in black dance pants and a yoga T-shirt. Reseda watched her reach under the quilt on the couch and squeeze Hallie's toes. "It smells heavenly, and it's the Lysol of essential oils."

Garnet was curled into a ball on the air mattress beside Holly, and she looked like she was already asleep. Reseda, however, knew that she wasn't. Her head was deep in the pillow and her eyes were shut, but she was merely feigning sleep while listening intently to the conversation around her.

"Will you keep the candle burning when you turn out the lights?" Hallie asked from her nest on the sofa.

"I was thinking that we might keep some of the lights on," Reseda told her. "I know I'd be happier if we kept at least the lamp on that table on. Would you mind?"

Hallie shook her head.

"Thank you."

"I know I want a light on, too," Holly said, and she giggled.

Hallie turned to Reseda. "Where are you going to sleep?" she asked.

The truth was, Reseda wasn't completely sure she was going to sleep. She had found that she was most receptive to visions when she was a little sleep-deprived. Everyone was. Healers and shamans and religious fanatics of all stripes knew the mind was most amenable to psychic visitation when it was exhausted. And she was feeling a little wrung out. Assuming the girls—especially Garnet, whose mind was particularly interesting to Reseda—eventually fell asleep, she thought she might visit the basement. She might see for herself the door that was of such interest to the captain and try to get a sense of what might have attached itself to him.

Emily had presumed that nothing could have been worse than watching the news footage of her husband's plane cartwheeling across the surface of Lake Champlain, or the images of the floating wreckage and the bodies as they bobbed amidst the ferries and dinghies and rescue boats. But this might have been worse. She wasn't sure how—she couldn't make distinctions that fine when the world was unraveling so completely—but at the moment she didn't even have the relief that came with the idea that the worst was at least behind her. By the time she'd seen the images of the destruction of Flight 1611, she knew that Chip had survived. Her husband was alive.

But now? Her husband was alive, but he had just had another very close call. He had, apparently, fallen down the basement steps and accidentally plunged a knife into his abdomen when he hit the mud floor. At least he said it was an accident. She would have been more confident that it was if the knife hadn't been the one the paranoid woman who had lived in the house before them had left behind in a second-floor heating grate. The young ER physician and an even younger nurse at the hospital here in Littleton had sewed him up, telling her that he was very, very lucky. The knife had not perforated the intestines. Nor had it nicked his left kidney, the pancreas, or—perhaps most fortunately—the iliac artery. There had been a lot of blood, but not a lot of damage. The principal concern, now that he was stitched up, was infection. But that should be manageable. Still, the hospital staff had decided to keep him overnight for observation, and now he was resting, sedated, in a room down the corridor.

Chip had insisted that he hadn't tried to harm himself, but he had seemed confused when he first appeared at the top of the basement steps. Had she not noticed all the blood, she would have wondered first how he could possibly have gotten so filthy: It was as if he had been rolling around on the dirt floor in the basement. But he had seemed to reacquire his bearings quickly, and then he had grown contrite and shaken. He kept apologizing for disappearing, and he kept trying to explain both to her and to himself what had happened. It still wasn't clear to her when he had fallen down the stairs. Had he stumbled while on his way to the water tank to check the pilot light? (There again was that excuse. Hadn't he claimed to have been checking the pilot on the furnace when she found him in the basement on Saturday night?) Or was it after the lights had gone out, on his way back up the stairs? He had offered both scenarios. And why was he even bringing that old knife with him down the stairs into the basement? He said he happened to have been washing it with the dinner dishes because it was a perfectly good knife, and he had had it in his hands in the soapy water when he decided to check on the water tank.

And so she was worried that this was, in reality, no mere accident. Whether it was self-flagellation or a suicide attempt, however, remained unclear. Obviously he had been depressed since the plane crash; obviously he had been enduring ongoing symptoms of PTSD. But there was a monumental difference between experiencing flashbacks of a failed water ditching and taking a knife and plunging it into one's own stomach. It was as if he had been in the throes of some new PTSD hallucination or nightmare. Moreover, something Chip had said when he collapsed at the top of the stairs, before he came back to his senses, made absolutely no sense. He was babbling that some child who had died in the accident needed company and he owed it to the passenger to find her a playmate. A moment later he seemed to understand fully where he was and what had happened: They had lost power, it was back on, and he was bleeding.

Emily sipped at the coffee, tepid and a little bitter, that she had gotten from a vending machine outside the hospital cafeteria, long closed for the night, and surveyed the waiting room. She wasn't alone because no more than a dozen yards away was command central for the wing, an island with four walls of chest-high counters, and nurses and doctors and administrators who were constantly racing among patient rooms and back behind it with clipboards, paperwork, and plastic cups filled with meds. But there were no other relatives or friends of patients at the moment because it was after midnight and visiting hours were long over. She recalled Jocelyn Francoeur's remorseless (though understandable) hostility. Before she had seen how badly Chip was hurt, the woman had been furious, nearly hysterical, and had hissed that she had been warned about the family. She had been told to steer clear of Emily and the twins the way she had always steered clear of Reseda and Anise and that whole perverted crowd.

Emily rubbed at her eyes. Clearly there was a schism in Bethel. There were her strange new friends with their greenhouses, and then there was the rest of the community. But who had reached out to her *except* for those odd herbalists? No one. No one at all. Consequently, she decided she was very glad to have that whole perverted crowd a part of her life tonight. John and Clary Hardin had appeared out of nowhere and had been sitting on this appallingly ugly, orange Naugahyde couch beside her until a few minutes ago, holding her hand and comforting her, until finally she had insisted they go home and get some rest. And even before Chip had been rushed to the hospital, Reseda and Holly and Ginger had descended upon her home, Reseda and Holly offering to stay with the girls as long as necessary. (She called, they came. *That* was friendship.) When Emily had phoned home a few minutes ago to check in, the four of them—Reseda and Holly, Hallie and Garnet—had set up a big slumber party in the living room, piling quilts and air mattresses and pillows onto the floor as if they were all teenage girls on a Friday night. Reseda didn't think the twins would want to stay alone in their bedrooms, and she was correct. The girls had sounded more tired than terrified when Emily spoke to them, and they were all finally going to sleep. According to Reseda, Anise had been by the house as well. She'd just left, though not before stocking the refrigerator.

The truth was, Emily knew that she didn't have anyone but these people in Bethel. Her mother-in-law? She might phone her in the morning, but then again she might not. What precisely would she tell her? And given her mother-in-law's drinking—given the reality that her mother-in-law was a drunk—what assistance could she provide? Absolutely none. After Flight 1611 had crashed, two days had passed before she called her son, and, though Chip wouldn't share with Emily the details of the conversation, he did say that his mother had told him fatalistically that it—an accident of this magnitude—was bound to happen. Emily imagined she could phone her theater pals in Pennsylvania or some of the lawyers with whom she was friends in her old firm, but what were they supposed to do? Drop everything and come to New Hampshire so they could hold her hand and help nurse her husband back to health? That was what mothers and fathers and siblings did, and she had none. Since her parents had passed away, she didn't have any family at all.

Emily realized that she desperately needed to sleep now, but there was one more doctor who wanted to talk to her, and that was Chip's new psychiatrist here in New Hampshire. Her husband had only met with him three or four times, but Chip had said that he liked him, and so Emily had called him. His name was Michael Richmond. He had arrived at the hospital just about when the ER physician and the nurse finished stitching up Chip, and he had been allowed to spend a few minutes with her husband after he was admitted. Now the psychiatrist was discussing her husband's case on the phone with a colleague in Chicago. Emily yawned again and was just about to curl up her legs and lie down on the couch when he returned. He was a tall man, roughly her age, in a white oxford shirt and blue jeans. He had thinning blond hair and a strong face made more handsome by the scars that remained from what must have been a titanic battle with acne as an adolescent. He sat on the couch beside her, in the very spot where John Hardin had been earlier.

"So," he began, his voice soft and melodic. "You must be exhausted."

"I am," she agreed.

"And, I imagine, pretty shocked."

"That, too."

"Do you want something to help you relax? Maybe even just a sleeping pill?"

She thought about this. "Yes. I will take a sleeping pill. I will even say yes to whatever you're offering in the way of antidepressants."

"You've been through a lot," he agreed.

"Well, let's start with what just happened to my husband. I really don't understand it. Did he actually try and hurt himself? I understand his guilt. But the flight was seven months ago. Why tonight? Why now?"

"We don't know for a fact that he did try and hurt himself. Maybe it really was an accident."

"You don't believe that."

He sighed. "PTSD is a complicated thing."

"There's more. There must be more."

"Has Chip had any issues with anger since the crash? Rage he couldn't control?"

"Not at all."

"Frustration that seemed, oh, a little off the charts?"

"Well, there was a door," she said after a moment, and she proceeded to tell the doctor about the barnboard door to a coal chute that Chip had turned to kindling with an ax. She wondered if that counted as anger he couldn't control.

"How about with the girls? How has he been with them?"

"He's been great. Always has been. The issue for me over the years was that he wasn't home half the time because he was a pilot. Do you have kids?"

"No."

"Try being a single mom with a job and twin toddlers three or four days a week. When he'd come home after flying for three or four days, the girls would swarm on him. We're talking seagulls on a Dumpster. And while I understood that it was simply that he'd been away, I always felt a little, I don't know, inadequate. And unloved. No, that's not right: less loved."

"But you realized this was an inaccurate perception."

"Intellectually. Not viscerally," she said, and she regretted that somehow this discussion was starting to become about her rather than about her husband. But it seemed that the doctor sensed her unease and brought the conversation back to Chip.

"And since the plane crash? How has he been as a dad since the accident?" he asked.

"Still great. He's a terrific parent. I mean, he's been a little spacey. How could he not? And, as you know, he's been depressed. There was a period when I don't think he was getting dressed until the girls were about to get off the school bus in the afternoon."

"Here in New Hampshire?"

"No, this was in those months right after the crash. Back in Pennsylvania."

He rubbed at his eyes, and she guessed that he was probably as tired as she was.

"How is he doing now?" she asked.

"Well, he's sticking with his story that it was an accident. He fell. And I guess it is possible that he happened to have the knife with him when he took a tumble while going downstairs to check on the pilot light. Or maybe he fell and didn't fall on the knife. Then, as he was sitting on the basement floor in the dark—he has no flashlight, remember—it all just overwhelms him: the accident, the move, the lack of purpose in his life right now. The flashbacks, the guilt. There is a lot going on inside his head. And so he hurts himself. I mean, we usually associate cutting with teen girls and young women. But it can affect anyone."

"He'd never cut himself before tonight."

"And perhaps he never will again. But it's still going to take a bit of work to answer your question: Why did he do this? And we may never answer that question, at least not to our satisfaction. But your husband has no history of schizophrenia or mental illness or violence, correct?"

"No," she agreed. "None. Trust me, they don't let schizophrenics fly planes. They don't let people who are likely to take a knife to themselves pilot commercial jets."

"That's what I mean."

"But what about that thing he said about some girl on his flight—his last flight—needing a playmate? What was that about?"

"Oh, it could mean any one of a hundred things. What I found interesting is that he only brought that up after he had given you the knife and collapsed."

"He didn't give me the knife," she corrected him. "He pulled it out of his stomach and tossed it on to the floor. It was like it was something that repulsed him."

The doctor stretched his legs out straight in front of him. She noticed he was wearing black Converse sneakers. "Your husband's contrition is profound. He is calm but ashamed. Appalled at what he did tonight. He is devastated that his girls saw him that way. But he is also continuing to insist that the water in the sink seemed a little cool when the two of you were doing the dishes after dinner. He says you went to the dining room to continue clearing the table and he went downstairs to the basement to see what was going on with the hot-water tank.

But he tripped and fell. Then the lights went out." He paused, thinking, and then turned to her. "Did that ER doctor check for a head injury?" he asked.

"I don't know."

"Before your husband goes home tomorrow—"

"If my husband goes home tomorrow—"

"Make sure he was checked for a concussion. There was no obvious sign of a head injury, but I wonder if maybe he hit the back or the side of his head in the dark and blacked out. It's just an idea."

Emily thought about this and about how Chip hadn't answered her when she had called out his name over and over, yelling for him as she went from floor to floor in the house. "Wouldn't the ER have looked into a concussion?" she asked.

"You had a pretty green doctor and nurse. I think he had graduated, oh, around three-thirty this afternoon. A lot would have depended on what he thought to ask your husband. And I'm not saying your husband even has a concussion. I'm only suggesting that he may have blacked out—if only briefly."

"You might be onto something," she said, and she told Richmond about her attempts to find Chip and how he hadn't responded when she had positively screamed for him during the blackout. She actually felt a little relieved at the idea that he may have been unconscious. "It would explain an awful lot," she told him when she was finished.

"See what I mean?" he said, and he gave her a small smile. "There are a lot of questions about what happened tonight that we'll never answer. Never. But some may have incredibly obvious solutions."

Reseda knew as well as anyone the stories—all suspect in her opinion—that Tansy Dunmore had not buried her son in the cemetery. The woman had feared that Clary or Sage or Anise or one of the herbalists long past would try again, even if it meant desecrating the boy's bloated corpse. Reseda gave little credence to the idea. Although Sawyer Dunmore had died before she was born (though only by half a decade, a reality that always made Reseda aware of her age since most of Bethel viewed Sawyer Dunmore's death as chronologically distant as the Peloponnesian War), she knew the women and she knew the tincture. She had always been confident that Sawyer Dunmore's body was in his casket in the family plot beside the two hydrangeas in the cemetery. It was only when the pilot had come to her office and mentioned that door in the basement that she had begun to wonder if she was mistaken.

Now standing perfectly still, hunched over, in the muddy chamber that Chip Linton had opened with an ax, she decided that Tansy and Parnell Dunmore had indeed turned a corner of their basement into a mausoleum. They had buried their child here, determined to keep even the soulless, rotting cadaver from the women. She had the sense that, if she took a shovel and dug, it wouldn't take long to find human remains. The notion filled her with despair for both of the parents, but particularly for Tansy. Her guilt just might have rivaled the pilot's.

Nevertheless, Reseda felt nothing attaching itself to her, nothing— no one—at all. If Sawyer Dunmore had remained here with his body (a distinct possibility, given how he died), he was now long gone. She ran her fingertips over the ravaged barnboard. It was appropriate that here was a doorway. A threshold. A liminal world.

She recalled the first time the dead had attached themselves to her and the trauma that had preceded it. She had understood even then, if only instinctively, how receptive the traumatized are to the dead. How open. Again, a doorway into one's aura—one's space. The dead will always find a passage. In hindsight, her twin sister had attached herself to her well before the police and the EMTs arrived. Reseda had been barely conscious and had presumed at first that she was dreaming: One minute she and Lucinda were walking on a path along Storrow Drive, and the next there was a man before them whom her sister clearly recognized and whose sudden presence she found terrifying. But all that had regis- tered for Reseda was that he was wearing a New England Patriots knit cap and that he was massive. It was late at night, and people would tell her later that they shouldn't have been out. But they were both juniors, Reseda at BC and Lucinda at BU. Soon they would be going home for Thanksgiving. Their family lived perhaps a mile from the ocean in Yarmouth, Maine. Lucinda had taken her sister's arm when she saw the man, but she had barely started to scream when he killed her. Just like that. Reared up like a stallion and stabbed her over and over in the chest and face. There had been so much of Lucinda's blood on Reseda's own white parka that initially the EMTs had been confused as they tried to find where she had been stabbed. And then he had attacked her. The next day in the hospital she would learn that her forearms had practically been skinned and the snow jacket sleeves shredded as she used her arms to ward off the knife blows and defend herself. A tendon in her hand had been sliced through, presumably because she grabbed at the blade while reaching for the knife. But the blade had neither hit her heart nor nicked her aorta, either of which in all likelihood would have been lethal. The knife had missed her liver and her spleen. She had lost a lot of blood, but she had suffered mostly puncture wounds, and nothing vital—no large-caliber veins—had been punctured. Unfortunately, in addition to gaping lesions along both arms and an especially cavernous maw on her right leg (had she kicked at her assailant as he stabbed her?), her left lung was collapsed.

And yet as she lay on the ground, her attacker disappearing into the night because he presumed she was as dead as her sister, almost right away she had the feeling that she wasn't alone. The sensation was so pronounced that even when she was being loaded onto the backboard, her neck in a cervical collar, she thought Lucinda was being carried into the ambulance beside her. She wasn't. At one point Reseda glanced at the trauma dressings and wraparound gauze that made her arms look like a mummy's, and she could have sworn that she saw her sister's slim wrist and the Georg Jensen bracelet with the moonstones she always wore.

Two days later she would be identifying Lucinda's killer from a series of snapshots. He was a deeply disturbed custodian at the university lab where Lucinda worked and had had a crush on her that had gone horribly wrong. Somehow Reseda knew details of the relationship—and the strange ways the young man had stalked her sister—that Lucinda had never shared.

The incursion into her aura would prove, in some ways, to be a penetrating injury. And though her sister had meant her no harm (which Reseda knew now was usually, but not always, the case with the undead), Lucinda's presence was at once debilitating and disorienting. Everyone in her family and at school noticed the changes in Reseda, and even when her internal and external wounds had healed, it would be a long, long time until she was fully recovered—until she was, quite literally, herself again. Everyone attributed this to the trauma, and they were right—though not in the way they meant. Had Reseda not been so traumatized by the attack, she might have resisted her sister's invasion of her aura.

Which brought her back to Sawyer Dunmore and his crypt here in the basement. It felt empty, save for whatever bones were somewhere in the dirt beneath her feet. Either he had made it to another plane or he had found another host on this earth. She presumed it was the former, since whatever was tormenting the pilot did not seem to reflect the little she knew about Sawyer. She wondered: Had Chip Linton found the bones? If so, he hadn't been thinking about them when he had been at her house for dinner. She hadn't sensed either Sawyer or a skeleton.

She circled back in her mind to the women. She thought of Anise. Of Clary. Of Ginger. Then she thought of John Hardin and Alexander Jackson. The original tincture was long gone, but now they had a fresh pair of twins at their disposal. The odds were good they would try again.

When she went upstairs, Holly and the girls were all sound asleep in the living room. She kissed each on the cheek and then perched herself on the deacon's bench in the kitchen, prepared to keep vigil until either Emily returned or the sun rose, whichever came first.

You know you are in a hospital bed. There are the metal rungs along the sides, there is a galaxy of small dots of light: distant stars, but not really distant at all. You listen to the sounds of the nurses, including the slim fellow with the immaculate, graying goatee, as they tend to you and whoever else is on this floor, passing by your half-open door. How long ago was it that Michael Richmond was here? An hour? Two? Three? You believe you are alone, but you are not completely sure. You hear no one breathing in that second bed, and there had been nobody there when you were first brought here from the ER. You recall that earlier your stomach hurt, but no more. They have given you something, and this is your principal source of frustration at the moment. You *should* be in pain. You *deserve* to be in pain. When you recall what you were contemplating, you grow a little nauseous. Would you actually have turned the knife on a child? Your own child? Apparently. It was close.

You fear that you will never be able to look your children in the eyes again. You almost did the absolute worst thing a parent can do. And the fact that you failed (thank God) doesn't mean that you can be trusted. You can't. Your daughters should never trust you again. You will never trust yourself. Ever.

You wonder what time it is and scan the hospital room for a clock. There doesn't seem to be one amidst all those pinpricks of light. But you presume that your girls are sound asleep right now. As is Emily.

At least you imagine that they are sound asleep. In your mind, however, you don't see them in their rooms on the third floor of the house. You hope, when you think about it, that they are not even in the structure: You like to believe that they have gone to a motel or an inn. That they are with John and Clary Hardin. Anywhere is better than that despicable place you now call your home. Three floors of malevolent timbers and plaster and pine board. Knob-and-tube wiring, every inch of which is as ominous as a snake. Rooms and corridors that are claustrophobic, wallpaper designed to make a man despair. Those sunflowers. The foxes. Weapons and cigarette lighters hidden throughout the house like Easter eggs, but evil. And then there is the basement. The pit of despair. Doors that lead nowhere. Whatever led you to nearly take a knife to a child was spawned in that pit. You need to get out. You need to get your family out.

Or is this just the morphine or whatever painkiller they're giving you? Are you being melodramatic, trying to shift blame? It's a house. It's not alive. Actually, it's a place that you are painstakingly making your own. You know people in Pennsylvania who would kill for a house just like this. The truth is, you are the problem. Not the house.

You have known all along that your future began to diminish last summer, on August 11. That was when the possibilities began to narrow. And now? Look at the way you are giving sentience and breath to bricks and mortar. You are becoming estranged from the world of the sane. You deserve nothing, and you have nothing.

You contemplate going home tomorrow and realize that you are afraid. The idea of being alone with your children terrifies you. What might you do when they climb off the school bus tomorrow afternoon— or the day after, or the day after that—while Emily is at work? Everyone fears you will hurt yourself. That should be the least of their concerns. Still, you find the notion of suicide growing real in your mind. You killed thirty-nine people back in August and nearly a fortieth this evening. You know this has to end. You tried to end it this evening, but wouldn't your death at your own hands scar your sweet girls even more? Of course it would. And look at the emotional wounds you have inflicted upon them already. Or would your death be a relief for everyone? In the long run, might it save your children's lives? Emily could take the girls back to Pennsylvania. Or raise them right here in Bethel with the help of Reseda and Holly and Anise. With John and Clary, with Peyton and Sage. Everyone here adores your daughters. They adore Emily. They say it takes a village to raise a child; well, this village loves your girls. So be it.

But you love them, too. You love Emily.

You stare at the horizontal blinds in the window and try to focus. A thought: You fly the plane until, pure and simple, you can't. Aviate. Navigate. Communicate. It's what you do. It's all about concentration.

Yes, tomorrow you will go home. You will try to stay away from the basement. You will try not to curl into a ball in the bone-ridden dirt in your own little pit of despair.

Outside your hospital room, you hear the nurse with the goatee laughing gently with another of the nurses, the stout woman with the button mushroom for a nose. She seemed very kind. They all seem very kind.

Yes, yes, the poor, dead Ashley Stearns does deserve friends. She does. But you can't do what it takes. You won't.

Aviate. Navigate. Communicate. Fly the plane until you can't.

You close your eyes against the stars in your hospital room, and eventually you fall back to sleep.

Part III

In the morning, John Hardin came to the house. The sun was up, and it was apparent that the last of the snow in the yard would be gone by lunchtime. There would still be snow in the woods, and a small, crunchy, knee-high ridge along the north wall of the carriage barn was likely to remain for at least a couple more days. And certainly more snow would fall at the end of March and into April. But the morning felt like spring when Emily opened the front door around seven-thirty. Holly and the twins were still asleep, but Reseda was upstairs showering. Emily had been so exhausted when she returned from the hospital that she hadn't bothered to climb into her nightgown and had instead simply collapsed on her bed in her clothes and pulled the quilt over her. She had somehow staggered to her feet when the alarm went off, and she had only set the alarm because she was a mother of ten-year-old girls who were going to need her rather badly when they awoke.

"Good morning," John said, his voice as cheerful as ever. She noticed that he was dressed more formally than usual. He was wearing a necktie with his tweed coat, and penny loafers instead of his usual L.L.Bean duck boots. She was impressed by how well rested he seemed; she hadn't glanced at herself in the mirror when she made her way from the bedroom to the kitchen, and so she presumed that she looked terrible—tired and messy and not even clean. But simply having made it awake and vertical seemed a monumental accomplishment at the moment—or, perhaps, a testimony to whatever antidepressant Michael Richmond had given her.

"Hi, John," she whispered, ushering him into the hallway and then into the kitchen. "The girls and Holly are still sound asleep in the living room."

He hunched his shoulders and nodded, as if making his body a little smaller would make him a little quieter. He sat down at the kitchen table in the seat nearest the counter with the coffeemaker as she started to brew a pot. "Giving the girls a day off from school?" he asked very quietly, enunciating each word with care. "I think that is an excellent plan."

"I wouldn't say it was a plan. It's just what's happening."

"Well, I hope you weren't intending on coming into the office today."

"No, I wasn't. I presume you don't mind."

"I would have sent you home the moment I heard you coming up the stairs. Your girls need you today. Chip needs you. What time are you getting him?"

"I thought I would call the hospital in a few minutes and see what's going on. But I guess I was hoping he would be back here by lunchtime or so."

"I want him to have the best care available," John said. "It's why I've come by. We both know in our hearts he didn't fall on that knife."

She closed her eyes for a moment and rubbed at her temples. She wanted this—whatever *this* was—to be a one-time aberration. She wanted Chip to come home and be fine and this latest phase in their nightmare to be behind them. "What do you have in mind?" she asked finally. "Is there a particular doctor or psychiatrist you would recommend?"

"I know Dr. Richmond spoke to him for a couple minutes last night—"

"Michael is his psychiatrist here in New Hampshire," she told him. "They have a relationship. It wasn't like he just dropped by the hospital."

"I understand. Not a problem at all. But there's another doctor I would love him to see, too. Her name is Valerian Wainscott, and you can have absolute faith in her. She's very, very good—an excellent therapist." He chuckled and shook his head slightly. "I remember watching her grow up."

"Any special reason you want Chip to see her?"

"Well, Valerian has a lot of experience with post-traumatic stress disorder. She works at the state psychiatric hospital two days a week," he explained. "Tell me: Has Chip been acting particularly odd lately—you know, before last night?"

"You mean more than the flashbacks?"

"And, I suppose, a measure of guilt and depression."

She watched the coffee drip into the glass pot and breathed in the aroma. "Yes. He has been a different person since the crash—which is to be expected."

"Anything specific?"

"He . . ." She floundered for a moment, trying to find the right words. It had been much easier talking to the psychiatrist around midnight, when she was at once exhausted and in shock. When she resumed, she said, "As I told Michael last night, he went a little nuts on this door in the basement. It was just the old coal chute. But it was nailed shut, and he took an ax to it."

"It was a violent act?"

"An act with an ax usually is."

"I see your point."

"And I think he was more disturbed than I was by Tansy Dunmore's paranoia. At first I was pretty shaken—more than Chip. But I guess I got over it." The night before she had told John and Clary that the knife Chip had brought to the basement was one of the items Tansy had left hidden in the house. "He was a little obsessed by it."

"Her paranoia."

"Yes."

John shook his head ruefully. "She was a very ill woman toward the end."

"So I gather."

"And Chip's therapist knew about all this?"

"Michael? Oh, absolutely."

"Good," he said, but the word caught just the tiniest bit in his throat. Then he smiled. "Tell me: How are the world's most adorable twins?"

Before Emily could answer, Reseda appeared in the kitchen entrance from the dining room, a towel on her head like a turban. "They're fine, John," she told him. "I just peered into the living room, and they're still sound asleep."

"Reseda, God bless you," John said, rising from his chair, a small eddy of laughter in his voice. "Well, I think that coffee is just about ready. May I help myself, Emily?"

"Go ahead."

"You were suggesting Valerian to Emily?" Reseda asked him.

"I was, I was. Doesn't this coffee smell heavenly? Ladies, may I pour? Reseda?"

"Thank you, John," Reseda said, "but I think I'll have tea."

"Of course you will," he murmured, "of course. You know, Emily, on the bright side, at least you're here in Bethel right now and not in West Chester. I don't know what sorts of friends or support group you had back there, but here you have a whole big family waiting to care for you and those two precious children of yours. Imagine: You had Reseda and Holly staying the night. You have Anise's magical cooking in your refrigerator. And you have people like my own lovely bride and Sage and Peyton at your disposal."

"And you, John," she said, taking the mug of coffee he was handing her. "Really, I'm so lucky to have you, too. You're such a gift."

He rolled his eyes. "Some folks would say I'm more of a curse. Wouldn't you agree, Reseda?" Her friend raised her eyebrows but otherwise didn't respond. "But, yes, I do try. We all try here in Bethel." He paused for a moment and then said with great earnestness, "It's a bit like all of you have come home to a big family, don't you think? It must feel a bit like coming home."

Garnet had seen greenhouses as large as this one, but they had all been commercial nurseries—not someone's personal greenhouse. There had been a nursery like this not too far from where they lived in

Pennsylvania, and two or three times she and Hallie had gone there with their mother, and Garnet recalled trying (and failing) to convince Mom to buy one of the stone gargoyles or garden trolls the place sold. But she had never been inside a greenhouse this large in someone's backyard—or one that had grow lights on stands above many of the tables of plants. It struck her as longer than any of the ones she had seen from the roads as they drove between the highway and their new home. It belonged to Sage Messner, the older woman she and her sister had met at Mr. and Mrs. Hardin's house a couple of nights ago. Saturday.

It was a little hard to believe that Saturday night was only a couple of nights ago. It was Tuesday morning, but in some ways Saturday night felt as far away as when her family had lived back in West Chester. Maybe it even felt as far away as before her dad's plane had crashed in the lake. She and Hallie hadn't been expected to go to school today, and now their mom was off meeting with doctors and bringing their dad home from the hospital, and Reseda had taken her sister and her here to Sage Messner's to see the greenhouse. Sage and Clary had been fussing over her and Hallie for over an hour, giving them lemonade with chlorophyll—the greenest beverage she had ever seen in her life, but it turned out to be pretty good—and chocolate brownies. Then Sage had shown them the guest bedrooms in the house, where she told them they could stay whenever they wanted. When she had shared the bedrooms with them, it was like when Mom and Dad had taken them last summer to Mount Vernon in Virginia, where George Washington had lived, and they had been shown his bedroom: Sage's enthusiasm was just about off-the-charts crazy as she went on and on about some amazing herbalist who had lived in the house before her. Garnet had half-expected the bedroom doorway to have a red velvet rope in front of it. Consequently, she had been a little relieved when Reseda had taken just her and her sister out here to the greenhouse, leaving Sage in the kitchen to make them yet another snack.

"And this is memoria," Reseda was saying, running the tips of her fingers gently along the purplish leaves of the plant. The memoria was about five inches high, the leaves the size of her thumb and roughly the shape of the spade on a playing card. There were seven of the plants side by side in small terra-cotta vases.

"Feel the leaves," she added, and so Garnet did and then Hallie followed.

"It feels like puppy fur," Hallie said, and Garnet thought this was the perfect description. Indeed, there was a light down on the leaves that felt like it should have been the coat on a cute little animal, not a plant. Garnet was wearing a small silver bracelet that resembled ivy around her wrist—Reseda had given it to her a few minutes ago—and Garnet noticed it once more when she gazed down at her fingertips against the memoria. She loved the bracelet as much as she had loved any jewelry she'd ever been given—even more, she realized, than the unicorn choker her parents had gotten her at Disney World just about two years ago now. It felt like a more adult piece of jewelry. Hallie had been given a bracelet, too, also silver, though the design on hers looked like Egyptian hieroglyphics. Garnet could tell that Hallie appreciated her gift as well.

"What do you do with it?" Garnet asked Reseda, referring to the memoria.

"It's a healing herb. Medicinal."

"What does it cure?" her sister wondered.

Reseda smiled at the two of them. She was wearing a suede duster, unbuttoned and open, that fell below her knees and blue jeans that clung to her legs. She really didn't need the coat because the greenhouse was heated and there were steamers hard at work in two of the corners. The glass there had filmed over with droplets of water. But it wasn't a very heavy jacket, and she looked elegant in it: Garnet liked the way it billowed around her like a sail as she walked. "Bad dreams," she said simply and then, after a moment, added, "And bad memories." Then she walked beside the long table and paused at another plant, beckoning for the twins to follow. "This one is despairium," she said, and for a second Garnet presumed the long tendrils were dead because they were as black as the moldering coal that sat in a dank corner of their basement. But apparently they weren't. "I don't want you to touch it," Reseda said. "But have you ever felt shrimp? The stems here feel just like cooked shrimp, except they leave a resin on your skin that is a bit like poison ivy. Only worse. It lasts considerably longer. That's why you shouldn't touch it with your bare hands."

"Then why does Mrs. Messner grow it?" Hallie asked.

"If you know how to harvest a pinch and steep it in tea—with a little honey and a little lemon—it can give a person a new perspective on life. It can cause a person to see things, well, differently. And some of us like to bake with it. Anise, for example, uses it."

"Anise is always baking us stuff."

"Is she now?"

"Uh-huh. She even labels the treats. Puts our names on them."

Reseda nodded, a little pensive. "She just arrived."

"You mean here at Mrs. Messner's?"

"That's right." Garnet decided Reseda must have amazing hearing, because she herself hadn't heard a car pull into the driveway.

"So, this greenhouse isn't just for Mrs. Messner?" Hallie asked.

Garnet was glad her sister had asked this. It was beginning to dawn on her, too, that this was a sort of communal nursery. She had a feeling that Mrs. Messner wasn't the only one who grew plants here.

"That's right," Reseda said. "Some of us have our own greenhouses, but not everyone. Holly, for instance, keeps her plants here. And none of us has a greenhouse quite this large. So, yes, this one is a sort of shared space. We all help tend the plants here. And you must call Mrs. Messner *Sage*. I know she'd prefer that." She brought the girls slowly up and down the long rows of tables, and occasionally Garnet recognized the name of an herb or a flower, but more often it was a plant that she had never heard of before. Some looked a little frightening, even when their names were rather comforting, such as the hoja santa: The leaves were the size of her face, and she imagined being smothered by one. Her favorite names, she decided? Elderberry. Fenugreek. False unicorn. One corner of the greenhouse had a series of raised dirt beds instead of tables, and the magic here, according to Reseda, was beneath the soil. Eventually someone would pull up many of the roots that mattered, but in some cases—such as the dangerously poisonous mandrake—only select, very experienced gardeners would be allowed to handle the harvest.

"Did the woman who lived in this house before Sage share the greenhouse, too?" Garnet asked.

"She did. And she actually bred some of these plants. Some she brought from other parts of the world, but others she created herself—like this rather potent despairium."

Just then the greenhouse door opened, and Sage entered with a plate of small tea sandwiches in her hands, and Anise and Clary beside her. Garnet decided she was right about Reseda's hearing: She had never heard Anise's pickup pull in or the truck doors slam shut. The sandwiches were made with watercress and chives and cream cheese, and some also had cucumber. The white bread was almost as thin as a cracker, and Garnet thought they were absolutely delicious.

"Is the watercress from this greenhouse?" Hallie asked, after Sage had listed for them the ingredients.

"It is, absolutely," Sage told her, and she surprised Garnet by putting the tray of sandwiches on one of the long tables with plants and sitting down on the dirt floor of the greenhouse. Anise and Clary, despite their ages, sat on the ground, too, and Clary patted the earth, signaling Hallie and her to join them. Garnet looked at her sister and saw that the girl was already sitting down, so she did as well.

"Reseda?" Sage asked, when the younger woman remained on her feet. "Going to join us for our . . . our picnic?"

"I'm fine," Reseda answered simply, but Garnet detected a slight sharpness to her tone. She noticed that Anise was staring intently at her, the woman's face curious and probing.

"What have you shown the girls so far?" Anise asked.

Reseda motioned vaguely at the long columns of tables behind her.

"The rosemary and the calandrinia?"

"No. That felt rather premature to me. Remember, all we discussed was showing the girls some plants. We did not discuss a naming ceremony."

"Not a ceremony. Just a . . ."

"A chance to eat finger sandwiches and learn our new nicknames," Sage chirped agreeably, cutting Anise off, clearly desirous of easing the tension that seemed to exist between the two women. "All right then, Anise, do you want to begin?"

The women who had sat down only a moment ago all rose up to their full heights, Clary rubbing the small of her back but still grinning expectantly. Her eyes sparkled, and she and Sage held out their hands, and Garnet realized that she and Hallie were each supposed to take one. And so they did, Hallie taking Clary's and Garnet grasping Sage's slightly gnarled but soft fingers. Then Anise led them down an aisle between the tables from one end of the long greenhouse to the other. Reseda followed, but Garnet sensed it was only grudgingly. Finally they stopped almost at the farthest wall of glass, and Anise motioned toward a pair of pots beneath grow lights at the edge of the table. One held an herb and one a flower with a great fan of red petals. "Do you recognize either of them?" she asked.

Garnet looked at her sister. Hallie shrugged, as unsure of what the plants were as she was. "No," Garnet answered simply.

"Well, we have a lot to learn then, don't we?" Anise said, and there was a waft of judgment in the remark. "This is rosemary. Smell it. Inhale the aroma. Lovely, isn't it? It looks like a little evergreen. And this is calandrinia. Feel the dirt it's in: sand, peat moss, and loam. And the flower—this one in particular—has a coloring that reminds me a little of your hair, Garnet. Clary here was the first person in this area to grow it. She brought the seeds back from Chile."

Anise used her thumbs to push her own untamed hair back behind her ears. "Hallie," she said, bending over with her hands on her knees so she was face-to-face with the girl, "I appreciate the idea that you are named for your grandmother. It was such a lovely gesture on your mother and father's part. I like genealogical legacies. And Garnet, I love the idea that you are named for that magnificent hair of yours. That was so creative of your parents and, at the time, so perfect."

Garnet nodded and waited for more, well aware that this was a pre-amble to . . . something.

"But," Anise went on, "when we're together, I think we would all like to call you Cali—short for calandrinia—instead of Garnet. You are, like this flower, a little mysterious, and you clearly have a depth that is both grand and uncommon. And Hallie, how would you like to be Rosemary? You are fragrant and proud and make the world a little more savory."

"But why?" Hallie asked. "Why these new names?"

"See what I mean? Already you are living up to the name. And the answer is simple: They're terms of endearment. Of affection. That's all. Many of us here in Bethel have taken names of interesting herbs and remarkable plants. It shows we're . . . friends. You may have noticed. And we want you two girls to be our friends."

Garnet didn't mind having a nickname, though a part of her wished that she had been given Rosemary and her sister Cali. She had to hope it would grow on her. And it sounded like only her mom's women friends were going to be using it anyway. She'd still be Garnet at school. Nevertheless, she wondered what Mom would think of this. Would her feelings be hurt? Would she feel it was some sort of intrusion into the family? Almost as if Reseda could read her mind, the woman knelt before her and said, "In time, your mother will be very happy with your names. Your father, too. And here is something that might make you feel a little more comfortable with this change. When your mother is with us, she is going to be called Verbena. Verbena is all about courage and friendship. Loyalty. It suits your mother." She brushed a strand of her own lustrous hair off her forehead.

"Thank you, Reseda," Anise said, but her voice was strangely curt. "I wasn't planning on going into that much detail today."

"And I wasn't anticipating a naming ceremony."

"Not a ceremony—just a preview. But I can't tell you how much it pleases me that even around you I can be a little unpredictable," she said. Then she reached for the leather shoulder bag that she had placed on the ground where they had been sitting and announced, "Girls, I have a present for each of you."

"More jewelry?" Hallie asked.

Anise glanced at their wrists, noticing the bracelets for the first time.

"I can be unpredictable, too," Reseda said, a wisp of a smile on her face.

But Anise only nodded agreeably and reached into the bag. "Do you two like to read?" she asked, and Garnet knew instantly that, instead of presents, they were both about to get homework.

Chapter Eleven

You contemplate all the hours you sat attentive and alert on the flight deck, and how you never grew less enamored of the niveous white magnificence of clouds as you gazed down at them from thirty or thirty-five thousand feet. Their exquisite polar flatness: fields of pillowy snow that stretched to the horizon. As the shadow of your plane would pass over them, you would imagine you were gazing down on an arctic, alabaster plain, and in your mind you could see yourself crossing them alone in a hooded parka and boots. (You wonder now: Why were you always a solitary man in this daydream?) If you were flying at the right time of the day and the sun was in the right spot, the vista would be reduced to a splendid bicolor world: albino white and amethyst blue.

And then there was that moment when you would skim across the surface of the great woolpack before starting to descend underneath it, and your plane would feel more like a submarine than a jet. It was like going underwater—deep underwater—right down to the darkness that abruptly would enfold the aircraft once you were inside the clouds. One minute the sky would be blue and the flight deck bright, and the next the world outside would be gray soup and the flight deck dim.

You know the technical names for clouds as well as a meteorologist, just as you know the federal aviation definitions for ice: Glaze. Intercycle. Known or observed. Mixed. Residual. Runback. Rime. You have always loved the alliteration that marks those last three, the poetry of the memorized cadence. And you can do the same thing with clouds.

You know the names of the ones that grow in the low elevations and the ones that exist in much higher skies. Even now, sitting in the backseat of the Volvo as Emily and John Hardin drive you home from the hospital, you can see perfectly in your mind the leaden sheets of gray stratus as the nose of your plane would start to nudge through them; the fleece of the cumulus, bright and cheerful when lit by the sun, dark and shadowy when not; the ominous towers and anvil plumes of the cumulonimbus you would steer your plane around when the traffic and the tower permitted. You close your eyes and see once again the gauzy layers of cirrus, their wisps strangely erotic, or their cousins, the rippling cirrocumulus. (Some people call these clouds a mackerel sky, but a flight instructor you liked very much called it a lake sky because it reminded him of the days he would spend with his own father fishing.) You see the rain on the flight deck windows and feel the bump as you break the plane of a layer of dark nimbostratus.

And now you open your eyes and the clouds disappear and you stare at the back of John Hardin's head. It is an indication of the toll your breakdown is having on Emily that she needed cavalry help to bring you home from the hospital. It is a sign of how ill they think you are that they have squirreled you into the backseat. John has pulled the passenger seat so far forward that his knees are pressed against the glove compartment, though you have told him over and over you are fine. You have been telling people precisely this all morning long. *I am fine. Fine. Just fine.*

You still have in your mouth the taste of the oatmeal cookies that John Hardin handed you when you first climbed into the backseat. Immediately you ate two. Anise had baked them. Of course. You are aware of raisins and cinnamon and a bitter spice you don't recognize. The truth is, you were never an especially creative cook, and you don't recognize very many spices and seasonings.

There is midday sun coming in through the car window, and you stare up into it. Into a cloudless sky. Apparently a psychiatrist—not your psychiatrist, not Michael Richmond—is going to come visit you tomorrow afternoon. Examine you. At your house. Imagine, a psychiatrist making house calls. You have no idea what to make of that, none at all.

But she's a friend of John's and, like all of John's friends, seems to want to help you. To help you and Emily and your girls.

You run your tongue between your teeth and your gums. You decide that you don't honestly understand the appeal of Anise's cooking. She seems to be a hit-and-miss baker. Of course, it may simply be that you will never be interested in vegan cooking and vegan desserts, and apparently everything the woman cooks is vegan. Or, maybe, she really isn't especially talented in the kitchen. Maybe people abide her cuisine simply because they like her. Even those oatmeal cookies you just polished off have left a sour, vinegary aftertaste that seems to smother the cinnamon.

"Chip?"

You face forward and see that John is speaking to you.

"The hospital pharmacy gave us a couple pills for pain. You may not need them, but we have them."

Us. We. "Thank you."

"How are you feeling?"

"I am fine." *Fine. Just fine.*

"Well, if you need something more, Clary gave me a tincture that I can assure you works wonders."

"A tincture."

"Her own little potion. Skullcap and willow bark. I can't tell you how much it has helped me when my knees get cranky after a day skiing or hiking." He reaches into his front blazer pocket and removes a small brown bottle the length of a finger. It has an eyedropper for a lid.

"Thank you."

Now it seems to be Emily's turn: "Chip?"

"Yes, sweetheart?"

"Is there anything special you would like from the grocery store? We can stop before heading up the hill."

"No, I'm good." *I am fine.*

"Okay."

You want to ask about the twins. You want to ask Emily what they believe happened last night and what they think of you now, but you won't with John Hardin present. You can't. You will wait until you and your wife are alone. But they are smart girls. They know something has happened. Something has happened to you. You have—choose an expression—gone off the rails. Left the reservation. Gone broken arrow.

But do they know that, for whatever the reason, you can't be trusted?

For the briefest of moments you recall the will—the monumental determination—it took to press the knife into your abdomen, and the agony that finally forced you to stop. You wince, but neither John nor Emily notices.

You didn't see Ethan or Ashley or Sandra last night in the hospital. You were alone with the distant stars that made up your room. But you have a feeling they will be waiting for you tonight.

Chip went upstairs to shower, and John climbed from the station wagon into his immaculate green sedan and drove back to their office in Littleton. The girls were with Reseda somewhere. And so Emily found herself alone in the kitchen, staring out the window over the sink at the greenhouse and, beyond it, at the meadow and the edge of the woods. She closed her eyes and fought back the tears. She tried to push from her mind her memories of last night or, even more recently, the image of her husband in the rearview mirror of the car that morning, chewing cookies without evident pleasure: He was eating them, it seemed, only because John had offered them. He insisted he was fine, but he wasn't. The Chip Linton she lived with now was a frightening doppelgänger for her husband. The fellow was a mere husk of the man she had married. It wasn't merely that this new catatonia was different from the walking somnambulance that had marked the months after the crash: This one was both the result of whatever tranquilizers he'd been given last night at the hospital and the reality that the self-loathing he'd experienced after the failed ditching of Flight 1611 paled compared to the self-hatred he was experiencing now. Whatever had happened to him last night—whatever he had done—had left him staggered: He'd slouched as they walked to the car in the hospital parking lot this morning, unshaven and his hair badly combed, like one of the murmuring homeless men Emily had seen on the streets of Philadelphia. She recalled something he had said to her last night in the emergency room: It was something nonsensical about the pit of despair that awaited him, and how it would be a relief to be walled up inside it.

It all left her wondering: What had been happening to him since they arrived here in the White Mountains? What had she been missing over the last month and a half? What had been occurring at the house while she'd been at work and the girls had been at school? She felt she had been a derelict wife, and she considered if this was, in some way, her fault. Had she been inattentive? So it seemed. Michael Richmond had been unable to reassure her that it was safe to leave Chip home alone. She wasn't certain it was even safe to leave him alone with the girls. It wasn't that he might harm them—though the idea had now entered her mind, and she knew as a mother it was going to lodge there—it was that he might harm himself when they were present.

She remembered something John had said to her that morning, before they picked up her husband. "This will all seem less surreal as the days pass," the older lawyer had told her. "I mean that, Emily. Everything's different now, nothing will ever be the same. But eventually you'll find a new normalcy. We all do."

She thought about this. She saw her experience as unique—horrific and peculiar to herself. But he'd seemed to be viewing it as a rite of passage. Unpredictable and certainly unanticipated, but in some way universal. "You make it sound like you went through something like this," she had said, staring straight ahead at the entry ramp to the interstate and the pine trees now clean of snow.

"No, of course not."

"That's what I thought."

"But my mother used to talk about passages and, once in a while, about ordeals. We all have them; we are all shaped by them. She thought the key was to find the healing in the hurt. Someone must have told you that by now."

"No. Right now I am far more desirous of finding the healing in an orange prescription vial."

"I imagine Clary or Anise has something much better for you: more effective and safer," he'd said, smiling, his eyes a little knowing and wide.

She listened to the water running in the shower above her and turned her face toward the spring sun. She breathed in deeply through her nose, the air whistling ever so slightly, and tried to focus on nothing but the warmth on her face.

Hallie hadn't planned on going to the basement. She hadn't even planned on getting out of bed. But she awoke in the night and thought she heard noises downstairs in the kitchen and presumed that her parents were sitting at the table and talking. She knew her mom was really worried about Dad. Then she decided that Garnet must be down there, too; it was why, in the hazy logic of someone awoken from a deep sleep, she hadn't peeked into Garnet's room before heading downstairs. But the kitchen was completely empty. The overhead lights were on, but probably because her mom had left them on by mistake before going upstairs to bed herself. The digital clock on the stove read 12:15.

She realized she was a little scared to be downstairs alone at night and was about to scamper back up the two flights of stairs to her own bed when, for the briefest of seconds, she heard a voice again—a single voice this time—and understood it was coming from the basement. The door was ajar, and a light was on down there as well. And so she stood for a long moment at the top of the stairs, listening carefully, aware because of the cold drifting up from the cellar that she hadn't bothered to put on her slippers. Now she regretted that: Her toes were cold. She ran her fingers over her bracelet, which she had begun to view as a good-luck charm. That afternoon Anise had said she would like her second present even more, but the truth was that she loved this bracelet much better. The second gift was a very old book about plants and what Anise called natural medicine. According to Anise, it had belonged to another herbalist a long time ago. Then Anise had given her sister an even fatter book titled *The Complete Book of Divination and Mediation with Plants and Herbs*—again, apparently, a favorite of an herbalist who had passed away.

Finally, when Hallie was just about to shut the basement door and race upstairs, she heard someone mumbling and she was sure it was her sister.

"Garnet?" she called into the basement. "Is that you?"

But no one responded, and so she tiptoed onto the top step, the wood coarse against her bare feet, and peered underneath the banister. Sure enough, there was Garnet, all alone, standing in the shadows before the remnants of the wooden door that their father had destroyed last week. She was ankle deep in the coal and staring into the black maw of the tiny room that their father had found behind that door.

"Garnet," she said again, her voice reduced by incredulity to a stage whisper. "What are you doing down there?"

The girl looked up at her, blinked, and then rubbed at her eyes. She looked down at her feet and seemed to realize for the first time the grotesque mess in which she was standing. She jumped away from it, landing in the moist dirt of the floor, which was a marginal improvement at best. Hallie understood that her sister had just—as one of their teachers back in West Chester once put it, infuriating their mom—zoned out. She had gone into one of her trances and lost herself somewhere inside her head. Hallie feared that it might have been a full seizure, and the fact that she was having a second one so close on the heels of another alarmed her. Garnet had never before had two in a week. Moreover, until the other night, it had been a long while since she had had even one.

"Come upstairs," Hallie said. "Get out of there and come back to bed!" she added, though she guessed that first her sister would have to run her feet under some hot water in the tub.

Instead the girl shook her head and said, "No. You have to see this first. You have to see what I found." Then she raised her arm and pointed into that little room.

"You went in there?" Hallie asked.

"I think so. I . . . I don't know."

The last thing Hallie wanted to do was go down those stairs: It wasn't merely the cold and the dirt and the coal on the ground there. It was the reality that she was scared. Her sister had always been able to freak her out; the idea that it was inadvertent didn't make the sensation any less real. Still, it was clear that Garnet was not going to come upstairs until she went downstairs, and so Hallie held on to the banister and descended the steps, wondering as she went if instead she should have gone upstairs and awakened their mother. But, she decided, she didn't want to leave her sister alone here; she wanted to retrieve her twin (and here she was surprised when she heard in her head the name Cali instead of Garnet) and get the two of them back into their beds.

"This floor is gross," she grumbled. "It's bad enough with shoes on. Have you gone crazy coming down here barefoot?" Her feet made soft squishing sounds as she navigated her way over to the coal.

"You're barefoot, too," Garnet reminded her.

"Duh. But only because I was in bed when I came to look for you." She exhaled in exasperation.

"Look," said her sister. "See it? I think I dug it up." Her right hand was indeed brown with dirt, as were the knees of her pajamas.

Hallie peered in, but she didn't see anything at first, just more dirt inside the cubicle and the wooden framing darkened by earth and coal. "What do you mean you dug it up? Dug what up?"

"That," said Garnet simply, and the word stuck a tiny bit in her throat.

And so Hallie squinted, reflexively rubbing at her new bracelet, and she leaned in more toward the doorway. Then, a little maddened, she decided that her feet were already a mess so what did it matter if they got even dirtier, and she plowed ahead, crossing the coal and walking right up to the remnants of the hacked door. There she held on to one of the dangling boards, realizing only after she had grabbed it that she was lucky she hadn't gotten a splinter, and gazed into the dark. And there it was, the object that Garnet in one of her unpredictable though characteristic stupors had dug up. For a second Hallie stared at it, convinced this was some strange Halloween prank, because it couldn't possibly be real. But it was. Had to be. There on a pile of dirt, beside a hole deep enough to bury a small dog, if necessary, was the unmistakable top of a human skull: the coral-colored Wiffle ball of the cranium, the deep sockets where once there had been eyes, and the tiny beak that she knew was the only part of a nose made of bone. There didn't seem to be a jaw, and, when she turned back to Garnet, she understood why: There in her sister's left hand was that piece of the skull, and it was evident that she had used it like a trowel to scoop out the dirt.

"Garnet," she whispered, "how?" She didn't know what she meant by the word, she wasn't precisely sure what she was asking. But then the presence of the skull and the night and the idea that a body had been buried in their house all came crashing down upon her and she batted the jawbone out of her sister's hand as if it were some sort of violent animal and dragged the girl as fast as she could up the stairs, screaming all the way for their mother.

The state trooper who arrived in the middle of the night was a slim young woman with short dark hair and an aquiline nose. Her badge said c. PAYNE. She knew all about Chip Linton, and not merely that he was *that* pilot. Emily had the distinct sense that she was aware that he had spent the night before at the hospital. The trooper acted surprised when Emily told her, but she wasn't much of a thespian.

"Tomorrow morning the state will send a team from Concord," she said matter-of-factly, referring to the State Police's Major Crime Unit. Her voice was pleasant but laconic: Emily recognized a trace of a Yankee drawl. The trooper was leaning against the kitchen counter, explaining to Chip and her what was next, while the girls sat wrapped in a blanket on the living room couch. It was evident that they weren't going to let their parents out of their sight, and Emily presumed that the two of them would be sleeping tonight with Chip and her in the queen-size bed in the master bedroom.

"The mobile crime lab will search for any remaining bones and probably nose around the basement—especially behind that door—for anything that might have been a murder weapon. Even a big rock," she said.

"This house seems to be filled with them," Emily observed.

The trooper smiled at the small, dark joke and said, "I guess you mean murder weapons and not big rocks."

"Yes."

"You want to be more specific?"

Emily looked at Chip to see if he wanted to answer, but he remained silent. And so she described the crowbar, the knife, and the ax.

"And you really found them hidden around the house?" the trooper asked.

"We did."

"Well, be sure to give them to the investigators tomorrow. And I know you've probably handled them a bunch, but try not to handle them anymore. Okay?"

"No problem there."

"That Tansy Dunmore was quite a piece of work."

"That's what I hear," Emily agreed.

The trooper turned to Chip. "So, you took down that door," she said.

"I did."

"Why?"

He shrugged and smiled. "Same reason men climb mountains, I guess. Because it was there."

"And you never found any bones in the dirt on the other side?"

"I did not."

"Okay." Then she peered through the doorway into the living room at the twins. "Really, there's nothing more to be scared of," she told the girls. "It's just a skull. We all have one. You're not in any danger."

Her daughters were staring at the woman, their faces a little blank. Emily couldn't imagine what they were thinking. "Whose body was buried down there?" she asked, lowering her voice, though she feared that her girls could still hear her. "Do you have any idea at all?"

"My guess? And it's just a guess from growing up around here. But

I'd say it was Sawyer Dunmore. We'll see if there are any open homicides or missing persons going back a long while. But my money would be on Sawyer. He killed himself years and years ago, and became the sort of ghost story we'd all tell each other at sleepover parties and Girl Scout campouts."

"You were a Girl Scout?" Emily asked.

The trooper grinned a little sheepishly. "I guess I've always liked uniforms."

"I was, too."

"There you go," she said. "You probably had your share of ghost stories founded on nothing."

"Well," Emily said, "this was something."

"Yes and no. I mean, it's real and it's scary. But it's all explicable. Everything you're going through is explicable and, soon enough, will be behind you."

"Tell me more about 'explicable.' I want my daughters to get a few hours of sleep tonight. I want to get a few hours of sleep tonight."

"Sawyer's parents were, I gather, a little . . . off. Especially his mother. And when Sawyer killed himself, she really lost it. At least that's what people say. I mean, it must be awful to lose a child like that. Just awful. I know I would have been willing to cut her a bunch of slack. Know what I mean?"

Emily thought about the weapons she had found in the house. She thought about the paranoia the woman had been enduring at the end of her life. "Go on," she said.

"We all used to try and scare each other by saying that Sawyer wasn't really buried in the cemetery. We used to go on and on with stories straight out of *Psycho*. You know the movie, right?"

Emily nodded. "Absolutely."

"We'd tell ourselves that Tansy and Parnell had kept their son's body around the house. They'd talk to it, dress it up. But his actual death was before my time, and we didn't really believe it. Not a word. After all, his twin brother had grown up in that house, too, and when I was a kid he was an adult living not all that far from here. St. Johnsbury, I think."

"Yes," Emily said. "It is St. Johnsbury."

"Anyway, it seems that maybe they really did bury their boy right downstairs. Built a little vault. But the Major Crime Unit and the medical examiner will look at what we have here. They'll make sure the skull and whatever bones are down there really are Sawyer Dunmore's. Dental records, most likely. If that doesn't work, then DNA. As you said, the brother still lives in St. Johnsbury. I just guess, Mr. Linton, you hacked your way into a personal crypt."

"But wouldn't Hewitt Dunmore have told us there was a body buried in the basement of the house?" Emily asked. "Wouldn't he want the grave respected?"

"I don't know. I'm not even sure it's legal. And, somehow, I don't think leaving a corpse in the cellar does a whole lot for a property's resale value," the trooper said, and she actually chuckled just the tiniest bit as she started walking toward the front hallway. She paused for a moment and waved at the girls. "You'll be okay," she told them, and she sounded a bit like an older sister. "You'll be just fine."

As they were saying good-bye, the porch light caught the badge with the woman's name, and it sparkled. "Tell me," Emily said, "What does the *C* stand for?"

The trooper looked her straight in the eye and said—just a hint of a smile on her lips—"Celandine. It's an herb." Then she turned and marched down the slate walkway to her cruiser.

Chapter Twelve

Again today the girls are not going to school. Not after last night. But you're not worried, they're smart. They'll catch up. Instead Emily has taken them shopping in Hanover and West Lebanon for the day. Anything to get them out of the house. She didn't want them here when the state troopers from the Major Crime Unit appeared, and she didn't want them present when this new psychiatrist makes her house call.

The Major Crime Unit came first, soon after the girls left, and you found that you rather enjoyed giving the four investigators in their crisp uniforms a tour. The men were roughly your age, and you took pleasure in showing them the door in the basement you destroyed and that strange back stairway between the kitchen and the second floor. You shared with them your work spackling and sanding and painting, and you showed them the new wallpaper you have started to drape upon the walls. You moved carefully because of your stomach, but it was only when you twisted your torso in that back stairway that you felt a real spike of pain—and even that was rather minor compared to the ago-nies you experience when Ethan or Ashley or Sandra is present. For a time you sat on the basement steps and watched as they dug and sifted through the dirt in the chamber. You were there when they exhumed more of the skeleton and when they found the small brown medicine bottle—uncorked, empty, and perhaps three inches long. It's just like the one with the homemade pain reliever John gave you. They took that old bottle with them, as well as the bones they unearthed and what they presumed were remnants of clothing. They placed in Ziploc bags the skull and the jawbone that Garnet dug up last night. They labeled and brought to their van the crowbar and the ax that Tansy Dunmore left for you. But they did not leave with either the bones you found or Tansy's knife. They did not know to ask about those other bones, and you did not volunteer the information that they existed and were stored at that moment in your bedroom armoire. And the knife? It must have gotten lost when you were brought to the emergency room. At least that's what you told them. The last time you saw the knife was here in the kitchen, you explained. You worked with the troopers to search the kitchen and your car and the basement. You suggested that, perhaps, it had wound up in Emily's station wagon, because that was the car your wife had driven when she followed the ambulance to the emergency room. You told the troopers you would be sure to look there when she and the twins returned later that day. And then they left, the van rumbling down your driveway, and they were out of your life—at least for the moment. You waved to them casually from the porch, the wind seeming to slice through the gray sweatshirt with your airline's logo on the chest.

Now, before going back inside, you stroll to the greenhouse, where you gather up three of Hallie and Garnet's American Girl dolls. Your own children won't be back for hours, and Ashley might enjoy them. The dolls have been out there since the night Molly Francoeur was over for a playdate. Sadly, Molly won't be back. That is painfully clear. A lost opportunity. Despite the pain that comes with grasping the dolls like bags of groceries—you can feel the pressure against your stitches—you carry them in precisely this fashion back into the house. No sooner have you pulled open the screen door than your skull starts to throb and you feel that daggerlike pain in your lower back, and you know from experience that, at the very least, Ethan and Ashley have returned. Perhaps Sandra, too.

And, sure enough, there is Ashley in the den, her face melancholy, sitting before the woodstove. Already a small puddle is forming beneath her on the brick hearth. She looks up at you when you walk into the room, and instantly she notices the dolls in your arms.

"Here," you tell her, and you place them on the floor before her, watching as the white bonnet on one of the dolls soaks up the lake water like a sponge. "I thought it might be fun for you to have some more dolls. My girls wouldn't mind."

She smiles, and it dawns on you that you have never before seen her smile.

"Your breathers," she says.

You move her Dora the Explorer backpack so you can sit beside her. "Yes. My breathers." And then, just the way you did with Hallie and Garnet before Flight 1611 crashed into Lake Champlain, you suggest a story line for the dolls, the barest outline of a tale about three sisters—triplets—who all fall in love with the same prince. Then you step back from your role as creator and allow Ashley to add the details that will bring the story to life.

You look up from Ashley and the dolls when the doorbell rings. Apparently, you had been so engrossed in the game that you hadn't heard the vehicle as it bumped along the gravel driveway. When you turn back to the child, planning to tell her that you'll be gone just a moment, she has vanished. And so you nod to yourself and climb to your feet. You pass through the kitchen, peering once down the stairs to the basement as you cross the room to the entry hallway, and then open the front door. The woman there introduces herself as Valerian Wainscott, the psychiatrist John Hardin wants you to meet.

You tell her you are sorry for the muddy footprints that you and the troopers from the Major Crime Unit have left in the hallway and the kitchen, but she waves off any apology. The woman is roughly Emily's age, slight, with short blond hair in natural ringlets and dark eyes that seem to be laughing. She smiles easily as she pulls off her Windbreaker and motions toward the kitchen table.

"Shall we talk here?" she asks.

You consider the other possibilities, including the living room with the wet American Girl dolls. You would love to show her those. But she

would presume they are damp for any one of a variety of reasons, none
of which begin and end with the water from Lake Champlain and a dead
girl named Ashley.

"Here is good," you agree, and you offer her coffee. Which she
declines. She tells you she is tea drinker, though she doesn't want a
cup right now, thank you very much, and you find yourself smiling. Of
course she drinks tea. Her name is Valerian. And valerian is a plant or a
flower or an herb of some kind. Valerian root. A sedative, maybe. A muscle relaxant. You wonder how much you should trust her, whether your
misgivings are grounded in anything tangible. But then you ask yourself
whether tangibility really matters. Is Ashley Stearns tangible? Or Ethan?
No, not at all. But their pain is as real as yours. Ethan's anger (and grief)
is as profound as any father's.

Valerian slides onto the deacon's bench, and you sit in one of the
ladder-back chairs.

Despite the reality that Valerian has come to see you for the businesslike purpose of trying to assess your mental health—to offer your
wife a second opinion—she has brought with her four chocolate cupcakes. She unveiled them from inside the large shoulder bag that seems
to double as both her pocketbook and her attaché case. Your regular psychiatrist here in New Hampshire, Michael Richmond, only offers you
coffee and water when you see him. Same with the therapist you saw
back in Pennsylvania.

"I was baking for my daughter's class," Valerian is saying. "Today's
her seventh birthday, and so I brought the class cupcakes. Still, I think I
went a little cupcake crazy. I had extras. But how is it possible to make
cupcakes from a box and wind up with extras? I actually needed to find
an extra cupcake tin. That's what I mean by cupcake crazy."

Given the reason why the two of you are meeting, you have the
sense that she wanted to wink when she said *cupcake crazy*. But she
restrained herself. Instead she sighs. "Please, have one. You must. I'm
starving, and there is nothing more pathetic than eating cupcakes alone.
Now *that* is sad."

"Okay. I never had lunch."

"God, me, too," she says. "What's that bumper sticker? 'Life is short. Eat dessert first.'" And then she takes one of the cupcakes and peels off the paper and takes a very healthy bite for a woman who otherwise seems so petite. She licks a bit of chocolate icing off the tip of her index finger. Her nail polish is the red of a maple leaf in early October.

You reach for the one nearest you and take a bite, too. It's delicious, much tastier than most of Anise's confections.

"Really, thank you for letting me dive into one," she says. "I didn't plan on attacking the cupcakes like this, but I realized when I got here that I was completely, totally famished. And let's face it: Buttercream frosting is irresistible—if I say so myself."

Cupcake crazy. Attacking the cupcakes like this. There is something almost taunting about her terminology. As if she knows what you have been asked to do by the dead. But then again, perhaps you are reading more into her remarks than really is there. Maybe she is merely linguistically clumsy. Isn't it possible you are hearing things in this conversation that she honestly hadn't meant as gibes? You recall Reseda's offhand remark about the geese when you were in her office last week. The truth is, Valerian really did attack that cupcake just now. She certainly seemed ravenous.

"I wish I had brought some of the ones I decorated for the kids. Sprinkles and jimmies and faces made out of M&M's. Trust me: Those bad boys were seriously tricked out."

"I'll bet they were. I've seen my share of cupcakes at elementary school birthday parties."

"With twins? I'll bet you have."

The two of you then finish your cupcakes in a strangely companionable silence. You recall that this woman works a few days a week at the state psychiatric hospital. She probably has lots of experience with patients who don't say very much. "So," she says finally, "shall we get down to business?"

"Why not?"

"Indeed, why not? Do you understand why I'm here, Chip?"

"I do."

"Good. That's a start." She wipes her hands on a paper napkin and daubs at her lips. Her demeanor visibly changes as she pulls a pad and a clipboard and a fountain pen from that bag.

"I don't see a lot of people using fountain pens these days."

"That's because you've spent so much of your time in the air. You want to see a mess? Bring one of these on a plane. You have not seen a mess until you've seen a fountain pen explode at ten thousand feet."

"Probably not," you tell her, marveling at the way she can make everything sound vaguely disturbing. Explode. Mess. Ten thousand feet. Some people are capable of making innocuous sentences sound sexual—they can twist everything into a double entendre. Valerian seems to have a similar, perhaps inadvertent, talent when it comes to breathing life into your own particular subconscious fiends.

She motions with both hands at the room in which you are sitting and out the window at the carriage barn and the greenhouse and the sloping meadows beyond it, and continues, "Okay, then. How are you doing here? How are your neighbors? They treating you well? Tell me honestly."

"They are. Honestly." You wonder: Did your repeating the word *honestly* sound like you were being flip? And if it did, should you care? You wonder why this woman's opinion should matter more than Dr. Richmond's. Again, you experience a wave of misgiving. What do these women whose names belong in a garden want from you? Do they want anything, anything at all? But Valerian simply nods. She doesn't seem to find your response in any way impolite. She simply asks whom you have met and where, and what sorts of plans you have for the house. She asks, parent to parent, what you think of the school system here in this secluded corner of the White Mountains, since of course she has a girl only three grades behind Hallie and Garnet. Finally she gets around to the issue that matters most to Emily—the reason Valerian is here. She glances ever so slightly at your stomach, barely moving her head. It's all done with her eyes.

"Tell me about the other night," she asks.

"Well, without wanting to be glib, there are at least two 'other nights' that didn't end well. There was the night when the girls had a friend over for dinner and a playdate and I wound up in the hospital. And then there was last night, when Garnet found a human skull and jawbone in the basement. Which?"

"Let's start with the night of the playdate. What do you recall of your accident?"

You think about this. She said *accident* without a trace of sarcasm. Good for her. And so you tell her, as you have told others, about having Molly over for dinner. How you and Emily asked Molly a lot of questions about what she liked about the school and what she didn't. She seemed like a good kid. A nice kid. Then you pause, recalling where everyone sat around the table in the dining room. There once again is Molly's face, her elbow on the table and a fork balanced on the ends of her fingers. Behind her, on the wall, is one of those menacing sunflowers.

"I'm sure she is a good kid," Valerian agrees, and the sound of her voice brings you back. "Go on."

And so you do. "I felt we were running out of hot water after we ate," you hear yourself saying, "which didn't make any sense. One extra set of dishes? Oh, please. Besides, we were just putting the plates in the dishwasher."

"What did you have for dinner?"

"It was all very easy. Mexican food. Rice. Beans."

"Where were the girls?"

"By then they were out in the greenhouse. Hallie and Garnet view it as their playhouse."

"A waste," she says, and you can't decide if she is kidding.

"They've had their dolls out there ever since we arrived."

"Well, they'll outgrow that soon enough," she adds, as if she is trying to reassure you. "So, you and your wife were washing the dishes in the kitchen."

"Yes. And the water felt lukewarm to me," you explain, and then you tell her about the pilot light and going downstairs with the knife in your hands, and how you must have fallen down the wooden steps. You add that everything after that is now a bit of a fog. You shrug, hoping the motion does not appear theatrical.

"Did you hear Emily calling for you?"

"Not for a long while. Emily thinks that maybe I knocked my head and was unconscious for a few minutes. Do you think that's possible?"

"Sure."

"Anyway, when I did hear her, I started back up the stairs, and the next thing I know, I'm in the kitchen and I'm covered in blood."

"With the knife inside you."

"Yes."

"You never reached the pilot light."

"I don't believe so."

"But you didn't relight it."

"I don't think I did."

"So it probably wasn't out," she says. She seems to be thinking about this, but in reality you understand she is watching you. She is trying to decide if you're lying. You realize at some point that your shoulders have sagged and you are hunched over with your hands in your lap. Once, a long time ago it seems, you had exceptional posture. You take a breath and sit up straight in your chair, inadvertently pulling at the stitches.

"What shoes were you wearing?" she asks.

"Slippers. Suede moccasins."

"You're certain?"

"I am. I always wear those slippers when I'm in for the night in the winter."

"I like slippers," she says, writing. You look down at her boots. Leather, small, solid heels. Her skirt is made of denim and falls just about to her knees. Her panty hose—no, these are tights—are black. "I'm just curious, did you ever wear slippers in the cockpit?"

"It's a flight deck. We call it a flight deck."

"Not a cockpit?"

"No."

"Okay. I won't ask why."

"You can."

"No, I'm good."

"Why would you think we wore slippers while on the flight deck?"

"Well, not when you were actually flying the airplane. But once when I was flying from Philadelphia to Rome, the seat beside me was empty and the captain or the copilot came out and put on a pair of those eyeshades and slippers they give you when you fly and took a nap."

"You were flying first class."

"Business. Anyway, I can see you doing that."

"No, you can't. I never flew overseas. I flew regional jets."

"The small ones?"

"Yes. The small ones." Somehow, even this exchange has left you unsettled. It's as if you were a failure because you never flew a jet bigger than a CRJ. Did she do this on purpose, too? Again, your mind recalls Reseda and her remark about geese; again, it circles back to the idea that you are being oversensitive.

"Can we talk about 1611?"

"Yes." And you patiently answer the sorts of questions you have answered for other therapists (in two states), as well as investigators and lawyers and the FAA and the pilots' union. Finally Valerian asks you if you blame yourself for the deaths of the thirty-nine people on the plane.

"I blame the geese," you answer simply. "I blame the ferryboat captain who turned his boat too hard too quickly and created that wave. And, yes, I do blame myself."

"But no one else does . . ."

"Blames me."

"Right. The crash wasn't pilot error. What Sully Sullenberger did was a miracle. You know there isn't a soul in this world who thinks it's your fault. You know that, don't you?"

In this world. You try to decide what that means, because certainly Ethan Stearns views the crash as your fault. So did the families of some of the passengers who died who came to the hearings. You saw it in their faces. *Why couldn't you do what Sully Sullenberger did?* they seemed to be asking. And you can feel Ethan's presence right now, right here in the kitchen, in the way the top of your head is starting to throb. And although you try to restrain yourself, you can't help but turn around in your seat—and there he is. He is in the doorway to the dining room, framed by those ghoulish sunflowers, and he is glaring at you. Shaking his head in disgust. And this only makes the pain in your skull worsen, and you fear that while this doctor is sitting across from you it might become the searing, white-light agony you have experienced around Ethan in the past.

She deserves friends. Do what it takes.

"Chip?"

You rub your eyes. You turn around. "I'm sorry," you tell Valerian, wondering how it is that only you know Ethan is here with you. Valerian seems to be staring right at him.

"You looked a little peaked there," she says. "A midafternoon sugar low?"

"I guess. My head hurts."

She sighs. "Feverfew and cayenne," she tells you. "I have just the tincture. Sadly, I have just the tincture at home. In the meantime, have another cupcake. You'll feel so much better. I promise." And she hands you another of those remarkable confections.

Chapter Thirteen

"You disappear, except for your name," explains Sandra Durant. "I'm just a name on a passenger manifest. In the newspaper. On a crawl on the cable news." She motions with her finger—and you notice the polish is salmon, every bit as vibrant as Valerian's but perhaps more girlish and childlike—toward Ashley, who is sitting rather primly on the couch. "She used to love to eat canned peaches in heavy syrup. She tells me she mastered the can opener in first grade and would snack on them after school and on weekends. Now no one will ever know that. Soon, no one but her mother will recall that she could make an origami swan—and eventually her mom will forget that detail, too. She'll forget what it was like watching Ashley learn to ride her bicycle. And some new technology will replace the video that her father made of her doing cannonballs into a swimming pool one afternoon, and no one will duplicate the disk onto whatever comes next. And so that splash and the girl's laugh will be gone, too. Gone forever. Eventually, all that will remain is her name."

You ask, "And you?"

"And me? Orange marmalade. I loved it."

"There's more."

"Of course there is."

"Tell me one more. Tell me one more thing that no one will know from your name on the passenger manifest."

"No one will ever know that at the end of my life my favorite color happened to be pink." She holds up her hands and spreads wide her fingers, her palms facing her, so you can see those nails you already have noticed. "But who knows," she adds, raising her eyebrows in mock earnestness. "Maybe that's a good thing. Maybe I was already too old for Barbie pink."

Garnet watched Hallie crushing the small purple seeds with the mortar and pestle, a little surprised by how much pleasure her sister was deriving from the chore. The seeds were about the size of sesame seeds, but they smelled like blueberries when they were mashed: The more of them Hallie turned to powder, the more the kitchen smelled like a fruit smoothie. Garnet had a sense that a big part of her sister's contentment came from the obsessive amounts of attention Anise and Clary and Sage were lavishing upon the two of them. Garnet, on the other hand, found the women slightly annoying; their presence was growing invasive. She and her sister seemed to spend three or four days a week after school with them. The only days they didn't wind up at Anise's or Clary's or Sage's (and most frequently it seemed to be Sage's) were those days when they had dance class or music lessons. Again today Clary Hardin had picked them up at the school entrance precisely at three o'clock and brought them to Sage Messner's home to make tinctures or bake or tend to the seemingly endless tables of plants in that massive communal greenhouse. Garnet thought that she and Hallie spent more time in Sage's kitchen or greenhouse than they did after school with kids their own age.

Which, maybe, was okay. Maybe they were fortunate to have the attention of these ladies. After the stories that Molly and her mother had told everyone of the blackout and their father's disappearance—and then, far worse, his reappearance covered in blood—there was no way that any kids were going to be allowed to come to their house anytime soon. Maybe forever. And now the girls (and even the boys) in their classroom seemed to be a little scared of her and her sister. It was like they were the ones who made the strange potions—not the women.

Their mom had tried to reassure them that over time the kids in their class would come around, but Garnet wasn't so sure. She saw how they kept away at dance class and school. Still, her mom was confident. In the meantime, she and Hallie spent time with their mother's new friends, either this group of women or Reseda—and sometimes Reseda and Holly. It seemed there were two separate cliques. Clearly Reseda was an herbalist and a friend of these other, older women, but there was also some tension. She kept her distance; it was like she didn't completely approve of them. And while Reseda's greenhouse was much cooler—it had a comforting shape and small statues that reminded Garnet of fantasy creatures—she found that she had to be careful about what she was thinking when she was around Reseda. It was as if Reseda knew.

One time Garnet had asked her mom why she and Hallie didn't just go home after school when they didn't have dance class or music lessons, the way they had before that night when Dad tumbled down the basement stairs and fell on the knife. And her mom had explained that their father was working hard on the house and his stomach needed to heal. Garnet didn't completely believe this: Either he was working on the house *or* his stomach needed to heal. Not both. It was like the old joke about why the little girl didn't turn in her homework: Either she forgot it at home *or* the dog got sick on it. Both were overkill.

In any case, Garnet had now decided that she would ask her mom that night about moving. She decided that she'd had enough of Bethel. Maybe they could go back to West Chester. Sure, she and Hallie were always going to be the kids whose father's plane had crashed into a lake. And she would always be the kid who had the seizures. (It hurt her feelings when kids would talk about her that way, but they did. Sometimes people presumed she was in a trance when she was having one, but she wasn't. She was just, as one doctor liked to say, in her own world.) But at least she and Hallie had friends there.

"Lovely, Rosemary," Sage Messner was saying to her sister. "The powder is finer than salt, isn't it? It's as wispy as talc." The woman was hovering over Hallie with her hand on the girl's shoulder. It still left

Garnet feeling a little uncomfortable and disloyal in some way when these women called her and her sister by their new names. Mom didn't seem to mind. And Hallie said she actually preferred being called Rosemary. But Calandrinia—and Cali for short? Over the last couple of weeks, she had grown to hate both the long and short versions of her new name.

"Now, your turn, Cali," Sage said, her voice that singsong river of condescension. She always talked to Hallie and Garnet like she thought the two of them were preschoolers. So did Ginger and Clary. Anise tended to speak to them more like grown-ups. But she was also far more stern with the two of them.

"My turn to do what?" she asked. "I think the seeds are all ground up."

"The hypnobium seeds are. But we still need to add the yarrow and the rose hips. If you only add hypnobium to a tea, you are likely to give someone a headache along with very scary—"

"Sage, that's a lot more information than the girls need at the moment," Anise said, cutting the woman off before she could finish her sentence. Garnet hadn't realized that Anise had returned to the kitchen from the greenhouse.

"Along with what?" Garnet decided to ask, partly because she was curious but also because it was clear to her that Anise didn't want her and Hallie to know.

"Instead of making them feel better, Cali," Anise said simply but firmly. "Now you want to wash your hands thoroughly after working with hypnobium and completely rinse both the mortar and the pestle." She barely glanced at Sage as she carefully poured the powder into a small glass spice jar. The ground-up seeds now resembled the old-fashioned sugar candy that some people gave away in straws on Halloween.

"I'm sorry, Anise," Sage murmured, her voice low and soft, as if she hoped that no one else would hear her. But Anise seemed to ignore her as she screwed the lid on the spice jar and then ran hot tap water over the mortar and pestle. The moment the water hit the wood, the room was infused with the aroma of the herb and the kitchen smelled like some-one was baking a blueberry pie.

"Next we need to prepare the rose hips," Anise said, gazing out the kitchen window. "I think Sage thought that might be a nice task for you, Cali."

"My name is Garnet." It was an impulse; correcting Anise had been as instinctive just now as batting a mosquito. Still, she regretted the short sentence the moment the words had escaped her lips. Her sister poked her surreptitiously in the side.

"It is," Anise agreed, turning off the water and using a dish towel with a rooster on it to dry the inside of the pestle, and for a second Garnet thought she might have worried for naught. But then Anise leaned over her, her face only inches away—Garnet could inhale the mint on the woman's breath—and said, "But not when you're with me."

"Why?" Again, it was a reflex, and Hallie turned to her and silently mouthed her regular name, drawing out each of the syllables: *Gar-net*. Garnet didn't usually like confrontations, but she didn't understand the desire these women had to change her and Hallie's names. She simply didn't get it.

"I've told you, it's a term of endearment. A term of inclusion. Of solidarity. Do you know what those words mean, Cali?"

She couldn't have defined them in a spelling test, but she under-stood more or less what Anise was saying. She nodded. She wished she were back in her bedroom in West Chester that moment. She saw in her mind the windows there and her bed with the blue and gold com-forter that matched the wallpaper: planets and stars and a cow jumping over the moon. She wondered where Mom had stored that comforter these days. The attic? A guest bedroom closet?

"You are now a part of my world, Cali," Anise continued, emphasiz-ing her new name, an undercurrent to her voice that was vaguely menac-ing. "You are a part of Sage's world and Clary's world and the world of some striking people who can make a difference for good or ill in all that you know. You are not a part of your precious Pennsylvania. You're in

New Hampshire. In Bethel. So don't cross me. Not this afternoon. Not ever." She brought her fingers to Garnet's cheeks and gently grazed the skin there with her nails; when she did, the silver bangles on her wrist jingled like chimes. "Think of that skull you found in your basement. The bones you touched with those little fingers of yours. The next time you are pondering whether you like your name or whether you should follow one of my instructions, I urge you to recall that skull. Recall the eye sockets. Recall the jaw. Recall the very idea that someone was buried in your new house and how scared you were when you found the remains. You, too, Rosemary. Now, do you have any other questions?"

Garnet thought she was going to cry, and so she bit her tongue and breathed in deeply through her nose. Then she glanced at Hallie, who was staring down at her feet. Her sister was wearing blue jeans and what she called her cinnamon toast socks: They were brown with yellow spots.

"Good. And if it makes you more comfortable with your new names, rest assured that your mother is taking one, too. And she rather likes hers." Abruptly Anise stood up to her full height. Garnet noticed that Clary and Sage were now standing beside Anise, the three of them looking like severe and demanding teachers, their eyes ominous and their arms folded across their chests.

"So, Cali," Anise said finally, her voice once more sounding calm and caring and kind. "We have the rose hips to prepare. I believe Sage will show you how."

When Emily walked into John's office, he was pressing his phone against his ear with his shoulder, finishing a conversation with a client. He was rubbing a cream onto his hands. He smiled at her, motioned for her to sit, and said good-bye to whomever he was speaking with.

"Want some?" he asked, tipping the small compact with the cream toward her. "My hands are chapped raw after a White Mountain winter. Between the woodstove and the time I spend on the mountain, they're an absolute disaster."

She dipped two fingers into the compact and took some. She wondered if it was the same sort of cream Ginger Jackson had rubbed near her eyes that night at Reseda's. "Did Ginger make this?" she asked.

"Nope. Clary."

"Ginger makes something similar."

"Of course she does. All the women do." He paused and smiled. Then: "You must think we are all awfully vain."

"No." She decided to try a small joke, hoping she might learn from it. "But I do think you're all witches."

He laughed ever so slightly and shook his head. "More like chemists," he said. "It's not about spells and magic. It's not about pendants and charms and"—he waved his hand dismissively—"crystals. It's about chemistry. It's about natural medicine."

"Potions."

He pretended to shush her, his eyes wide. "Tinctures," he said, aware this was a semantic difference at best. Meanwhile, she felt her skin tingling where she had massaged in the cream. Already her hands looked better.

On the first spectacularly warm day of spring, you sit on the walkway outside your front door and watch the ants, which built a small hill between two edges of slate overnight. It is lunchtime, and you have brought with you a piece of banana bread that Anise baked. You decide that you really know nothing about bugs. Really, nothing at all. But in the past you have watched ants eat. Everyone has. You have watched them move crumbs that look proportionately like boulders. An efficient, almost robotic swarm. They break apart what they can and move what they can, carting the bounty above their heads and their trunks, disappearing either into anthills in the ground or nests behind the walls. They move in lines. You have seen it as you sat on the front stoop of your old house in West Chester and, years and years ago, as you would lie on the grass in Connecticut when you were a small boy.

And you are quite sure that you have never seen ants do this. Never.

The small ones die within inches of the banana bread morsels. They take one of the minuscule crumbs you have broken off and collapse under its weight seconds after starting off. And the larger ones? They last a little longer. They stagger in circles as if they have grown disoriented—panicked—and then they wobble and crumple. It's as if their tiny legs have just buckled.

You tell yourself that they were not really panicked. Not even scared. You know that an ant's nervous system isn't built that way. Most likely, they were merely confused, suddenly unsure of what they were doing or why they were dying. It just looked like they were scared.

Still, you cannot help but wonder what herbs would poison an ant—and what those herbs might do to a human.

It was sixty-five degrees outside, but Reseda could feel the temperature was about to plummet. The sun had been high overhead at lunchtime, but now a great swash of gunmetal gray clouds was darkening the sky, rolling in from the northwest and stretching deep into Canada. She gently shut the door to her greenhouse and turned toward Anise, who was misting the tentacles, nacreous as marble, that were branching out from the poisonous acedia. The acedia was spreading like a spider plant, and its tentacles were dripping over the sides of the pedestal on which it resided. Reseda knew that Anise didn't approve; she felt it should be trimmed back, the shoots chopped and the toxins harvested. But Reseda was so pleased with her success with the plant that she couldn't bear to don gloves and take a knife to it. Not yet. No one had ever had such a triumph with acedia. The plant was named after the Latin word for sloth because it was a sedative and, used improperly in a tincture, lethal. She wondered how she would feel about her achievement if it had been named for the Latin word for pride.

"What are you feeding the pilot?" she asked Anise now.

Anise continued to circle the plant, careful not to make eye contact with her.

"Crumpets," she answered evasively, her voice uncharacteristically light. "Always vegan. Always delicious."

"I'm serious."

"I am, too."

"I don't see what good could possibly come from poisoning him."

"Me, neither," said Anise, and she put down the mister on one of the gardening tables and stroked the stone Baphomet's beard. "Do you ever find it odd how out of touch a pilot is with the earth? Oh, they see how beautiful it is from twenty or thirty thousand feet. But their whole purpose is to separate themselves from the soil. To be above the ground, rather than one with it. You grow beautiful things, Reseda. That pilot never will. I'm really not all that interested in him."

"But you have been constantly filling the Lintons' refrigerator. Bringing them small confections with *his* name on them."

"I'm a one-woman Welcome Wagon. You're a real estate agent: That should make you happy."

"Just because you put the captain's name on it doesn't mean he's the only one eating it. I am sure the girls have eaten some of your . . . confections."

"Perhaps. But it's not like they're hash brownies. Anything special in them would demand, well, repeat exposures."

"Hallie had nightmares."

"We all have nightmares," Anise said, dismissing her concern. "I find both girls very interesting. Don't you? I find them curious. Or do only the dead inspire you these days?"

"I worry about them," she said, ignoring the dig. "They have endured an awful lot."

"I agree. And that's what makes them so . . . special. So receptive. It changes the brain chemicals. You know that as well as anyone."

"You're not trying to up the level of trauma?"

"Maybe a little. But mostly I'm just an observer. I've been watching them. We all have. I had them working at the communal greenhouse again this afternoon. And I know you've been watching them, too,"

Anise said, and she turned to Reseda, though she did not meet her eyes. "Oh, don't look at me like that. You pretend you're above that sort of thing: It's too dark, it's evil, it's cruel."

"A boy died. That seems to me far too high a price."

"You weren't there. You don't know what happened. You've only heard the story from Clary and Ginger."

Reseda gazed at a pair of water droplets descending the glass window near the steamer. "I know what Clary saw," she said.

"You know what Clary *thinks* she saw," Anise corrected her. "You know what Clary recalls. There is a big difference, Reseda. Remember, I was there, too; you weren't."

"I don't want you to try again. They're little girls."

"If it makes you feel any better, I don't even know which one we would use. I really don't," Anise said, and she strolled over to a long table with cooking spices, inhaling the aroma from the basil. "But you know something?"

Reseda waited.

"If you were my age—good heavens, if you were Clary's and Ginger's and Sage's age—you would view the twins more the way I do. You really would. It's human nature."

"Tell me: What are you feeding the captain?"

Anise smiled, but then she shook her head and her eyes grew narrow and reptilian. "You really think I'm a witch, don't you?"

"Are you?"

"I just like to bake," she said, refusing to answer the question. "That's all. I just like to bake."

Garnet had both books that Anise had given her sister and her open on the rug in the living room. She was lying on her stomach before them, near the warmth from the radiator, resting her chin in both hands. The books were so old and so heavy that the pages wouldn't flip shut when she laid them flat on the floor. Whole sections had thick pages with nothing but handwriting—somebody's cursive lettering. Recipes and formulas and diagrams, and some beautiful watercolor illustrations of flowers and ferns. They were more like scrapbooks than published books, she decided. They smelled a little musty and a little like one of the plants from Sage Messner's greenhouse: maybe the one that had the red leaves that were shaped like the points on the wrought-iron fence by the cemetery. She found a picture of it in the book that had been presented to her, *The Complete Book of Divination and Mediation with Plants and Herbs,* but it didn't appear in the botany book that had been given to Hallie. The plant was called *Phantasia.* Much of the biology in her book was over her head, but Garnet found the elegant and precise drawings more interesting than she might have expected and the uses for the plants absolutely fascinating. She had, of course, thought about flowers as decorations and gifts; she had been aware that her mother used herbs as seasonings when she cooked; and certainly she understood the role that fruits and vegetables played in her health. But this was completely different: It was as if some plants and some herbs were medicines. It was as if others were—and the word lodged itself in her mind—*magic.* They affected how people behaved if they ate them or drank them. But it wasn't like the way alcohol or drugs might change your behavior; that was random and unpredictable. She had seen adults drunk at her parents' parties, and she had seen what alcohol did to people on TV shows and in movies. According to this book, however, some plants or combinations of plants, properly cured or steeped, could make people fall in love. Grow violent. Have visions. The book talked about making people act on their *dreams,* and dreams in this case had nothing to do with ambition. It was as if, with the right herbs in the right doses—the right *tinctures*— you could make someone's nightmares feel real by the light of day.

Moreover, she realized that her book was part of a small encyclopedia. It said VOLUME I on the spine. She went to the back of the book to see how many volumes there might be and had to read something twice because it looked so strange. It seemed there was at least a second book. This one was called *The Complete Book of Divination and Mediation with Animals and Humans.* It was Volume II. She made a mental note to ask Anise about that, if she ever got out of Anise's doghouse. These women seemed to be interested only in plants—just look at all those green-houses. But maybe she was mistaken. Maybe they did have other . . . interests.

Over her shoulder she heard Hallie coming down the stairs in her clogs and then joining her in the living room. Her sister sat on the carpet beside her and glanced at the books, but she wasn't especially interested. She rolled her fingers around her bracelet and then touched Garnet's wrist.

"How come you're not wearing your bracelet?" she asked.

"I don't know. I'm just not."

"You should."

Garnet put her forehead down on the rug and closed her eyes. She breathed in the aroma of the books. She was home, the women weren't here right now. What did it matter if she wasn't wearing her bracelet?

"How does Dad seem to you?" Hallie asked. "He seems to talk less than ever."

"I know."

"He talks even less now than he did, like, two or three weeks ago," said Hallie.

"Since the night he got hurt in the basement."

"Yup. But you know what's weird?"

Garnet waited. Everything these days was weird.

"He's changed, but maybe it's just who he is now. I'm getting used to it. In some ways, it's like when he was still flying planes and gone a lot of the time. Know what I mean?"

Garnet knew precisely what Hallie meant. Before Flight 1611 had crashed, it was more normal having their father gone than it was having him home. Or, at least, it was as normal. The reality was that, for most of their childhoods, their father had been away from home three or four days a week. They—Mom and Hallie and she—were accustomed to being a household of three, and their mother had the single-mom drill down to a science. She knew how to run the house just fine when Dad was flying. In some ways, things even went a little easier when it was just the three girls. Dad wouldn't suddenly be there wanting to bring them to and from dance class when their friend Samantha's mom was already planning to pick them up at school and bring them to her house until Emily was finished at work. Dad wouldn't suddenly want dinner to be a perfect replica of what the school nurse said dinner was supposed to look like, with just the right combination of meat and vegetables and grains. They could eat dinner in the den and watch TV. And Dad wouldn't suddenly be checking to make sure they had made their beds before going to school or practiced the violin or the flute before going to sleep. The truth was, regardless of whether Dad was flying or he was sitting silently at the table and staring at something no one else seemed to see, the three females had figured out long ago how to manage.

Still, Garnet felt guilty even thinking such things, and so she found herself answering, "I know what you mean. But Mom says it just takes time. He'll get better. You think he will, right?"

"Yeah. I'm sure he will," Hallie said, but she sounded dubious. Then: "Want me to get you your bracelet?"

Garnet pushed herself to a sitting position. "Fine. Get me my bracelet. It's on the top of my—"

But before she could finish, Hallie handed it to her. She had already retrieved it and brought it downstairs. "I saw it on top of your bureau," she said. "And I figured you should be wearing it. You just never know when Reseda or Anise or someone is going to drop by the house."

It had been clear to Emily throughout dinner that something was troubling the girls, though Garnet had seemed more out of sorts than her sister. (But wouldn't it be worse, she asked herself, if something *wasn't* troubling her children?) She watched them pick at their food, Garnet always seeming on the verge of bringing something up. Now Emily was going through their vocabulary words with them in Hallie's bedroom on the third floor, helping them complete the workbook pages they had been assigned as homework. Chip was downstairs taping the frames of the doors in the entry foyer, because he was planning to paint it tomorrow. His stomach, he insisted, felt pretty good.

But she studied her girls as they worked. Hallie was sitting on her bed, while she and Garnet sat on the floor with their backs against it. She tried to focus, but as she watched the twins together in a moment of such comforting normalcy—upstairs in a bedroom doing their homework—she found herself wondering how so much of their life as a family had gone so terribly wrong. Actually, not how. The how was easy. It was the why. The why seemed almost Job-like. Inexplicable. Unreasonable. But the how? A person could trace the steps with ease. There was the plane crash, of course, that was where it all began. It was Flight 1611 that had led to Chip's depression and PTSD, which in turn had resulted in their moving to northern New Hampshire. And then it was here in Bethel that his mental illness had worsened, perhaps—according to Valerian—because of the solitude. Not that taking a yoga class or volunteering at the library would have made a difference. But all those hours alone in this house scraping wallpaper and slathering paint on kitchen walls? It had exacerbated his disconnection from people other than his wife and his daughters. And so whatever demons he already had were transformed into the self-loathing that had led him to hurt himself.

And then Garnet had found the bones. Good God, her children would have had to have been mannequins not to have been out of sorts. It was a miracle that they could put one foot in front of the other and function at all.

No, it wasn't precisely a miracle. It was Reseda. Anise. Holly. Clary. Ginger. Sage. It was all those remarkable women. It was John Hardin. It was all those remarkable *people*. They were strange, there was no doubt about it. They were obsessed with their greenhouses and gardens and quaint little remedies. But they were caring and giving and intellectually engaged. While the girls might feel a little ostracized at the moment by their classmates—though Emily honestly was convinced this would improve over time—they had been embraced by the most interesting women of Bethel. *Verbena*. This was the name that Clary and Anise were calling her now. John was, too, though for some reason she found his use of it a little troubling: It suggested a more public transformation than she was prepared to make at the moment, because he wanted to call her that at work. Moreover, she wasn't enamored of the name—the connotation in her mind was the men's talcum and soap she had sometimes placed under the Christmas tree for Chip, though Anise had reassured her that it had a long and rich feminine history as well. A mystical history. Anise had told her that another term for *verbena* was Juno's tears, and she thought it might be a fitting name for Emily as she coped with the heartbreaking loss of Flight 1611 and her reawakening into a future she had never anticipated.

When Emily had told Reseda that some of the women now wanted to call her Verbena, her friend had shown absolutely no emotion, and for a moment she thought that perhaps Reseda didn't approve—which made her fear that perhaps Reseda didn't believe she was worthy of having a new name. Of becoming one of them. But then Reseda had nodded and said, "Yes, of course. We should have a christening. A rebirth into Verbena. It might be fun. We'll view it as an excuse for a party."

"Mommy?"

She looked over at Garnet. "Yes, dear?"

"What were you thinking?"

"I was thinking about vocabulary words. At least I should have been. Sorry."

"I wasn't thinking about the words, either."

"No?"

"No. I want to move back to Pennsylvania."

Emily rested her hand on her daughter's shoulder and rubbed it softly. She was surprised by both the bluntness and the suddenness of her daughter's request. "Sometimes I do, too," she said, and she was about to say more: explain why that idea had its appeal but why, in the end, she would prefer to stay here in Bethel. At least for now. The reality was that there was a support group here. Moreover, she didn't believe that her husband—their father—was capable of uprooting his life once again. In some ways, the man she had fallen in love with and married and raised the two of them with had died that awful afternoon last August. He had become a ghost of his former self, a wisp: He had become, sadly, the pilot who wasn't Sully Sullenberger.

Meanwhile, she wasn't even sure she was capable—not emotionally, not intellectually—of returning to a practice as demanding as the one she had left behind in Philadelphia.

"Then we might move back?" Garnet was saying. "There's a chance?"

"I don't want to," said Hallie, and she glared down at her sister from the bed. "I know things have been kind of weird here. But it's not like West Chester was so great."

"You *loved* West Chester," Garnet corrected her. "You were, like, the most popular girl in the class!"

"I was not!"

"You were! You totally were!"

Hallie sat back against her headboard and folded her arms across her chest.

"Let's talk about this calmly," Emily said. She gazed back and forth at her daughters and recognized in the two of them the odd penumbra of resemblance that strangers noted when they first met the girls. "Garnet, you go first. Why do you want to move back to Pennsylvania? And then Hallie, you can tell us why you don't. Okay?"

Hallie gazed angrily out the window into the night, and Garnet nodded slowly, marshaling her ideas. Before she started to speak, however, the phone rang and Emily made a T with her hands, signaling a time-out. "Hold your thoughts," she said to Garnet, and then she rose and ran down the stairs to the second floor to get the phone in her and Chip's bedroom. She figured she reached it about a half second before the answering machine would have picked up.

"Good evening, ma'am. Is this Emily Linton?"

"Yes." She didn't recognize the male voice.

"My name is Sergeant Dennis Holcomb, I was one of the investigators from the Major Crime Unit who examined the remains your daughter found in your basement. We met your husband, the captain, that morning."

"Yes. Of course." She felt her heart thrumming in her chest; she feared this could only be more bad news.

"Well, we went and got a DNA swab from Hewitt Dunmore. There's a match. He still claims he had no idea that his twin brother had been buried down there. Insists the bones must have preceded his family's purchase of the house: Abenaki remains or fur trappers or loggers. He still says that door was just the old coal chute. But it's pretty evident the remains are Sawyer Dunmore."

"So what does that mean?"

"It means the case is closed. The twelve-year-old's death was ruled a suicide years ago; there was never any suggestion there may have been foul play. And New Hampshire law allows for burial on private property. Why the parents wanted the world to think they buried their boy in the cemetery—and how the mortician was or wasn't involved—is anyone's guess. But they're all dead, and no laws were broken."

"So we're done?" she asked.

"More or less. I will tell you this: The medical examiner's office said some of the bones are still somewhere in your basement—in that homemade vault. They couldn't build a whole skeleton. So, you might want to discourage your little girls from playing down there. I know I wouldn't want my little boy digging around that cellar."

"Thank you."

"You're very welcome, ma'am," he said, and then he gave her his number in case she ever had any more questions. She, in turn, murmured her gratitude and hung up. When she went back upstairs to Hallie's bedroom, both girls were sulking—clearly they had bickered while she had been gone—and neither wanted to discuss the pros and cons of leaving Bethel.

You hang up the kitchen phone only after both Emily and Sergeant Holcomb have hung up their receivers. You make sure that there is no one on the line to hear your click. Then you lean against the counter beside the oven. You glance down. The knife that Tansy left you is still underneath it. One time Desdemona pawed at a dust bunny there and Emily watched the cat while she was chopping an onion, but other-wise you have had little fear that someone will notice it there. Never-theless, you are relieved the sergeant didn't ask about it—that he didn't ask Emily whether it had turned up. He might have. He might have said something as simple as *We'll get that crowbar and that ax back to you soon enough. They weren't murder weapons, so we don't need them.* Or, *Did you or your husband ever find that knife? Just curious.* And then Emily would have asked you where the knife was, since clearly it wasn't with the State Police. Yes, you were lucky. She might not have trusted you after that.

You hear a noise in the den and stroll there. As you expected, Ashley is playing with your daughters' dolls, while Ethan watches. He glances at you and then back at his little girl. He tries not to share with her his utter contempt for you. But he is relentless, his judgment unforgiving and harsh. Why is it that the presence of this other father and daughter causes you such intense physical pain? It is not merely sympathy for all they have endured and all they have lost. For their unspeakable loneli-ness. It is the racking pain in your head, your abdomen, and lower back that causes you to close your eyes and breathe in deeply and slowly until the Advil kicks in and takes the edge off.

Ashley looks up at you and then drops the doll in the Civil War–era smock near the brick hearth for the woodstove. She looks a little dis-gusted, a little sad.

She deserves friends. She does. Yes. She does . . .

Clary Hardin switched on the dining room light in her home and heard the loud pop. She knew instantly that one of the bulbs had burned out and hoped it wasn't the smiling cherub. They had absolutely no smiling cherubs left. When she surveyed the chandelier, however, she saw that it was indeed one of those bulbs that had blown. They'd have to replace it with one of their two remaining faces of despair.

"Another bulb go?" her husband asked, when he saw her stand-ing underneath the chandelier, staring, her hands on her hips. He stood behind her and wrapped his hands around her waist, and she allowed her arms to fall to her sides.

"Yes," she said. "We have got to get back to Paris."

"Honey, you know that store closed in 1941. It was never going to survive the occupation. It was never going to survive the war."

"Nevertheless: We have got to get back to Paris."

"I know." They had gone there on their honeymoon in 1934 and brought back that chandelier with them on the boat. It had dominated their first home, a two-bedroom apartment near the promenade in Brooklyn Heights. "Tell you what: We'll go this autumn?"

"Once we're revived?"

"Absolutely," John agreed, and he kissed her on the back of her neck.

A t night, after their parents had tucked her sister and her in and gone back downstairs to the second floor to get ready for bed themselves, Garnet watched the cold spring rain slap against a windowpane in her bedroom. She tried to study each of the water droplets as they ran down the glass, hoping to clear her mind of the moment when Anise had chastised her once again in Sage Messner's kitchen. But she couldn't escape the memory. It wasn't merely that she didn't want to be called Cali. It seemed like she was always getting in trouble. It wasn't merely that she was jealous of the idea that these women wanted to call Hallie something normal like Rosemary. It was that she didn't like the way the women looked at Hallie and her. She didn't like the way they wanted her sister and her to be so interested in plants. And it seemed like Anise wanted to scare her—and, yes, that the woman usually succeeded. She realized that she was frightened of Anise, which was precisely why she hadn't told her mother what sometimes occurred in the greenhouse. Before dinner she had considered telling her, but Hallie had argued successfully that this could only get the two of them in even more trouble when their mother confronted Anise—and, in a way that

Garnet couldn't quite fathom, she understood that this would endanger their whole family. The closest she could come to the issue was asking if they might move back to Pennsylvania. They couldn't have their old house back, but maybe there was something for sale in a neighborhood just like the one they'd lived in most of her life. Maybe there was a nice house available somewhere that was far away from this creepy Victorian and Bethel and Anise. From all those kooky women.

For a long moment she stared at her dresser. She knew what was behind it. She had found it. Or, more accurately, Desdemona had found it. It was a small door—a hole, really—in the wall that connected to the attic on the other side. A few days earlier, Garnet had watched the cat sniffing there and then pawing at the edge. When she went to see what was so interesting to the animal, she had noticed it. It was a rectangle and it was just big enough for her to crawl through, but she only discovered it with Desdemona's help because the edges were cut to blend into the red and green plaid of the wallpaper. And still, she had to slip a wooden ruler into the seam to dislodge the square, discovering that someone had cut away the plaster and horsehair and even sawed off a part of a beam, but the result was a passage into the attic. There was a six-inch length of twine stapled to the attic side of the doorway that served as a handle: Once inside the attic, a person could yank the block into place so it would blend into the wallpaper. The afternoon she found the small door, she had crawled through on her elbows and stood up in the attic. What struck her most wasn't the idea that here was yet another disturbing quirk in the house—up there with those rickety back stairs from the kitchen and the door in the basement behind which she'd found the bones; rather it was how frigid the attic was compared to the rest of the house. After all, it wasn't heated. So she had stood there with her arms around her chest, noting their old moving boxes, their old living room carpet rolled up in a tube, and that monster of an antique sewing machine that came with the house, and then crawled back through the passageway into her bedroom. Her instincts told her that this was, in some fashion, an escape hatch: A person would only travel from the bedroom to the attic this way, never the reverse. And it was nowhere near wide enough or tall enough to move anything from the attic to the bedroom. Nevertheless, once she was back in her bedroom that day, she had moved her dresser nearly two feet farther down the wall, so the door would be blocked by the piece of furniture. It threw off the symmetry of the room, but her mom clearly had enough on her mind that she hadn't asked why her daughter had ever so slightly rearranged the furniture. And although the passageway was a little frightening, it was also interesting. A little magic. She had decided she would share its discovery with Hallie, but not yet with their mother.

Now she kicked off the comforter and climbed from bed and walked down the short hallway to Hallie's room. They slept with their doors open and the hall light on these days, and so she figured that, if Hallie was awake, she was already aware that her sister was on the way to her bedroom. Just in case, she stood for a moment in the doorway, watching the shape of her twin huddled underneath her own quilt.

"Hallie?" she asked, her voice barely above a whisper. "You awake?"

The body didn't move, but she heard her sister grumble. "I am," she said. "And I told you that, when it's just us, I want you to call me Rosemary. Anise said it would help me get used to it. And you should start trying to be Cali."

Garnet knew that Hallie was not going to be receptive at all to what she wanted to discuss, and she feared that she would probably wind up retreating to her own bedroom with her feelings hurt. But she also knew that she didn't want to "start trying to be Cali," and so she crossed the bedroom floor and climbed into bed beside her sister.

"I don't want to be Cali," she said once she was settled there, wrapping herself in a section of the quilt. Hallie sat up and yanked a part of the comforter back over her own shoulders. Garnet couldn't quite make out her sister's face in the dark, but she could tell that Hallie was glaring at her.

"Don't be a pill. You don't want to be left out again. Don't make me have to take care of you here, too."

Garnet knew what Hallie meant; she understood the lengths to which her sister had gone to include her in West Chester—to make sure that she was neither ignored nor picked on. But she also knew that her sister derived a measure of satisfaction from looking out for her. Hallie was going to grow into either one of those adults who took great pride in being needed or a mean girl who took pleasure in the fealty of her friends.

"I was doing fine here at school and at dance class. I was making friends just like you until Daddy . . ." She didn't finish the sentence, though she really didn't have to. *Until Daddy freaked out Molly Francoeur.*

"Well, none of that means anything anymore. We don't have a lot of friends at school. We don't have a lot of friends at dance class. We really don't have anyone but the plant ladies. No one. Those people are our friends right now, they're what we've got."

"Great. A group of middle-aged and old ladies as friends. I'm so glad we live here. Let's stay here forever."

"Reseda's not middle-aged. Holly's not middle-aged."

"The rest are like grandmothers."

"You really don't like them?"

"No," Garnet said firmly. "I don't."

"Well, you're making a mistake. I do like them. I want to be one of them."

One of them. Garnet thought about what that meant and realized that she honestly didn't know. She had heard of ladies' garden clubs where the women made floral arrangements and tried to spruce up parks and neighborhoods; there was one in West Chester and there was probably one in Littleton or Bethel. But these plant ladies were different. She thought of the books they had given her sister and her. These women wanted to make potions and tinctures and teas—not arrangements.

"Hallie?"

"It's Rosemary," she reminded Garnet, her voice flat and blunt.

"Why do you think they want us to take new names?"

"God, will you let that go? What is the big freaking deal?"

"It's just—"

"Would it make a difference if they didn't want to call you Cali? Would you stop making waves if you had a name you liked?"

She curled her bare feet underneath the quilt and accidentally grazed Hallie. "Your feet are freezing," her sister cried out.

"I know. Sometimes I just can't get warm in my room," Garnet said.

"One more reason why you should accept the fact that, from now on, you're Cali."

"My room will suddenly warm up like yours?"

Her sister shrugged. "Everything is easier. Everything is better."

Garnet tried to imagine a plant name she might like, but she could only come up with the names of ordinary vegetables and fruits and trees. And the women didn't seem to use them very often. "There will still be that hole in the wall," Garnet murmured. "The one that goes to the attic. There will still be that draft."

"The door fits tight. There is no hole. There is no draft."

She knew Hallie was right. But, still, her room always seemed chillier than her sister's. "It scares me."

"The little door? I think it's cool. You know I'm jealous. Someday I think we should switch rooms."

"Maybe," Garnet said, but she knew in her heart that they never would. She understood that there was a certain amount of bluster to Hallie's confidence. Her sister was frightened by the door, too. "When will you tell people at school?" she asked after a moment.

"You mean about my new name?"

"Uh-huh."

"I don't know. Anise says to wait until September. We just come back after the summer and tell everyone we want to be called by our new names. And we'll have had some sort of cool naming ceremony in the summer—outdoors, when it's warm."

"Assuming Mom doesn't mind."

"Obviously."

"And we're still living here."

"Which we will be."

Garnet sighed unhappily. "Do they scare you?" she asked after a moment.

"The plant ladies? No. I can see why they might scare you—because you're still being stubborn. But once you get over that stubbornness, you'll see. They only want us to be happy."

"I think there's more to it than that."

"Like what?"

"They need us."

"They need us?" Hallie repeated, her tone incredulous and condescending.

The idea was vague and not wholly comprehensible to Garnet; she was still formulating the notion in her mind. Volume II. *The Complete Book of Divination and Mediation with Animals and Humans*. She had found nothing about it on the Internet. "Yes. I think they need us more than we need them."

"Well, we need them a lot," Hallie said. "I told you, they're all we have."

"Maybe. But do you see them spending time with any other kids? Wanting to give any other kids new names? I don't."

Hallie curled her knees up to her chest under the quilt and wrapped her arms around them. "So?"

"Why is that? Is it because we're new and everyone else knows to stay away? Or is it because we're twins? And, really, why *do* they want to rename us? You and me. Why do they want to teach us to make all those potions and teas and things?"

Outside, the rain continued to thwap against the window, and occasionally the glass rattled in its frame. Hallie seemed to consider this. "Mom said she might take a new name, too."

"I know. It begins with a *V*."

"You scared?"

"Sometimes. I wish we had houses nearby."

"Like in West Chester."

"Uh-huh."

"You want to sleep in here tonight?" Hallie asked. And while this wasn't why Garnet had come to her sister's bedroom, she knew now that she did. And so she nodded and curled up under the sheets, and soon both girls were sound asleep.

Your plane is, finally, a triple-seven heavy. A Boeing 777. You know the flight deck, even if you have never flown one before. And you know this is a dream because you are alone as you do the preflight check-lists from the captain's seat and because this peculiar airport is in the middle of a harbor. Literally. All of the planes are floating on the water, a row of skyscrapers rising up from the ground along the edge of the surf in the distance. But the belly of the plane is also hooked on to a conveyor belt, and the belt runs on a track just beneath the surface of the water. It is like a train track. No, a roller-coaster track. Because a quarter mile to your right a camelback rises from the salt water, the track sum-miting higher than any roller coaster you have ever seen in your life—higher than any roller coaster ever built anywhere. Is it fifty stories high? Maybe. One of the skyscrapers along the beach is Boston's Prudential Center (though clearly this is not Boston because all of the other towers are unrecognizable totems), and the track's peak is about the same height as the Prudential. But the descent doesn't go all the way back to earth, to the gently rolling waves. If the vertical climb is fifty stories, the drop is only twenty-five. Then the track angles up again, but the pitch is gentle, no more then five degrees. This is, you understand, the runway. A chain lift locked into the bottom of your plane will pull you along the surface of the water and up to the peak of the camelback. Then, like it would a roller-coaster car, gravity will send your plane plummeting down the other side, the antirollback locks disengaged. You will be traveling two hundred miles an hour, your engines will click on and you will feel the plane hurtling along this runway track in the sky. And then you will be flying, leaving the edge of the track as if it were the end of an aircraft carrier. This is how you take off. You watch a 737 do it. Then a CRJ. Then an Airbus. Then another CRJ. It's beautiful the way these planes are launched. They leave the track roughly thirty stories in the air, turn right into the departure corridor, and grow smaller and smaller as they disappear into a soft blue sky, an egg-colored setting sun in the distance. And then it is your turn. The tower has cleared you, and so you inform your passengers and flight crew that you are number one for takeoff.

You sit straight in your seat, your hands on the yoke, and feel the plane lurching forward, jerking just like a roller-coaster car at first, and then you are climbing up the track. The plane rests at the summit for a second or two, the tower says go, the antirollback struts slip away, and the nose of your aircraft dips. And then you are rumbling down the far side of the track, the passengers behind you screaming—but not in terror, in delight, because this is, apparently, the tradition in this particular aviation culture. You have the feeling their hands are over their heads.

When you hit the bottom—and the start of that gently angled runway itself—your engines kick on. On the instrument panel you can see the turbines are spinning. All good. And then, a moment later, you are flying, angling into the departure corridor high over this bay and getting clearance from the tower to climb to five thousand feet. And there isn't a bird in sight. Delightful.

But this is a dream, and do your dreams ever end well? Not these days. A flight attendant knocks on the door, and even though you are in the midst of your initial climb, you unbuckle your harness and see what he needs. He is a young man and his face is colorless. You walk into the first-class cabin and gaze at the floor where he is pointing: This plane seems to have a long row of baseboard heaters along the floor, and what is occurring is most visible before the feet of the passengers in the first row—the bulkhead seats—but is happening the entire length of the plane. Waves of what looks like woodstove or fireplace ash are spewing from the grates on both sides of the jet, rolling from the openings like lava and coating the floor and the feet of the passengers.

Meanwhile, the plane continues to climb, though there is no one on the flight deck piloting the aircraft, and you and the flight attendant conjecture amiably about the location of the fire. You seem to believe that the blaze must be out, because this is ash and it doesn't seem to be causing the passengers any pain, so it must be cool. But then the plane begins to dive. Not only is it not climbing—or even gliding—it is plummeting, almost nose down. And so you leave the flight attendant to see if you can prevent the aircraft from breaking the surface of the water like an Olympic diver.

You climb into the captain's seat on the flight deck and pull the yoke back as hard and fast as you can, and instantly the plane starts to rise; you hit the vertex of the parabola, the very bottom of the U, and you resume your climb. But in your haste to save the jet, you pulled back too fast and too hard. Yes, you are climbing. But it is only a slingshot effect. You pulled the triple-seven heavy out of its dive so quickly that you asked more of the metal than it could handle: You sheared off the wings. You are now in the front of a long tube, not a plane, that is going up but in a moment will reach the top of its arc and then fall headfirst into the earth. Into that bay. And behind you the passengers scream once again. They, too, have seen the wings ripped off, and this time they are screaming in horror at the imminence of their death.

And then you wake up.

You always wake up before your plane augers in.

You listen to Emily's breathing beside you, her hair on her pillow wild like Venus's when she was born in Botticelli's painting. You feel your head pounding, and you know instantly that Ethan is with you. You turn toward the doorway, and there he is, beckoning you with one finger. It's time. You climb from beneath the sheets, careful not to untuck them because Emily sleeps best when the sheets are tight, but tonight this is not merely because you are such a considerate husband. It is because you can't risk her waking when you do what you have to do. This can't continue. This can't go on for you or Emily or your beautiful daughters. This can't go on for Ethan or Ashley. God, poor, poor Ashley. You are all in pain. You are all unhappy.

Together with Ethan you go downstairs. You peer into the den, and there are Sandra and Ashley playing with Hallie's and Garnet's American Girl dolls on the floor. Sandra looks up at you and shakes her head no, but Ethan takes you by the elbow and pulls you along into the kitchen. There you fall onto your hands and your knees and reach underneath the oven, finding the blade of the knife with your fingertips. You pull it along the linoleum floor and then grasp the pearl handle in your palm.

"Let's take the back stairs," Ethan suggests, and you agree. You know why. It is because he does not want you to see Sandra again when you pass the den. He does not want you to be dissuaded from this hard, hard task by her disapproving eyes and, perhaps, her desperate entreaties. But there really is no danger of that. Not tonight. She is not connected to you the way Ethan and Ashley are. You don't feel as profoundly what she feels; you don't know as precisely what she thinks.

Still, you move gingerly up the back stairs and then as silently as you can along the second-floor corridor and up to the third floor. To Hallie's and Garnet's rooms. You hold your breath for long moments as you walk, the knife wrapped tightly in your fingers. The pain in your head and your side is excruciating. You will begin in Garnet's room, for no other reason than it is nearer to the top of the stairs. You will place your left hand on her sleeping mouth so she cannot scream when she is awoken by the knife, moving in your right hand like a jackhammer. You will stab her in the chest and the abdomen. Then you will move to Hallie's room.

You wonder: Are you dreaming now? Still? Perhaps at this moment you are in fact in bed beside Emily.

It was raining earlier tonight. No longer.

You gaze into Garnet's room, and the idea that you might still be asleep becomes more pronounced when you see that she isn't in bed. She should be. It's the middle of the night. And so you go to Hallie's room, presuming you will simply begin with her. *Begin*. Not *stab*. Did you want a euphemism? Is the actuality of slaughtering your twin girls really becoming too much for you?

Just in case, Ethan wraps his wet arm around your shoulder and guides you to Hallie's room. And there you see your daughters together. At some point, for some reason, Garnet has gone to Hallie's bedroom to sleep. So be it. Besides, there is a symmetry to handling it this way: They were born within moments of each other, and they will die within moments of each other. Born together, dead together. You cross to the far side of Hallie's bed and stare down at them. You try not to view them as beautiful children, though you are their father and so the idea that they are is inescapable. But so is Ashley. So are all the children who died or were made orphans or lost a parent when you crashed Flight 1611 into Lake Champlain.

You are contemplating precisely how to begin, the knife at your side, when you hear your name.

"Chip?"

You look up. There in the doorframe is Emily. She is lit by the hall light behind her, but she has not turned on Hallie's bedroom light. Her hand is near the wall switch. If she does, she will see the knife. You hold your breath.

"Chip?" she whispers again, her voice a little more urgent this time. She clearly has no plans to risk waking the children by turning on the light. You press the knife against your side, shielding it from her view. You join her and wrap your free hand around her waist. You pull her against you.

"I was watching them sleep," you murmur, the words catching strangely in your throat. You look for Ethan, but he's gone.

"Come back to bed," she says.

"Yes, of course," you agree, and together you return to your bedroom. There you slip the knife between the mattress and the box spring when you tuck back in the sheets. And you are thorough when you tuck them back in, because Emily likes a tight bed.

Chapter Fourteen

When the girls are at school and Emily is at work, while you are painting the entry foyer, you are surprised by a visitor. It is Hewitt Dunmore. He is wearing a red check flannel jacket and leans on his cane on the front steps of your house in much the same way he did when you visited him at his home in St. Johnsbury. Behind him, in the trees at the edge of the meadow beyond the greenhouse, you notice that the wisps of green shadowing the tree branches have become actual buds. Alabaster white clouds float against the blue sky like islands.

"This is a surprise," you tell him, extending your hand.

"I was going to call, but since I am apologizing, I thought I should do it in person. Seemed like the right thing to do."

"Apologize?"

He peers over your shoulder at the masking tape protecting the trim in the front hallway and surveys the way you have already coated one wall with a shade of paint called sunset coral. "Looks like you're making some changes," he says, ignoring your question. "Good for you."

"I guess." You shrug, not wanting him to feel insulted by the ways you are redoing virtually every room in this house that once belonged to his family. "But that's only because we have little girls and—"

He waves you off. "The paper was tired. The paint was tired. Makes sense to spruce up the old place."

"Would you like to come in?"

"I'll just stay a minute," he agrees, and together you walk carefully

over the newspaper along the floor in the hall and around the paint-
brush and roller and the open can of sunset coral paint. You sit in your
kitchen now, just as you did once before in his, though this visit feels
more companionable. He drapes his flannel jacket on the back of the
chair and hooks his cane over an armrest. Behind his shoulder, in the
dining room, you gaze at those disturbing, nearly dead sunflowers.

"I want to tell you I'm sorry."

"So you said. What for?"

"For my parents' strangeness. For the things my mother left around
the house. And, yes, for their burying my brother in the basement," he
says, and you have the sense by the forcefulness of his response that he
has rehearsed these words.

"You knew?"

"About my brother? I did not know for a fact. But I suspected."

"Did you know about the knife and the—"

"No. That was a surprise. I would have told you about those things
if I'd known, since you have children. But Sawyer's body? I figured it
was long gone by now—you know, deteriorated—assuming anyone
even wanted to break down that blasted door. Still, I should have told
you. But I needed the money from the house. It's just that simple. I have
health issues, I don't have much of a retirement nest egg. And so, well, I
looked the other way. Told myself my parents hadn't really buried Sawyer there, and, if they did, it wasn't a big deal. And here's the last thing: If
I had known your girls were twins, I would never have sold you the old
place. I swear it."

You think about all that he has just shared with you, unsure where
to begin. "So, your parents never told you they had buried your brother
here," you observe after a long moment.

"Nope. But then the State Police called and I knew."

"Why did they do it? Your parents?"

He sighs. "I was never here."

"I don't understand."

"I was never here—at your house, in this kitchen. That's what I
mean. What I am about to tell you? You can tell no one I told you."

"My wife—"

"No one. I presume you are the sort of man who tells his wife everything. Am I right?"

"Yes," you agree, though these days you know that's a lie.

"Well, you cannot tell her this. Act on the information as you see fit. But you cannot tell her I was ever here or we ever spoke. She works for John Hardin. I know Reseda sold you this house. So, can you promise me that?"

"Yes. That's fine."

He seems to think about whether he really can trust you. Finally: "I suppose you've seen a lot of the women."

"The women?"

"The herbalists. I suppose they've been here a lot."

"No. Not really."

"That's surprising."

"I mean, they haven't been strangers. I've been to John and Clary Hardin's house for dinner. And Anise is constantly feeding us," you tell him, although ever since you saw the effect of her baked goods on some ants on your walkway, you have done all that you can to prevent your family from eating any. You have certainly eaten none yourself. If you could be absolutely sure that Emily had not already been commandeered into the group, you would share with her your suspicions. "And, of course, Reseda became our real estate agent after Sheldon died," you continue.

"'Course she did. She saw you had twins. You may recall, she was not my first choice in a real estate agent."

"And you did not come to the closing."

"I try to steer clear of them—the women. They showing interest in your girls? The twins?"

"I think my girls see a lot more of them than I do. My wife has them go to their houses all the time after school." Again, there it is: that vague fear that Emily already is one of them.

At this Hewitt sits forward in his chair and grasps the edges of the kitchen table with both hands. "They think they're witches."

You have had this idea, too, but not in such a literal sense. In your mind, it was always hyperbole. Exaggeration. Even, early on, condescension. "Go on."

Hewitt repeats himself, enunciating each word perfectly, no contraction this time: "They think they are witches. That is what they believe. They call themselves herbalists, but it's all witchcraft. Most of what they do is harmless. But not all of it. Not all the time."

"How big is the group?"

"How many have you met?" he asks, his voice growing a little more urgent. You realize he hasn't answered your question.

"I don't know. Maybe five or six."

"My mother was one. She was always in that greenhouse. Always."

"You said most of what they do is harmless. What isn't?"

He looks straight at you, his eyes locked on yours. "They're crazy," he says, his usually laconic voice growing urgent and intense. "They believe in blood sacrifice. I would not put it past them to try again to kill a child."

"One of my girls?"

"One of your girls. That's why I should never have let you buy this place."

"Tell me the truth: Why was your mother hiding knives and hatchets all over the house? Who was she afraid of?"

"I told you, I didn't know she was hiding those things."

"She wasn't trying to protect you and your brother?"

"No. She did that long after my brother was gone. She was probably trying to protect herself."

"From?"

"Who do you think?"

"Well, the women. The herbalists. But you said she was one of them."

"She was until they took her son. My brother."

"Your brother slashed his wrists."

"I don't think so. I think something went wrong."

"With a ritual?"

"A ceremony. While they were making one of their potions. I'll never know because Sawyer died and my mother would never talk about it. She was never the same after that night. How could she be? She saw her son slaughtered—and there is no other word for it. But she was there. Had to be. And even if she wasn't, she was the one who led him there in the first place. Her own boy. I don't know what went wrong that night or whether the other women knew he was going to die. I believe Clary Hardin was there. Sage Messner, too. And Anise. And I know for sure that my mother's guilt drove her mad."

You want to reassure him that you are no stranger to the notion of guilt driving a person mad. You feel that pain in your side and know instantly that Ashley is present. You are imagining her in the den with her dolls—no, that's not right; those are your daughters' dolls—when you see her standing in the doorway to the dining room, the sunflowers towering over her. She is listening intently. You nod at her. You have to restrain yourself from waving.

"Their potions are an inexact science at best," Hewitt continues. "The women think they have more control over them than they do. They all seem to have more confidence than they should in what they steep and stew."

"Why would they want to kill one of my girls?"

"Most of their potions and tinctures come from plants. You've seen their greenhouses. But not all. Some potions demand animal parts, too. Or blood. Sometimes it's animal blood and sometimes it's human blood. And sometimes it's a heart. I know of one tincture that demands a deer heart. I know of another where they use the hearts of bluebirds. Yup, bluebirds. I don't know what they did to Sawyer the night he died, but I presume they did not cut out his heart. Even in a part of New England as rural as this, I think someone in the medical examiner's office or the funeral home would have noticed. But they did need his blood."

"And my girls?"

"They're twins. That was what was so important about Sawyer. Could have been me, you know. But the recipe, it seems, only needs one twin. And for some reason they picked him and not me. Maybe"—and here he waved one of his arms dismissively—"they liked his blood more than mine. Or maybe they thought he wasn't as far along as I was."

"Far along?"

"Puberty. The twin is supposed to be prepubescent." He turns around abruptly and glances out the window. Churning up a trail of dust on the gravel and dirt driveway is Anise's old pickup. When he looks back at you, his face has become ashen. He shakes his head ever so slightly, and you rise to go and greet Anise. You watch her gaze curiously at Hewitt's automobile as she exits her truck, and then welcome her into your house. She has brought a casserole dish and a plate of brownies.

"You have company," she says in the doorway. "I hope I'm not intruding."

"Not at all."

"I've brought you a cassoulet—vegan, of course."

"Of course."

"It begins with dried haricot beans. But you'll recognize lots of other vegetables. And the thyme and rosemary and bay leaf are from my greenhouse."

"That was sweet of you. Thank you."

She bustles past you into the kitchen without asking. "Hewitt Dunmore," she says when she sees him, her voice flat and unreadable, her lips curling up into a withering smile. She places the brownies and the cassoulet on the counter. "It has been aeons. How are you? How is life in the big city?"

"I wouldn't call St. Johnsbury a big city."

"Oh, but it dwarfs Bethel. You must love it there. You never, ever seem to come back here."

He remains silent.

"So, tell me: What has brought you back today? Old home week? Leave something behind in the house?" she asks, her face hard, and she rolls her eyes toward the door to the basement.

"I happened to be driving this way and thought I would see the old place," he says, his voice a little shaky.

"That's all? Really?"

He looks down at the tabletop, a small child being chastised. "Really," he mumbles.

"First time back?"

"First time."

"Well, I know the captain appreciates visitors enormously."

"Actually, Anise, I was just leaving."

"Oh, I'm so sorry."

"Errands," he says vaguely.

"Well, I hope you two had a nice visit."

"No complaints," Hewitt says, reaching for his cane and standing. He clumsily pushes his arms through his jacket sleeves. And then he is gone, limping along the front walkway to his car.

"I'd say he's a bit strange," Anise remarks, her voice a little conspiratorial—as if you two are the closest of friends. "Wouldn't you?"

"I don't think I'm a real good person to make that call."

You watch Desdemona pounce upon the circular plastic ring from a milk carton. Accidentally she bats it underneath the stove.

"Are your daughters cat people?"

"Not especially. I think they are ambivalent about Desdemona," you tell her. "When they were younger, they played with her more."

She seems to think about this. Then: "How is your stomach? That injury must be pretty well healed by now."

"It is, thank you. I feel pretty good."

"I suppose they still have you on some antibiotic?"

"Not anymore."

She nods, offering no opinion on whether she approves of antibiotics, but you have a feeling that she would have prescribed instead a tincture made from some exotic herb that she grows in her greenhouse. The idea crosses your mind that these women steer clear of doctors, but you don't honestly believe this. After all, isn't Valerian a psychiatrist?

Anise hands you one of the brownies. "I baked them this morning," she says. "Try it."

You take it and stare at it for a brief moment. When she senses your hesitation, she delicately breaks off a piece and puts it into her own mouth. "I am a fiend for my own cooking," she says when she has swallowed it. The gesture is oddly intimate.

And so you take a breath. But still you can't bring yourself to take a bite. "I had a big lunch," you tell her.

She nods. "Suit yourself," she says slowly. "I'll be seeing your girls later today. They can tell you what you missed."

Reseda was moving among the mad-dog skullcap and the ashwagandha in her greenhouse, tending them with a brass watering can shaped like a crouching gargoyle (the water flowed from its large, round eyes) and a plastic mister with a falcon's head (in this case, the water emanated from its beak). She was listening more carefully than it might have seemed as Clary and Sage prattled on behind her about how far along her St.-John's-wort was and how healthy it seemed by comparison to theirs. She understood why they had come by this afternoon, and she suspected they knew that she knew: They were struggling mightily to mask their real thoughts with their enthusiastic blather about the state of her herbs. Moreover, Clary was blinking senselessly, which the woman believed (mistakenly) in some fashion shorted out the connection between her mind and Reseda's.

Finally, when Reseda turned off the spigot beside the greenhouse hose for the last time, Clary got around to the actual reason for their visit. "You know, Reseda," she began, hoping her voice sounded offhand, "Anise wants to try again. She thinks the Linton girls offer real potential after what their father went through. The trauma of the plane crash and all. So, we were wondering if perhaps you two could, I don't know, enter into a period of détente?"

"Anise was over here just the other day," Reseda said. "You make it sound like the two of us don't play nicely together in the sandbox."

Sage chuckled nervously and ran two dry, gnarled fingers underneath the first cerulean blossoms on the memoria. Neither she nor Clary was accustomed to speaking so candidly about Reseda and Anise's relationship. "Of course you do. You both do. But . . ."

"Go on."

"Everyone knows you two aren't as close as we'd all like. I am about to be completely honest because—" And she paused here. Finishing the sentence as she had originally planned would have meant acknowledging that Reseda knew always what they were thinking and this made it hard for Sage to trust her as deeply as she wanted. And so she switched gears and said instead, "Well, I think Anise is a little threatened by you. And I think you two sometimes work at cross-purposes."

"Thank you for being so candid, Sage. I appreciate that," Reseda said agreeably, and she meant it. "Anise doesn't know you're telling me this, does she?"

"No. But you can tell her. It isn't a secret."

"And what are you planning to say to Anise? I suppose, as part of your shuttle diplomacy, you're seeing her as well."

"We are," Clary admitted. "And we are going to ask her to do nothing without your involvement."

"She won't agree to that."

"You weren't there the first time we tried," Clary said. "It was horrible. Everything went wrong. Just . . . everything. That wouldn't happen this time."

"Besides, it wasn't Anise's fault," Sage continued. "It was Tansy's."

Reseda watched a block of sun on Baphomet and strolled into the center of the pentagon. She closed her eyes and stared up at the ceiling of the greenhouse for a long moment, savoring the feel of the warmth on her skin. "Have you decided which twin?" she asked, opening her eyes.

"No," Sage told her. "But Anise is enjoying her afternoons with the girls and getting to know them."

"I am, too," Reseda said. "And I like their mother a great deal. Don't you?"

"She's very nice. But I can't say for sure if she'll ever be one of us."

"Move too fast and she won't be. I think it was a mistake to try and start calling her Verbena so soon. Same with the girls."

"The problem is that Anise doesn't think she has all that much time. And we have even less. I had given up before the Lintons came into our lives. I had absolutely given up. The first tincture is long gone. And then, magically, they appeared."

"I would not read too much into the idea that Emily contacted Sheldon Carter in the autumn and wanted to see a house. This was neither some cosmic plan nor one of mine."

"You don't have as much interest in the second volume, that's the problem," Clary told her, raising her voice slightly in her excitement. "You don't care as much for the blood potions. But the fact is, the tincture worked. Yes, the child died. But the tincture worked."

Reseda was struck by how old the pair seemed, how physically decrepit. They weren't, not really; the truth was, they were in absolutely remarkable shape for their age. But they were aging rapidly now, and that was what Reseda was sensing: their panic that, for them, time was running out. The tincture had worked forty years ago, but now they needed more. One of the Linton twins probably represented their last chance. "No," she admitted, "I don't care much for those potions. Those, in my opinion, are witchcraft."

"We know more now than we did with the Dunmore child. And we have you. This time nothing would go wrong," Sage said, pleading.

Reseda looked back and forth between the women. "I am more interested in their father."

"For a tincture?"

"No, of course not."

"Then why?" Clary asked, her puzzlement evident in the way she drew out that one short sentence.

"Something is going on inside him. I don't know what precisely. But I don't believe he's the man he was before he came here."

"Of course, he isn't!" Sage said, seemingly nonplussed by Reseda's uncharacteristic denseness. "He was the captain of a plane that crashed. It must be horrible."

"It's more than that."

"More than PTSD?" asked Clary.

"Perhaps."

"Well, John and Valerian and Anise have that under control," Sage told her, and then busied herself by inhaling the rosemary. "Valerian is having lunch with Emily tomorrow. I am very confident that Chip Linton won't have any effect on what we want."

"Please, Sage: Be judicious with your use of the word *we*."

"Does that mean you won't help us?" Sage asked.

Reseda noticed the woman's jaw working as she tried to control her annoyance. Her earrings were bunches of green grapes. "I'll speak to Anise," she said finally, and she watched as both older women relaxed, their shoulders sagging a little forward, and their minds focusing more on the possibilities held by the future than on what they had witnessed that night long ago when Sawyer Dunmore died. Reseda was glad for them—and for herself. That vision was, she decided, among the most disturbing things she had ever seen in someone else's mind.

You feel Ethan Stearns putting his cold, wet hands on your shoulders as you kneel in the front hallway, pressing the lid on the paint can. You close your eyes against the pain in your head.

"Chip?"

"Yes?"

"Keep your word to Hewitt. Do not tell Emily he was here."

You push yourself to your feet, and he releases your shoulders. You rub your eyes at the bridge of your nose and you massage the top of your head, but it does nothing to ease the pain. In a minute or two you will take a couple of Advil, but you know that won't help, either. At least not very much. The throbbing will cease only when Ethan Stearns leaves.

"I won't tell her," you agree. "But, please, don't threaten me."

"I wasn't threatening you."

"Okay."

"And don't tell her that Anise was here, either."

"I wasn't planning on it."

"If Anise wants her to know, Anise can tell her."

Outside, through the glass window in the storm door, you notice two very large robins landing on a thin branch of the bare lilac near the front walkway. They are so large that you half-expect the branch to bow. But it doesn't. Birds have hollow bones. It really is hard to believe it was birds that brought down your plane.

The next morning, John Hardin strolled into Emily's office in the Georgian beside the bicycle shop and sat down in the chair opposite her desk. "Verbena," he said, his voice a little wan. "How are you?"

"Still Emily," she corrected him. "Not Verbena yet."

"I'm sorry," he murmured, sipping his coffee. "Sometimes for a sleepy little corner of New Hampshire, we move too quickly, don't we?"

"It's fine. I'm just not prepared yet to make that . . . that leap."

He shrugged. "And you should feel no pressure to," he said. "None at all." He paused and then took a deep breath. "This has been a very strange spring, hasn't it?"

"I would say that's an understatement," she said.

"I just got a piece of news that makes me a little sad. It really has nothing to do with your family, but—"

"Then do I need to know?" she asked, cutting him off. "Honestly, John, I really don't want to begin the day with bad news."

"Sad—not bad. There's a difference. And you'll be fine. It just makes a man my age wistful. But it's not tragic. You know that fellow you bought the house from? Hewitt Dunmore? Well, it seems he died last night."

The news made her a little dizzy, a little nauseous, and she couldn't say why. "I'm so sorry. How?"

"Natural causes, apparently. He was found in his garage. A heart attack, most likely. He wasn't well. It might have been days and days before he was found, but, fortunately, the garage door was open and the light was on."

"I never actually met him," she said. "We spoke on the phone, but that was it. He didn't come to the closing."

"I know. I remember."

"Who found him?"

"The fellow who delivers his newspaper. I guess he saw the light on in the garage and the garage door wide open. And then he saw the poor man."

"How did you hear?"

"Old-fashioned grapevine, I guess. Someone told someone who told someone."

"And who was the someone who told you?"

"Anise. I ran into her at the coffee shop. She was getting some tea." He gazed out the window. "On the bright side, it's going to be another beautiful day. God, I love spring." He raised his coffee cup in a mock toast, stood up, and continued down the hall to his office.

Chapter Fifteen

Valerian Wainscott asked only for tea and honey at the booth in
the diner, waiting until after Emily had ordered a chicken salad
sandwich and a diet soda to put in her small request.

"That's all you're having?" Emily said to the psychiatrist.

"Oh, no, not at all," Valerian reassured her, and she reached into her
handbag on the cushion beside her and pulled out a Ziploc plastic bag
filled with granola. "Voilà! My lunch."

"They don't mind?"

The woman shrugged and smiled cherubically. "It's homemade,"
she said. Then she removed a black leather portfolio case and opened
it on the table between them. On the inside front cover Emily saw a
pocket with pages of handwritten notes about her husband. "There's a
lot I want to talk about," Valerian said. "I have strong opinions about
your husband and strong thoughts on how to help him."

"Go on." There was no doctor-patient confidentiality. Chip had told
Valerian he wanted her to share with Emily whatever Valerian thought
his wife should know.

"First of all, I worry that if we don't, well, get him under control, he
may hurt himself."

"You mean again?" Emily said, seeing once more in her mind the
knife in his stomach that night as he had stood at the top of the stairs.

"I mean worse than what was, in essence, an instance of especially
violent cutting."

"You're suggesting that he might make another attempt to kill himself."

"Yes."

Emily sat back against the vinyl cushions and tried to focus. She reminded herself that Valerian was only verbalizing thoughts she had already had and things she and Michael Richmond had discussed. Nevertheless, the reality of her husband's deteriorating mental state was still hard to hear. "I leave him alone with the girls as little as possible," she murmured.

"Oh, he would never hurt the girls," Valerian reassured her. "Never. This isn't about that."

"I didn't mean to suggest he would," she said. "I just worry that he gets so . . . so distracted. I just worry that one afternoon Hallie or Garnet might do something dangerous and silly—they're only ten, after all—and Chip would be completely oblivious."

"I see."

"So, tell me: What do you want to do?"

"Well, remember, I am just the second opinion," Valerian began. "Michael is still his doctor, and he seems perfectly competent in most ways."

"Go on."

"But your husband and I are starting to build a good rapport, too. And my sense is that I would like to admit him."

"Admit him?"

"So we can observe him."

Abruptly Emily understood what Valerian was telling her, and she felt as if she was on a plane and had just dropped a few thousand feet in sudden turbulence. She felt as if her whole body had lurched, and she was frightened. She heard the clatter of silver and plates and the din of conversation all around her through the thick French drapes of a theater. Everything sounded muffled and far away. "You want him institutionalized?" she asked when the idea had sunk in.

"Just temporarily. And he would have to agree to it. But all those beams that keep a person sane and functioning are about as stressed as they can get without snapping in two. And if they do snap, it won't be pretty."

"How long?"

"At the state hospital? I don't know."

"Best guess?"

"Maybe a month. Maybe less, maybe more. You both should view it as a time-out from life."

"Then couldn't the same effect be achieved with, I don't know, a really restful vacation?"

"He needs treatment and observation."

Emily was vaguely aware that the psychiatrist had opened her bag of granola, and now the woman popped a few pieces into her mouth. Her chewing reminded Emily of a rabbit.

"Have you talked to my husband about this?" she asked finally.

"No. I wanted to talk to you first."

"What about Michael?"

"I'll talk to him."

"Can you tell me what's involved?"

"With institutionalization?"

She nodded.

"Since it's voluntary, it's mostly about making sure there's a bed. John Hardin would not even need to help us prepare committal papers."

In her mind Emily saw her calm and gentle boss. "I keep forgetting: You know John."

"Like a godfather, Emily. I love that man. There's nothing I wouldn't do for him."

"Can I think about this?" she asked.

The waitress returned and, smiling, placed the chicken salad sandwich on the table. She was an older woman with bluish hair and large tortoiseshell eyeglasses that dwarfed her nose. She didn't seem troubled by the idea that Valerian was eating food she had brought from home into the diner, and so Emily reflexively looked at the badge on her smock dress. Maggie. So, the waitress wasn't one of them. Emily was surprised.

"Of course you can think about it," the psychiatrist said after Maggie had left them alone. "And I will respect whatever decision you make. Just . . ."

"Just what?"

She pushed her little bag of granola aside and put her hands on the table, palms open and up. "Give me your hands," she said to Emily, and—a little reluctantly at first—Emily did. Then Valerian grasped them, gently massaging Emily's fingers with her thumbs. "I just worry about you. All of us do. We all just worry about you so, so much."

The cat watched the birds here in New Hampshire, making no distinctions between the ones that she'd stalked in Pennsylvania and the ones that seemed to be everywhere in this new world. There were more of them now that the snow was gone and the days were growing long. She was finding the field grass beyond the greenhouse a considerably better place to stalk them than the manicured lawns around her previous home, even though it was nowhere near as tall as it would be in another month. Unlike other cats, she felt no need to share the remains of her kills with the four people around her. She needed their approval in some ways, but she tended to eat the birds she caught wherever she found them. Same with the field mice and moles.

Likewise, she watched the insects, and was particularly fascinated by the ants that would swarm upon the small pieces of the breads and confections that the people she didn't know brought into this house. She made no connection between the people and the way some of those foods seemed to poison the ants; that sort of cause-and-effect leap was beyond her.

Among the humans whom she did not view as part of her family but was starting to recognize, there was one with gray hair that was long and thick, and who seemed to bring more food into the house than any of the other strangers. Today she had come by again when only the man was home. It was early in the afternoon, and the girls and their mother had disappeared, as they tended to most days, and the father was working around the first floor of the house. The woman had knelt down in the front hallway and made kissing sounds, and so Desdemona had walked over to her while the father went to retrieve something from the kitchen. She'd pressed her head into the woman's fingers and the palm of her hand, enjoying the way this individual knew precisely how to rub her ears and scratch her neck. She'd purred.

Then the woman had opened a plastic bag and pulled out a mouse by its tail. It was already dead, and for a moment Desdemona had eyed it carefully. No human had ever given her an animal before. And there was a scent to it that she didn't recognize. But a mouse was a mouse, and it was fresh. And so she took it and raced into the corner of the den nearest the woodstove. There she devoured every bit of it, despite its unfamiliar but not unappealing flavor, even the tail and the liver and the head.

Michael Richmond hadn't known Valerian Wainscott well before their meeting that afternoon at his office in Littleton, but their paths had crossed at a pair of conferences and once they had been at a cocktail party together. That was three years ago. Richmond had been struck by her name the moment they'd met, since, he presumed, it signaled that she was a part of that bizarre cult of herbalists centered in Bethel. But she seemed almost too much of a flake to be one of them; moreover, she worked at the state psychiatric hospital. She was a lovely young woman whom he recalled nibbling on a homemade cupcake during a lecture in one conference and whose questions betrayed a deep distaste for most pharmacological interventions in the other—which, he supposed, made her a very rare bird at the hospital. Given how many beds were filled with the mentally ill who were violent or delusional or both, it seemed inconceivable that some days she wouldn't want to pass out risperidone and valproate like M&M's on Halloween. The fact was, chamomile tea wasn't going to sedate a raging schizophrenic.

The two other women Richmond had met who he was convinced were part of the cult were a pair of real estate agents, and they seemed considerably more focused and intense than Valerian. One of them was so preternaturally composed that she was a little intimidating. He had met the two when he'd been searching for a small home near the ski resort. After spending a day looking at property with the composed one, he'd decided to work with another agency—and, eventually, through that firm had found an A-frame with a magnificent view of Cannon Mountain. He couldn't recall the original real estate agent's name now, but she had explained to him that it was some rare and exotic flower. Later people would tell him about the strange cult—a coven, they had said, only half-kidding—and he would realize that he had met one of its members.

Well, Dr. Valerian Wainscott was in all likelihood a member, too.

And now she wanted to commit Chip Linton—or, to be precise, recommend to Chip that he commit himself. And while that notion alone had infuriated Michael, he had to admit that he was also annoyed with her presumption that she was better trained than he was to care for "a middle-aged male cutter" like Chip Linton.

"You make it sound like that's a type," he had told her, incapable of hiding his incredulity.

"It's uncommon, but not unseen," she had replied, her voice downright chipper. "I see men like the pilot at the hospital periodically."

"You do?"

"Absolutely," she had assured him.

"Well, he does not need to be committed."

"Is he getting better with you?"

"He's making progress."

"No," she'd said, her voice pert, "I just don't see it. And are you really that confident that he won't kill himself? Tell me: Could you live with yourself if he did?"

"I simply do not believe hospitalization is in his best interests," he had told her. "I will argue against it. I will tell Emily that her second opinion is a wrong opinion."

Valerian had smiled and raised her eyebrows and shrugged. He'd decided she was absolutely beautiful and absolutely insane. He'd decided she was completely unqualified to do what she did for a living. And he'd decided he would tell Emily and Chip to give this Valerian

Wainscott as wide a berth as they could. They should have nothing to do with her and—if they ever met any others—they should avoid those Bethel women who spent way too much time in their greenhouses.

"I'll bet your father has finished hanging the wallpaper in the dining room," Emily told the girls, handing Hallie a half gallon of milk and Garnet a brown paper grocery bag. On the way home from dance class, they had stopped at the supermarket and done the food shopping for the next few days. "I really won't miss those sunflowers," she added, trying to sound cheerful. She was looking forward to seeing the room brightened by the new wallpaper patterned with roses, but mostly she was preoccupied with Valerian's belief that her husband should be institutionalized. She wasn't sure if she had stopped thinking about it for more than a few minutes since Valerian had rendered her opinion. She wanted to meet with Michael Richmond to see what he thought, and didn't want to broach the subject with Chip until she knew more.

"Me, either," Hallie said, leading the way into the house even though she was burdened with the milk, her dance bag, and her school backpack. "They were creepy."

Emily called out to her husband that they were home, a grocery bag in each arm, figuring in her mind that she had two more trips. "Chip?" she called again when he didn't respond. She thought she needn't necessarily worry that he hadn't answered, but she did.

The three of them went straight to the kitchen, put the bags down on the counter, and then Emily followed the twins as they peered into the dining room. But instead of hearing the girls either coo over the new wallpaper or remark on the reality that there was still a whole section of the west wall with those gloomy, dispiriting sunflowers, she heard Garnet calling out the cat's name quizzically. "Dessy?" Garnet was saying, her voice not much more than a murmur. "Dessy?" But then the voice grew to one long, loud shriek, and Hallie was wailing the animal's name, too. There was the family cat on the floor by the credenza—half on the Oriental rug and half on the hardwood planks—her eyes wide open and her tongue protruding like a small pink stone from her mouth. There seemed to be dried froth on her nose and a small stain of dried vomit on the floor beside her.

"Is she dead?" Hallie was asking, trying to sniff back enough of her tears for her words to be clear, and even before Emily had knelt on the floor by the cat and touched the cold fur, she knew that the animal was.

"Chip?" she called again. "Chip?"

"Be right up!" he yelled, his voice somewhere in the basement below them.

"He's always down there," Garnet murmured, still crying softly, speaking to no one in particular. She was sitting on the floor and running two fingers gently along the cat's side. "There, there," she said, as if the cat were alive and needed comforting. "There, there."

In a moment Chip was standing in the doorway, his face grimy and his shoulders sagging just a bit, but looking rather cheerful. He had a glass jar in his hands with what looked like soapy water. "Hello, girls," he said. "I didn't hear you get home!"

"We were calling for you," Emily said, trying to read him. "What were you doing?"

"Oh, I was in the basement. I guess I didn't hear you. I must have been in my own little world."

"Something's happened to Desdemona," she said.

He walked around her and crouched like a baseball catcher between his daughters. He stroked the cat once and then lifted the animal's head so he could see her dead eyes and the way the tongue protruded from her mouth.

"Oh, Dessy," he said. Then: "She must have gotten into something. The poor, poor thing."

"You think she ate something that poisoned her?" she asked him.

"I do. Look at the tongue and look at the vomit."

"And she's dead, Daddy?" Hallie asked. "Definitely?"

"Definitely," he said sadly.

"What's that in the jar?" Emily asked him.

He looked from the cat to his fingers and seemed surprised to see anything there. Then he shrugged. "Paint thinner. I got tired of wall-papering in here and touched up the trim. I was cleaning the brushes when you got home."

"In the basement."

"That's right," he said, and once again he stroked the cat behind her ears, the way he had countless thousands of times before. Emily couldn't imagine why he would have poisoned the cat, but the idea crossed her mind that he had. And then she looked back and forth between her girls, and the notion of her husband taking—to use Valerian's expression—a time-out from life seemed more and more logical. She decided in the meantime that under no circumstances would she leave him alone with their daughters.

Reseda thought that Sage Messner's greenhouse—the largest in Bethel and the one the women who did not have greenhouses used—needed statuary. She was watching Anise and Sage work with the twins, and she imagined a marble sculpture of the girls near the parsley, basil, and echinacea. She recalled a Renaissance statue of twin children she had rather liked that she had seen one afternoon on a third-floor corridor at the Uffizi. A cat was rubbing her side against one of the girls' marble shins, and so Reseda made a mental note to leave out that detail if she should decide to mention the statue to the children. Their cat had died two days earlier, and she knew the loss was still fresh. Right now the twins were standing around a table, hunched over a copy of *The Complete Book of Divination and Mediation with Plants and Herbs,* while Anise and Sage stood behind them and pointed out where in the green-house they could see the actual plants that were pictured in the text. This was the first of the two-volume encyclopedia that the women used for most of their tinctures, and some approached the book with an almost biblical reverence. There were only four copies of that first volume in the group's possession, all from 1891, and the women were constantly photocopying pages from it or scanning them into PDFs on their computers, and it was an indication of Anise's interest in Emily's daughters that she had shared with them her own personal copy.

Reseda had been about to say something complimentary to the girls about what lovely models for a statue they would make when she paused: She sensed that one of the twins was aware that there was a second volume, and already the child had skimmed through enough of the first book to know its name: *The Complete Book of Divination and Mediation with Animals and Humans*. Only a single copy of that second volume existed, and Anise kept it in an ornate, reliquary-like cherry cabinet in her bedroom. Frequently the women searched used bookstores and online auction sites for an additional copy, but one had never appeared. Like their four copies of the first volume, the copyright of the second volume was 1891.

And so instead of making a random suggestion that someday the girls pose for a statue, Reseda said, "I have always preferred this first volume to the second."

Both girls looked up at her.

"I hadn't told Cali and Rosemary about the second volume," Anise said, her tone a little clipped.

"The book talks about it right here," Garnet said, and she showed Anise and Sage where in the encyclopedia she'd seen that second volume referenced. "See?"

"Aren't you the diligent student, Cali," Anise told her.

"What does *diligent* mean," Hallie asked, oblivious to the slight edge in Anise's voice.

"It means she works very, very hard," Sage explained. "I imagine you do, too."

"No, she works harder than me," Hallie said, and she smiled at Garnet with what Reseda knew was genuine sisterly pride. The pride a twin has in her twin. A lover had once told Reseda that he presumed the bonds twins shared far transcended the more common sibling rivalries. He'd been right. "Dad says she's going to be a teacher or a professor someday."

"Both are worthy aspirations," said Anise.

"How is your father?" Reseda asked. She wasn't as interested in what either child might say as she was in what thoughts would pass through Sage's head when the woman envisioned Captain Chip Linton. But almost instantly Sage started counting the massive leaves on the hoja santa—which, in a fashion, was itself revealing.

"Mom is a little worried about him, I guess," Hallie answered, looking down at a diagram of hypnobium in the book rather than meet her gaze.

"We all are," Sage said.

"Is there anything in particular?" Reseda asked the girl, but carefully she gazed at Garnet as well. "So far, I don't feel Bethel has been especially healing for him. I know the move to New Hampshire has been hard on all of you."

"You do?" Garnet asked.

"I do. I really do."

Garnet seemed to think about this. Then Hallie began to answer: "The other day I caught him talking to someone. I was in the kitchen and Mom was upstairs, and I heard—"

"Hallie!" said her sister, cutting her off, and she took the girl's arm. "No!"

"It's Rosemary," the child snapped. "And, yes, I will tell them! Someone has to know! And just because you don't want to scare Mom doesn't mean I can't talk about it!"

"Go ahead," Reseda said. "Tell me."

"The other day I caught him talking to himself," Hallie said, and then she took a deep breath. "He was in the basement near that weird door, and it was like he was talking to me or Cali. But he wasn't, because we weren't with him. We had been upstairs. And another time I found him sitting in the den with my dolls, and it was like he was inventing a game with them for us. But again, he wasn't. He was all alone."

"They're my dolls, too," Garnet said, and she shook her head.

"And I think . . ."

"What do you think?" Reseda asked.

"I can tell Mom thinks he might have killed Dessy."

"Do you think he did?" Sage asked, bending over with her hands on her knees.

"I don't know. Mom started to say something about maybe taking her body to the veterinarian so he could tell us what happened, but Dad just wanted to bury her. And the ground was just soft enough now that we could."

"Is there more?" Reseda said.

Hallie nodded. "I guess."

"Tell me. You can."

"Well, he's gone from being kind of spacey since the accident to being really cheerful one second and then really angry the next. But he never gets mad at us. He just gets mad. He also has headaches, and I know they're getting a lot worse. Mom doesn't want us to know, but I've heard them talking. And he has some really bad pain in his side."

"He's depressed," Anise said. "That's all. And he should be depressed. What kind of man would your father be, if he weren't?"

"Is that your way of comforting the children, Anise?" Reseda asked.

"It's my way of comforting everyone," she said, and then the whole room seemed to grow quiet, except for the gentle hiss of the humidifier. Sage counted soundlessly, moving her lips, and the girls thought of their father, and Anise merely smirked. And then Garnet's head cleared, and she looked at all three women around her but directed her question at Reseda.

"Can I ask you something?" the girl said.

"Yes, absolutely."

"What are the potions in the second volume?"

"I think he did poison that cat," Anise told Reseda, once Emily had picked up the girls and taken them home. The two of them were walking from Sage's greenhouse to their vehicles at the edge of the woman's long driveway. "I think Verbena and the girls will be much, much safer when he is properly hospitalized—as Valerian suggests."

"Perhaps."

"Perhaps?"

"I don't see that sort of unreasonable malevolence in the captain. I think the cat just ate something that did her in."

"I'm not sure Valerian would agree. And she's the doctor."

"But she's not his doctor."

"She will be."

"I don't think a hospital can treat what ails him."

"And that is?"

Already Reseda regretted saying as much as she had. She didn't trust Anise. The woman wasn't necessarily dubious of Reseda's work as a sha-man, but she also craved the tangibility that came with a tincture. She saw magic largely in plants. But, then, Reseda wasn't fully confident in her own diagnosis, either, since it was based only on very limited obser-vation and what one of the pilot's daughters had told her. Moreover, she herself had stood in Sawyer Dunmore's crypt and felt nothing. Nothing at all. It didn't seem likely the captain was possessed by the Dunmore twin who had been killed. "I'm honestly not sure," she said finally. "I just don't think he should be institutionalized."

Anise shrugged. They had reached her truck, and the rusty front door groaned when she yanked it open. Before climbing in Anise added, "We will do this, Reseda. You know that, don't you? You can't stop us. We will try again."

"Because they're twins," she said.

"Yes. And because of what they've endured."

"Do you know which one?"

"I don't. Not yet. But I will."

"No good ever comes from that second volume."

"Not true," Anise said, settling into her seat and staring down at Reseda from the full height of the truck cab. "I may be vegan, but just the other day I whipped up something absolutely magic with a field mouse." Then she turned the key and the engine roared to life. She barely missed Reseda's toes as she sped down the driveway.

*   *   *

"He simply doesn't agree that hospitalization is the right course," Valerian told John Hardin, as they sat across from each other at his kitchen table. "I don't know Michael well, but I know his type."

"Even after the captain killed the girls' cat?" John asked, sipping his coffee. He could tell that Valerian, like his wife, did not approve of coffee. But he viewed it as his only vice. Besides, he had yet to find a tea he enjoyed half so much. "He really doesn't think the man poses some sort of danger to his family?"

"So it would seem. But, then, he doesn't believe the captain poisoned the animal."

"Well, Verbena does."

"And that's something. Nevertheless, he called me today to tell me he's going to report me to the State Board of Medicine. He's going to suggest that I have some . . . some sort of agenda . . . for wanting the man committed."

"Well, you do," John said, and he allowed himself a small smirk. As he hoped, it seemed to cheer the young woman a bit. "So, hospitalization isn't really the recommended protocol?"

"Of course not!"

"No arguable gray area?"

"None."

"Well, you're the doctor. I'm merely a lawyer. But sadly, in addition to getting you in a wee bit of hot water, this could be a bit of a cause célèbre, couldn't it? Given the captain's history and that ditching in Lake Champlain, arguing over his competency could draw more attention to us than any of us desire."

"I know."

"Tell me: In your opinion, would Verbena be able to convince the captain to admit himself to the hospital if Michael were no longer his physician?"

"Absolutely," she answered. "I have no doubt."

"So we need Michael gone."

"Yes, but we really don't have the time to convince him to . . . take care of himself."

"Well, that doesn't matter because I'm not much of a sorcerer. Just had the good sense to marry one. Besides: It's not as if Anise has managed to convince the captain to take care of himself."

"These things take time. And unfortunately, I really don't have a lot of it."

"Everything is so much easier once the captain is committed. Verbena is dependent upon us and enamored with us. There's a term for that, isn't there? A psychological term?"

She nodded. "The Stockholm syndrome. It's when a captive or a hostage starts thinking well of his or her abductors."

"Well, I like to believe she would think highly of us no matter what. I think most of the time we're rather good eggs."

"John, sometimes I just can't tell when you're pulling my leg or being deadly serious."

He reached across the table and squeezed her arm. "This time? I am being deadly serious," he answered, smiling, and his eyes had the twinkle she loved.

That night Emily skimmed through the local phone book. Even though it was but a fraction as thick as the one back home in Pennsylvania, there were still nearly two columns of people named Davis. Fortunately, there were only two in Bethel and only one Rebecca. Paul and Rebecca Davis. Clearly this was the woman who had buttonholed her at the diner in Littleton soon after they arrived in New Hampshire. While the girls were doing their homework she phoned her. That afternoon, Anise and Sage had each tried calling her Verbena, just as John Hardin had earlier in the week. Meanwhile, Valerian Wainscott wanted to institutionalize her husband. And so now Emily decided that she needed another opinion about these self-proclaimed herbalists. She wanted to speak with someone who, clearly, wasn't one of them.

A man answered the phone at the Davis household, and she

introduced herself to him. She said she was Emily Linton and she was hoping to speak to Becky Davis. Although she was quite sure she heard the woman in the background speaking with that high school–age son she had mentioned at the diner, Paul Davis said his wife wasn't home. But he said that she would call Emily back in the next day or two.

"Would you like my work number?" she asked.

"We know your firm," he said, an edge to his voice that hadn't existed when he first answered the call.

"That's right," Emily said simply. "Your wife mentioned that she knew I worked with John Hardin."

"We all do," he told her, and then added curtly, "Good night."

You wonder: These days, does Emily ever fall into a sleep so deep that she will not remember her dreams in the morning and no mere rustle will wake her? You know what she thinks about you. You know what they all think. The women. Their husbands. You know what they all believe.

The truth is, now whenever you climb from beneath the sheets— before you have even thrown your feet over the side of the bed onto the cold wooden floor of your bedroom—Emily is awake.

Chip? she will murmur, and then she will ask you where you are going.

Oh, just getting an Advil, you will reassure her, and sometimes that has indeed been the case, because sometimes Ethan or Ashley or even Sandra has joined you in your bedroom in those smallest, darkest hours of the night. Other times you have simply gone to the bathroom. Either way, Emily will sit upright in bed and await your return. You know she is listening carefully to the sound of your footsteps along the corridor and awaiting the sound of the bathroom door closing and opening. If your toes so much as touched the steps to the third floor and Hallie and Garnet's bedrooms, she would be out of your bed like a shot.

The result is that those same demons that have you contemplating the deaths of your own children have you contemplating her death as well. She has no idea that you have brought Tansy's knife upstairs, none at all. Right now, you could lie on your stomach and drape your arm over the side of the mattress, dangle it casually as if you were getting a massage, and find the knife held to the inside wall of a horizontal slat with one wide piece of duct tape. Or you could simply smother Emily. The original Desdemona—Shakespeare's, not yours—died that way. And, in fact, your Emily once played Desdemona and she was remarkable. You were able to rearrange your flight schedule that month so you could be in the audience opening night, and you may never have been more proud of her as an actress than when you witnessed her final scene with Othello. You watched her die at the hands of her husband.

You have to hope it will never come to that in real life. You have to hope you can resist. But the physical pains grow worse, as does Ethan's incessant prodding. If you ever hurt either Emily or your girls, you know that next you would kill yourself. That has always been clear.

And so once more you contemplate the knife you have brought to your bed. Perhaps you should simply use it upon yourself first and ensure that nothing happens to Emily or Hallie or Garnet. This time, instead of plunging it into your abdomen—trying, in some way, to eradicate the pain you already are feeling—you should slash your wrists. Long cuts along your forearms, from your elbows to the wrinkles at the palms of your hands.

"Chip?"

"Yes, sweetie?"

"Were you having a bad dream? One of your plane dreams?"

"No. I wasn't even asleep. I was wide awake."

"You were?"

"I was." You pull your legs out from under the sheets and feel her sit up in bed. You knew she would.

"Where are you going?" she asks.

"Just getting an Advil."

And then you walk to the bathroom, leaving the door open so she can hear exactly what you are doing. She can hear the mirrored cabinet door with its small squeal and she can hear the rattle of the red pills in the plastic bottle when you shake three more tablets (yes, that is how many you will take now; sometimes you even take four) into the palm of your hand. When you return to bed, her head is on her pillow, but you can tell that her eyes are open. She is alert. Vigilant. But, of course, she is not as vigilant as she thinks she is. She has no idea that on the other side of the bed—her side of the bed—Ethan Stearns is watching her. He is watching you both. And your head? It now feels like it will explode, and, despite those three Advil, you shut tight your eyes against the pain, grimacing into your pillow in the dark.

Chapter Sixteen

Michael Richmond flipped the windshield wipers on the car to a faster speed because the rain was relentless and navigating the tortuous two-lane road up the hill to his A-frame was proving a challenge. The thermometer on the dashboard said it was thirty-eight degrees, so he wasn't worried about the rain turning to sleet or this stretch of road becoming a long sheet of black ice that glistened in the light from his car's headlamps. But it was nearly ten-thirty at night and he was sleepy, so he sat back against the seat to concentrate and took another sip of his Red Bull. (Valerian, he had to assume, did not approve of Red Bull.) Then he grasped the steering wheel with both hands.

He kept thinking about Valerian's appalling and absolutely irresponsible belief that Chip Linton should be institutionalized. There was something going on with the captain, there was no doubt about that, but the answer wasn't confinement in the state hospital. It made absolutely no sense, no sense at all. "The person in this write-up in no way resembles my client," he had told Valerian.

Tomorrow he was going to contact the Board of Medicine. He considered whether his anger was reasonable and decided it was. Valerian had overstepped her bounds and, worse, was going to try to convince a fundamentally sane man to commit himself. He knew also that she was going to pay: He was going to go after that lunatic's license.

"Michael," she'd replied at one point when, yet again, they were arguing, "he may have stuck a knife in his stomach. He has phantom pains that are off the charts. He may have poisoned the family cat. He went berserk over a coal chute door."

"And that door turned out to be a crypt," he had answered, though he knew this really didn't exonerate Chip. The man hadn't known the Dunmores buried their son there. And so quickly he'd added, "He's calm and reasonable now, and we don't know if he poisoned the cat—and we probably never will. Imagine if we were discussing whether the man was competent to stand trial: Well, perhaps he wasn't competent the night that Molly Francoeur was over at their house and he hurt himself. But you know as well as I do that a person can become competent. And he is definitely competent right now."

Though they had argued for nearly thirty minutes—their third debate over the past five days—it was clear that she wasn't going to budge. And neither was he.

Up ahead he saw a vehicle pulled off to the side of the road with its hazard lights flashing, and he thought about what a miserable night it was to have car trouble. He slowed as he approached and saw the car was a new-model hybrid and there was a person in a hooded yellow slicker standing beside it, waving at him with a flashlight. He coasted to a stop ahead of it, wishing his sheepskin coat was waterproof or he kept an umbrella in the backseat. But there was nothing to be done about that now, and so he braced himself for a foray into the chill rain and climbed from his car.

He saw that the individual was a tweedy, athletic-looking older man with a great shock of Robert Frost–like white hair and wire-rimmed eyeglasses, now spotted with rain. He guessed the fellow was in his late sixties or early seventies.

"Thank you so much," the gentleman said, and Michael realized that he was shouting to be heard over the wind and the rain.

"Not a big deal. What's the problem?" he asked. The guy must have been desperate to stand out here in the storm.

He shook his head and extended his hands, palms up, signaling his absolute befuddlement. "And there's no cell coverage here—at least I have none," he said.

"Yeah, I don't, either," Michael told him. "What happened?"

"I heard a beep and then got a mass of flashing warning lights on the dashboard. One for the ABS system, one for the battery, one for the pressure in the tires. I pulled over to turn off the car and turn it back on, hoping it was just some computer glitch that needed a restart. Nope. Now the car won't even turn over. When I looked under the hood, I saw nothing obviously amiss."

"Where do you live?" Michael asked. "At the very least I can give you a ride back to Franconia. Maybe something will be open there. Or you can call someone from my house. I only live about two miles up this road."

"If it comes to that, I'll certainly hitch a ride. Thanks a bunch. But would you mind first seeing if you can get it started? It would save us both a lot of trouble."

Michael grinned. "My auto mechanic training begins and ends with adding wiper fluid. Sorry. You probably know a hell of a lot more about what goes on underneath the hood of a car than I do."

"Well, maybe you'll have better luck turning it over," the man said, and he handed Michael the keys. "Would you mind trying? Maybe something will catch."

"And I thought I was an optimist," Michael said. "Get in with me and we'll see what happens. Is the door unlocked?"

"It is," the fellow said. Then: "I think I have some gloves in the front seat. My fingers are a little numb from the cold." And already he was racing around the front of the car and escaping the rain in the passenger seat, where he retrieved his gloves. Michael slid in behind the steering wheel, amazed at how already the rain had soaked through his coat and sweater and shirt. He could feel the wetness against his back when he leaned against the seat in the car.

"I'm Michael," he said as he settled in.

"John," the older man said. "Pleasure to meet you." Then he added, "Excuse the blankets on the seats. My wife and I have two very big dogs at home, and sometimes they travel with me."

Michael looked down now and realized that, indeed, both the

passenger and driver's seats were covered by old, badly stained blankets. "Well, here goes," he murmured. And almost out of intellectual curiosity, he turned the key in the ignition. He tried twice, and both times the engine made almost no noise. Once he thought he might have heard a dim clicking somewhere under the hood, but otherwise there wasn't even a gurgle from the engine.

He turned to the older gentleman, shaking his head, his eyebrows raised, and saw him smile. But it was an odd grin, the smile Michael had seen before on patients he'd visited at the state psychiatric hospital—a smile unconnected to normal stimuli or responses. It was a little manic and disturbing. "I tried," he said sheepishly. "I was—"

He never finished the sentence. He was aware of the fellow's right arm rising up out of nowhere, and even in the dark of the car he saw the long, wide blade of the knife. But it all happened so fast. One second he was telling him that, as he had expected, he had no magic touch that was going to start the engine. The next? Vicious, stinging pain and he knew he was going to die. He hadn't even had time to raise an arm in defense. The knife hacked deep and far into his neck, not once, not twice, but three times, and it felt like his throat was full of fluid, a melting glacier in his esophagus. Intellectually he understood that his carotid artery had been slashed wide open on that first, violent pass and he was going to bleed to death within moments. *Exsanguination* was the medical term. Odd that in these last seconds of life he should think of that. Or, as his head was all but decapitated and balanced briefly on his shoulder before his chin toppled forward against his jacket, the colloquial term: Bleeding out. Bleeeding . . . out.

Then, he felt nothing. Absolutely nothing at all.

When it was done, John Hardin took a washcloth from a pocket of his raincoat and wiped the blood off the window beside the driver's seat, and then dabbed at the steering wheel a little delicately. He wrapped the body in the blanket on which it was sitting, pulling the corners up and over the lolling skull and the limp arms. He was a strong man, but it still took enormous effort to drag the corpse from the driver's bucket seat to the passenger's—he had to stand on the pavement in the rain and pull—and one of the psychiatrist's hands fell from the blanket and got blood on the cushion. He used the washcloth to clean that, too. Clary hated bloodstains. He couldn't blame her. They both liked a tidy house and tidy cars.

When he was done, he turned off the blinking hazard lights on the psychiatrist's vehicle, locked the door, and then climbed back into the driver's seat of his hybrid. He reached under the steering wheel and aimed his flashlight at the fuse box. Before leaving home he had taped small, bright dots of yellow paper beside the fuses for the fuel pump and the ignition so he could spot them easily. Now he pressed the fuses back into place and started the vehicle. As he did, a tremendous milk tanker barreled up the road, seemingly out of nowhere, and he spotted its lights at the very last moment. The trucker slammed on his horn, veered into the other lane, and continued on. Had he pulled out a split second earlier, the tanker probably would have killed him and totaled the car. And that, John thought, would have done no one any good. No one any good at all. So he took a breath to compose himself, though he really hadn't lost his composure until he had almost pulled out without looking. Then he flipped on the car's radio to the local public radio affiliate—the station played jazz this time of the night, which he liked—and started home. He glanced back one time at the psychiatrist's vehicle through the rain, but, without its lights on, it grew invisible quickly. The road curved to the left, and the empty car disappeared into the night.

R eseda returned to the real estate office after showing a pair of married bond traders intent on early retirement what they thought might be the bed-and-breakfast of their dreams. The old inn had been for sale for nearly eighteen months, and the asking price was a fraction of what it had been when the widower first put it on the market. But Reseda ended up talking the traders out of the property. It was clear to her that the couple wouldn't be happy in this backwater corner of New Hampshire. Neither was the sort who was capable of aimlessly chatting up weekend guests about the foliage, maple syrup, or the perils of mud season. They still needed the frenetic chaos of the trading floor, even if they thought they were burned out.

When she arrived, Holly was waiting for her with a stack of pages from the Internet listing the names of the people who had died on Flight 1611, and any demographic information she could glean from news articles.

"Who do you think it is?" Reseda asked as she sat at her desk and began leafing through the papers.

"I have no idea. I thought about what you told me the girl had said," she answered, "and there are some distinct possibilities. But there were still thirty-nine fatalities."

"That's how many died? Thirty-nine?"

Holly nodded.

"Well, I would say it's this child," Reseda said after a moment, touching the name Ashley Stearns with the tip of her pen, "because Rosemary was quite sure that, when he was talking to himself, he was imagining a girl. He was, in fact, playing with one of her and her sister's dolls."

"But a little girl couldn't be that controlling. Could she?"

Reseda thought about this. "If Ashley is with the captain, she's probably not alone."

"I wish we knew how they had died in the crash. After all, we know where the captain is in pain."

She smiled approvingly at Holly. If what she did demanded an apprentice, she would want Holly to be hers.

Hallie watched Anise intently as the woman turned her face up into the April sun, her eyes closed and her hands clasped behind her. The light was raining down upon her like a shower. With her halo of gray hair and a thin smile on her face, she looked, Hallie thought, like an angel. She was standing toward the western wall of the Lintons' greenhouse and staring up at the western ceiling. At her feet were three supermarket cartons filled with seedlings (most from either her greenhouse or Ginger Jackson's), a forty-pound bag of potting soil, and a plastic watering can she had filled from the outdoor spigot near the house's wheelbarrow ramp. The seedlings, according to Anise, were among the more common herbs and flowers—not the exotic ones that Hallie had never heard of before they moved to Bethel. The cartons were filled with basil, parsley, peppermint, sage, and thyme, but she wouldn't have been able to say which seedlings were which without the small Popsicle-stick signs that had been speared into the dirt.

Today was the warmest the greenhouse had been since they moved here, two months ago. Hallie and her sister were wearing only hooded sweatshirts over their T-shirts, and Hallie felt she would have been comfortable in here even without the hoodie. They had been picked up after school by Anise and brought home so they could start setting up their very own greenhouse. Once more, instead of doing homework or attending a dance class or having a music lesson, the girls were going to be gardening. Their mother would be at the office for another two hours. Meanwhile, their father had finally finished the dining room, the living room, and the front hallway, and this afternoon he had gone to the hardware store and the lumberyard. He had been nosing around those back stairs behind the kitchen—wondering what, if anything, he should do about them—and decided he wanted to replace some of the rotting steps and try to add a handrail.

"It's not polite to stare, Rosemary," the woman said, emerging abruptly from her reverie. She was smiling at the girl, but still Hallie felt scolded, and so she quickly formulated her defense.

"Oh, I wasn't staring," she said, though she was well aware that she had been. "But I did think you looked pretty in the sunlight, Anise," she added. She sounded in her head like a kiss-ass, a term she had learned the night before on a TV show, but she was confident that Anise wouldn't see through her. Reseda would; Reseda seemed to know precisely what a person was thinking. Hallie had figured out that, when she was around Reseda, she should keep her mind as blank as possible or she should tell the absolute truth. But Anise? She wasn't as bright. Or, maybe, she wasn't as (to use the word she had overheard Clary once use) *gifted*.

And, indeed, Anise smiled at her. Then the woman put her hands on her hips in a businesslike fashion and surveyed the tables and the toys in the greenhouse. "First of all, a greenhouse is no place for a lot of dolls," she said. She lifted one of the American Girl dolls roughly by its ankle and started toward the greenhouse door. Garnet had been kneeling before one of the cartons, peering in at the rows of plants there in their tiny plastic pots, but she was instantly on her feet when she saw Anise treating the doll so roughly. She pulled the doll from the woman's hand and held it against her chest as if it were an actual infant.

"Cali, really. It's a doll," Anise scolded her. "You are ten years old. Isn't it time to—forgive me—stop thinking like a child and reasoning like a child? Isn't it about time you put aside your childish ways?"

Hallie was pretty sure the quote came from the Bible, but she couldn't have begun to explain the context or the meaning or why Anise had decided to cite it. She had a vague sense that the woman was using it ironically: Anise had meant what she said, but quoting the Bible was almost a joke to her.

"I like that doll," Garnet said. "I like all my dolls."

"You're too old—"

"I'm not too old! I'm ten!" She motioned at Hallie with her hand. "We're ten!"

"It's okay," Hallie said, hoping to calm her sister. "We'll bring the dolls inside and put them back in the den. They probably shouldn't be out here in the greenhouse anyway. I'll take a couple and you take a couple. Anise, is that okay? We'll bring them to the den or even upstairs to our bedrooms, and it will just take a minute. Cali and I will—"

"And I'm not Cali! I'm Garnet! I don't want to be Cali!" Suddenly she was shouting, and Hallie could see from the corner of her eye that Anise was more intrigued than angered by the outburst. She seemed to be studying the two of them, almost curious. She had no intention of jumping in as a grown-up.

"Okay, you're Garnet. Fine. Not a big deal," Hallie reassured her sister, and Garnet seemed to calm down. They would each take an armful of dolls, and then they would each take an armful of the dolls' furniture. In two trips they would have cleared the greenhouse of what Anise considered the childish things. "Anise, we'll be right back, okay?" Hallie said.

Anise nodded, and Hallie turned back to her sister, expecting to see her rounding up more of their toys. But she wasn't, she was just standing there, her gaze stonelike, and Hallie knew instantly that the girl was in the midst of a seizure. Her eyes were open but absolutely oblivious to the world they were taking in. She was standing perfectly still, holding the American Girl doll named Addy in her arms; she might have been mistaken for a wax model of Garnet Linton, except for the reality that Hallie could see her sister breathing slowly and evenly.

"Garnet?" she said, but only because she felt she had to say something. She knew her sister wouldn't respond. "Garnet?"

And, just as she expected, her sister didn't say a word. And so Hallie gently removed the doll from her arms and took Garnet's hands in hers. Then she sat her sister down on the ground where she was, the dry dirt warm, and knelt beside her.

"What is she doing?" Anise asked. The woman was towering over the twins, and Hallie couldn't tell what to make of her tone.

"She's not *doing* anything," she answered. "At least nothing on purpose. But she has these seizures. It's a brain thing."

"An illness?"

"Sort of. I don't understand it really. But my mom and dad have tried to explain it to me. It has something to do with how the synapses fire in her brain. Sometimes they just fire like crazy all at once, and it's like when a computer freezes."

"And you know what a synapse is, Rosemary?"

"No, not really. All I know is that it has something to do with the way the nerves communicate and the brain sends messages to the body."

"And her brain has . . . a problem?"

"It's not a problem. It's just how she is."

"You likened it to when a computer freezes. I'd say that constitutes a problem."

"She hasn't had one in a really long time."

"Interesting."

Hallie looked up at Anise, annoyed that this was how the woman was going to respond. Hallie knew there was nothing to be done and that eventually Garnet would come out of it. She knew that her sister wouldn't stop breathing and her heart wouldn't stop beating. But whether it would be ten minutes or an hour until she was back was always a mystery, and so she hoped her dad would return any second now from the hardware store. Meanwhile, the idea that this grown-up who'd never before seen one of her sister's seizures wasn't fretting—not insisting that they call 9-1-1 or leave right away for the hospital—was disappointing. No, it was more than that: It was irritating. Weren't these plant ladies supposed to care about her and her sister? Weren't they supposed to be freakishly motherly and doting?

"She's going to be fine, you know," she said to Anise, unable to mask the disgust in her voice.

"This happens with some frequency?" Anise asked.

"I told you: No. This is only the third time it's happened here in New Hampshire."

"Three times in two months?"

"They're usually not that common."

"And she takes . . . pills?" the woman asked, the word *pills* spoken as if it were an obscenity.

"Yes. But they're not perfect."

"Pills never are."

Her mother had made a joke a week earlier about how some of the women here were not especially enamored of modern medicine, and now Hallie understood what she'd meant a little better. "There's nothing we should do but stay with her," she said after a moment.

"You mean watch her?"

"Yes."

"Why?"

"To make sure she doesn't wander off."

"Does she do that when she has one of these seizures?"

"She never has. But the doctors say she could. Like a sleepwalker."

Finally Anise squatted beside the two girls. "Rosemary?" she said, questioning Hallie though she was staring straight at Garnet's slack face.

"Yes?"

"Do you have any problem like this?"

"No."

"You're fine?"

"Uh-huh. And Garnet is, too. She—"

The woman put her finger to Hallie's lips. "Cali when you're with us. Remember? Her name is Cali."

"And Cali is, too," she went on. "She just has this . . . this thing."

"But you don't have it."

"No."

"Well, thank you."

"For what?"

"For telling me. Someone had to. We had to know. And now we do." Then she stood up and started to unpack the cartons of seedlings as if absolutely nothing was wrong in the world. "You always want your ingredients to be flawless," she added, apropos of nothing, as Hallie sat alone on the ground with her sister.

Part IV

Chapter Seventeen

Y ou sit on the couch in the den with Emily beside you and feel
her entwining her fingers in yours. Emily has asked the girls to
run along to their rooms upstairs to play or do homework, but
you would not be surprised if they are sitting on the stairs right now and
trying to listen. If you were ten years old and a pair of state troopers had
appeared yet again at your house, you would want to know why.

At first you had presumed this was about Sawyer Dunmore's bones
and the crypt in the basement you opened. Then you thought it might
have something to do with the recent death of Hewitt Dunmore in
St. Johnsbury. You were completely mistaken in both cases, and the reality of why they are here this evening—interrupting you and Emily as
you prepared dinner—has left you a little shaken and stunned.

"I understand you only knew Dr. Richmond professionally and
hadn't even been one of his patients all that long," the older of the pair
is saying, his hands on his knees as he sits forward in the easy chair.
His badge says R. PATTERSON, but you cannot recall whether he told you
his first name was Roger or Rick. He has an immaculately trimmed
mustache the color of copper—a more restrained version of your own
daughter's red hair—and occasionally he lifts one of his hands and
abstractedly runs a finger along it. The younger trooper is clean-shaven,
which makes their age difference even more pronounced. You peg the
older of the troopers to be somewhere around forty and the younger to
be a mere twenty-five. The younger trooper is taking notes as you speak,

while the older one listens. "But did he ever say anything that might be helpful in our understanding of what's happened to him?"

You have noticed that they do not say "his death." He is merely missing. The other day his car was found about two miles from his house, the doors locked, and no one has seen him since. He did not show up at his office that day or the next or see any of the patients on his schedule. The troopers clearly presume that a crime has occurred, but at the moment they do not know this for sure.

"No," you tell them. "Mostly we talked about me." You offer a small, wan smile.

Although she is not a defense attorney, Emily has already told the troopers that, if she thinks a question is inappropriate, she is not going to allow you to answer it. They have assured the two of you that you are not a suspect in the doctor's disappearance; they are only, to use the older trooper's words, nosing around at the moment, and they saw that you were among his patients.

"Can we ask you why you were seeing Dr. Richmond?" Patterson asks. But before you can respond, Emily squeezes your hand.

"There is no reason to answer that, sweetheart," she says, her voice gentle, though her gaze is intent. She looks at you squarely in the eyes.

You shrug. "I don't mind," you tell her. And then you turn to the troopers: "I am being treated for depression and PTSD. As you might have heard, I lost an airplane."

"Yes, sir, we did know that," the trooper says. "I'm sorry."

"Me, too."

There is an awkward pause; there was a flippancy to your tone that you hadn't expected when you started to open your mouth.

"Did he ever mention any enemies?"

"No."

"Any personal problems of his own? I know you were talking about the things on your mind, but did he ever relate them to something going on in his life?"

You grimace involuntarily at a sudden pain in your side, the wince traveling all the way down your arm to your fingers. Emily turns to you, and you nod you're okay. Then you gaze at Ashley as she stands on the brick hearth by the woodstove. At the moment she seems oblivious to you and Emily and these two state troopers. She is uninterested in dolls or a playmate. She is focused solely, almost quizzically, on the long, daggerlike triangle of metal fuselage on which she is impaled, the piece of your airplane that has sliced through the side of her abdomen. She is fingering the smooth, blue edge, careful to keep her fingers from either the point or the pieces of muscle and stomach and rib that garnish the jagged lip. You find yourself wondering: Was there water in her lungs when they did the autopsy? Or had the metal killed her instantly?

B ecky Davis never did call Emily back, so Emily decided to phone her. But this time she called the woman at work, remembering from their one cryptic conversation in the diner that Becky had said she did something at Lyndon State College. From the school's automated phone system, Emily learned that the woman worked in the library. There Emily asked to speak to Becky Davis.

"Speaking."

"Oh, I didn't recognize your voice," Emily said.

"Who's this?"

"Emily Linton."

There was a long pause at the other end, and Emily could imagine the woman sitting a little straighter in her chair. Rubbing the bridge of her nose, perhaps, the way Emily knew she herself did when she was in the midst of a phone call that she found either stressful or unpleasant. "What do you want?" she asked finally.

Emily took a breath. Becky sounded far less friendly than she had at the diner. "Well, I'm not sure. Tell me: How was your parents' visit? Didn't you tell me they were coming up from North Carolina for a bit?"

"That was a long time ago. They've come and gone."

"Okay."

"Are you at your office?"

"I am," said Emily.

"You're calling me from the law firm," Becky said, unwilling to hide a small wave of incredulity.

"Why is that a problem? It's not like our phones are bugged or you and I are about to share state secrets. It's—"

"Fine. You're in John Hardin's office. I get it. My husband told me you called the other night. What do you want?"

"I'm honestly not sure. When you introduced yourself to me at the diner, you were very nice. But you also kept talking about *them,* and you called *them* the herbalists. And then you left when you saw Alexander Jackson coming into the diner. Clearly you knew who he was. I didn't at the time, but I do now. He's married to Ginger. What was it you wanted to tell me that day about *them*—about the herbalists? Can you tell me now?"

"Have you ever been inside John Hardin's house?"

"Yes."

"Did you notice the pictures?"

"Do you mean the paintings? No, I—"

"I meant the family photographs!"

"What about them?"

"He doesn't age! Clary doesn't age! At least it seems that way. It's not . . . natural. It's . . ."

"It's what?"

"And where is your husband's doctor? His psychiatrist?"

"You mean Valerian? Well, she's at—"

"Valerian? You know who I mean. Michael Richmond. He sometimes skied with my husband. They were friends. *We* were friends. Where is he now?"

"Look, I know something is going on. That's why I'm calling. I have a house with bones in the basement, Hewitt Dunmore is dead, Michael is—"

"He's dead, too. My husband and I are sure of it."

"You were telling me about the photos in John and Clary's house. Can you—"

"Really, there's nothing I have to tell you. I love Bethel and I love my family and I think it's great that you're here."

"Becky, please," Emily said. But she heard a click and the line went silent.

"Everything okay?"

She looked up, and there was Eve, the firm's young paralegal, standing in her doorway and looking a little concerned.

"I'm fine," she answered.

"You looked like you'd seen a ghost," Eve said.

"Nope."

"If you need something, you'll ask?"

"Tell me something."

"Sure."

"Why is your name Eve?"

"I seem to be rather talentless when it comes to plants. I seem to have the opposite of a green thumb," she said with absolute earnestness, and then she continued on her way down the corridor.

"It's for the best," Valerian said to Emily later that afternoon, sitting across the desk from Emily in her office. John leaned against the wall, ever the sage, avuncular presence. "And it's not for long."

"I just don't know," Emily said. "I'm not sure Michael would have agreed."

Valerian turned around and looked up at John. "Do they know anything more about Michael's disappearance? The police, that is?"

He sighed wearily. "No. I haven't heard a thing, I'm sorry to say. And while I like to believe he's just—what did that South Carolina governor once do?—disappeared to be with some hypnotic young siren in South America, I think we can't help but suspect the worst." He shook his head, looking uncharacteristically morose. "We like to believe we're exempt from that sort of violence here in the White Mountains. Apparently, we're not."

"I want to think about it some more," Emily said finally. "I don't want us to broach this subject with him just yet. Okay?"

"Absolutely," Valerian said. "Let's revisit the idea later this week. I'm seeing your husband tomorrow. Maybe we'll have a better sense of what we should do after that."

You replace the empty battery in the drill with the charged one, grab four long screws, and drop into place another new step on those rickety back stairs behind the kitchen. It takes about a minute because you measured twice and cut once. You like that expression.

Inside this back stairway, you have found that you do not hear the birds. It feels as if there are more of them here than there were in West Chester. This is probably a delusion. There were plenty of birds in Pennsylvania. But the cheeps and coos and trills sometimes seem to surround you here when you walk between the house and the carriage barn or when you stroll down the long driveway to the mailbox on the road into Bethel. You do not hate the birds. You blame them—but you do not hate them. At least this is what you tell yourself, struggling to be reasonable. You wish you could talk to Michael about this distinction between blame and hate, but you can't.

You have come to suspect that the women were involved in Michael's disappearance, just as you have come to suspect that they were involved in Hewitt Dunmore's death. But you can't see why or how. You have the sense now that they are plotting something involving you, and that Emily is complicit. She seems to be seeing more of Valerian. There are phone conversations that end abruptly when you enter a room or descend the stairs to the first floor. Emily brought home some papers from work, and when you aimlessly wandered into the kitchen and saw her reading them, she thrust them into her briefcase.

This morning Ethan visited you soon after Emily and the girls had left for the day, and he told you in no uncertain terms that your suspicions were accurate: Emily is becoming one of them. People don't tell you things, but you are aware that secrets are rising like distant thunderclouds. A new name for Emily and new names for your daughters. When were they planning on telling you? It is possible that Emily already is one of them. Just look at the plants that have appeared in your greenhouse. Her greenhouse. The *girls'* greenhouse. Ethan tried to reassure you that all of the pain you are experiencing will stop once Ashley gets a playmate—your guilt, too, will melt away—but you told him you would rather live with the pain and the guilt and the debilitating sense of failure. He reminded you that it wasn't a question of character. It was a question of strength. And he was stronger. The fact was, someday the two of you would do it together. It was inevitable. Think back to the evening when Molly Francoeur was over for dinner and a playdate. Or that night when you tiptoed up to the third floor with Tansy's knife. You would do it, he told you. You would.

Meanwhile, outside the house the birds dart among the trees—the evergreens and the maples and the mountain ash alike—and savor their return to the north. Even the geese are back now. But at least they have the kindness to steer clear of your yard.

You have three more steps to repair on this back stairway when you hear someone calling for you from the front hallway, a woman, and you believe it is Reseda's sultry voice. So, you adjust the collar of your denim shirt, smooth your hair, and emerge into the kitchen.

"Well, Reseda, this is a surprise. Lovely to see you," you say. You hadn't realized how sunny it had become while you were working in the dark of that back staircase.

She stares at you in that slightly odd, inquisitive manner that had led you to presume initially that hers was a mind that tended to wander. You have since decided that nothing could be further from the truth. It's almost as if she can read a person's mind. But of course she can't. No one can really do that.

"What home improvement am I interrupting this morning?" she asks. She is wearing a waist-length black leather jacket and jeans.

"The back stairs. I have no idea if we'll ever use them, but you never know. A fire exit, maybe. So, I'm repairing the scarier-looking steps."

"Do you have a couple of minutes?"

You motion toward the deacon's bench where once the family cat would sleep, and Reseda unzips her jacket and sits.

"I don't know if I've told you, but I am very, very sorry about Desdemona," she says. "That was her name, right?"

"Thank you. It was a bit of a blow," you admit, taking the ladder-back chair across from her. You wonder: Does she think you killed the cat, too? It's so clear that Valerian does. And Anise. And, perhaps, even your own family. And yet you didn't. At least you don't believe that you did. These days, you seem capable of almost anything.

"Cats—and dogs—poison themselves all the time. It wasn't your fault," she says evenly.

"Thank you. You want some tea?" Somehow you know she doesn't drink coffee. Did you learn this when you were at her house for dinner, or is it merely a suspicion that all of these herbalists prefer tea?

"No, but you're kind to ask. I want you to tell me something."

"Sure." You realize you have folded your arms across your chest. You try to casually bring them onto the kitchen table.

"Tell me about the voices," she says.

"The voices?"

"Who are you talking to when you're alone?"

"Good Lord, what makes you think I talk to anyone when I'm alone?"

"One of your girls told me."

You pause, your stomach turning over once. This is devastating news. You had no inkling that they had seen—that they knew. "And both know?"

"Yes."

"How long have they known?"

"I couldn't say. But they seem to comprehend you are experiencing something rather different here from what you were enduring back in West Chester. Is that accurate?"

You feel the first twinge in your side, the first indication that Ashley is near.

"Yes. It's this . . ."

"This house. I know."

He shakes his head. "I'm not angry at you because you didn't know . . . but you and that Sheldon character sold us a house with a body in the basement."

"If I could do it all over again, I would never have allowed you to buy this place. Never. I would have stopped Sheldon from showing it to you. That's the truth. I'm sorry," she says. "But the voices—"

"The visions," you say, correcting her. "I wish it were voices only. Then you could diagnose me a schizophrenic and drug me accordingly."

"But the visions do not involve Sawyer Dunmore. It may have been his bones in the basement, but he's no longer here. You've never seen him."

She is watching you, and you find yourself swallowing uncomfortably. "No. Never him."

"There were children who died on Flight 1611. Is it one of them?"

You nod. "Ashley Stearns."

"Who else?" she asks. "Are there others?"

"Yes." The word catches in your throat and the syllable grows elongated.

"How many?"

"Two—plus Ashley."

"Do you know what they want?"

You see in your mind the knife by your bed, and then you have to close your eyes against the first migraine-like spikes of pain along the top of your head and behind your eyes. Ethan is coming, too.

"Do you want to get some aspirin?" she asks when you remain silent.

"Maybe in a minute," you answer. Then you take a deep breath and tell her in as reasonable a tone as you can muster of your visits with Sandra Durant, the PR executive who liked orange marmalade, and of Ethan Stearns, the father with the serious guns for upper arms who is so angry at the death of his daughter. And, of course, you tell her lots more about Ashley. That child, it seems, is the reason why your own family is in danger. Someday, when it all becomes too much, you may savage one of your children with the knife you keep by your bed. But you don't tell Reseda that. It is impossible to say such things aloud. Instead you finish by murmuring, "I had never believed in ghosts. But they're real, you know. Either that or I've lost my mind once and for all."

"They're real," she agrees simply.

"You believe in ghosts?"

"I do."

"You've seen them?"

"I have."

"The thing is . . ."

"Go on."

"The thing is, they were my passengers and they died when my plane was brought down by a flock of geese. There were thirty-nine people who died. Why those three?"

"Versus your first officer or the flight attendants or anyone else who was onboard?"

"Exactly! Why not Amy Lynch or Eliot Hardy?"

"The rest of them have gone on."

"To heaven."

"That word is as good as any," she says. "When we're living, we're shielded from possession by an aura. When an aura is sound, it's difficult for a spirit to penetrate it and become one with us."

She says this as if she is explaining how the immune system or a jet engine functions. A year ago, you would have assumed it was New Age nonsense. Now? You tend to have a more open mind.

"And you know all of this . . . how?" you ask finally.

"*Know* is a very loaded word in this case. The truth is, I *know* nothing. I am certain of nothing. But that's what faith is, isn't it? We believe things we can't prove and have some confidence that we're right."

"They want things from me."

"I am sure they do. But if you want me to," she says, leaning in to you in a fashion that is at once provocative and intense, "I can try to make them leave."

"You can?"

She nods. "I can try. And if I succeed, I want you and your family to move away."

"Leave this house?" You are surprised by the loyalty you have to the Sheetrock and plaster. To the rooms you have made new and to the rooms that await new wallpaper and paint. You have changed the house dramatically. Made it yours.

"Bethel," she answers. "The White Mountains."

"You don't think we belong here?"

She shakes her head. "I think you belong here too much."

In the morning, John Hardin gazed up at the wondrous penumbra of lime green on the tips of the trees: not leaves yet, but waves and waves of buds. That moment when life moves from mere mist to a tangibility that swallows the twigs. It was weeks past the equinox now, and the days were starting to feel pleasantly long. He and Clary were likely to have dinner when it was still light out, which was rather nice, they both agreed. And there had been one last, torrential sugar run the day before. A person could have stood at the top of Mooseback, the squat little mountain just east of Bethel, and seen steam from sugarhouses in all directions. Over the weekend he had taken Verbena and her girls to Claude and Lavender Millier's sugarhouse to witness boiling firsthand. As John had expected, the Milliers' son had driven up from Salem for the weekend. And the girls had loved it. Verbena had been positively entranced. Said it brought back memories long dormant of visiting one of her grandmother's neighbors in the woods near the lake in Meredith.

He was just about to get into his car and drive to the office when he heard the front storm door squeak open and saw Clary walking briskly across the slate to the driveway. Like him, she usually rose and dressed early, even though she didn't have a law practice to tend to, but they had made love this morning and she was still in her ankle-length red nightgown.

"What did I forget?" he asked her, though her hands were empty.

"Phone call," she murmured, and he could see the worry on her face.

He nodded. The cordless phone didn't work this far from its base. He tossed his briefcase onto the passenger seat of his car, thought of the body of the dead psychiatrist that once had lolled there in mangy old blankets, and strolled back to the house. He noticed that there was a perfect line on the grass where the rising sun had melted the frost: The grass was white where it was still masked by the shade from the house and green where the rime had turned to water.

"Who is it?" he asked.

"Anise."

"Ah. Thank you."

In the kitchen he reached for the phone. "Good morning," he began, "though I have the distinct sense based on the scowl on my wife's usually lovely face that you haven't rung me with good news." Clary was standing in the doorframe, her arms folded across her chest. Her lower lip was quivering with anger; she looked profoundly unhappy.

"I just saw Reseda. She came by my house this morning."

"Wonderful! I always want my girls to be friends." He was absolutely sincere in that he did want all of them—the women as well as the men—to get along. But there was also a layer of black humor rippling just beneath the surface of his remark. He knew that Reseda and Anise would never be close, at least not in the way that most of the women were. Reseda was always going to be something of an outsider.

"It wasn't wonderful at all."

"No?"

"No, John. It wasn't. She believes we killed both Hewitt and the psychiatrist. She said the death of the doctor—"

"Not dead, my dear. Only missing."

"Presumed dead. It's been a while."

"And he has, more or less, fallen off the radar. There was nothing on the news last night—again—and nothing in the paper this morning. He had no wife, no children. A deceptively easy man to forget. That sounded rather harsh—certainly harsher than I meant. I'm sorry."

He heard her sigh on the phone. "Reseda might not let him be forgotten."

Once more it crossed his mind that in their enthusiasm they had all moved too quickly. The idea had been gnawing at him. The reality was that half the town already thought everyone in their small group was a little nuts. And while he viewed most of what they did as, well, rather a freedom of religion issue—a First Amendment issue—homicide represented an arguably unnecessary part of their practice. It was one thing to risk sacrificing one of the girls. But homicide? Now that was nasty.

"Well, I'm glad she went to you and not me," he said finally, knowing—as they all did—that Reseda seemed incapable of reading Anise's mind.

"She will come to you. Reassure me: There is no evidence?"

He chuckled. "Oh my, Anise, there is almost always evidence if you look in the right place. I'm quite sure if the State Police ever checked my car, they would find traces of the psychiatrist. A tiny hair. A piece of skin the vacuum missed. But they would need reasonable cause to search the car. And I tend to doubt any judge would approve a warrant because Reseda pulled a memory from me and went to the police."

"She wants this over with now."

"I do, too."

"I meant something different."

"I know what you meant. Reseda wants us to leave the twins alone and move on. Accept the inevitability that a person ages and dies. Well, that's easy for her to say, given that she is still on the smooth side of forty. I'm on the deeply wrinkled side of . . . never mind. So are Clary and the Messners and the Jacksons. And you are precariously close to that Rubicon."

"I think we should do it tonight."

"Interesting. I was just thinking how we may have been moving too quickly. And now you want us to move faster still."

"Tonight. Before Reseda can intervene."

He stood a little straighter. He felt himself growing frustrated and shook his head. He had always tried to view Reseda like a daughter. Lately he had even begun to hope that someday she and Verbena—who still, much to his disappointment, insisted on being called Emily— would both be like daughters to him. And if Verbena was like a daughter, then her twins were like granddaughters. And why would he want to hurt one of his granddaughters? He wouldn't! Really, what kind of man did Reseda think he had become? No, in theory nothing bad was going to happen to either of Verbena's girls. Nothing at all. There was a risk. Sawyer Dunmore was proof that there was a risk. But look how the tincture had worked! There was every reason to suppose it would work again. It demanded a lot of blood, no question about it, especially given the number of adults who would be present this time and how much of the tincture would be necessary. But both girls were young and strong. And they fit the recipe perfectly: They were twins, they were preadolescent, their blood had been leavened by trauma.

"Intervene," he murmured, repeating the word. "That would suggest that Reseda shouldn't be present. That she really is no longer a part of our little group."

"I don't think she is."

The answer made him wistful; he couldn't imagine proceeding without her—though clearly they would.

"So, should we?" Anise went on. "I really do want us to try tonight."

"Yes," he said finally. "Make the arrangements."

"But I also don't want Verbena to wind up like her"—and here the old lawyer heard Anise pausing as she chose her word carefully— "*predecessor* in that house. I don't want her to wind up like Tansy."

"Heavens, none of us do! But maybe that won't happen to Verbena."

"I hope not. I rather like her."

"I do, too. And she's a very good lawyer. Good, solid work ethic."

"But if she does lose one of her children . . ."

"It will be a shattering blow. Absolutely staggering."

"Do you think she'll leave us?"

"She might. But now we know more how to handle such an . . . an eventuality. And I suspect that she'll need us more than ever if something should happen to one of the twins. She really hasn't any family."

"She still has the captain. At the moment, he is neither dead nor committed."

"No. But I think you're correct: We do it tonight and we do it without Reseda. I don't think we have a choice, as much as I wish the captain were out of the picture. Tell me, have you decided which girl?"

"Absolutely. We should use—"

"No, don't tell me! Surprise me!" he said, an almost childlike giddiness in his voice. "It will be more interesting that way. It will be more interesting for all of us." He looked at his watch and realized he would be late for a real estate closing if he didn't leave soon. "Anise, I need to skedaddle. And I meant what I said: Don't fret. We'll iron out the details this afternoon, but go ahead and start preparing for the ceremony tonight." Then he placed the phone back in the cradle, kissed Clary on the cheek, and strolled out to the car. He noticed the line of frost on the grass had moved a few inches while he was inside and smiled up at the spring sun. He really wondered how anyone couldn't be happy just to be alive.

Chapter Eighteen

E mily thought Jocelyn Francoeur was more polite than she needed to be—and, perhaps, more polite than she had to be, given the circumstances. Although the idea initially had made Jocelyn uncomfortable, in the end she hadn't prohibited Emily from bringing her girls over to the Francoeurs' modest ranch that afternoon after school with the small birthday present they had picked out for Molly. The last time Emily had seen Jocelyn, Chip's arms and shirt were awash in blood and Molly was sobbing. This was not precisely the way any mother wanted a playdate to end.

Still, it was almost as if the woman's original rage toward the Lintons had been replaced by wariness and unease. Jocelyn seemed more frightened than angered by the idea that the Lintons were in her home; it seemed to Emily that the woman had only agreed to see them because she thought not seeing them would be worse.

Yet the purpose of the visit, in Emily's mind, was simply to apologize once again as a family and to bring by the birthday present. She presumed that Molly was having a party on Saturday and her children weren't invited, which was fine, but she still wanted to do all that she could to make sure the twins were invited to any party Molly had next year.

Now the five of them—two mothers and three daughters—were sitting awkwardly but politely in the living room. Emily sensed that Jocelyn was eyeing the twins and her a little guardedly and hadn't said very much. Really, no one had said much but Emily, as she struggled to find things to talk about (which shouldn't have been hard with three girls roughly the same age) and topics they might discuss. "Well, this is the main reason we came," Emily said brightly, after she had run out of things to say. She smiled as broadly as she could and watched as Hallie handed Molly a small box wrapped in silver paper. "It's a birthday present from all of us."

The girl looked at her mother, and Jocelyn seemed to be thinking about whether she wanted her daughter to have it. Again, there was that ripple of anxiety on the woman's broad face. Then, much to Emily's embarrassment for her own children—Hallie, especially, who had offered the present—Jocelyn took the box from Molly and held it for a moment. She seemed to be weighing it, trying to decide what might be inside. The box was not quite the length of a pack of playing cards and half an inch deeper. She didn't actually sniff it, but Emily could tell that she was inhaling the air around it to see if whatever was inside had an aroma.

"Not a plant," she said to Jocelyn, hoping to reassure her. "Nothing herbal. I promise."

Emily saw a small swell of dread pass over the woman's face, but Emily had only meant to be glib—not terrifying. Quickly she added, "They're earrings. That's all." She turned to Molly and her girls and added, "Sorry. I guess I just ruined the surprise."

Jocelyn handed her daughter the box, and Molly opened it with unusual delicacy for a child: She slowly untied the ribbon and peeled back the tape on the wrapping paper. Then she opened the lid and held up one of the silver earrings for her mother to see. "It's pretty," she said. "What does it mean?"

Emily knew the interlocking circle of vines was a Celtic symbol of friendship: Reseda had told her. It was why she and her girls had picked out this particular pair of earrings for Molly when the three of them and Reseda visited the jewelry store. She was just about to explain this to the girl when Jocelyn took the earring from her daughter and placed it back inside the box. Then she stood, and Emily was struck by just how tall this woman was; there was a reason that Molly was such a big girl.

Jocelyn towered over her, and Emily wanted to rise up off the couch, but she was afraid that she would appear defensive or confrontational if she did. And so she remained seated as her hostess handed her the earrings and said firmly, "No. We will not have these in this house. We will not have your . . . your beliefs . . . in this house. Go. Go now."

"They're just earrings," Emily said. "They're Celtic earrings. That's all." She looked at her girls, but clearly they understood. Already they were standing up and slinking toward the front door like chastised puppies. And so Emily stood, too.

"I want no part of your group or their symbolism, and I want my daughter to have no part of it, either," the woman insisted.

"My group? Really, what group am I a part of? I know you don't mean my law practice," Emily argued, though she understood precisely what Molly's mother was driving at. "I'm serious, Jocelyn, tell me: What group?"

The woman put her hands on her hips and was visibly shaking. Then she took her daughter by the hand and pulled her beside her. "You know better than me. You live in the house where one of them lived. You work for John Hardin."

"I know next to nothing about Tansy Dunmore. And most of what I know about John Hardin begins and ends with his legal expertise."

"There are two kinds of people in Bethel. And someday your kind will go too far. Frankly, I think you already have."

"My kind? Jocelyn, look, I am—"

"Fine," the woman said, interrupting her. "I believe you. There's no group. None. There's no witchcraft and there's no weird religion. Now, Molly and I have some things to do to get ready for . . . Well, we just have some things to do," she said, and Emily understood that Jocelyn was not going to discuss this any further. Clearly the woman was afraid that she had said too much. And so Emily took the girls, who looked no less sheepish as they stood by the front door pulling on their boots, and left the Francoeur house with the little box of earrings in her hand.

*   *   *

Reseda stared up at the looming Victorian from the seat of her car, watching the afternoon sun on the western windows. She couldn't decide whether the dead would have grown so invasive had the captain remained in West Chester. Probably they would have, but he had been more isolated here—more separated from friends and neighbors and a support group of other pilots—and that seclusion, more than this house, was what may have given the spirits such access. Such command. There was also the possibility that whatever Anise was feeding Chip was exacerbating their control and making their presence more disturbing. But Reseda would never know for sure. Finally she heard another vehicle rumbling up the driveway. She looked into the rearview mirror and saw Emily's station wagon approaching. A moment later, Emily coasted past, waving, and came to a stop before one of the carriage barn's two bays. She had the twins with her.

"Coming or going?" Emily asked, as Reseda climbed from her own car.

"Coming," she answered.

"Does Chip know you're here?"

"I don't think so. I just arrived."

"Well, let's go inside," Emily said, and together they started up the front walkway.

"You're not returning from something pleasant like a dance class or a music lesson, are you?" Reseda asked the twins.

Garnet shook her head no and Hallie sniffed derisively.

"We just tried to make peace with Jocelyn Francoeur," Emily explained. "Remember the earrings you helped us pick out? Giving them to Molly didn't go well."

"I'm sorry."

"She doesn't approve of you herbalists."

"She really doesn't know us well enough to approve or disapprove. I told you that."

"She would disagree," Emily said. "She has mighty strong feelings. And . . ." She stopped midsentence and said to her girls, "Run ahead and tell your father we're home and Reseda is here. I'll be right behind you."

"Are you going to tell Reseda what happened? What Molly's mom said?" asked Garnet.

"I may, yes. But please don't you tell Daddy—or at least wait for me. I'll be right in," Emily said, and the girls ran into the house. Then she pulled the box of earrings from her shoulder bag and shook it at Reseda, unable to mask the disgust on her face. She recounted for her how Jocelyn had refused to allow her daughter to accept the gift that they had chosen together and how she had all but called the herbalists witches. Finally Emily put her hands on her hips, and her gaze grew earnest. "Tell me," she demanded of Reseda, "are you a witch?"

"No."

"Then what are you?"

"A real estate agent."

"Don't be coy. I want to know what's going on here in Bethel and I want to know right now. I want to know why your little group wants to change our names and what you want from me and my girls."

"It's why I've come here."

"Okay then, tell me. Now."

"First we need to begin with your husband."

"With Chip? He has his share of problems, but—"

Reseda cut Emily off, pressing one finger gently but firmly against her lips, silencing her. Then she took her hand and started leading Emily away from the house, walking her in the clean spring air into the meadow, where the grass was, suddenly, almost knee-high. There she told Emily of the dead who were with her husband and the dangers they posed for her daughters, and how she wanted to bring her husband to her own greenhouse that night to perform a depossession—and how she already had broached this idea with Chip and he had agreed. She told Emily that there was a second volume of recipes in their group's canon, and it included a particular tincture that the herbalists wanted to make that also represented a danger to her children.

"What do they all want to do?" Emily asked, her voice facetious. "Graft some of their skin? Harvest a little blood?"

"Not a little," Reseda said, and for the first time in her life she verbalized aloud what she had seen one night in Clary Hardin's mind when she pressed for details about the death of Sawyer Dunmore.

The twelve-year-old boy was drugged with a tincture that Anise had made from valerian, skullcap, and California poppy, his body resting flat on its back on the makeshift wooden altar in the communal greenhouse, his hands folded across his chest as if—and his mother had to have noticed this—he were a corpse. Anise was a decade and a half younger than the others, but every bit as committed. The child's hair was the color of wheat, and it was damp from sweat, the perspiration a side effect of the tincture. His eyes were shut, and he breathed with the slowness of a seemingly sound, untroubled sleep. But he was not as sedated as everyone thought, the sleep not nearly as deep, and that would be a part of the problem and why everything went so horribly wrong. It was well into the night, and the greenhouse was lit entirely by candles— Sage had rounded up easily a hundred of them, tapers and blocks and votives from the church outside Boston where she and Peyton had been married one summer Saturday in 1932, and now the candles were lining the tables with the plants or ensconced in hurricane lamps on the ground—and the walls were alive with the shadows of the six herbalists. Outside the air was bracing and crisp, as late autumn rolled inexorably toward winter. Parnell had taken Hewitt hunting, and the father and son were with Parnell's brother at a friend's deer camp in Danville, Vermont, though there was no question that Parnell knew what his wife and her friends had planned for Sawyer. He had seen how well their tinctures worked—even the ones from the second volume—and, like Tansy, supposed this one would, too.

And so the herbalists surrounded the body in the greenhouse. They edged closer all the time, especially when Anise finally raised the child's right arm from his chest and Clary held a cast-iron stewpot beneath it while Tansy—the boy's own mother—took one of her own kitchen knives and made a single cut along the wrist. The boy flinched. Certainly Clary saw that. Probably Anise did, too, and she must have worried that she had either mixed the sedative improperly or—fearful of killing the child with an overdose—given him too little. But the boy did not awaken. At least not yet. Sawyer Dunmore awoke only after Anise and Sage had both observed aloud that the slice had been neither deep enough nor long enough and already the coagulants were starting to stem the tide. They needed far more than a few drops of blood; this wasn't homeopathy, after all. They needed enough blood to reduce it like a sauce with the ashwagandha and eternium. And though Tansy paused with the knife at her side, summoning the courage and deciding whether she was indeed capable of cutting her own child a second time—and making this gash far more pronounced—she didn't pause long. Had she been tranquilized, too? Clary didn't know and so Reseda didn't know. Clary had never been sure whether the stupor that initially had enveloped Tansy Dunmore like a shawl and made her eyes less animated than the rest of the herbalists—all of whom were electrified by the idea that finally they were preparing this particular tincture, the one that demanded the blood of a traumatized, prepubescent twin—was the result of massive doses of passionflower and schisandra or unease at the reality that she was slashing her own child's wrist. Regardless, she raised the knife once more and this time made the cut deeper and longer and, intentionally or not, she ran the knife lengthwise along the ulnar artery, rather than across it, and blood geysered up into the air, a punctured hose with the spigot on full, and the boy awoke. He screamed and struggled to sit up, but Peyton Messner and John Hardin were there before he could, the two men pressing the boy's shoulders back against the altar. But Sawyer fought hard for his life, and his cries pulled Tansy from the somnambulance that had allowed her to forget for a period who she was and what she was doing to her own son. She lashed out at Peyton and John, and managed to tear the sleeve from John's robe, but Clary dropped the heavy pot—spilling the little blood they had collected onto the dirt floor of the greenhouse, where it disappeared into the earth—and she and Anise together clenched Tansy's arm and pushed her away from her son and then onto the ground. But Tansy heard Sawyer crying as he bled out (and he really did bleed out very, very quickly), and she wailed his name over and over. The adults might have saved the boy's life if they hadn't been working at cross-purposes: Peyton was hoping to stop the bleeding, trying to press the cloth from the cuff of his robe against the deep gash, but Anise and John were squeezing the child's forearm, trying to keep the vein open. Moreover, at some point someone had toppled one of the candles and set Anise's long sleeve on fire, badly burning her arm before she was able to smother it. She seemed oblivious to the pain, but the small blaze only added to the distraction. Still, Clary eventually managed to right the cauldron and capture Sawyer Dunmore's blood as it flowed and flowed, puddling in the bottom of the cast-iron pot and saturating John's and Anise's robes.

Meanwhile the boy cried out for his mother until he grew too weak and the mother screamed for her son and their pleas were unbearable.

When the boy was dead and the adults saw what they had done, they brought him home and placed him in a bathtub and allowed the world to believe his death was a suicide. The blood, they forever insisted, had turned the water salmon pink and then disappeared when they opened the drain.

Chapter Nineteen

You know that Emily has doubts that the dead from 1611 have attached themselves to you, but she has convinced herself that because *you* believe this is the case, perhaps Reseda's little New Age ritual (and, in her mind, there is nothing sillier than a little New Age ritual) will help you. In her opinion, it can't possibly make your mental illness any worse. You, however, have absolutely no doubts that you are—to use Reseda's word—possessed. And, because you have faith in Reseda, you agree to the depossession, confident that this is indeed more than a little New Age ritual, in terms of both the likelihood of its effectiveness and the upheaval it will cause in your soul. Your (and this is a new word for you in this context) *aura*. Reseda has made the depossession sound troubling for a great many reasons, but largely because she has warned you that while under hypnosis you may relive the crash.

"Can we make the outcome a little more promising?" you ask, hoping to lighten the moment, but she answers that the end will be every bit as terrifying.

"I was never terrified," you correct her.

"Then you won't be now," she says. "Your passengers, however, might be. The outcome will be the same, because it's all you know of the experience and it's all they know of the experience. It's what happened."

"How long will I be hypnotized?"

"Until everyone inside you has left."

Emily rubs at her upper arms as if she is cold. "And there's no danger?" she asks again.

"The spirits represent a danger to others while they have access to your husband—and they may represent a danger to him. But I think the element of the actual depossession that is most dangerous will be the effect on your husband of experiencing the crash once again. But he says he'll be fine," Reseda explains, and then she turns her gaze upon you, gauging your reaction. You shrug. Yes, you'll be fine.

And so tonight when the girls are asleep you will go to Reseda's. There, in the midst of the statuary and the plants in her greenhouse, a small world where, she insists, she is strongest and most persuasive, she will attempt to drive out the dead. Or, as she puts it, drive them home. It may all be over in an hour, but it may also take all night. When the Santa Fe shaman performed the depossession on her, liberating her twin sister, it had taken no more than forty-five minutes (though at the time, Reseda says, it felt as if it were taking all night). Twice before when Reseda herself has performed depossessions, once on a firefighter who was saddled with the dead from a house fire—an angry teen boy and his father, a man who had placed the very space heater in his son's bedroom that would cause the electrical blaze—and once on Holly, who was coping with the dead from a car accident she had witnessed, it had taken hours. Reseda suggested this was because there had been multiple spirits trying to cohabit with the living. But she will take whatever time is needed.

"Is this an exorcism?" Emily asks as she walks the woman to the front door of your house.

"I don't believe so," Reseda replies.

"You don't *believe* so?" Emily says, unable or unwilling to mask the bewilderment in her voice.

But Reseda merely shakes her head. "An exorcism would suggest that your husband has been possessed by demons. I'm not sure I believe in demons." Then she smiles ever so slightly and adds, "I try not ever to be too sure of anything."

As she speaks, you feel the throbbing in your head and understand that, at the very least, Ethan is listening. Perhaps Sandra and Ashley are, too. You have the distinct sense that Ethan is not going to leave quietly. He may not be a demon in any literal sense, but having to watch his daughter's unquenchable loneliness in the purgatory he shares with her—a three-story Victorian to most of the living—has turned his anger to madness and made him by any definition more than a little demonic.

E mily put down the book she was reading—staring distractedly at words, she thought, because she was assimilating nothing—and leaned back in the blue easy chair in the living room. She contemplated what Reseda had said about her husband and then about the other herbalists. Early on, she had sensed a certain remoteness between Reseda and Anise, and today the woman had confirmed her instincts. Emily didn't focus long on whatever schism might exist between Reseda and the other women, however, because she heard something outside—something other than the wind—and she sat forward, alert. She hoped it was Chip and Reseda finally returning. This was, after all, why she was waiting up. And then the house went dark.

For a moment, she remained perfectly still, trying—and failing—to convince herself that this was a power outage. The gusts of a fierce spring storm were rattling the windowpanes, and for all she knew there had even been thunder. Although it was only April, the weather reports had suggested there might be thunder that night. And up here on the hill, they seemed to lose power a lot, a detail of the house that neither Sheldon nor Reseda had ever mentioned. She told herself that the power would return any second, and well before it was time to get the girls out of bed and ready for school.

But she didn't believe that. She didn't believe that for a moment.

And then she thought she heard a thump, either below her in the basement or in the kitchen on the other side of the house, and she felt her heart drumming in her chest. If the cat had been alive, Emily would have attributed the sound to her. She listened intently, her feet flat on the floor in front of her rather than beneath her—the proper position for one's feet when bracing for impact. Chip had told her that she should never put her feet below the airplane seat when a crash was imminent, because there was every chance that the seat would collapse on her ankles and crush them, making it impossible to exit the aircraft even if she survived the primary impact. Instead she would die in the firestorm that was likely to follow, choking on poisonous air or being burned beyond all but dental recognition. At the time, she had thanked him sarcastically; this was considerably more information than she needed to know. But then, of course, her very own husband's plane would crash.

She cleared those thoughts from her mind and tried to recall where they kept a flashlight here on the first floor; she knew there was one beside her bed upstairs. She wondered if she had something nearby that could serve as a weapon—if, dear God, she needed one. Then she heard a noise above her as well, the sound of footsteps. It was the creak of the floorboards just outside Garnet's bedroom. Already she knew that the boards there were more likely to wheeze when you walked upon them than was the flooring on the other side of the third-floor corridor or even the half-rotted boards on the attic side. She said a small prayer that her girls were awake, that was all it was, perhaps aware that the house had lost power, and it was only their footsteps she was hearing. Then she placed the novel on the floor and climbed silently from the chair, pressing her feet into her slippers. The house felt chillier than she would have expected, and she wondered if she had transitioned from a wool nightgown to a cotton nightshirt too soon. She thought she smelled the not unpleasant aroma of the musky, softening earth and the idea crossed her mind that the front door had been opened, but she tried to reassure herself that this was unlikely. Even though the door was on the other side of the house, she was on the first floor. Wouldn't she have heard it opening? But the sad fact was, nothing was unlikely in this old house; even its acoustics were peculiar. The truth was, she should worry. She should be terrified. For all she knew, Garnet had opened the front door and was out in the greenhouse or the meadow right now. Once before the girl had wandered into the cellar in the middle of the night; what was to prevent something from drawing her outside now?

Emily didn't like the way her mind had phrased that: *something drawing her outside*. It sounded either conspiratorial or suggestive of a belief that the house was haunted. Which it wasn't. She didn't believe in

ghosts. Reseda did. Her husband did—at least he did now. But she did
not. The issues dogging her family were mental illness and seizures and
a group of neighbors who were either well intentioned but sociopathically intrusive or less well intentioned and interested in her daughters
in a way that was delusional and macabre. Neither possibility seemed
inconceivable to her. She hoped she had simply failed to lock the front
door before settling in the chair to await Chip's return, and one of those
northeaster-like squalls she was hearing now had blown the door open.

After rooting around the kitchen in the dark, feeling her way across
the room with her fingertips, she finally found the heavy metal flashlight. It was too long for most of the drawers and so stood upright like a
column in a crevice between the Sheetrock and the side of the refrigerator. Then Emily went to the entry hallway and her heart sank: The front
door was wide open and the glass storm door was an inch or two ajar,
prevented from swinging shut because the entry mat was bunched up
beneath it and serving as a doorstop. Some of the downpour was whip-
ping into the hallway, and the frame looked to Emily like the side of
a shower stall. She leaned outside into the pelting rain and waved her
flashlight haphazardly, unsure precisely what she hoped to accomplish
but starting to panic. Although it probably wasn't much below forty
degrees outside, the rain felt almost like ice when she pushed open the
glass door and called out loudly into the dark—her voice filled with
tears that she hadn't even realized had started welling up in her eyes—
"Garnet? Hallie? Girls?" But her words were lost to the storm well
before they reached the greenhouse and the slope of the hill. She saw the
greenhouse was dark.

Still, she cried out her girls' names once again, only then remembering that she had heard at least one of them upstairs on the third floor.
She tried to convince herself that they both were there and she was
becoming hysterical for naught. Any moment one was going to appear
at the top of the stairs, rubbing the sleep from her eyes and asking why
in the world she was screaming their names into the night and whether
she thought the power would come back on soon. Still, Emily shut both
doors and raced up the stairs herself, taking them two at a time.

She stood on the second floor a long moment, not sure whether she should be frustrated or relieved that now the house was quiet; she was aware mostly of the smell of mud and the chill in the air. In one of the empty guest bedrooms at the top of the stairs, her flashlight beam caught a pile of rags on the top of the stepladder, and for a split second a rope of cloth had resembled a cat's tail and she screamed, terrified at the idea that Desdemona was back from the dead.

"Girls? Hallie? Garnet?" she shrieked again. She tripped as she started up the thin steps to the third floor and fell forward, cutting open the palm of her hand on a jagged sliver of wood when she landed. Then she shone her flashlight into Hallie's room and saw no trace of her daughter; nor was either of the girls in Garnet's room. The beds clearly had both been slept in—she felt Garnet's sheets and they were still warm—but otherwise the twins had vanished into the night. And so, once again, she howled out their names, knowing she couldn't even call 9-1-1 on the telephone because the electricity was gone and this horrible house on this nightmarish little mountain had absolutely no cell phone coverage at all.

G arnet had only told Hallie about the hole in the wall. She hadn't yet told their mother, and neither had Hallie. But when Garnet smelled the cold, outside air wafting up the stairs she sat up in bed, fully awake, and she thought of the passage. She couldn't have said what had awakened her. And while she wasn't positive that she was hearing footsteps—they were largely muffled by the rain on the roof and the sudden way the wind would rattle the storm windows—she was confident that someone other than her parents and Hallie was inside the house. And so she tiptoed into her sister's bedroom.

"Someone's downstairs," she whispered.

"Yeah, Mom," said Hallie, and she sat up on her elbows in her bed, her hair wild with sleep. "And maybe Dad's back." Neither she nor Hallie knew precisely where their father had gone, but at dinner Dad had said he was going to a meeting that night and probably wouldn't be home until after they were asleep. They guessed that it had something to do with the depression and strangeness that had marked him since Flight 1611 crashed, but what that meant precisely neither could say.

"I don't think so," Garnet said.

"What?"

"It's someone else. I think we should go hide."

"Really?"

"Yes! Just till we know. We could hide in the attic. Through that hole in the wall. It's there for a reason."

"The attic scares me," Hallie said, a rare quiver in her voice.

"It's just dusty and cold," Garnet reassured her. "That's all."

She could tell that Hallie was starting to think about this, and then they both heard a small thud in the dark two floors below them and her sister crinkled her nose. Hallie, too, was smelling the cool, damp air. "Maybe that was Mom," she whispered, but it was clear that she wasn't confident.

"Come on," Garnet urged her, and Hallie nodded and climbed from her bed. For one of the few times in the sisters' lives, she followed her redheaded twin. The girls returned to Garnet's bedroom, where Garnet pushed her bureau a few inches toward the window and then knelt and pulled open the door to the passageway. She pushed Hallie through it first and then followed her sister into the dark of the attic. As she was on her stomach on the attic floor, pulling the door back into its slot with the twine so it would disappear into the wallpaper, she could feel the vibrations of someone—some people, she thought—walking just a few feet away on the other side. Then, somewhere far off, she heard her mother calling out both her and her sister's names. She didn't believe the people in her bedroom were friends; she didn't believe her mother even knew they were there. She wished there was a way she could warn her.

You are surrounded by the sounds of the chimes. Here they are once again, the relentless tweets and rings you heard (but only vaguely at the time) in the cockpit as Flight 1611 descended inexorably back to earth. They are meant to alert you that the ground is rising up toward the aircraft. As if you don't know. As if you need a synthetic voice urging you to "pull up, pull up, pull up." Or another one informing you that you are too low, too low, too low. That there is terrain. You know as well as anyone that there is terrain, as the small boats on the lake grow more distinct and the forests on the foothills of the Adirondacks on the New York side of the water come into focus and suddenly seem to be higher than the wings of your plane. And yet somehow you and Amy Lynch remained more focused than you would have thought possible when you listened to the cockpit voice recordings with the NTSB. Somehow, despite the noise from the automated warning systems and the radio traffic that filled your small space at the front of the doomed aircraft, you worked the problem until, it seemed, you had solved it. And then there was that wave from the ferry and you were done.

Now it is all back, including the chimes. It is all before you once more, including the sound of Amy's voice, an unmistakable but absolutely understandable tremor coursing through each syllable. But like you, she worked the problem. She skimmed through the emergency handbook, she tried to reignite the engines, she implemented the ditching procedures.

You couldn't save her.

Now you try to open your eyes, but you can't, and it takes you a long moment to recall where you are. Slowly the details of the pentagonal greenhouse become clear in your mind's eye, despite the strange mugginess that has engulfed you. You wonder what was in the sweet tea you drank and then the bitter tincture you swallowed immediately after it in two great spoonfuls. The greenhouse had been illuminated by long rows of grow lights, and at one point it was so bright that you found yourself squinting as your eyes adjusted. You remember turning your head and gazing at Baphomet, at his beard and his wings, and you inhaled what you thought was incense. Your fingertips felt for the edge of the gurney. No, it wasn't a gurney. Nor was it a massage table. It was a long, antique pumpkin pine table, on which the plants had been replaced with a futon.

You sigh. You decide that what you just experienced of Flight 1611 was a dream, not a flashback. This distinction seems to matter, even now.

"Where is Sandra?"

You turn your head the other way—at least you believe you do—toward the sound of Reseda's voice, and you have the sense that Holly is standing beside her. Perhaps it is the aroma of lilacs that reminds you Holly is assisting Reseda. Doesn't the woman always smell slightly of lilacs? You cannot recall what the three of you might have discussed when Reseda was steeping that strange tea in the kitchen. When you first lay down here in the greenhouse, over Holly's shoulder was a pipe with hanging plants, the leaves of which were shaped like Valentine hearts; the colors were an orange and a purple more vibrant than your twins' Magic Markers.

"Where is Sandra?" Reseda asks again.

You try to find your voice, to tell her you don't know, you don't feel the specific pain you associate with Sandra's presence, when out of nowhere you hear her. You hear Sandra. You hear her with the same perfect clarity that you heard her that first time she spoke to you in your basement.

Here, she says simply.

"When did you join the captain?" Reseda asks, and you realize that Reseda heard her voice, too. Or did she hear yours? You have read about out-of-body experiences and you long for one now. You want to be both in and above that former pilot on the pumpkin pine table, because you want to witness this. You want to see where Sandra is standing this second. Is she visible to the two other women?

I don't know, she is telling Reseda, *but I think I joined him in the water. I couldn't breathe.*

You try to sit up, to find her. But you can't. You recall the mind-altering crumpets infused with God-alone-knows-what that Anise and Valerian had been feeding you and start to panic that now Reseda and Holly have paralyzed you from the neck down. Is this, you wonder, what it is like to be hypnotized? Or is this something else entirely?

"Shhhh, you're not paralyzed," Reseda says. "Don't struggle. Let Sandra speak."

You try to relax, at least a little. Do you nod? You believe that you do, but, again, you are not completely sure. No matter. No . . . matter.

Reseda runs a clay pestle under your nose with a shallow puddle of hot oil bubbling inside it, and you inhale what might be juniper. Then Holly—yes, you can hear her and sense her—is lining the head of the table, just beyond the futon, with burning votives. Each time she places one on the pine, Reseda dips her fingers into the hot wax and presses a single drop onto your forehead and murmurs a name you recognize from the passenger manifest. The sensation is not unpleasant, and you wonder if she will do it forty-eight times. She stops at twelve, however, listing the names of the nine survivors (including yours) and the names of the three people who died but have attached themselves to you. The melting wax in the votives is flecked with aromatic herbs, but the scent is unfamiliar to you. Again she asks Sandra a question, and you are listening to the woman's response when suddenly there is the water from Lake Champlain that awful August afternoon starting to wash over you in a single great wave. And so you take a deep breath, your cheeks ballooning like a toddler's, though the air in those pockets is largely irrelevant. And then, before you know it, you are upside down and the lake water is in your nose, the pain stinging, and you are desperate for air, desperate. When you open your eyes to see where you are, you are completely underwater. It happened that fast—the blink of an eye. You are vaguely aware of the blue leather on the seat ahead of you, of slick emergency information cards, glossy in-flight magazines, digital reading devices, and paperback books floating amidst the bubbles like tropical fish, and the way the fuselage is falling, falling, falling through the lake. You see the wide-open eyes of the young businessman in the brown suit, his hair floating up in the water like saw grass, his arms frantically lashing out as he tries to swim. Then he turns away, kicking you with his wingtip shoe. You release your seat belt—not a five-point shoulder harness, a mere steel buckle linking a thick nylon ribbon—and abruptly the eddies of whooshing water slam you hard into first an armrest and next the jagged floor of the jet, which somehow is above you. You probably would have been forced by the pain in your chest to open your mouth in another second anyway, but when the side of your head is cleavered by whatever is protruding from the floor, reflexively your lips part into a wide, silent O, and the lake water pours in, and your throat spasms shut—the laryngeal cords trying desperately to keep all that water out of your lungs. It is an agony more pronounced than anything you have experienced in your life or, now, ever will. And it seems to last an eternity. You want this over, you want to die now rather than in minutes—because you are conscious of the reality that you are indeed going to perish, there will be no miracle—but it takes time for the brain to black out. The last thing you see before the pain and terror and whiteness obliterates all thought? The white shirt of, you believe, the captain of the aircraft.

The idea crossed Emily's mind to get in the car and drive for help, but that would demand that she stop searching for her girls. And because there didn't seem to be a strange vehicle on the property now and she hadn't heard one earlier, she told herself that the girls were somewhere nearby. They had to be. And so she raced downstairs and screamed once more for Hallie and Garnet, shouting their names into the storm from the front hallway, the screams desperate, biblical wails that made her throat hurt. Only when her voice had grown hoarse did she finally grab her keys and run for her car, stumbling once on the slate walkway and feeling the sting acutely on the hand that already was cut. But it barely slowed her. She was hysterical and she didn't care. She climbed into her car and switched on the headlights and the wipers and was just about to throw the Volvo into reverse and glance behind her when she saw it. She saw it for just a fleeting second, and she saw it only because the car had been facing the greenhouse and all that glass acted like a mirror, causing her to look away from the solarlike luminescence of the vehicle's headlights. She flinched and reflexively turned to her left, back toward the house. And in a window on the second floor, the guest room down the corridor from her and Chip's bedroom, she saw the halo from a flashlight. It moved briefly but clearly, and she was reminded of the massive fog lights that would cut through the mist at airports. It was that distinct. And then it was gone.

An idea crossed her mind, cryptic but meaningful: This was why Tansy Dunmore had kept a small arsenal hidden throughout the house. This explained the crowbar, the knife, and the ax.

Well, she had weapons, too. She had knives. In the kitchen.

For a moment she watched the wipers and tried to think. If someone was in the house right now, they had known she was there, too, because of the way she had been frantically screaming and searching for her girls. But they had left her alone. They hadn't hurt her. They hadn't drugged or sedated her. Apparently, they hadn't even been interested in her. They had only been interested in her children: It was Hallie and Garnet they wanted. And if someone was still inside her home, then perhaps her girls had hidden themselves somewhere in the house or in the woods and hadn't been discovered yet.

And so she kept the car running and the headlights on, figuring that whoever was inside might presume for a few more seconds that she was still in the vehicle. At the same time, if she could find the twins, they could race into the station wagon and speed off the property. Leave this despicable house and this despicable town . . . forever. So she closed the car door as softly as she could and ran back through the rain into the house.

A thought crossed her mind: *I am like a firefighter. I am running into a burning building.* But it passed quickly as she tried to imagine where her girls might be hiding.

Far below them, Hallie and Garnet saw the station wagon headlights bounce against the greenhouse and then watched their mother emerge from the car, barely shutting the door as she returned to the house. They had been sitting absolutely still, curled into small balls, when the strangers were just across the wall from them in Garnet's bedroom, barely daring to exhale until they heard the sounds move away from them into Hallie's bedroom and then down the stairs to the second floor. Only then had they stood up and moved to the window, where they waited now, surveying the world below them.

"They're in the guest room," Garnet murmured.

"I know," Hallie agreed. "I hear them."

"I'm scared."

"Me, too."

"How many are there?"

"I don't know. Two, I think. But maybe three," Hallie answered. The attic floorboards were cold and her toes were starting to freeze.

"I was hoping it was just one person," Garnet said. Then: "Think they'll hurt Mom if they catch her?"

"They haven't yet."

"No. I guess not."

"It must be us who they want," Hallie said. "I think they want to kidnap us."

Garnet thought about this, and she realized something she should have understood earlier—the moment she had heard the strangers inside the house. "No, that's not it," she said. "It's not like they're strangers who want to kidnap us for money. It's Anise."

"What?"

"Well, maybe not Anise herself. I don't know. But it's the plant ladies. They've come for us. I know it."

"Then why wouldn't they have just taken us any of the times we've been at their houses or greenhouses—or when they've been over here in the past? And why would they come in the middle of the night? Why would they be sneaking around? There aren't any other cars outside."

"I don't know. But we can't just stay up here if Mom's looking for us downstairs," Garnet said, and she heard her voice growing a little more urgent. Hallie pushed a finger against her lips to shush her. "We have to help her," Garnet whispered. "We have to do something."

They could no longer feel anyone moving anywhere inside the house: not the strangers in the guest bedroom below them or their mother in some other corner or on the stairs. The house went absolutely

still. And so for a moment they both stood where they were, staring out
the attic window at the storm and contemplating what they should do.
Just then the trapdoor was yanked open from the second floor and a
flashlight beam rose like a waterspout into the attic.

This time, the captain's white shirt starts to fall away. Or, to be precise, you fall away. You drift, swaying as if the wrecked fuselage of
the jet were a hammock, rocking you, as you and the others descend
toward the muddy bottom of Lake Champlain, your back against the
aircraft aisle floor. Once before you grabbed that white shirt and clung to
it. Not this time. Someone in the distance is calling to you. Urging you
to go home. Someone else—your grandfather—is leaning against his
vintage white Mustang with the black vinyl hardtop. Tony the Pony he
called that car, and you would laugh and sink deep into the vehicle's red
leather seats. You sat on his lap when you were a little girl in Ridgewood,
New Jersey, and other times you would sit beside him on the couch
when he would read to you, while your grandmother sat near you both,
doing her crewelwork. Their home often had the welcoming aroma
of your grandmother's homemade Swedish meatballs or, as Christmas
neared, her holiday sugar cookies. After your grandfather retired, he
played an organ at Macy's in the weeks before Christmas. That was how
he would spend his Decembers: playing Christmas carols. He died in his
sleep when you were in the second grade, and you cried at his funeral—
the first you ever attended—but he and his Mustang are considerably
closer to you now than that other voice, the woman encouraging you to
go home. Soon that captain's shirt is above you, far above you and growing small, and then it is gone completely and all that remains is blackness
and the beckoning sound of the department store organ.

Emily had switched off her flashlight and now held it against her
thigh like a club. She pressed herself flat against the kitchen wall
beside the pantry and waited for her eyes to grow accustomed to the

dark. She held her breath and listened, trying to hear or feel movement anywhere in the house, but heard and felt nothing. When she could make out the details of the kitchen more exactly, she gazed at the counter with the wooden block with the knives. She couldn't tell if they all were there, but she saw at least three long handles, and so she knew the most dangerous ones were still in place. She moved quietly across the kitchen and pulled out the carving knife. Then she paused once more, waiting. Above her she thought she heard the groan of the trapdoor to the attic—a prolonged creaking that accompanied the descent of the stairs—but she wasn't sure. It might simply have been the house shuddering in the wind. She considered taking her knife and going straight up the stairs and challenging whoever was there—assuming someone had indeed just opened the door to the attic—but even if she made it to the second-floor landing without being heard, she would lose all surprise when she ran down the corridor toward the trapdoor. She needed another approach.

And the answer, she realized, was that bizarre back stairway at the other end of the kitchen. She almost never used it. She had ascended it exactly two times since they had moved in—the second time only because Chip wanted to show her how he'd replaced the worst of the steps—but it was still windowless, unlit, and too thin to be of practical use if you were carrying anything of any size. It still felt half-finished. But now it might offer the element of surprise, and so silently she opened the door and started up those steps, the flashlight in her left hand and the carving knife in her right.

The primary impact rarely kills everyone in a plane crash. This is especially true in the case of a planned water ditching. Reseda recalled Chip telling her in a voice that was almost numbingly clinical that underwater disorientation, drowning, disorderly evacuation, and injuries from not bracing properly were what killed many people, and Flight 1611 was tragically typical in that regard. Moreover, he feared it was likely that some passengers had an unreasonable faith that they would walk away from the disaster as easily as had the passengers on Flight 1549, Sully Sullenberger's successful ditching of an Airbus in the Hudson River, and those individuals may not even have braced properly. They had, he presumed, been staring enrapt out the windows, as if this were a mere carnival ride.

He had no idea whether Ashley Stearns had braced properly, he said, but it probably wouldn't have mattered: If Sandra Durant was one of those who did not die on primary impact, then Ashley was one of those who did. Compared to Sandra, she was fortunate, in that her death was almost instant. From what Reseda could see in Chip's mind and from what he had told her of his encounters with the child, the girl had been all but cut in half—imagine a guillotine blade slicing through the abdomen—by a part of the aircraft when it finished its somersault and slammed upside down into the lake. Based on the airline's colors and the portion of logo Chip could see on the metal, he had presumed it was either a part of the rear fuselage or a piece of the vertical stabilizer. There was so much more that he could have told her, but he didn't. He didn't have to. He didn't have to tell her of the child's eyes, open but listless, the light of the living there gone, because she saw the girl in his mind. Ashley's skin was waxen, a ghost's right away. The gaping wound—chasmlike, the great, triangular shard ripping through muscle, intestine, and kidney (the blood and urine rising amidst the bubbles like ribbons), until finally it severed even the vertebrae and spinal cord—reminded her of a painting she'd seen once in a San Gimignano torture museum of a specific medieval form of execution: A person would be suspended upside down so there would be as much blood flowing to the brain as possible, and thus the victim would remain conscious through far more of the agony. The heretic's or prisoner's ankles would be bound to separate posts to shape the body into a Y. Then he would be cut in half with a two-person saw, the blade starting in the groin and slicing first through the perineum. The difference for Ashley? She had been killed in a heartbeat. Thank God.

She deserves friends, someone said bitterly, and Reseda knew this was the girl's father. Even now he was out there somewhere, angry and poised for a fight.

"This will be a long evening," Holly murmured, her voice a wisp, and Reseda nodded. She had been so focused on Ashley Stearns's imminent death that she had nearly forgotten Holly was beside her and might hear Ethan, too. Still, Reseda opened a vial with an oil composed of valerian leaves and retreatus and put a line of drops along the captain's upper lip so he would inhale the potion as he breathed. She pressed her fingers against his temples and asked to speak to Ashley. She feared briefly that the girl's father was going to act as a buffer spirit, a barrier, and he might have tried, but the child had heard her instantly and come forward.

I can't talk to most breathers, she said.

"You can talk to me," Reseda said gently.

If Ashley's mother had died in the crash with her, Reseda would have sent the child to her—instructed her to go home with her. But her mother had survived, and that was a part of the problem. And while her father had died that afternoon, he may have been the very reason why the girl had not gone on but had instead remained attached to the pilot; her father had stayed, and so she had stayed with him. Consequently, that afternoon Holly had researched which of the child's grandparents were living and which ones were dead. She'd learned that Ethan's mother had passed away from cancer last year, which meant that Ashley had known her. That woman might be the spirit guide the child needed, the escort who could take Ashley by the hand and lead her to her destined next life. So Reseda had Holly fill the air of the greenhouse with fresh, pungent ayahuasca and enticium leaves, sprinkling the plants like confetti, while she summoned the spirit of Ashley Stearns's grandmother.

It might have been possible to find places to hide in the attic if they had had more time. There were boxes, some empty and some filled with old blankets and quilts or half-filled with ancient high school yearbooks and aviation manuals. Perhaps they could have buried themselves in a couple of them. But it hadn't crossed either of the girls' minds that whoever was in the house would think to search the attic. And so the best they could do now was to crouch together behind a tall cardboard wardrobe container near the window where they had been standing. They both understood it wouldn't take long for them to be found.

And then? Garnet didn't imagine she would fight, but she thought Hallie might. And as scared as she was, she believed that struggling was a bad idea. As she had told her sister earlier, the women—and whoever was now in the house—wanted them. They *needed* them. It didn't make sense that they would hurt them. But, then, there seemed to be a whole world of things swirling just beyond their understanding. She saw in her mind the jawbone and the skull she had found in the basement in this very house, three floors below them. She wondered where her mother was now; she was no longer yelling out their names, which might mean that she also knew there were intruders in their home.

"You're shivering," Hallie whispered.

Garnet nodded. Her teeth were chattering, too, and her bracelet was vibrating against the tall cardboard box. She wrapped her other hand around it.

"What do we do?" her sister asked.

She saw Hallie was watching her, wide-eyed, her cheek pressed against the wardrobe. Her sister was so scared that she was panting, and just as Hallie had shushed her with a single finger a few minutes ago, now Garnet silenced her. She clenched her teeth to stop them from clicking. Then she puffed out her cheeks to convey the idea that they both should be holding their breath. They listened, aware that any moment they would hear someone or some people climbing the steps and the light in the attic would grow brighter. They would be discovered and then . . .

And there Garnet's imagination failed her. She tried to reassure herself that the plant ladies couldn't possibly want to harm them.

But the attic didn't fill with light. Instead they heard below them what sounded like someone grunting—gasping, perhaps—and the attic went completely dark as they heard something fall to the pinewood floor, a thump so heavy that, even a floor above, they felt a slight quiver along the crude wooden planks on which they were cowering.

*   *   *

Reseda knew that her own energy was starting to flag. She had felt the agony in her throat and chest and had nearly blacked out herself before Sandra Durant's soul found its way beyond Chip Linton, and she had wound up gasping and then reduced to whimpers as she experienced Ashley Stearns's sudden evisceration when the CRJ broke apart in the lake. She wondered how the captain had lived with it all for so long and whether the physical agony was actually worse than the psychological torment of myriad second guesses and what-ifs, of having not gone down with his ship—of having lived when so many of his passengers had died. Nevertheless, she kept searching for the girl's grandmother, entreating the spirit to guide her young granddaughter home. Finally, there in the fog, she saw a heavyset older woman in a leopard-print bathing suit and a diaphanous beach cover-up, barefoot. The powdery white beach on which she was walking was dotted with sand dollars and shells from sea urchins, slippers, and fighting conchs. She had a whelk shell in one hand but was beckoning toward someone else with the other, smiling. She was wearing dark sunglasses because recently she had had a cataract removed from her right eye. Then she took Ashley's small hand in hers. Ashley, it seemed, was whom she was waiting for. The child was in a bathing suit, too, a little girl's two-piece patterned with cartoon butterflies, and she was no longer impaled on the jagged remains of a wrecked airplane. She gazed quizzically up at her grandmother, a little confused, but then she rested her head against her grandmother's arm as they walked down the beach, the low tide lapping at the sand a dozen or so yards away, while the whitest sun Reseda had ever seen burned off the last of the early morning fog.

"Verbena, no! No, no, no! That was a monumental mistake."

Emily was on the floor, kneeling over the broad-shouldered stranger in the wool cap and the yellow slicker she had just attacked, and there before her—towering over her, it felt—were Anise and John. Emily was almost hyperventilating, and she wasn't precisely sure where she had stabbed the fellow: She had seen him from the top of the back stairs no more than three or four feet away and leapt at him, trying to plunge the knife into him. And now the man was facedown and Emily could see a great streak of blood along one of the jacket shoulders.

"We were going to fetch the girls and then you," John continued, the irritation evident in his usually avuncular voice. "Really, what in heaven's name would possess you to assault a person like that?"

"Where's Hallie? Where's Garnet? What have you done with my children?" She spat the words out in a frenzy as she rose to her feet, and now she held up the knife, pointing the tip at John as if it were a fencing foil. She saw that Anise looked every bit as perturbed as the older lawyer—perhaps more so. She was wearing a parka so wet that it glistened in the beam of the flashlight. "Tell me right now or I will kill you just like I killed him," Emily continued, motioning at the body on the floor.

Anise rubbed her eyes with her fingers, clearly exasperated and tired. "No, I don't think you will. Especially since, thank God, you didn't kill Alexander," she said. And just as the realization was registering in Emily's mind that she hadn't recognized the powerfully built older man because of his wool cap, she felt her bare ankles being grabbed and her legs pulled out from underneath her. She lost the flashlight as she fell onto her knees, the bones thumping hard on the wooden floor, but she might have been able to hang on to the knife if John hadn't grabbed her arm and whisked it from her fingers. Then Alexander rolled her onto her back and knelt on her chest, one of his knees pressing hard against her sternum. She barely could breathe beneath his weight.

"That's fine, Alexander," John said. "That's enough. Are you badly hurt?"

"Well, I could bore you with the details of what could have been the damage to my rotator cuff," he answered, grimacing. "But I won't. Shoulder wounds can be nasty, so suffice to say I dodged a bullet—or, in this case, a knife. I have a bulky sweater under my raincoat, and that helped. She only got my upper arm. I'm bleeding, but mostly she knocked the wind out of me."

"We'll be sure to tend to your wounds," Anise said as she crouched before Emily.

"I'll be fine," he said simply in response.

"Trust me, Verbena, this will all go so much easier if you just tell us where Cali and Rosemary are hiding," John said. "Will you do that, for us—for them?"

"They're in the attic," Alexander said. "At least I think they are. I thought I heard them scurrying around up there when I pulled open the trapdoor."

"I hope so. Really, I do. I hope it wasn't just a couple of very large mice," John muttered. "Verbena, call your girls. Tell them to come down."

"I won't," she grunted. "I can't yell with him on me anyway," she stammered.

"If I ease up, you'll call them?" Alexander asked.

They beamed a flashlight onto her face, and she shook her head no.

"Good Lord, what do you think we plan to do with them?" John asked. "Cook them in a stewpot?"

And so Alexander sat back on his heels so she could breathe deeply and yell, and Emily did call out to the girls. But she screamed precisely the opposite of what John and Anise desired. "Hallie, Garnet, wherever you are, stay hidden!" she screamed as loud as she could. "Don't let them find you!"

Alexander cupped his hand over her mouth, and Emily was astonished at the fellow's strength. "All you are doing is postponing the inevitable," John said to her. Then he turned his gaze upon Alexander. "I think you can let her go. Really, I do. She's not leaving. But would you mind going up to the attic and retrieving the children? Anise, you, too? Give me the knife and I'll wait here with Verbena. This already has taken far, far too long. We have people waiting."

"And it has been a long wait," said Anise, and Emily understood that the woman was speaking of something entirely different from what John Hardin had meant.

But the partner in her law firm smiled at Anise's remark and added, "Indeed, it has." Then he looked straight into Emily's eyes and told her, "We've been waiting since Sawyer Dunmore died. Now: Let's go get the girls from the attic. Shall we?"

*   *   *

There is nothing you would not do for your daughter. Nothing. Or is it daughters? You find yourself watching the CRJ descend toward Lake Champlain, but the view is not from the flight deck, it's from one of the passenger cabin windows toward the left rear of the aircraft. Meanwhile, you struggle with this one strangely unanswerable but profoundly important question: Where on the aircraft is your daughter? Or, again, daughters? You see in your mind the round face and blond spit curls of one girl, but shouldn't there be a second child? Or (and here the mind feels truly unmoored) a third? Briefly you envision a girl with red hair, but the image grows hazy fast. And then it is gone. She's gone.

The seat beside you is empty, but you are absolutely certain that your daughter—the blond girl—was there just a moment ago. She was in that window seat. Her Dora the Explorer backpack is still nearby, one of its straps and a nylon handle peering out from underneath the seat ahead of you. But that little girl? Gone. You scan the rows of people in the seats before you, but there is absolutely no sign of her. There is absolutely no sign of any children at all.

At the very least, you must find the child with the blond hair before the plane belly flops into the lake and—as somehow you know it will—breaks apart. You must, because you love her and she needs you and there is no more powerful, more poignant cord. But then the plane is down and for the barest of seconds seems to be skimming along the surface of the lake. This may, in the end, turn out all right. Suddenly, however, the aircraft plows into a surface as solid as a medieval castle wall and is stood upright on its nose, and your head is whipped into the seat before you and then, as the fuselage crashes back into the water, into the collapsing ceiling. Or is it the floor? You have no idea. You know only that the cabin has come alive with the sounds of screaming and ripping metal, and already you can smell the lake water that is rolling like a tsunami down the aisle, and—this doesn't seem possible, this can't possibly have happened—a metal pike has pierced your skull like an arrow. You run the fingers of your right hand over the shard, and they come away bloodied. And then you try to take a breath, but already the water is over your mouth and nose and you start to gag.

So you struggle, you thrash, even as you grow weak, even as the water is flooding your nose and you are aware that you will never survive your head wound. You try to rip the seat belt in half because something has dented the metal buckle and now it won't open. And somewhere very far away someone is calling your name. Someone closer is, too.

But, still, you have no idea what happened to your daughter. Or those other girls. Twins? Yes, twins. You know for sure only one thing: Your daughter didn't deserve this, and the realization has you enraged. She didn't deserve to die this way. She deserved more than eight years. She deserved a lifetime. She deserved friends.

And so, once again, you lash out, even though it is futile, even though there is absolutely nothing that can be done.

But the anger is all and so you fight.

Holly tried holding down the captain's left arm and shoulder and Reseda his right, but he was thrashing violently—great, convulsive heaves—and the greenhouse was filled with Ethan Stearns's rage as he died once more in the warm August water of Lake Champlain.

"Go, you have people waiting for you!" Reseda tried to reassure him, the words rushed and, she knew, slightly fearful. He would have none of it. "She's gone. Your daughter is gone. You can't stay. You shouldn't stay, your daughter is waiting—" she said, and she would have continued, *Your daughter has gone home, she has gone to her grandmother, she has gone where she belongs and is happy,* but she never got to finish the sentence. He broke free and slammed the back of his hand hard into the side of her face and her ears registered the hollow bang of his knuckles on the bones in her cheek, and she was reeling, falling into a table beside her, toppling the plants, one of the clay pots shattering and another spilling its dirt and the small, pink hysterium that was just starting to bloom. From the floor she saw him sitting up and Holly desperately trying to push him back down, but her ears were ringing from the blow and it was as if she were suddenly deaf or watching a movie with the sound off. Then he was on his feet, standing, and, with more strength than she had imagined he had, he was lifting Holly under her arms and hurling her into the glass wall, shattering it into thousands of pieces. Reseda pulled herself off the ground and tried to grab him, but already he was running toward the greenhouse entrance, angrily toppling Baphomet as he wheeled among the statuary and tables, one of the statue's horns breaking off when it crashed to the dirt. He grabbed something on his way out, but she couldn't see what it was. She crawled like a crab to Holly and found the woman's hands and arms were bleeding where reflexively she had tried to shield her head from the glass. The rain and cold air whipped inside and stung the side of her face. Holly was breathing rapidly, and she sat upright and stammered, "He was out like a light, wasn't he? I mean, where did that come from? I thought he was practically paralyzed."

Reseda examined the woman's wounds. They were bloody, but they weren't deep. "He was," she said, aware that her own words sounded slightly garbled because it hurt so much to speak. Her face still smarted where he had struck her. "But it wore off. It's been a long night. There were three of them."

"Can you stop him?" she asked.

"I don't know," she said.

"Go," Holly insisted, "go!" She rolled her eyes up toward the ceiling and added, "I think he took my bag."

And Reseda understood instantly what the captain had grabbed on his way out—and why. "Call Emily right now!" she said. "Tell them to leave the house right this second." Then she stood, but already she heard a vehicle engine starting and outside she saw its headlights illuminating the trees. A second later, Chip was spinning Holly's car into reverse, the trees went dark, and he was gone.

Chapter Twenty

E mily knew the communal greenhouse from those afternoons
that spring when she had picked up the twins there after
school—when, ostensibly, they had been learning about plants
and herbs with some of the women at Sage Messner's. But she had never
been inside it at night and she had never seen it so crowded: In her mind,
it was always just her girls and two or three older women, and the skies
high above the glass ceiling were likely to be blue.

Not now. The wind and the rain were lashing the great panes of
glass against their metal framing, and there were at least three censers
burning what John had told her with unrestrained pride was frankin-
cense Clary had transplanted from Oman. There must have been twenty
or twenty-five of her neighbors present tonight, women and men she
was likely to meet on the streets of Littleton and Bethel—the people
she had viewed as an extended family of sorts throughout the last couple of months—though now they were all dressed in what looked like
burgundy-colored choir robes. There were Anise and Clary and Valerian
and Sage and Ginger—who gave Alexander a vaguely chaste kiss on the
cheek and then insisted on looking at the wound on his upper arm, her
eyes going back and forth between the puncture wound and Emily—
and Celandine, the female trooper who had come to Emily's home that
frightening night when Garnet found the skull in the dirt in the basement. She saw her girls' schoolteacher. In addition, there were another
three or four women Emily didn't recognize. And there were the men,
their spouses and partners, and John quickly climbed into a robe and

joined Peyton and Claude, where they stood beside a waist-high black marble basin, the column a spiral of interlocking carved vines. There was something unrecognizable about all of them this evening, something far more profound than the reality that they were dressed in red robes: They'd stood and swayed and stomped their feet in a barely controlled frenzy when Anise and John had first nudged the girls into the greenhouse. They were all a little giddy, and Emily couldn't decide if it was more like a religious rapture or the adrenaline rush that accompanies a nighttime bonfire at a beach in high summer. Some of the assemblage were drinking from identical ceramic goblets with leaves carved into the cups and the stems, dunking their goblets into that basin as if it were a punch bowl.

The electric heaters were warming the greenhouse, but it was illuminated only by clay oil lamps with corked wicks and tall candles in hurricane vases in the corners. The blue flames from the lamps lined the floor and the edges of the tables, all of which had been pushed against the walls, and the flickering light seemed to lengthen all the shadows. It made everyone look about seven feet tall. And at the end of the greenhouse, where some of the group was gathering now in a great semicircle, beside a pane of glass that opened out, was a wrought-iron cauldron that had to have been at least three feet high, suspended on five squat legs that Emily thought were as thick as her ankles. Beneath it was a small fire, and she couldn't help but recall John's cryptic words: *What do you think we plan to do with them? Cook them in a stewpot?*

Her girls looked more stunned than terrified, but she knew how frightened they were and she thought there was nothing she wanted more than to be able to go and comfort them. No, there was something she did want more than that: She wanted out. She wanted to take her girls and run from this greenhouse and from Bethel. She would stop by Reseda's and get Chip and then leave northern New Hampshire forever. But two younger men she had never seen before—sons or grandsons of the herbalists, she imagined—stood on either side of her, each grasping one of her arms by the elbow.

The idea crossed her mind that Reseda and Holly were involved.

Clearly they were herbalists. But had they convinced Chip that he was possessed and brought him to Reseda's greenhouse so it would be easier to abduct the twins? Or were those two women unaware of what the rest of the group was doing right now? Emily wanted Chip—the old Chip, the man who had overcome a nearly disastrous childhood and wound up an airline pilot—back and beside her.

She could feel her heart racing; if she weren't so determined to try to find a way to get her girls out of this greenhouse, she thought she might die. Literally, she might collapse with a heart attack. Her girls were standing on the other side of that massive cauldron, Anise's and Sage's hands resting like great bird claws upon their shoulders. The twins were wearing their matching winter jackets, which they really didn't need because, despite the dampness and chill outside the greenhouse, despite the pane that was open to vent the cauldron, the heaters and the small fire were keeping the place almost toasty. But the girls were still in their pajamas, and Emily was struck by the sight of their baggy pajama pants between the bottoms of their parkas and the tops of their boots. She noticed that Garnet had tucked her pajamas into her boots, but Hallie hadn't bothered. Anise had allowed Emily to put on a pair of blue jeans, but she was still wearing her nightshirt underneath her coat.

Finally John worked his way through the crowd until he was standing beside her, while Anise stepped forward and smiled at everyone as if she were hosting a cocktail party and wanted to welcome her guests. She pulled her robe tight around her neck, and Emily noticed that, unlike the other robes, hers had a silver clasp. She couldn't make out the design from where she was standing, but she had a feeling it was some kind of ivy.

"Welcome," Anise said, spreading her arms and smiling. "The earth is with you!"

"And with you!" responded the gathering.

"We merge blood with seed!" she cried, staring down at the dirt floor, enraptured.

"We merge seed with soul!" they replied.

"And soul with earth—"

"To be born anew!"

"Yes," agreed Anise. "To be born anew." She looked up and gazed at the gathering and shook her head in wonderment, and everyone watched her expectantly. "We did it. You did it. We have earth. We have twins. And we have . . . our recipe." Valerian held open before Anise a thick book, and Emily thought it resembled the one that Anise had given Garnet, and the crowd in the greenhouse murmured their approval.

"To the earth and seeds!" John cried out in a toast, raising his goblet, and everyone drank with him. "To the twins!" he added. "Hear, hear!"

"To the twins!" the gathering shouted back, a loud and powerful and almost orgiastic chorus.

Emily craned her neck to read the title of the book, and her heart sank: *The Complete Book of Divination and Mediation with Animals and Humans.* She watched the flushed faces of the adults as their eyes darted back and forth between Anise and her girls and started to cry. Anise noticed but was unmoved. Then she pulled from a pocket at the front of her cape what looked like a bouquet of Italian parsley, but Emily was confident it was instead a plant that was both venomous and rare— something discovered or bred by these women from seeds they had found in some exotic corner of the planet. Anise pulled off the leaves and dropped them into the cauldron, as if they were merely bay leaves for a stew.

"John," Emily whispered, her voice urgent and quavering, "please, let us go. If we can help you, we will. You know that. But, please, please let us go. I'm begging you: Please don't hurt my girls."

John's eyes looked a little watery, too, and his profile a bit less regal: She wondered if perhaps he was weakening. But it was only age. His hands were clasped behind his back, and he smiled and shook his head firmly. "This is hard for all of us. I understand. I really do. But we only need one and it will all be over soon."

Emily recalled what Reseda had told her, but still it seemed too cruel to be true. "You only need one . . . what? One of my children?"

He nodded. "It's a very intense ritual, a very complicated process.

A complicated recipe. You need the right person—the right genes—and the right plants. You need a twin, and, according to the formula, the blood has to have been forged by a great trauma." He raised his eyebrows and breathed in deeply through his nose. "Tansy never forgave us—or herself. But our intentions were good, Verbena. You have to believe me. And the fact is, it worked with Sawyer. It was awfully effective. I am so sorry about what happened to the boy, but the tincture worked. Sadly, nothing from nature lasts forever, and now we need, well, boosters. We need more."

"Did you kill Sawyer? Are you saying he didn't kill himself?"

"You must think we're absolute fiends," John said, and he actually chuckled. "Besides, I'm a lawyer. You can't possibly believe that I would confess to something like that! Now, you should pay attention," he admonished her. "We both should."

Celandine was approaching Anise with a potted plant, the leaves cochleate and yellow as daffodils, with one spear-shaped bulb rising from the center. The plant was perhaps eighteen inches tall and the bulb the size of a grown-up's fist. Clary Hardin and Ginger Jackson fell to their knees, their heads thrown back, nearly swooning with anticipation, as did another pair of women Emily didn't recognize. They dropped their goblets onto the ground and spread wide their arms in ecstasy.

"They've been waiting a long time for this moment," John murmured. "Many of us have. To be so very, very close to the end and get a second chance? What a delightful notion!"

Sage Messner began herding the twins forward, edging them closer to the cauldron. Then the girls' schoolteacher, Mrs. Collier—Yarrow Collier, Emily remembered—knelt before the children, handed them each a goblet, and said in a voice as soothing as a lullaby, "Enjoy this. Drink, girls, drink up."

They both looked across the greenhouse at their mother, wondering what they should do, and so Emily violently shook her head. They looked tiny to her, more like big dolls than small children. Even in their winter coats they appeared waiflike. "Don't," she yelled to them, hoping she sounded more resolute than panicked—because she knew she was panicked. But she knew also that whatever herbal potion these women had prepared for her children would only harm them. She was as sure of that as she had been of anything in her life. "Don't drink it!"

"Verbena, that's enough," Anise said, speaking to her for the first time since they had arrived at the greenhouse, and the two men tightened their grips on her arms. Her voice was absolutely inscrutable to Emily. Then she crossed the greenhouse and placed her long, cold fingers on Emily's cheeks and looked directly into her eyes. For the briefest of seconds, Emily was brought back to that first Sunday morning when the woman's rusted pickup truck had rumbled up their long driveway and she had appeared with a casserole and brownies.

"Send her away," hissed one of the women Emily didn't know.

"We don't need her!" added Lavender Millier.

"No, I would rather she watched," said Anise simply. Then she looked directly into Emily's eyes, brusquely wiped the tears off her cheeks, and added, "Now: I must insist you behave." Then she released her and went to Hallie and Garnet, kneeling beside Mrs. Collier so the girls were actually a little taller than she was. She seized the goblet from Garnet and took a sip, gazing at the girl and smiling. After that she took a sip from Hallie's chalice, too, running her tongue over her lips after she had swallowed. When she was finished, she stood up and turned back toward Emily. She raised her eyebrows high above her eyes as if to say, *See? Satisfied? I'm still standing.* Then she motioned for the girls to drink up, and, much to Emily's despair, they did, draining the two chalices that had been given them.

"Thank you, girls," Anise said. "That was very grown-up of you."

The twins glanced at each other and then at Anise and Sage and their schoolteacher. Emily thought Garnet looked like she might collapse, and she wondered what the group would do if her daughter had a seizure right now. She studied both girls and decided that Hallie looked a little wobbly as well; whatever was in that goblet had acted quickly. When Anise asked them to take off their snow jackets, both twins fumbled spastically with the zippers.

One of the women Emily didn't recognize, a petite, square-faced blonde her age who would have fit in well at a Junior League luncheon back in Philadelphia, approached Anise and bowed her head ever so slightly. Then she gave the woman a leather sheath, from which Anise pulled a long, ancient-looking dagger with a T-shaped handle that appeared to be made of dull iron. It looked vaguely Celtic to Emily, and had a moonstone nearly the size of a golf ball at the edge of the grip and smaller ones along the handle.

"Blood meets seed," Anise cried out.

"And seed meets soul," the herbalists proclaimed together.

With two fingers and her thumb, Anise snapped off the bulb from the yellow plant, and the sound was reminiscent of a cat's squeal immediately before a catfight. Then she took the bulb and held it above the black cauldron and slashed it open lengthwise with the knife, and a white milk waterfalled into the pot, and the smell—gardenia-like, and yet somehow it conjured for Emily the image and aroma of a just washed baby—overwhelmed the incense in the greenhouse. Then Anise dropped the empty husk into the mixture, too, and stirred it around with the tip of her dagger.

"And the last ingredient?" Valerian asked, though it was clear that she and all the other herbalists knew precisely what they would add next. Still, Anise glanced once at the grimoire that Valerian was patiently holding open for her. Then she signaled for the psychiatrist to shut the book.

"And so we finish," Anise proclaimed. "To those we once were—"

"And to those we shall be!" the herbalists finished.

"To the youth of the earth and the power of the seed!"

"To the youth of the earth and the power of the seed!" they repeated.

Anise raised the dagger over her head, and Emily realized that these people who posed as her neighbors and friends were about to execute one of her children—slaughter a ten-year-old girl. And so she screamed for her girls to run, to run away, as she threw herself violently at Anise, dragging those younger men with her. She was aware of the two of them and John Hardin trying (and failing) to pull her back, but she was enraged and fell upon the woman—*the witch,* she heard in her mind, *the witch*—tackling her onto the greenhouse floor, all the while howling for her children to flee. She'd reached for the knife, unsure what she would do with it if she wrestled it from the woman, when she was violently lifted up and off of Anise, her arms wrenched so far behind her that she feared one of her shoulders had been ripped from its socket. She turned, and there was Alexander Jackson and there was his heavy fist coming toward her face, and then all was black.

You had stood over each of the beds in the girls' rooms on the third floor of the house, the pearl-handled knife in each case raised in your hand high over your head. And yet each bed was empty. Emily had vanished as well, the bed still made (and the knife, fortunately, still held by duct tape to the horizontal slat on your side). Her station wagon was in the driveway, which suggested that, when they left, they had left in someone else's vehicle.

You wonder if they left because of the blackout. You noted in the kitchen that the digital clocks on the microwave and the oven were dark, and then in the girls' bedrooms that the automatic night-lights were off. But again, someone would have had to have picked them up.

Since they are not with Reseda, the Hardins are the most likely possibility. And so you drive to their place, peering at the tortuous road before you, the wipers on Holly's compact battling to keep up with the downpour and the lights no match for the darkness. But then, as you are approaching the Messners', you spy a conga line of cars parked off to the side of the road and snaking their way up the driveway.

Of course. You are not alone in wanting the twins. You know what the captain knows and he knows that the herbalists want them for . . . something. You crush the brakes hard and park.

Reseda hadn't realized that John and Anise were taking the twins that very night. She presumed they would wait for the new moon, since the book suggested the tincture should be prepared when the moon was waxing, and now it would be waning for three more days. She knew only that the twins were in danger because Ethan Stearns had attached himself to the pilot.

Yet as she was approaching the Lintons' driveway, before she had even pulled in, she saw headlights. She saw Holly's car speed from the driveway onto the two-lane road, nearly sideswiping the mailbox in the process, and race away from her toward the village of Bethel. He must have accelerated to eighty or ninety miles an hour. Maybe more. Briefly she considered going to the Lintons' as she had planned, but either they were already dead or they weren't there. And she guessed it was the latter because Holly must have reached them by phone. She saw no lights on down the driveway.

And so she accelerated, hoping she could keep up with the captain, but she wasn't sure she would succeed as she watched his red taillights disappear into the night. But she drove on as quickly as she could, the engine so loud that she could hear it even over the pounding drumbeat of the rain on the roof of her car. And then, as she was nearing the Messners' home, she felt a powerful spike of unease rise up side by side with her frantic worry for the twins: In her mind she saw tall pillars of cedar mesa sandstone spiking straight into the air in the Southwest. There was an enormous amount of activity just beyond her aura, and she had the sense, despite the electricity in the air from the storm, that a gathering was nearby. She felt the presence, inchoate but organizing, of a crowd. And so she pressed hard on the brakes, the car swerving slightly on the slick pavement, and discovered instantly that she was correct. There was Holly's car, empty, the front door wide open, the downpour saturating the seat and the upholstery on the inside of the door. It was last in the line of vehicles, most of which Reseda recognized. The Messners' house was dark, but even through the storm she could see a weak penumbra of light emanating from the south side—the side where the large communal greenhouse was built—and so she started running across the yard, the rain-soaked grass saturating her canvas sneakers.

When she got to the greenhouse, she saw a window was venting steam from Clary's cauldron, a massive wrought-iron pot that Reseda always viewed as a melodramatic affectation. But Clary loved it. A black-smith had made it for the woman perhaps a decade ago, and she had an almost fetishistic attachment to it. Reseda gathered herself, unsure what she would say or do, and pushed open the glass door. She saw no sign of the captain, but there were the herbalists gathered in their robes, while one of the twins was teetering on her wobbly legs before the cauldron. They had pulled up the sleeve of her pajama shirt and were holding her naked arm above the kettle. Anise had the blade of the group's ancient boline poised at the crux of the girl's elbow.

"Anise, don't do it!" Reseda commanded, aware that her voice could be firm and it could be cryptic, but rarely—if ever—was it menacing.

John Hardin took a sip from the chalice he was holding and then handed it to Peyton Messner. "I am one hundred and three years old," he said quietly. "You know that, my dear."

"And all of your extra time was at the expense of a twelve-year-old boy. I know that, too."

He waved a single finger, correcting her. "All of *our* extra time," he said, and then he motioned with his arm at the Messners, his wife, and Anise.

She looked at the group—the whole group—at the way their eyes were glazed and their skin was burning with anticipation. None of them would ever get any younger, that was a fact; but they all believed they could stall further aging for . . . years. The first tincture, built from the blood of Sawyer Dunmore, had given all of them who had gluttonously drunk from the chalice an extra three and a half or four decades. For someone like Clary Hardin, the best to be hoped for now would be to survive another three or four decades feeling seventy—but she was prepared to strike that bargain, especially since, like her husband, she was in fact well over one hundred years old. Meanwhile, someone like Celandine, the young state trooper? She would remain thirty, and what woman wouldn't accept the energy and strength and firmness that came with being thirty for an extra third of a century?

"Where is Emily?" she asked.

Anise nodded toward the rear of the greenhouse. The woman was sitting in a wooden chair, slumped over, with Alexander standing behind her, his hands resting heavily on her shoulders. She stared at John, reading him, and saw in his mind what had occurred a few moments earlier: She saw Alexander throwing Emily to the ground and knocking her unconscious for a brief moment. The girls' mother was still stunned. John looked away, but before he did Reseda thought she saw also what had happened to Michael Richmond last month: She hadn't seen John's entire recollection, but she saw that the old lawyer had used the very same knife on the psychiatrist that Anise was about to use to slice open a little girl's arm.

"You can't do this," she said, speaking to everyone and to no one. She knew in her heart that they weren't going to listen.

"Enough!" Anise told her. "This is not your decision. It's ours." And then she took the boline and scored the child's arm from her elbow to her wrist, flaying the skin and allowing it to dangle over the cauldron as the blood spurted like a water fountain—Sage Messner, who had been helping to restrain the girl, dunked her mouth into the stream and swallowed a mouthful voraciously—before slowing to a steady rivulet.

"Blood meets seed!" Anise declared.

"And seed meets soul!" the herbalists raved.

And then as one they edged ever closer. The child was so drugged that she only looked down at her arm, a little curious as her blood trickled into the cauldron, but clearly she had felt very little pain. Still, Reseda rushed forward and wrestled the girl from Sage and Ginger's grip, pushing the child's thin arm into a V to try to stop the bleeding. But it was doing nothing, nothing at all. She needed a trauma dressing and stitches. Eventually, the child's knees would buckle and she'd collapse onto the greenhouse floor. Still, Reseda wrapped her own arms around her, trying to protect her, as the circle of herbalists closed in upon the two of them.

"You're killing her," she said to them. "You're killing a child."

"Give her back to us, Reseda," John demanded. "You know you can't stop us. We're going to finish this. Besides," he wavered, his voice softening, "you're one of us. You're a part of us. You know that, too."

They had, she realized, become animals. They were selfish,

insatiable, violent animals. They needed blood, and they needed enough for all of them. She wasn't going to be able to reason with them. Nevertheless, she said, "I'm not one of you. I was once. But I'm not part of this."

"Reseda, really. The child is losing blood fast and it's being wasted. Wasted! You're a New Englander, how can you abide that? Besides: The more she loses now, the less she'll have when we're finished and the less chance she'll have of—to use a term you're fond of—going home."

Anise was still holding the dagger, and so Reseda looked around for another weapon, her eyes scanning the tables and the floor of the greenhouse. On a wooden bench in the corner near her were a pair of one-handed garden clippers. There were shears just like them, it seemed, on most of the tables. The safety was open, which meant the clippers were splayed into a slender Y, ready to harvest herbs or trim dying leaves. With one thrust she could slam them into either John's or Anise's eyes, certainly blinding them and—if she drove the blades hard enough into the brain—in all likelihood killing them. The problem, of course, was that there were far more herbalists around her than only Anise and John. They would swarm upon her the moment she attacked either of their leaders, and she knew well how ruthless they could be.

Besides, she wasn't built that way; she didn't believe that she was capable of lodging the steel blades of a pair of garden shears in anyone's eyes. Not even to protect a child. And so instead she did the only thing she thought she could do. "I'm a twin, too," she reminded them.

"Yes, of course, you are. But you are also rather—and you'll forgive me if this sounds ageist—old for our purposes," John told her, his voice knowing and smug. "The tincture demands the blood of a prepubescent twin."

"And you have some," she went on, nodding at the cauldron. "You already have a lot. I know the recipe. Use what you've harvested from the child and then supplement her blood with mine."

John turned toward Anise, his eyebrows raised.

"We'll need a good amount, Reseda," Anise said, a crooked smile on her face. Reseda knew that Anise did not especially like her, but she was unprepared for how happy the woman was to augment the tincture with her blood.

"I understand."

Anise nodded and turned to Clary. "Put a compress on the child's arm," she said. "We have plenty of her blood already."

Only after Reseda had watched Clary Hardin press a white hand towel against the child's forearm for a long, quiet minute did she extend her own arm over the cauldron and allow them to roll up her sleeve and gouge a deep trench into the veins there. Anise made the incision, roughly and inexpertly, but Reseda didn't watch. She focused instead on the moonstone at the tip of the boline handle. The cut hurt every bit as much as she'd expected.

T here they are. There are the playmates your wondrous daughter deserves, standing perhaps a dozen yards apart, separated by a cauldron, each in the arms of those self-absorbed breathers. You stand at the entrance of the greenhouse as Reseda, looking uncharacteristically shaky, stares at something far away. Her arm is held over that massive black kettle, and the blood drips like water from a rusted-out rain gutter. They have not noticed you yet because they are focused only on Reseda and the girls, and they are in the midst of a euphoric chant about seeds and souls.

And so you charge, running across the greenhouse, oblivious to anyone and anything but the idea that Ashley will no longer be alone. But before you have reached the first of the girls, there is their mother, up and before you and throwing herself into your arms.

"My God, Chip!" she wails. "Stop them! They're going to kill them!"

For an instant, you recall something. Them. Garnet. Hallie. They're going to kill your children. The instant passes, because they're not your children. Your child is Ashley. But that still doesn't give them or you the right to kill . . . anyone. The whole notion has left you muddled, confused, and you find yourself staring at the knife as if you have no idea

how it got into your hands. And just as you are starting to regain a modicum of your focus and your anger smothers your momentary befuddlement, the men in the robes—some, it seems, very old yet strangely
strong—have a hold of your arms and the knife, and the greenhouse is
filled with their admonishments to drop it, to stop struggling, to be still.
You cry out against them, but there are so many and they are so forceful
that they are able to pry the knife from your fingers. Your eyes rest on
the women on the far side of the cauldron, and they stare at you, even
Reseda, whose complexion is growing pale—as if the color is literally
draining from her face and streaming into the cauldron. She murmurs,
"Bring him to me," and you are pushed forward so aggressively that only
your toes are touching the greenhouse floor. She looks deep into your
eyes across the black kettle and says, "I am telling you, she is gone. Your
daughter is no longer here."

She has said this before, and she will say it again. She will—

"I am telling you, your daughter is fine—but she needs you."

She does need you. You are sure of this. A pitchfork leans against
a glass wall, and the moment you spy it you rear up, bellowing like a
wounded animal and breaking free from these old men. You grab it with
both hands and jab at the crowd as they surround you. Once more you
focus upon the children, standing a little stupefied with two of the older
herbalists and their mother. And so you charge, the pitchfork a bayonet
in your mind, only to be restrained again by the men and women in
their robes. Their hands are everywhere upon your shoulders and waist
and arms, and they are wrestling the pitchfork from your grip. And then
abruptly they stop. You follow their eyes, but it must have happened so
quickly that you are not precisely sure what occurred. Still, it appears
that Anise and Reseda have collided and fallen to the ground as they
tried to get out of your way. Or, perhaps, Reseda pulled Anise out of the
way, trying to shield her, and the two women tumbled in a heap onto
the greenhouse floor. Either way, when Reseda looks up at you, her face
is oddly vacant. Almost bewildered. And then you understand why, as
Anise is repeating "No, no, no!" over and over. Reseda's blouse is black
with her blood, and extending from that beautiful, swanlike neck is the

long, elegant handle of the boline. When she fell, she fell on Anise's hand and impaled herself on the knife.

"It was an accident, I swear!" Anise cries out, drawing the long blade from Reseda's neck as if she is prying a carrot from soil, and a geyser of blood sprays the two herbalists in the face. Then, ever so slowly because Anise is trying to pull her up by her shoulders—as if she believes that so long as Reseda is sitting upright the woman will live—Reseda chokes out one last rivulet of blood and collapses, a marionette freed from its cross-bar and strings. John Hardin falls upon her, though she's already dead, as do Ginger and Clary and Sage.

And almost in that instant you see Reseda, alive and standing before you. She is offering you that unreadable smile, her blue eyes beckoning. She motions behind her, and there is Ashley, your beautiful daughter, the straps of her Dora the Explorer backpack looking a bit like suspenders against her summer shirt. She is grinning happily, her eyes alight, the way she did when she was beside you on the runway at Burlington International Airport and all that loomed was a fifty-five- or fifty-six-minute flight to Philadelphia. She waves. You wave back. And the moment you start toward her, all of the rage that has been burning inside you since Flight 1611 cartwheeled into the lake vanishes. You kneel before her and embrace her. Then, the sky brightening as if the sun is rising in June, you stand up and—still holding Ashley's small hand—follow Reseda into the welcoming daylight.

Somewhere very far behind you stands a pilot. An airline pilot. He looks a little haggard—they all look a little haggard—as one of his girls is led back to the cauldron. You hope someday there is someone back there for him, too. Someone just like Reseda.

Epilogue

In all the years that you have lived in Bethel, you have to admit: Clary Hardin has never looked better. And while there are some people who presume that both she and her husband, John, have on occasion resorted to chemical injections and peels that minimize lines, you know them well enough to understand that they're just not the type. Neither is that vain. Both are wary of inorganic toxins. Verbena also looks considerably younger than her peers. Maybe she escaped the pressures of that Philadelphia law firm just in time. The two of you have a daughter in college now, but still Verbena's hair hasn't begun to gray. Oh, she hennas it. She likes that look, as do you. But you are confident that underneath that color not a single follicle has turned white, and this despite the crash of Flight 1611 and then the death of a child—the single worst thing that can happen to a parent—a decade ago. Verbena misses the girl. As do you. You miss her madly. You see the child in the cheekbones and the shape of the eyes of your remaining daughter, her twin, when the girl is home from college or when you visit her there.

But somehow you and Verbena both moved on. You survived. In the end, neither of you wound up like Tansy Dunmore. Thank God. You are, clearly, a survivor. You survived a plane crash, didn't you? Of course you did. Somehow, you survived even the stultifying guilt that had paralyzed you in the aftermath, the what-ifs, the visions, the ghosts.

Nevertheless, for months—for over a year, until well after the anniversary of the girl's death had passed—you had indeed been smothered by mourning; it was all you had. No, that's not completely true. You had the herbalists and their strange concoctions and desperately needed friendship. They were constantly feeding both you and Emily. Their foods and their tinctures were what kept you both upright and functioning, their medicines were what made the memories bearable—and, then, what made the worst of the memories recede so far into the backs of your minds that it's almost as if they never happened.

And, yes, they needed you, too. Holly was especially devastated by her friend's death, but even Anise and Ginger and Sage—mature enough to have seen a great many of their own friends pass away—seemed to have been scarred by the accident that took the woman's life.

And your daughter's.

"What do you think, Chip?"

You turn toward Anise, sipping the Syrah that Peyton discovered this past February in Argentina, when he and Sage were escaping a White Mountain winter. Sage was looking for specific herbs and roots in the foothills of the Andes, while Peyton insisted he was interested only in grapes. You guess they are each at least eighty now, as are John and Clary. You will turn fifty in a month. Peyton is helping you convert what had once been a coal chute in your basement into a wine cellar. The space is ideal, a fitting spot to indulge your new passion. What else could a person put in that space but wine? It's perfect.

"Oh," you answer, no longer worrying about whether you need to choose your words carefully, "I think a green thumb is just an expression. Either no one has a green thumb or everyone does. Sure, some people are destined to be ballerinas and some people, no matter how hard they work, will never be recruited by the American Ballet Theatre. But I think gardening is more like . . . cooking. Some people are better than others, but, with a little patience and a little practice, most people can make a pretty adequate lasagna."

"I disagree," Anise says, and she reaches across the large pouf in John and Clary's living room and squeezes your knee. You savor the hint of patchouli in her perfume tonight, and for a moment the aroma from the kitchen is lost beneath it. Rosemary. The main course is a stew of some sort, simmering right now on the stove, and you smile when you recall what Clary had said when you first arrived this evening and inhaled the delicious scent from the great copper pot: *A pinch of rosemary makes everything better.* "You really don't believe that your Verbena here is such an extraordinary gardener because it's in her blood?" Anise asks.

"I think she's an extraordinary gardener because you and Clary and Sage are very good teachers."

Verbena sips her wine, and her eyes are shining. She is wearing a black velour sweater tonight that clings to her and a string of pearls. She couldn't, it seems to you, be more beautiful.

"And your little girl?" Anise continues, pulling her hand back and folding her arms across her chest. She raises her eyebrows a little impishly and smirks.

Indeed, you wonder about your little girl, though she is no longer little. She is majoring in plant biology and minoring in anthropology. She grew up, it seems, in that greenhouse beside your home, and the communal one at the Messners'. Nevertheless, in your opinion that was more about nurture than nature—it was proximity, not genes. Had you remained in Pennsylvania, there is no reason to believe that your daughter would have wound up an aspiring botanist and herbalist. Still, the evening is too pleasant to waste energy debating whether her interest in plants was genetically inevitable or a self-fulfilling career path once you landed here in northern New Hampshire.

"Well, she also had some exceptional teachers," you answer simply and sip your wine. The goblet has the crest of the coven (there really is no other word for it, though they insist they are nothing but botanists of a sort), and your eyes pause on it for a brief moment. Really, what would you and your wife and your daughter have done if it had not been for these remarkable people? You contemplate this almost unthinkable what-if, as you do periodically: How much does Verbena recall about that night? Supposedly very little. The women have seen to that. Memorium. Delirium. Their magical tinctures. The car was totaled in the rainstorm. They told you it's a miracle that Verbena survived when your daughter was killed and Reseda was all but decapitated. Celandine was the first on the scene.

"I'd say she had miraculous teachers," Sage purrs, saying something that sounds prosaic but you know in reality is really very profound. Then she turns to Clary and says, "Do you need any help getting supper on the table?"

Clary rises from the sofa with the serpentine arms and nods. "You're positively psychic," she says, smiling at her friend, and bustles into the kitchen. Verbena—so placid at midlife, so free from anxiety, it's as if in addition to discovering a fountain of youth in this northern New England backwater she has also found here the secret to calmness and serenity—stands up and joins the women, kissing you on the cheek as she passes. She is wearing black lace ballet flats, and you are struck by the erotic elegance of even her small feet. Have you ever been more in love? No. Clearly not.

Anise follows the women, leaving you alone with Peyton and John.

"You're a lucky, lucky man, Chip," Peyton says.

"I think we all are," John adds agreeably.

"When does Cali come home from school for the summer?" Peyton asks.

"Oh, that's still a month away. The Friday before Memorial Day weekend most likely."

"Does she still have those seizures?"

"Rarely. But every once in a while, yes."

Peyton nods and glances at John, but John doesn't look up from his Syrah. He seems lost in thought.

"She spending the summer here in New Hampshire?"

"I wish. Nope, she is only here through the end of June. Then she's off to the Southwest for just about six weeks. Desert plants, mostly."

"There's a lot to study there," Peyton says.

"Indeed. She'll be in Santa Fe, Sedona, Bisbee, Las Cruces—though not necessarily in that order. But it is a pretty packed itinerary."

"Ah, to be young and to have all that energy," John says, smiling and suddenly returning to their conversation.

"We do all right," Peyton says.

"We do now," says the older lawyer. This is, it seems, a small but important correction in his mind.

"Hear, hear. A toast to health and to youth!" Peyton says, raising his voice as if he were in a bar, and you hold the goblet under your nose and breathe in the fragrance from the wine. And you agree: You haven't felt this young or this healthy since well before a plane hit some geese and fell from the sky. But even that now seems but a distant, nebulous recollection: the details that for a time you knew so well? Either vague or gone. It is a bit like the death of your daughter. Rosemary—though when she was alive, weren't you likely to call her Hallie? Yes. Yes, of course. But somehow the image of a girl named Hallie floats in the heavens just beyond the reach of your memory.

Like so much else, apparently. Like all of those thousands and thousands of hours you once spent on the flight deck of an airplane.

"Chip?"

You glance up at John and his raised chalice.

"You seem to have your head in the clouds tonight," he says.

"Not anymore," you tell him, holding high your glass, "those days are gone." Then, after you have taken a slow, comradely sip, you sigh.

Acknowledgments

Once again, I could not have written this novel without an enormous amount of help. First of all, there were the pilots who shared with me what their lives are like on the ground and in the air: John Weber, Carol Lynn Wood, and Judy Bradt (who is a shaman as well as a pilot, a rare combination indeed). In addition, I am grateful to J. J. Gertler, a thorough and uncompromising reader, and a font of all sorts of esoteric information about aircraft. And then there was William Langewiesche, one of the world's great aviation experts and a wonderful writer, who examined the scenes in this novel that involve flying (and crashing) and gently pointed out my particularly egregious errors.

And when it comes to crashing—or, at least, ditching—an aircraft, I am not sure that there are many people who know as much about surviving that sort of disaster as Maria Hanna and Richard Martin at Survival Systems USA in Groton, Connecticut. May I never need to use all I learned that day in the dunk tank, when the simulator was turning me upside down on the flight deck and I had to find my way to the surface of the water.

I learned an enormous amount as well from the shamans: Mary Alexander, Anthony Patrick Pauly, Jr., and Hilary Raimo.

And then there were the doctors, psychiatrists, and EMTs: Dr. Mike Kiernan, Dr. Richard Munson, Dr. Marc Tischler, and James Yeaton.

The books that were my Emergency Information Cards while writing this novel included *Medicine Woman* by Lynn V. Andrews; *The Unquiet Dead* by Edith Fiore; *Fly by Wire: The Geese, the Glide, the Miracle on the Hudson,* by William Langewiesche; and *Highest Duty: My Search for What Really Matters,* by Chesley Sullenberger and Jeffrey Zaslow.

And, of course, I am deeply indebted to the whole team at Random House and at Gelfman Schneider. First at Crown: Domenica Alioto, Shaye Areheart, Andy Augusto, Patty Berg, Cindy Berman, Sarah Breivogel, Jacob Bronstein, Whitney Cookman, Jill Flaxman, John Glusman, Kate Kennedy, Christine Kopprasch, Jacqui LeBow, Matthew Martin, Maya Mavjee, Donna Passannante, Philip Patrick, Tina Pohlman, Catherine Pollock, Annsley Rosner, Jay Sones, Molly Stern, Kira Walton, and Campbell Wharton. At Gelfman Schneider: Jane Gelfman, Cathy Gleason, and Victoria Marini. And no list would be complete without Arlynn Greenbaum at Authors Unlimited and Dean Schramm of the Schramm Group.

Finally, there is my lovely bride of a quarter of a century, who reads all my work in more drafts than anyone should have to endure, Victoria Blewer.

I thank you all so very, very much.

THE NIGHT STRANGERS

A Reader's Guide by Amy Clements

A Note to the Reader

In order to provide reading groups with the most informed and thought-provoking questions possible, it is necessary to hint at certain aspects of the plot—as well as the ending. If you have not finished reading *The Night Strangers*, we respectfully suggest that you wait before reviewing this guide.

Introduction

Both a chilling page-turner and a moving portrait of a family's struggle to heal, *The Night Strangers* raises provocative questions about the nature of survival and the world beyond our own. Showcasing the storytelling power of Chris Bohjalian at the top of his game, this is the tale of airline pilot Chip Linton, who is suffering from severe emotional trauma after his regional jet crashes in Lake Champlain.

When both engines fail soon after takeoff after a double bird strike, he attempts a water landing reminiscent of Captain Chesley Sullenberger's "Miracle on the Hudson." The landing goes tragically wrong for Chip, however, and most of the passengers die on impact or drown.

Hoping for a fresh start, Chip and his family move to a rambling Victorian house in rural New Hampshire. But the house and the new neighbors soon present some unsettling revelations—including a basement door sealed shut with thirty-nine bolts, precisely matching the number of passengers who died on Chip's doomed flight. A group of local women eagerly help the Lintons settle in, but they seem a little too obsessed with their herb gardens and greenhouses, and they clearly know more about the house than they are letting on. For Chip's wife, Emily, and their twin daughters, their new home in Bethel begins to test everything they ever believed about life and about one another. Is this "coven" of herbalists evil? Or are they shamans offering the Lintons their best chance for recovery?

A pitch-perfect thriller with a cast that encompasses the living and the dead, *The Night Strangers* will keep your reading group riveted. We hope this guide will enrich your discussion.

Questions for Discussion

1. How sharp were your detective skills as you read *The Night Strangers*? Did your assumptions about the basement, Chip's visions, and the herbalists prove to be correct?

2. Chris Bohjalian wrote Chip's scenes in the second person ("you"), present tense. How did this affect your reading? What was it like to be in Chip's mind?

3. Discuss the portrait of marriage and family conveyed by the Lintons. We're told that before the plane crash, Emily and the girls were self-sufficient while Chip was away on flights. What else stayed the same after the crash? What were the greatest strains on the family as a result of Chip's PTSD? How does Emily and Chip's marriage compare to Clary and John's?

4. Discuss the plants from which the herbalists take their names (reseda and anise in particular). Throughout the book's "recipes," what did you discover about nature's ability to heal or poison, and to bring clarity or hallucination?

5. As Chip teeters on the brink of insanity, what are the benefits and limits of conventional psychiatry?

6. As the breadwinner, Emily wistfully remembers the days when she had time to be a community theater actress. How does her experience in theater eventually help her in Bethel? How does she cope with the stress of essentially becoming a single parent with a full-time job?

7. Ultimately, what could have saved Sawyer Dunmore's young life? What does his family represent in a town where the herbalists have considerable power, despite being despised by some?

8. What does the novel show us about the guilt of survivors? Haunted by Ethan's line, "She deserves friends," how is Chip's guilt reflected in the bonds between fathers and daughters?

9. Did Garnet (Cali) and Hallie (Rosemary) remind you of your own siblings? Was your childhood marked by a sibling or friend who was different from you in many ways but nonetheless stayed close to you?

10. How did your impressions of Reseda shift throughout the novel?

11. How far would you go to attain eternal youth?

12. Explore the images of flying that appear in the novel, from Chip's exuberant memories to his nightmares. Do you enjoy flying, or do you fear it? What do our attitudes about flying say about us?

13. In the epilogue, Chip and Emily seem to feel gratitude to their community. Did this surprise you? Does *The Night Strangers* have a happy ending?

14. In his acknowledgments, the author lists many people who helped him in his research, including several shamans. How does this add to

the realism of the novel? If you were to consult a shaman, what spiritual resolutions would you seek?

15. What emotional themes in *The Night Strangers* are echoed in previous Bohjalian novels you've read? What makes this particular story line unique?

A Conversation with Chris Bohjalian

Q: The seed for your new novel stems from two events that occurred years apart. Tell us about those events and how they became the foundation for *The Night Strangers*.

Chris Bohjalian: Along one of the basement foundation walls of my house, belowground, is a door about five and a half feet tall and three feet wide. It's made of rough, unfinished wooden planks, and it was added at some point after the 1898 Victorian above it was first constructed. When my wife and I moved into the house, it was nailed shut. There was a moldy pile of coal beside it, a decomposing little mesa, and so I convinced myself the door was merely a part of an old coal chute.

A few years later, in the early 1990s, I decided to man up and pull the door open. The project demanded a crowbar, a wrench, and—at one point—an ax. After hours of toil, behind that door I found . . . nothing. In no way did it resemble a coal chute. It was more like a closet—or a crypt behind which you might wall up a neighbor alive. So I nailed the door shut and made a mental note to steer clear of that corner of the basement for as long as we lived in the house. Nevertheless, on some level I understood even then that the basement door was going to lead to a novel.

It would take an Airbus ditching one January afternoon in 2009 in the Hudson River before I would begin to understand what was going to exist behind that door. Like many thousands of other people, I raced to my television set and watched the evacuation as it occurred, staring enrapt as passengers stood on the wings and the plane floated, nose up, amid the waves.

Perhaps it was the shape of the jet's cabin doors, but at that moment I thought of the door in my basement two floors below me. The next morning, I wrote the following sentence: "The door was presumed to have been the entry to a coal chute, a perfectly reasonable assumption since a small hillock of damp coal sat moldering before it." So begins *The Night Strangers*, a novel about a plane crash and the ghosts—literal and metaphoric—who dog the surviving pilot.

Q: *The Night Strangers* **is in part a ghost story. You have always enjoyed ghost stories, but you haven't written one in more than twenty years. What was holding you back?**

CB: If you look at my personal library, you will notice that it ranges from Henry James to Steig Larsson, from Margaret Atwood to Max Hastings. There's Jane Austen and Edgar Allan Poe and volumes of letters from Civil War privates. It is pretty eclectic. The reality is that I rarely read the same sort of book in a season. And, I hope, I will never write the same book twice. Look at my most recent novels. *Secrets of Eden* (2010) is about domestic violence, a double murder, and a minister's guilt. *Skeletons at the Feast* (2008) is a love story set in Germany and Poland in the last days of the Second World War, and one family's complicity in the Holocaust. And *The Double Bind* (2007) is an exploration of a young social worker's descent into madness after a violent sexual assault; the book moves between a very real Burlington, Vermont, and Jay Gatsby's fictional West Egg, Long Island.

So why a ghost story? Well, I love them. They're fun to read—and, yes, fun to write. And when I imagined the subject matter of a plane crash and a pilot's post-traumatic stress disorder, ghosts seemed as good a way in as any.

Q: In order to better understand your protagonist, Chip Linton, a commercial airline pilot, and what he might have gone through in the opening pages of this novel, you visited Survival Systems in Groton, Connecticut. Can you tell us about that experience?

CB: I loved everything about my day at Survival Systems. One of the first things I did when I started this novel was to go there, climb into a flight suit, get strapped inside a Modular Egress Training Simulator (METS, for short), and then lowered into a 100,000-gallon tank of water. I was rolled 180 degrees so I was upside down. The point of this was to get a taste of what it's like to exit a plane that has just crashed in the water.

The METS is a cylinder that resembles an aircraft cabin. It has interchangeable exits, so Survival Systems can replicate egress from most types of fixed and rotary wing aircraft. The device is lowered into the tank, submerged underwater, and then rolled upside down or to an off-angle, depending upon the scenario. The ceiling can be set on fire because, let's face it, when your plane or chopper has become a lawn dart, there's a chance that something is ablaze. The day I was dunked, there were three National Guardsmen being trained as well. I had an instructor in the simulator with me, and there were divers in the water around it to make sure that all of us got out with, worst case, a snootful of water. Altogether I was dunked three times, twice rolled until I was upside down. Escaping the simulator the two times I was strapped into a seat and had to push out exit windows while upside down was particularly satisfying.

Q: Like many of your previous novels, *The Night Strangers* is set in New England. The area really seems to draw you in. Was there a time when you were first starting to write this novel that you thought about setting it elsewhere?

CB: Not really. I have no objections to venturing beyond New England in my work. *Skeletons at the Feast* is set in Poland and Germany. My next novel, *The Sandcastle Girls,* is set in Armenia, Turkey, and Syria. But I do enjoy writing about northern New England. It's my home and I understand the landscape and the people. And let's face it: the New England ghost story has a long and distinguished literary pedigree.

Q: In *The Night Strangers*, you introduce a peculiar group of women whom the locals refer to as herbalists. When did you know they would play such a prominent role in the novel? Are you a "green thumb" yourself?

CB: I rarely know precisely where my books are going when I start them. I depend upon my characters to take me by the hand and lead me through the dark of the story. *The Night Strangers* was no exception, and the herbalists changed dramatically from their first involvement.

I am a pretty good gardener—especially vegetables. I grow flowers, too, but I couldn't tell you the names of most of the flowers I grow. I'm not kidding. So, I guess there is no chance I will be recruited anytime soon by the local garden club—or any herbalists with ulterior motives.

Q: In *The Night Strangers*, some of the most interesting characters are not among the living. Was there any difference in how you crafted these characters and their personalities?

CB: I tended to approach my ghosts with the same basic criteria I have for my breathing characters: If presented with certain stimuli, how will they respond? What will they do, given who they are? That was what I was thinking about most often. I wanted their behavior to make sense to readers.

Q: You often talk about how one of your greatest joys in life is being a father. Was it difficult for you to imagine some of the scenes between Chip and his twin daughters after it becomes clear he's suffering from post-traumatic stress disorder?

CB: The scenes that were most interesting to write in that regard were those in which Chip is contemplating his sense of failure—what his daughters think of him now and how they will see him in the years to come. I would hate to disappoint my daughter and my wife. And while there might not in reality have been anything that Chip could have done to prevent his plane from cartwheeling in the lake, he is nonetheless nearly incapacitated with self-loathing.

About the Author

CHRIS BOHJALIAN is the author of fourteen novels, including the *New York Times* bestsellers *Secrets of Eden, The Double Bind, Skeletons at the Feast,* and *Midwives.* His novel *Midwives* was a number one *New York Times* bestseller and a selection of Oprah's Book Club. His work has been translated into more than twenty-five languages, and three of his novels have become movies (*Secrets of Eden, Midwives,* and *Past the Bleachers*). He lives in Vermont with his wife and daughter.

Visit him at chrisbohjalian.com, find him at facebook.com and goodreads.com, and follow Chris on Twitter.

Aldine 401 is Bitstream Inc.'s version of the old-style serif font Bembo, and it was first seen in 2000. Bembo is based on the typeface cut by Francesco Griffo for Aldus Manutius's printing of *De Aetna* in 1495. Today's version of Bembo was designed by Stanley Morison for the Monotype Corporation in 1929. In the 1980s, Monotype produced the Griffo revival as a digital font. Bembo is noted for its classic, well-proportioned letterforms and is widely used because of its readability.

Also by CHRIS BOHJALIAN

SECRETS OF EDEN
$15.00 paper (Canada: $17.00)
978-0-307-39498-9

SKELETONS AT
THE FEAST
$14.95 paper (Canada: $17.50)
978-0-307-39496-5

THE DOUBLE BIND
$15.00 paper (Canada: $18.95)
978-1-4000-3166-5

BEFORE YOU
KNOW KINDNESS
$14.95 paper (Canada: $19.95)
978-1-4000-3165-8

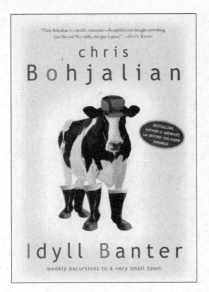

IDYLL BANTER
$13.99 paper (Canada: $15.99)
978-1-4000-5236-3

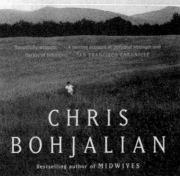

THE BUFFALO
SOLDIER
$15.00 paper (Canada: $17.00)
978-0-375-72546-3

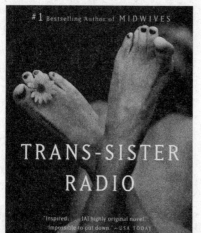

TRANS-SISTER RADIO
$14.95 paper (Canada: $21.00)
978-0-375-70517-5

THE LAW OF SIMILARS
$13.95 paper (Canada: $17.95)
978-0-679-77147-0